THIS
SAVAGE
WORLD

ANNA HOUSEGO

This novel was written on the island of lutruwita/Tasmania, on the southern land of the muwinina people, with the mountain slopes of kunanyi on the skyline. I pay my respects to the Traditional Owners and acknowledge the Tasmanian Aboriginal people as the continuing custodians of this land. I honour their Elders, past and present, as the keepers of deep knowledge and culture spanning more than 40,000 years. They and their story live on.

This Savage World
copyright © Anna Housego 2024
www.annahousego.com

1st edition 2024, paperback
ISBN (paperback): 978-0-6456369-2-5
ISBN (ebook): 978-0-6456369-3-2

For sisterhood, and
dear sisters, Cheryl, Jackie and Trudy

LONDON, ENGLAND

TENERIFE

AFRICA

LAND OF
BRAZIL

ATLANTIC
OCEAN

RIO
DE JANEIRO

CAPE OF GOOD HOPE

N

W   E

S

SOUTHERN

PACIFIC
OCEAN

NEW
HOLLAND

NORFOLK
ISLAND

PORT
JACKSON,
SYDNEY
COVE

VAN DIEMEN'S LAND

OCEAN

Death borders upon our birth. And
our cradle stands in the grave.

Joseph Hall, Bishop of Exeter (1564-1656)

CHAPTER ONE

GREATER LONDON, 1776

S HE IS NOT QUITE FIFTEEN when she midwifes her first baby; as it happens her own mother's.

Maggie would not normally enter the room at midday when her ma rests, but she has managed to make a weak broth with a gristly piece of mutton, an onion, and turnip tops scavenged from behind a market stall. She hopes it may prove a tonic, for her mother has been flagging for days.

She opens the door to the sound of groaning. The pains have come on quickly and already sweat is beading on her mother's forehead. Maggie instinctively looks behind as though help may be waiting in the next room, yet only the two of them are home. No siblings tease each other or fight, no father shouts at them, there is only her mother's distress and a sickening sense of being rooted to the spot.

She cannot stand there fuddled. She'll run for the toothless woman who helped with the six other babies.

'No, there's not time. You'll have to do.'

Her mother writhes, trying to sit up as she attempts to take charge.

'Too late for spreading straw on the floor. I'll stay on the bed. Get the rags I set aside.'

Soon she gives herself over to her own animal sounds, the grunts and roaring punctuated by swearing better heard from the costermonger selling pickled whelks from his pitch in the Tower Hamlets.

Above the wailing and cries, Maggie hears the panicked thump of her own heart. Never again will she be so unknowing, will she understand so little about a woman's body, its flesh, the strength that has pure frailty at its core.

In a rush of blood, and the shock of it, she catches the purple-faced boy, her brother. He is squalling as she ties twine tightly around the navel string and cuts it with the carving knife.

'Did I hurt him, ma?'

A shake of the head says no. 'Wrap him in my shawl and give him to me while I wait for the afterbirth.'

The boy's passage was fast but after some time the afterbirth has still not emerged. Exhausted, Maggie's mother encourages her to tug on the navel string to help it out. It seems an eternity, though may only have been ten minutes or so, before the shiny big lump of tissue flops onto the bed. Maggie resists the urge to retch at the sight of the strange thing, which seems to have trapped handfuls of worms in its wet crust. On poking it, the wriggling pale lines reveal they are blood vessels.

She leaves it in an enamel bowl, where it will stay until she can dump it in the cesspit at the back of their building after dark, taking care to be rid of it before the nightman arrives and can object.

Her mother dozes on the bed with the dazed baby in the crook of one arm, while Maggie gathers the soiled nightgown and sheet, bundling them for tomorrow's washtub.

Suddenly, the older woman opens eyes filled with alarm and fixes them, unblinking, on her daughter.

'I see it now, the seed in you. God has marked you, Maggie.'

Her eyes scan her daughter's face as though searching for something lost, then almost immediately the lids snap shut, her head falling back onto the pillow. The room is still, dust motes caught mid-air in their dance, the moment undisturbed by the squeaking wheel of a barrow passing outside and the bellowing of the coal man.

Maggie goes to her ma's side, leans forward.

'How, ma? Tell me what you did see.'

She places an ear near her mother's mouth, straining to hear an answer, no matter how faint. It is then she looks towards the foot of the bed and sees the rose blooming red, unstoppable, across the mattress.

Had she been a seer perhaps she could have read the omens in the outline it left, could have seen into the future, caught a glimpse of the vision that afflicted her mother. And yet, perhaps it is its own gift that Maggie cannot prophesy and is confined to what she sees before her each day, surely burden enough to bear.

In the weeks to follow, after her mother's grey form is rolled into the grave, the baby, birdlike, soon after, Maggie learns she could have mixed the powder of ergot as a tea to slow the bleeding, and rolled rags, packing them in place to staunch the flow from the womb.

She discovers, too, that she can never forgive herself, the stony glances of her da, two sisters and three brothers only serving to confirm that she failed them all. She takes

3

to standing in the doorway eating her share of what little bread or potatoes they come by, or kneeling in the dirt of the cobblestones, the chill outside far kinder than the frostiness in the air of their two rented tenement rooms.

For three days a strong easterly keeps the East Indiamen from the Thames River, their unwieldy square rigs making them unable to tack into the wind. With no cargo to shift, Maggie's father is not needed as a porter in the warehouses near the docks, where for years he has submitted his back, bending beneath sacks of coal, sugar, malt for the brewhouses, loads of lumber heavy as his own bodyweight. Her mother's meagre earnings from stitching black armbands for mourning sailors are no more.

Titus Bloodworth waits till his children have risen from their pallets next morning and are gulping down oatmeal gruel and the last pieces of dark maslin bread. His head is thick from the previous night at the Rose and Crown, where he downed the better part of a pint of wine made into a negus. The hot water, lemon juice and spices in the mix have done naught to stop his stomach from turning sour.

He clears his throat loudly. 'Time for doin' things a different way.'

Each spoon stops between bowl and mouth.

'We'll not be living in Deaths Head Alley with the paupers, suffering for charity from the alms house. Not when I got you strappin' young 'uns.'

Their mother was opposed to the boys being forced into dangerous work as city sweeps, sent naked up narrow chimneys only to die young from soot wart on their bollocks, or forced to be hurriers harnessed to coal carts in mines up north. But she's not here to resist. When Titus points to his eldest son George, nearly thirteen, the boy jerks upright in his seat, eyes stiff with terror.

'The rector don't tolerate idleness in the likes of you. He be gettin' you bound to one o' the weavers over at Spitalfields.' George lets out the breath he is holding. He would rather be a pure finder scavenging for dogshit to sell to the tanneries, than jammed in a tight chimney.

Second daughter Fanny, now eleven, will look after the three little ones, freeing Maggie for gainful work.

'I've heard say there's call for a washerwoman at the upholsterer's house near the Minories.'

Maggie meets the news with dismay. She thinks straight away of her friend Audrey, a year older and apprenticed to Mrs Greeves, head of a household near Limehouse dockyards. Audrey's up at midnight, lighting a fire under the copper, taking care the water gets hot so she don't get whacked with a stick when the laundress arrives an hour later to sort the linen.

Poor Aud's always weary. Her hands are stiff, cracked from the caustic soaps. Her back aches from lifting buckets of hot water from the copper to the washtubs, the endless lifting and squeezing of wet sheets and heavy blankets. Pains run down her wrists from hours of beating out stains with the battledore.

The trials of her friend pass before Maggie in a flash. She nods in response to her father, walks away, and keeps walking.

The toothless one has a name, Mrs Grimes. She is surprised when the girl knocks on her door for the second time, the first being when she sought assistance for her ma, too late. This time the girl has a proposition.

'I know I'm young, but take me on, I beg you. I work hard, am wanting to be your 'prentice.'

The old woman makes a hissing noise, and Maggie can't tell if it's a means to send her away or simply the sound of the woman sucking air through her caved-in mouth.

'Don't need a helper. I be too old for draggin' round a girl, and what pennies I gain are not of a sum for paying you or t'other.' She begins to close the door but the girl thrusts her head towards the gap.

'I don't need payin'. I'll do it for the learning.'

Perhaps it is the earnestness in Maggie's voice or maybe the woman feels sorry for her, but she pauses, and Maggie has the good sense to hold back her words.

''Tis a job for an older one, a woman who's birthed a bairn already.'

Maggie sees the midwife is set to be rid of her as she might a scuttling cockroach. She won't let it happen, needs to show Mrs Grimes she is no weak creature, that she's a fighter.

'I've delivered a babe, it's of no matter that it were not mine. I need to learn, get things right.' The tears are coming. She must not let them make her crumble.

'My da will flay me, but my offer is true. I'll work for no pay till the end of winter, then you can say if I be worth takin' on.'

The onion hawker is making his way down the street with loud cries of *sixpence for a rope, London's finest,* but she ignores his racket and the pair of hollow-eyed streetwalkers stumbling past, cussing, still unsteady on the gin taken in the wee hours to make the threepenny upright coves tolerable.

The clank, rattle and heave of the parish of St Botolph Aldgate, on the eastern side of the old wall separating it from the City of London, is a vibration Maggie feels in the soles of her feet as she waits. It's the pulse of people pushing through dirty laneways with a leaden sky pressing down. Urchins scavenging for food or chased from church steps into dark streets by the watch. Rickety hovels leaning in foul air, worse when the wind blows from the open poor's pit at the burying ground near the church. Cinder smoke belching from breweries, the tannery, inns, and shops on the Middlesex side. Blood running in the street on Butchers Row, guts and gristle from each day's hacking and slicing tossed from stalls into the street, mixing with manure from passing horses so that carriage wheels spray foul muck over her skirts.

Travellers bless St Botolph, patron saint of wayfarers, as they leave the city walls, praying to be spared the dangers, the chaos of what lies beyond. The tumult they see is something else to Maggie, her birthright, an inheritance of grit, grind, and stink so strong it stains the skin. She questions none of it, the way a stone tossed into a pond does not resist.

Mrs Grimes says nothing, does nothing for the longest time. At the point where the girl is set to leave, the door cracks open a little more.

'Don't you go makin' me sorry, girl, for not giving you a good kick up the backside to send you on yer way.'

Maggie's father is not so forgiving, furious that his daughter would go against his wishes for paid work as a washerwoman.

'You ain't got yer head on straight. Any fool will take you if you're free labour. Go back and tell her you've changed yer mind.' He raises his hand to slap her.

'Think about it, da. I be paid soon enough, and once I'm done learning I'll never be out of work. Babies is always gettin' born.'

The talk of babies has turned Titus' stomach again. He drops his hand, suddenly certain he needs a hair of the dog at the inn more than he needs to be standing here butting heads with a daughter who's stubborn as an old goose.

Maggie proves to be a fast learner. How to use tinctures from the herbalist to ease birthing pains or keep up a woman' strength. Comfrey for loose bowels, horseradish root in a cordial to revive an exhausted mother. Ginger poultices for backache, linseed meal and mustard seed plasters for nausea. Oil of sweet almond as a lubricant to help stretch the quim for the baby's head.

She is shown which birthing positions are best to ease the baby's passage into the world, when to get the mother upright, on her left side, or have her kneel. How to use one hand to apply pressure, stopping the mother from tearing as the head emerges. Where to prod the stomach for a baby reluctant to be born. How to help a baby coming feet first.

Far better to send for the midwife than the doctor, even if he can be afforded, for Mrs Grimes knows all too well that women are more likely to die from childbed fever when he attends.

'It be the bad air that comes with him from the cadaver at the morgue, the sick room, wherever he was before he gets to 'em.'

She snorts loudly if anyone mentions Middlesex Hospital's two lying-in wards, funded by the wealthy for poor mothers.

'They only take respectable married women, Maggie. Gawdsakes, how many o' those do we see? I can tell you, even the rich ain't that respectable when you get to the bed chamber.'

Midwives have a bad reputation in London. Some are drunkards, others take money when they are no help at all or, worse, cause damage. Maggie soon sees that the toothless midwife and widow, despite appearances, has skill aplenty, the kind you only get with years of gaining the knowing.

Not the least, she is firm about any interfering by grandmothers or the gossips, whether friend or neighbour, who show up to dole out old wives' tales or fuss about in the confinement. Mrs Grimes urges Maggie to keep them busy fetching wood for the fire, boiling water, making tea, *anything to get 'em out from under my ol' bunioned feet*.

As the weeks pass, Margaret Bloodworth, barely out of childhood herself, is initiated into the rites of the childbed and the mysteries of a force that is life itself.

The arrival of each bonny, breathing baby fills her with joy in a way that nothing else in her short life ever has, each newborn a small counterbalance against the weight of responsibility for the mother and brother she failed.

Within the month she and Mrs Grimes attend a woman with bow legs and badly stunted height. The midwife immediately pulls Maggie aside, her voice low.

'Fetch the surgeon. The sooner this is done the better.'

'The surgeon? But you don't like him.'

Mrs Grimes grips Maggie's arm. 'Look at those narrow hips, not grown proper. She's had rickets as a girl. 'Tis a big babe, be jammed tight soon if it's not got out, and the ma could die as well. Now go, girl.'

Maggie runs hard all the way to the surgeon, arriving back breathless.

'Says he'll be here quick as he can.'

Almost an hour passes before the surgeon turns up, lackadaisical as you like, taking his time removing his jacket and rolling up his sleeves, ignoring the groaning mother.

'Well, Mrs Grimes, looks like I have work to do.'

He pulls instruments from his bag. Maggie wants to turn her eyes away but can't, watching with horror as he produces what looks like a butcher's hook, followed by long-handled scissors, and a strange instrument with two claw-like arms.

Mrs Grimes comes up behind her, hissing. 'Pull yerself together, girl. Yer not the one in his sights.'

The blood, the woman's screams, the baby's flesh and bones in pieces. Maggie wants the memories out of her head. It makes no difference that the ma lived, made to put up with the surgeon giving her a good talking to about staying away from the baby-making business from now on.

Maggie goes to Mrs Grimes two days later, tells her she's changed her mind, that midwifing's not right for her after all. The older woman fixes her with a withering stare.

'Wasting yer time with all the worry. Too late for that. You ain't the one to decide if this is yer calling, it found you. No quarrelling with that, lest you want to take it up with God hisself.'

At nineteen years she goes to the local ecclesiastical court to apply for a Bishop's licence, her future resting on the outcome. Without a licence she'll be no different to those using the dark arts to trick women out of their money.

Mrs Grimes was taught to write by her midwife mother and has helped with the papers, spurring on her pupil as she might one of her own daughters, had she been able to hold them in the womb until they were far enough along to live.

Maggie has with her a reference from the local parson, six references from matrons she has delivered, confirming she is a fit practitioner, and one from Mrs Grimes to prove she has served an apprenticeship.

The clerk is brisk, glancing over the papers. She pays the fee of one pound and fifteen shillings that took a year to save, then is told to return on Monday week to appear before the Bishop's chancellor.

'Bring your employer and at least three of the women who testify in your favour.'

She prepares carefully, memorising the midwife's oath and the liturgy to be used for baptising frail infants who will not live long enough for a parson or priest to be fetched.

Early on the Monday morning she washes, dresses in a clean shift, and gets Fanny to tie her into canvas stays, though not too tight. Then she slips over her head a pale green gown, bought second hand at the Rag Fair. She takes her time combing back her long brown hair, pinning it underneath a faded maroon bonnet. Her scuffed brown lace-up boots will have to do, they're all she has.

Mrs Grimes meets her at the cathedral, bearing her own licence in case she is required to prove she had the authority to take on an apprentice. Soon Maggie's witnesses arrive.

When it is her turn to enter from the nave, the apparitor, sitting on the left side of the courtroom well, gestures her forward into the wooden enclosure. The proctor bids her sit at the table below the Chancellor, next to him, where he can see if she tries to cheat.

Maggie trembles as she takes her seat before the elderly Chancellor, a crouching bird of prey on a high throne at the front, distractedly scratching his scalp under the side of his wig, then adjusting the neck of his black silk gown.

The diocesan registrar, at a lower bench to the right of the Chancellor, reads a summary of Maggie's application in a thin voice that can barely be heard. When he finishes, the Chancellor addresses Mrs Grimes.

'She is quite young for the heavy responsibilities of midwife.'

Maggie's left foot begins tapping of its own volition on the flagstones. The proctor glares. Immediately she presses her hand down, forcing the leg to be still. *I beg of you, Mrs Grimes, for my sake keep a clean tongue.*

She hears the old woman wheeze as she inhales.

'I been workin' in this calling for more than four decades, honourable sir. I tell you, no lie, this young woman has a gift in midwifing, and she not be one afeared o' hard work.' The witnesses nod in agreement.

The Chancellor mutters, his response inaudible. It would seem he has had a long morning and is keen to move on, waving a listless hand in Mrs Grimes' direction to stop her from saying more.

'Your papers are in order, Miss Bloodworth. Be warned, on pain of death, that you are not to use either sorcery or witchcraft in your work. You must remain true to the high moral values of the church and the sacred direction you are granted today. Stand now, and swear the midwife's oath.'

The proctor, zealous in his duties, studies her to ensure she has no scrap of paper in her hand as a prompt.

Maggie begins, promising faithfully and diligently to help childbearing women, watching as the Chancellor appears to fall asleep.

'Speak up, girl.' His head still rests on his hand. She is relieved she didn't embellish the oath by stating the truth, that morals are no use in the work she does, helping all childbearing women, married, unwed or whore.

'In time of necessity, I shall not forsake the poor woman to go to the rich, nor charge more than a family can afford. I shall not divulge matters that are private.'

She pledges to ensure all stillborn children are buried where neither man nor beast can interfere with them. She will not procure an abortion, nor connive at false claims of paternity or substitution of infants. Neither will she allow any woman to be delivered secretly and will always, where possible, ensure lights of some kind are in operation so that an unwanted child is protected from deliberate suffocation.

She forces back a smile. The Church of England has grave fears that midwives will steal the bodies of dead infants for rituals to Satan, one church leader famously declaring he would rather his child was baptised by an ape than a woman. Good luck to him finding a tame gorilla in London.

Finally, she solemnly swears to use only prescribed words when christening frail infants close to death.

The Chancellor stirs.

'Recite the liturgy, so I know you are in good faith. To make an error is to risk losing the soul of the infant to the devil.' He relishes spitting out Satan's name.

Maggie clears her throat and speaks slowly, as Mrs Grimes taught her.

'I will speak the following words: I christen thee in the name of the Father, the Son, and the Holy Ghost. I will use no other profane words. In such time of necessity, in baptising any infant born and pouring water upon the head of the infant, I will use pure and clean water, and not any rose or damask water, or water made of any confection or mixture, and I will certify the curate of the parish church of any such baptising.'

The Chancellor nods, pleased she understands she must not, under any circumstances, allow any contamination by Catholic baptismal practices.

'You are hereby authorised to practise midwifery within the St Botolph Aldgate parish. Wait outside. The registrar will bring you the signed licence at the noon recess.'

Afterwards, she and Mrs Grimes walk home laughing, Maggie carrying the precious certificate. The Chancellor had not really seen her, except as a slip of a girl, had not understood the profound nature of her work. She is helpmate to the sacred cycle of life, which starts between a woman's thighs and ends, for the most part, with a woman's gentle hand washing puckered skin. Even he is not exempt.

The heaving, filthy streets of Middlesex seem full of beauty, even the sway-backed horses and her mentor's gummy grin.

Within the month, Mrs Grimes is dead from a failed heart and her student has so much work there is little time for laughter.

Late nights, early mornings, two years of wearing out boots with all the walking to one mother in need, then another. It's all a blur, interrupted when Maggie's friend, Aud, marries the coachman at the house where she works.

'I'll be needing you soon enough, Maggs. I'm nearly four months gone.'

Aud cannot stay in her job as a married woman, cause for celebration on her part, now she has a man to support her. 'Let's go to the fair. I've a hankering to see a conjurer and ride the boat-swings.'

The first chill of autumn is upon them when they leave soon after daybreak for the long walk to West Smithfield, setting off with arms linked, in high spirits, pleased Aud's man is happy for her to have a day out.

The sound of fiddles, drums and hawkers' shouts reaches them well before they get to St Bartholomew's Fair, turning the final corner into full carnival cacophony.

Maggie watches spellbound, craning her neck to see two tightrope walkers balance on a high wire strung between tall buildings, before Aud drags her over to the fire-eater, where they gasp in amazement at his feats.

The smell of hot sheep's feet at a nearby food cart reminds Maggie that she hasn't yet had breakfast, but it's roast pork she wants. Pushing through the crowd they find the stall where tender meat cooks over a bed of coals. They eat their fill, then buy gingerbreads and wash them down with a half pint of ale, standing contentedly for hours after that, watching musicians, occasionally dancing.

Men gather near two tents marked 'Soiled Doves', waiting their turn with the whores inside. The two friends give the tents a wide berth, passing stalls selling puppies, toys, medicines with suspect origins, singing birds, all manner of goods that might bring in pennies. They hold their purses close to foil pickpockets aplenty on all sides.

Finally they reach the astrologer, seated on stool with a flimsy sheet tied up to shield her from the throng. Maggie waits while Aud goes in, hoping to hear about the bright future that awaits.

She is mindlessly watching the nearby queue for the dancing bears when a man's voice makes her startle.

'Beggin' yer pardon, miss. Didn't mean to be givin' you a fright.'

She turns for a quick gander at the fellow to see the bluest eyes looking straight into hers. He is the same height, with hair the colour of sun-bleached corn. He holds up a calloused hand, the giveaway he does labouring work.

'I'm Daniel Jarman, though folks call me Dan.'

'And beggin' your pardon, Mr Jarman, but I've not asked you to tell me who you might be.' She shams irritation, for the man's open, agreeable face has caught her eye.

He grins, ignoring her words in favour of the expression on her face. 'Would you give me the liberty of buyin' you a gin or an ale? Saw you dancing a while ago, and mighty fine with the footwork you was.'

Maggie wants to shake off this fellow, but in her line of work there's little chance to meet an admirer. The time is coming when she must marry, she knows it without her father's jibes, more frequent since younger sister Fanny found a husband, a saddler no less. She knows it in her flesh, too, a rising desire to meet a solid, kind fellow and maybe bear children when the time is right.

Aud emerges from behind the sheet, looking glum. 'Fat lot o' good that shilling were.' She spies the fellow standing with her friend. 'Ooh, got a fancy man then, Maggs?'

'Don't be stupid.'

Before Aud can reply, Dan jumps in. 'Can I buy you two lovely ladies a drink, and if you're agreeable, walk you home later?'

'We'd be obliged.' Aud laughs, slapping her friend on the shoulder. 'I could go a gin.'

When they leave the fair and are heading home to Middlesex, she takes charge for a second time. 'You two go ahead, suits me to follow.'

As they walk Maggie finds herself in a great tremble without knowing why. She barely knows the man, yet something about him says he is steady in his ways, that he has already lodged under her skin. Also, the fact that he's a looker is no bad thing.

Within a year they marry, pledging to delay having a child for as long as possible so they can both keep working and put some money by. Nothing has prepared Maggie for the delights of the marital bed, the wanton way her body moves and bucks of its own accord. Late one night, curled up against Dan, she runs her fingers down his chest and chuckles. 'Lucky I know a thing or two about keepin' babies at bay.'

Perhaps it is the pleasures of the flesh that bring her undone, but over time she often forgets to use the sponge soaked in astringent. When, at twenty-three, she realises she is with child, there is no question for either her or Dan that they will keep it. They are overjoyed, though each secretly thinks it will be a tad more difficult without the money Maggie's work brings in.

Michaelmas has long gone when the waves of pain begin at daylight on a chilly autumn morning, early frost still thawing in the lane outside their rented rooms. Aud is beside her as helpmate, with a midwife arriving in time for the final passage of the baby.

Maggie says nothing to the two women of images rising unbidden in her mind: babies with heads stuck fast, mothers labouring for hours to birth a baby that's perfect yet lifeless, others arriving with deformed limbs or misshapen heads swollen by water, one who arrived with no eyes and a nose like an elephant's trunk. She pushes away the memories, reminding herself she's no different to all the labouring mothers she's known, every single one in need of forbearance.

She stops groaning out the pain, instead finding her breath, travelling on it as her belly squeezes, her back curls in agony. Breathing all the way in to her centre, letting the pain out with each lungful of air, doing it over and over until there is nothing but her breathing and her body doing the work it was made to do.

Her daughter arrives peacefully at dusk, eyes closed as though not yet ready for the world. Dan has waited nervously in the next room for most of the day, cringing at the sound of his wife's guttural cries, and goes in to her the minute he hears the baby begin whimpering.

Maggie lies back on a pillow, too exhausted to do more than give a wan smile. Dan cries tears of joy, enough for both of them, as the girl is swaddled and placed in his arms.

'By all that is holy she be a fine baby, and must have a holy name.' He kisses the top of her head.

'Hannah, her name should be Hannah,' Maggie declares, alert now. 'May God's grace always be with her.'

CHAPTER TWO

SYDNEY COVE, NEW HOLLAND, 1790

SHE IS EVERY WOMAN WHO has been beaten down to the bones by life. She feels it in the ragged edge of her breath, the way it catches in her throat. The person she used to be matters less than all she owns, the shift and jacket she wears and a single dirty dress bundled under her arm while the marines shout.

She does not belong here and never will. In the swirl of uncertainty, that much is clear as she is herded off the stinking *Lady Juliana*, intended as a breeding mare for this new colony at Sydney Cove.

Maggie Bloodworth, you are an intruder in this foreign place. The land speaks to her and what it has to say is harsh, unyielding. As her feet touch the shore, the earth moves and for a moment she thinks she will buckle and drop to her knees. The ground before her rises up as if to slap her back to the ship. She throws out her hands to hold it at bay.

She must not weaken, for what is behind her are two demon years of cruelty and hunger in Newgate Gaol, then the hell of sailing ten months away from the one who carries her light. Had she the means she might have gone over the side with the women who bribed their way to freedom while the ship was in the Thames, or taken her chances with the Spanish sailors, like the four women who slipped away in Tenerife.

At almost twenty-nine years, she has been careful on the voyage to make herself look older, tearing at her face with jagged fingernails, leaving her brown tresses matted and scarcely covered by her cap, thankful for the shapeless shift she wears. The marines prefer the younger, fresher convict women, especially those with pleasing plump bosoms and hips.

Some seek to turn it to their advantage, coupling with naval or marine officers in the hope of gaining a relationship that might improve their standing. Maggie is no maiden, though, knows the perils of relying on a man. What wits she has gained might yet prove to be in her favour.

'Step lively. We've a show to put on.' The voice behind is mocking and when she turns she sees young Sarah Newcombe laughing, twirling her skirts, in an outlandish parody of a streetwalker.

'It's what they think we be. May as well have some fun with it.'

Maggie scarcely has a chance to flash a grin when a sturdy arm reaches out and a marine grabs the girl by the shoulder and shoves her forward.

'You'll not be laughin' when you see what you're in for.'

Two hundred or more of them are marched uphill along the pitiful semblance of a street, past the Governor's cottage on the eastern side of the cove, a modest dwelling, though the only one to have glass panes in the windows.

Some of the women are clutching newborns, one mewling as though it knows the despair in Maggie's heart. The rough dirt and stones punish the thin soles of her boots, and the male eyes, so many eyes on her, on them all.

Those who were first to arrive two years earlier have fought the wilderness, forcing it back up the hill where groves of fir-like trees wait to reclaim thin, sandy ground. Huts lining the street, and scattered in groups further away, have walls made of logs plastered in pale mud, roofs covered in wooden shingles or rough thatches. She barely notices their form, instead puzzled by signs of neglect everywhere she looks. Walls are water-stained, moss growing on some, flaps of bark the only covering on doorways.

The earlier arrivals in this Great South Land are rough in appearance, the women in tattered rags worse than those of gypsies, one in a skirt made from rice sacks. Maggie catches sight of convict men wearing animal skins lashed to their feet instead of boots, naval knobs and marines in faded, frayed jackets. Near a hut a man finishes making water and puts up his britches, brazen as you like.

The newly arrived women are in good health, much better than in gaol thanks to fresh vegetables, fruit and meat taken on board during lengthy port stays for ship's repairs along the way. While they fattened up, the settlement has grown lean, its folk gut-foundered, a steadily rising number starving to death in previous months.

It doesn't occur to Maggie, intent on getting her bearings, that her ship is the first contact with the Old Country for this ramshackle place since the Union Jack was first raised. The Government has jitters about French threats and internal politics, King George talks non-stop till foam runs from his mouth in the madness. What matter that seven hundred convicts and five hundred soldiers have been dumped on a godforsaken continent to fend for themselves, let alone more sent to follow?

Every soul, felon or not, has longed for a glimpse of a ship from England, dreaming of a cargo of food, spirits, live animals for meat and breeding, tools, clothing, crockery, medical supplies, and for the officers, small indulgences from families and friends.

'More damned whores.' The disgusted voice of a Lieutenant who cares not one whit that Maggie and the others can hear him.

Captain Aitkin, meanwhile, has disembarked from the *Lady Juliana* and is in full stride towards Government House. Maggie sees him peel away from the senior officers. She doubts his presence will be applauded, for he bears devastating news that the storeship *Guardian* hit an iceberg early in the journey, ripping a hole through both the ship's bow and the hopes of replenishment from two years' worth of supplies on board.

News filtered through to the convict women well before their ship reached Sydney Cove. The frigate was towed to the Cape of Good Hope, but only after the crew was forced to ditch most of its cargo. How Maggie and the other women crowed at hearing the officers' private goods were thrown overboard first, nudging each other with elbows, laughing in the faces of the knobs. With the ship still sinking, guns were rolled into the sea, though the women agreed the real tragedy lay with the livestock and crates of supplies that followed. The ship is moored, half-sunk, at the Cape of Good Hope. It will never arrive.

As Maggie crosses a small bridge over a stream to the western side of the cove, Governor Arthur Phillip is sharing his own bad news with the Captain. The infant settlement, after eighteen months, is at breaking point. Scurvy and dysentery are rife. Ship's damp spoiled much of the seed from England. Crops have failed due to sandy soil, a dearth of farming skills, and weather patterns hard to predict.

Rations are less than needed for survival, with convicts and soldiers alike eating whatever kangaroo meat, fish or wild greens can be secured. The occasional crow makes it into a cooking pot. Bakehouse workers use rancid flour in tough bread, unable to sift out tiny weevils threaded through it. The rice fares no better, infested so badly with flour bugs it is said to be more insect than grain.

Clothes and shoes have worn out, patches on cloth and leather mended, worn out, and mended again, while winter is bearing down. Those toiling in sawpits and brickpits need new tools, while convicts and marines alike hope for stronger axes to clear land, for the English ones are no match for the tough wood of the eucalypts.

The *Lady Juliana* has discharged more mouths to feed in what is little more than a miserable camp, so if eyes look at the women with resentment and mouths twist in disgust it is no surprise.

Maggie is led along a path around a rocky shore, wide ledges dropping down on her right to meet bright water, sun bouncing off it, so blinding she is forced to raise one hand to shield her sight.

Over at Government House, Governor Arthur Phillip risks a moment of honesty with the Captain.

'It is difficult to motivate anyone to work when people believe themselves forgotten by the mother country, abandoned like orphans to a hostile world, and no less vulnerable. Each is brought to the same level in this fundamental regard.'

All of this is unknown to Maggie, straggling along with the others. As she approaches the communal hovels of the convict women's camp, her mind searches for a positive sign, a small gain she can cling to.

Surely the huts can't be worse than sleeping on the orlop deck with the ship's bilge below, its foul odour thick with the smell of women sweating and bleeding their way to Rio de Janeiro, Cape Town, then across a vast nothingness of ocean. Days of endless sky and water, blank like an empty page yet with none of the promise that might come from a nib dipped in ink. Then the Southern Ocean rearing up against them, whipped by westerly winds, to thrash the ship's timbers till they feared they would be sucked down into its fathoms.

Maggie can still feel the shuddering, the rage of the storm as it came for them all, tearing through the numb state that descended with the last glimpse of England's shores. As the waves loomed up, thundering down like battering rams against the hull, women began to wail, fearful they were about to pay an even higher price for poverty, for the useless circumstances of their existence, while others dropped to their knees and prayed.

Water leaked through planking seams overhead, hour after hour. Deadlights covered the portholes, and the lamps kept blowing out, leaving them in blackness darker than night. At the height of the storm, the monster sea rushed into their quarters, giving strange life to every loose item. Plates, pannikins, cutlery, water barrels, chamber pots leapt and danced in the water, thrashing anyone in their way.

Maggie was with a scrap of a girl, no more than sixteen years, as labour pains reached a peak. The girl knew it was far too early, barely seven months gone, and with each contraction whined miserably above the ocean's roar. Maggie gripped the side of the narrow bunk with one hand, bracing as seawater rushed across her feet, slamming a wooden bucket into her legs, knocking her down.

She clambered up to examine the girl and as she reached for the lip of the bunk the ship pitched sharply. She fought to gain purchase with a wet hand but the wave that had surged through the hatch was a mighty foe, it was not finished with her yet. She felt a brief burst of air, then was thrown down onto the timbers, her mouth filling with saltwater before she raised her head and spat out its putrid brew.

Winded, she stayed where she had fallen, letting the chaos happen and be damned. Thunder cracked overhead, water seethed back and forth, the ship rolled this way then lurched another, a woman emptied her stomach while others shouted and scrambled to gather belongings.

Maggie continued to lay in the embrace of a siren song as old as time itself, sinking into its call, overcome by the temptation to cease all effort, to bend to fate, even as she knew she would likely be dashed on the rocks of its false promise.

The girl's screams rose and at the sound of her terror Maggie's arms and legs began struggling with the effort to stand. As the ship righted itself, she clung on beside the bunk, knowing full well the baby, when it came, would not have proper lungs to breathe. Knowing, too, a harsh truth, that within her she had the willingness to give up. It had not visited before; she saw at once it was a temptation she must fight with all her might.

The day of the storm is still fresh in her mind, shaking her adrift from the solid ground she's trusted in herself. Now she faces a new land intent on destroying what remains of who she is, of what she understands to be at the core of her character.

As she walks, the ground faintly beats in a different way to the familiar thrum of St Botolph's. It taps a message through the soles of her feet. *You are not mine. You are not of me.*

Does Dan feel it, in the far-flung place where he has been ensnared? The rhythm of a land that is not his own, that seeks to chew him up and spit him out as a rat-catcher's terrier might cough up a sharp bone. A land that cares naught for him. This land that cares naught for her.

It's not the time to think of him, she insists to herself, straggling behind the other women. Yet here he is, determined, not caring that she has more immediate matters to consider, his square face and bright blue eyes right there at the front of her mind, shoulders strong, tipping his head to the side like he does when listening to something she says.

Dan Jarman is a good man, a hard worker. He would never have consented to leave them if he had been in gainful work or in his right mind. She has said the words to herself often, polished them with great care till they glow, giving off a comforting warmth. Time and time again she has drawn herself up to them as a chair to a fire, the embers fit to thaw a freezing soul.

When he disappeared she walked for miles through twisting alleys, her three-year-old daughter sleeping on her hip as she sought out those who knew him, until eventually she found the truth.

He had been in low spirits, drinking in the alehouse, easy prey for the American ship's captain who offered him work and the promise of free passage.

Oh Dan, you should have known better, for we'd heard of vipers who tricked men into servitude. No doubt the captain signed him on while drunk, then with the indenture contract in hand locked him up. By the time he was sober he'd have been on his way to Virginia, a hostage for auction as labour for a tobacco plantation, treated worse than an ox.

She clings uselessly to the hope he is alive, yet is savvy enough to know he'll be thrashed till he does what is demanded to repay a trumped up debt to the shipowner. Three, four, five years—what does the nature of the contract matter? No one ever returns.

The grief of Dan being snatched away remains a festering sore, but the storm has challenged her with something that troubles her more as she walks. She feared death in the tumult of wind and water yet was shown something within that is a far greater danger, a weakness that must be resisted if she is ever to regain her daughter.

She must stop thinking of the past. She hurries ahead to Sarah's side and reaches for her hand, giving a brief squeeze the younger woman takes as reassurance, though Maggie means the touch for her own benefit.

Maggie and nine other women are directed to a hut that looks fit to collapse, long brown stains down the front wall, mould growing on one side of the roof. The shelter has walls of woven twigs plastered in a mix of mud and white pipeclay and is bare, except for wooden pallets on the floor, a few cooking pots, and three or four sacks with victuals. They are to be no different to alley cats, spitting and hissing over a few dried morsels.

The air crowds in on Maggie, dank, heavy, like it did in the room when her mother took a final breath. Her chest rises and falls in short, rapid movements, her palms sweat, a band of pain shackles her head. She ignores the women scrapping over the corner spaces of the hut and bursts out through the doorway into the light.

She leans against the wall, breathing in hard through her nose and out in long breaths through her mouth to tame the panic. A nearby line of small firs sigh in the breeze, their long needles swaying a little, shrunken trees, unlike the soaring pine she saw in a London churchyard. She imagines them breathing in and out in unison with her, feels their moist air pricking at her throat and lungs, bringing calm.

As her heart settles back to its normal rhythm she takes in the scene before her, over the sprawling harbour they call Port Jackson, where the work of unloading the ship's cargo continues. To the left she is startled to see, on a sandstone ledge, three or four naked figures gathered around a low fire, natives with skin dark as the hottentots at the Cape. The smell of charred fish wafts her way, and before she recognises what it is her mouth is watering after weeks of salt pork and sea biscuits tough enough to stop a musket ball.

She turns away from the tantalising smoke and scans to the right towards a loud voice barking orders at what is clearly a parade ground.

A group of red jacketed marines march up and down in formation, swinging arms and legs in unison, bodies close in tight rows, guns on shoulders, bayonet spikes pointing at the midday sun. A drummer sets the beat in grubby white jacket with red cuffs jerking up and down, like the pecking beak of the tightly wound toy bird a market man once tried to sell her.

She has seen many extraordinary, tragic, devastating things in her life, but this display by the Marine Corps is surely the most pointless. Little wonder the sailors call them lobsters.

All night she lies rigid on the grass-strewn hard pallet, at the mercy of the anxious hours beyond midnight. No matter the effort she summons, the fracture lines in her family grow ever wider, tearing away to all points of the globe and no way to unite them again.

Hannah in the London workhouse in Seven Step Alley or the Middlesex workhouse over on Nightingale Lane. Maggie shudders; dear God, let them not be working her in one of the match factories. She's seen girls with phossy jaw, bones eaten away by vapours as they dip matches in phosphorous. They don't last long.

Dan, even as she thinks of him, is maybe waking for a long day on a plantation, digging ditches or picking cotton, taking a thrashing when he dares speak up for food or rest for others as much as himself. The man she's loved would surely take that risk. She dare not imagine otherwise, that his spirit has become weak.

Her, trapped on the hem of the world, as far as she can go from either of them, at any moment losing her grip, spinning off into space.

The sun rises, the sun sets whether she is here or not. The tide washes in then out, paying no heed to Maggie Bloodworth, her needs or desires. The sun, the tide, the country from which she's been banished, none of them care that the only place she belongs is beside her daughter.

At daylight, after a breakfast of skilly with a few scrapings of wallaby meat, the women are sorted like ruined wheat from chaff, their skills giving them no advantage. Those already chosen as wives are spared to cook and clean for their men, whether officers, marines or convicts. Some are mistresses to senior ranks, though for the sake of appearances are called servants.

Milliners, lacemakers, glovemakers, all are now common labourers. Fishwives, hawkers, ladies maids, plain cooks, nursemaids, book stitchers, every single one is reduced to the lowest station, treated the same as skullions, pickpockets and harlots. Trained hands that crafted silk brocades and damasks with precision are sent to do washing in tannin-stained waters running into the harbour. Eyes that know exactly where to place a needle to create delicate flower trims must search out shells to burn for lime. Those who grumble are made to scythe grass to be dried for bedding, or stack bricks at the brickfields.

'Think yerselves lucky you ain't sent to the stone quarry.' The nameless marine speaks to the women as he might a pack of stray curs. *Careful mister high and mighty,* Maggie thinks, *like vicious mongrels we'd easily do you over.*

Sarah and a handful of others are put to work in the bakehouse. Another group is led away to whittle pegs for roofing shingles from timber fallen in an acacia grove on the edge of the settlement. Maggie is one of twenty or more assigned as hutkeepers for groups of single convict men.

'You'll sweep, cook and do the washing. Make sure every man has his clothes back, clean and properly mended, on Sunday mornings.'

She begins following one of the knobs around the shoreline as he allocates huts. Behind her a second marine glances at the ship's manifest.

'Hold up,' he shouts. 'Says here one of you is a nurse. Which one?'

Maggie raises a hand warily. He points at her, gesturing with his head back towards the hospital. 'Report to the surgeon, and be quick about it.'

She follows the rough track that links the women's huts to the hospital, before it continues on to the observatory on the point. To the right, Sarah disappears into a bakehouse. To the left a narrow wooden building, maybe eighty feet long, sits in a large garden, vegetable plots fenced off despite little growing there in sandy soil, while a lone goat is tethered to one side.

A smaller brick dispensary sits beside it, barely noticed by Maggie. She is caught in the thought that with meat in such short supply the goat will have a brief life, as will the seventy sheep their ship took on at the Cape.

Maggie enters the door of the main building and waits for her eyes to adjust to the dimness inside. The windows have no glass, covered instead with lattice shutters made of twigs woven loosely together. She stands in a small entry room with a ward running off each side, one marked for convicts and another for soldiers and civil officers.

'What is your business here?'

The accent is Irish, the face impassive. The pungent odour of the dying surrounds the lanky fellow appearing in the gloom.

'I were sent to help.'

'We've enough cleaners and washerwomen.' Contempt sounds the same in any accent.

A loud groan can be heard rising then falling. A man cries in the ward next door and pleads for his mother.

'That's not why I were sent, sir. I have knowing of birthing, tending the sick, layin' out the dead. Though if you've no need of me …'. She turns to go.

'You'll do. Come with me.'

He leads her into the convict ward where the sick are laid out in rows, some little more than a bag of bones. She holds her breath at the smell of rotting flesh as she follows his brisk steps towards a woman carrying a basin and cloth.

'I'm Assistant Surgeon Considen and this is Mrs Hoile. You're to do as she says.'

Maggie is put to work immediately changing the dressing on a young man's head. His skull has been fractured by an axe rebounding from hard timber when felling a tree. She has seen wounds bad as these on the head and arms of men injured by factory machines. Doubtless he will be dead before the week's out, yet it doesn't deter her from speaking in soothing tones, touching him gently as she works.

Next she cleans the ulcerated cut on the leg of an old lag while he grunts with pain. The leech gatherers are late returning from damp gullies where they search for the hundreds needed each month to clean impure blood. She is directed, instead, to a supply of maggots in a small wooden box, the stink of dead rats reaching her before she lifts the lid and scrapes up a few squirming grubs on her spoon. They will do wonders with dead tissue around the eruption of raw flesh that won't heal.

Her inquiry about laudanum for those groaning in pain is met with a shake of the head. Medical supplies have run out. There is not even honey to calm the pus of boils and wounds, though Mrs Hoile is hopeful a hunting party out at present will find a nest or two of native bees in tree hollows.

The no-nonsense head nurse keeps an eye out from a distance, in case her new worker has lied about her abilities to escape heavier labour.

Maggie ignores the woman's gaze and spoons elixir of vitriol into the mouths of those with scurvy, the sharp smell of the sulfuric acid solution of wine, vinegar and spices not strong enough to conceal the stench of flesh wasting away or gums swollen where teeth have fallen out. Some moan with pain that bites in their bones.

For those with hacking coughs or laboured breathing, Mrs Hoile hands Maggie a bottle of clear liquid and a spoon for administering it.

'Eucalyptus oil, a new medicinal for lungs and fever. The surgeon had it distilled from the leaves of local trees.'

Her frown belies her words. 'Seems to work.'

For the first time since Newgate Maggie feels a sliver of hope. If there's knowledge of local herbs and plants for healing then perhaps she can offer services as a handywoman, outside the toil her sentence requires. She may yet raise the fare for her passage back home.

'The surgeon, he know much about the uses of local plants?'

'Enough. Now get on with your work.'

Two women at the end of the ward have finished cleaning dysentery patients. As one passes by Maggie with her basin of filthy water, she slows a little to whisper.

'He watches the natives, gets 'em to show him what plants they use for ailments.'

A sudden downpour cuts off any chance of questions, sending every woman scurrying for pans and buckets to catch rain dripping through cracks in the roof. As Maggie returns to her duties she swears she can feel mould growing across her damp shoulders.

The air has cooled by the time Mrs Hoile dismisses her. She is wending her way towards her quarters when her attention is caught by a small group of women gathering outside a far hut. Curiosity takes her there.

The sight that comes into focus is a strange one. Sitting on a log sliced to form a seat is an old woman, maybe fifty, stringy white hair falling around her wrinkled face, suckling a child.

The woman closest cannot contain herself. 'Be it yours?'

The object of their attention takes her time in nodding.

'What evil magic is this?' another growls.

'No devilry in it.' The women turn to see the source of the forceful voice, a tall matron, ample-bodied.

'We who came first have a habit of drinking sweet tea.'

The conversation has taken a confusing turn. Maggie, like everyone, knows basic supplies have run out.

'Where do you get sugar?'

A couple of the women snicker, leaving the matron to answer.

'Not tea you'd know, but a local herb, bitter yet sweet. Native sarsaparilla they call it, grows on a vine in shady gullies. Many who drink it are soon teeming with child.'

Having announced her authority on the subject, she walks off. Maggie follows, plucking at her sleeve.

'Wait a moment. Tell me, have you knowing about plants round here?'

'No more than another. Now I must cook for my husband.' With that she hurries away.

Sarah is four months gone. On the journey to the colony she had a weakness for a midshipman, attracted by the cut of his dark blue naval jacket. Now he has sowed the seed he wants nothing to do with her.

'Help me, Maggie. Without a stoppage of nature I'll be carin' for a babe on my own. I can barely find the strength to look after myself.'

They sit on a mound of dirt near the rear of the hut, Sarah stuffing her fist into her mouth to muffle the crying. In this strange society tittle-tattle has a value, can be traded or used against you, and she doesn't want the others to know her predicament.

Maggie shakes her head gently, one arm around her friend.

'Oh dear girl, I've no herbs to help bring down the flowers.' She has long been distanced from her midwife's bag with its powders and potions, and she dare not ask the Chief Surgeon or his assistants for counsel. Aiding abortion could end in a whipping, or worse, a short drop from a rope.

She herself had been known to take a spoonful of pennyroyal oil to bring on bleeding—not a drop more, for it could kill. With Dan sometimes unable to find labouring work it was best not to risk another mouth to feed.

Now she's at a loss, what she learned of herbs and salves so long ago has no value in this strange land.

Two days later she returns to the hut at dusk, wearied by a long day with five new men to care for, holding the hand of first one then a second of her patients as they died, the last begging for her to smother him so his agony would cease.

Sarah lies limp on her pallet, the other women gone to the communal fire to cook their meal. Maggie touches her friend's forehead, clammy, slick with sweat. As she does, Sarah opens her eyes.

'What's wrong, dear girl?'

'I have done it Maggie, but I fear I've drunk too much.' Sarah closes her eyes.

'What have you drunk?' She shakes her friend by the shoulder, an old panic waking, churning her gut.

When there is no response, she taps the girl on the face, gently at first then harder, slapping one cheek then the other till she rouses.

'Benton, she looks after the fires in the bakehouse ovens. She made friends with a native woman, sneaks bread to her oftentimes.'

Sarah's voice fades for a moment and Maggie fears she will slip back into unconsciousness.

'Tell me what you've taken so I can help'.

'The baby's gone, Maggie, this afternoon. Such a tiny creature, not even a hand-span long, I buried it in the woods.'

The girl shudders, though no tears come.

'I did as the tribal woman told Benton, gathered green berries from the kangaroo apple bush. Strange things, shaped like an egg, as though they hint at what they can do to a hatching.

'I boiled 'em, drank the tea. I wanted to be sure, so I drank it all.'

She pats the girl's hand.

'It's okay Sarah. I just need to see what's happening.'

The petticoats are stained with dried blood, but Maggie is relieved to see there is no show her friend still bleeds. She fetches water and helps the girl rise onto one elbow, insisting she drink a full cup.

Afterwards, she seems more alert despite a groggy voice.

'You never told me what they got you for.'

Sarah waits for a response, eyes half-closed. She regards Maggie's silence for a moment.

'I expect it were sneak-thieving from your employer, same as most of us. Or were you one of the clever ones runnin' a snuff racket?'

Maggie shakes her head. The one-off thieving, and not much to show for it, was a long way from any plan to throw snuff in a shop-keeper's face, blinding him to nick a big haul.

She wants to take Sarah's mind off the griping pains in her belly, after all her own story is no more shameful than any convict woman's, sealed by the hot wax of an unfair law. It's not that she distrusts Sarah with the details of her past, the difficulty lies with another.

The story leads back to Hannah, for that reason she will not tell it. The sensation of being torn from her is so great she has consigned it to the farthest corner of her mind, locked it there behind a separate door for the beast of grief.

Yet here is a key turning against the bolt, even as she sits with her now sleeping friend, stroking her hair.

CHAPTER THREE

MIDDLESEX, GREATER LONDON, 1787

I T STARTS AS AN ORDINARY day, as these things often
do. She wakes earlier than three-year-old Hannah and
lies there, watching her soft face, hair pale and sweet
as meadow hay, same as her father's, listening to the girl's
butterfly breath before she stirs, never thinking it will be
the last time.

When her daughter wakes she dresses her, brushes her
hair and ties it with a dark green ribbon, the only new
thing they've owned in the months since Dan disappeared.

Soon after, she leaves Hannah with her neighbour, for a
share of the fee in the usual arrangement, to stay overnight
nursing the consumptive wife of a printer at St Giles In
The Fields. The girl clings to her leg. 'Mamma staaay.' She
cries, fat tears running down her cheeks. Maggie must prise
the pink hands from her thigh, and leave swiftly before her
own heart breaks and she changes her mind.

The walk takes her away from familiar sights, past gin
shops, overcrowded dosshouses, and through the Rookery
slums where poor Irish families, Greeks and Armenians
live more confined than her own kind. On the corner of

a wider street with brick houses a charity boy torments a dog, only stopping when she threatens to clip him under the ear.

She finds number twenty-seven, taking the stairs down to the servants' door at the side.

The one room Maggie inhabits with Hannah is in reality half a room, a flimsy wall hastily erected years earlier to divide it for two tenants. It would fit in the buttery of the two-storey house she enters.

John Reider has done well for himself making cheap broadsides and printed songs churned out on tea-paper blotched with lamp black and oil. Popular ballads rake in a steady stream of coin, coarse ditties for drunk men to sing. *The Wanton Wife of Bath*, *Beggar's Wedding*, *The Woeful Lamentation of Mrs Jane Shore*, Maggie's heard them all, knows her work earns more respect than her employer's.

Perhaps it is the grubby way he earns his money that breaks her, or the slightly shabby house pretending to be something more, with its faded oriental pattern on the wall tapestry and the smell of rabbit pie the cook bakes in the kitchen next day. The cause is of little consequence, for what matters is the sense of injustice that overcomes her, anger rising up that she and her child suffer with so little to keep them from the streets while this family has so much.

What happens next should have been a question of principle, which would have freed it of shame. Instead, as she approaches the servants' door to leave, the anger summons an impulse when she spies a bundle of clothes and linen left for the washerwoman. Her hand is a ladle, swiftly scooping up lightweight garments to hide under her skirt, a cotton dimity petticoat, two muslin aprons, and a child's linen cap trimmed with delicate lace.

Her feet hurry up the steps, one hand holding the garments tight against her body, already deciding to sell all but the child's cap to one of the traders at the Rag Fair in Rosemary Lane. She will wear her Sunday dress so she won't be mistaken for one of the stinking rag-pickers turning up with what they've scavenged from rotting rubbish piled up near the riverside breweries and in laneway corners.

She rushes down a soot-smeared alleyway, resisting the urge to break into a run and betray herself as a thief.

As she steps briskly, the next moment is upon her. Perhaps it is the one her poor mother had seen, staring through a crack in time as she approached death.

When Maggie turns the corner she comes face to face with Mr Reider, on his way home. In an instant he recognises her.

'What have you there?' It is not an inquiry, but an accusation.

She pushes past, running with him in close pursuit, dodging stalls, weary mothers, past the skittle grounds, and through the entrance to Cripple's Court, where a loaded cart pulls away from a storehouse and blocks her path.

She hurls the stolen clothing under the cart in an attempt to foil her pursuer, but he is on her, gripping her arms, yanking them painfully behind while he screams for the watch. The driver has no time for yet another filcher, sees them every day. He flicks his whip at the horse, the cart finishes turning and pulls away, crushing the white cap under one wheel.

Within the week Maggie is led from a dank, dim cell at Newgate Gaol along a basement tunnel to the Old Bailey sessions house. She has given her maiden name so she can be tried by it, not wishing to pile disgrace on Dan's family name.

She stands, a little unsteady, blinking in cold light from dirty windows up high in the courtroom. Members of the First Middlesex Jury sit behind a raised timber panel, observing without expression as she answers to the charge of stealing.

It is the twelfth day of December 1787, and Hannah will not know it is her fourth birthday. She will not understand why her ma doesn't come for her. It is a cruel thing to reach out a hand for what you seek to give a child only to find, too late, you hold a knife that will hurt them in ways that can never heal.

The courtroom has no rules Maggie can fathom at first, impossible as a dream where people abruptly appear or depart with no rhyme or reason. Maybe it's a zoo, the jurymen caged up above, some alert as trapped animals, others slumped as though defeated. Black gowned men sit behind a long table, ravens who take turns to preen and caw as each case is heard. Witnesses jostle for space, while ushers on the edges of the room shift from one leg to another in the manner of wading birds, or lean against wood panelling.

Her turn comes, catching her by surprise after days suspended in fog, and now she is a specimen in a glass jar, eyes staring at her. The prosecutor spits out the facts of her grand larceny, his voice rising at the end. 'The stolen goods are worth a sum total of seven shillings and tenpence.

Three days wages for a tradesman, though his earnings would come by honest labour.'

The verdict is swift, jurors and court officers keen to get through the day's business to avoid the gaol fever outbreak that has already killed at least ten people who work in the building. Her destiny is worth no more than fifteen minutes of their time.

The court recorder writes quickly in his book, her name and crime on the page for all time. Then the beak speaks from his bench.

'Guilty. To be transported for seven years.'

The court officer is rough as he attaches the chains, his breath hot in her face. 'Stand still so I can get this over with.'

She is marched back to gaol, too overcome to weep or tear at her clothes.

Hannah, light of my life. What have I done?

During the first year in gaol the neighbour brings the girl in twice. Hannah is growing fast and the woman complains about how much food she eats. Maggie's da is long gone, her brothers scattered to the winds by the quest for work. She is unlettered so a cellmate, a maid whose mistress taught her to write, scratches words across a page to Fanny, now with two children of her own.

Maggie pleads with her sister to take her dear girl, explaining the child's kindness, her gentle ways, a nature that's pleasing and easy.

She hears not a word from Fanny. The neighbour never returns.

The image of her sweet girl in the workhouse burns in her mind, a fire threatening to lay waste to any strength she has left. Hannah, so innocent, will likely be sent to work in the cotton mills up north, if she even survives till she's of age.

The thought of her daughter's neglect is far greater torture than sleeping on the hard floor of the cell, fighting for space with the rats amid the uncontrolled pissing of mad women, and the bellowing of drunks slowly poisoning themselves, going blind from cheap gin watered down by turpentine spirit or sulphuric acid.

The gut-burning *mother's ruin*, sold freely in the gaol, offers oblivion, but Maggie's lack of sponsorship by family or friends who might send money spares her from its ravages.

Adrift from the two pillars of her life, mother and wife, she's afraid to look within for fear of finding she has ceased to exist. There's no need of a mirror to show that even the hair on her head is disappearing. She wakes from fitful sleep with clumps of it tangled in her fingers. Perhaps her teeth will be next, she thinks, though by some miracle they hold fast in her gums.

Late in the second year the guards start emptying cells. Day after day women disappear, the sick and feeble still able to walk, girls with bodies as young as eleven but tongues as sharp as old slags, single women, married women; mothers, some with fretting babes or numb toddlers in their arms; and heartier souls gifted with endurance despite the meagre diet of salt meat, old bread, and watery skilly lacking a single oat.

She has ministered to many, advising on herbs to be smuggled in for healing, giving succour, closing the eyes of the dead even though they will not have the dignity of an eternity box. The women penned alongside her have occasionally paid with a few morsels loved ones have brought in, but mostly with respect, though it's poor currency in a gaol where even the vermin fight for scraps.

Soon she is bundled into the tunnels and chained in a line to others, marched through the streets while on either side jeering faces enjoy the afternoon spectacle.

A ruddy faced fellow in a coarse jacket spits at them, the glistening gobbet landing on her foot. She spins to catch his eye over her shoulder, two years of caged rage exploding, and lunges towards him, screaming. 'You filth. Next time you thieve may you hang.'

Her irons yank her up short, and he chortles as she is shoved forward.

'I be clever, not a beef-witted blowse who gets caught.'

At Blackfriars they are packed into a lighter and rowed to a transport ship moored at Gravesend, near the mouth of the Thames, the river sluggish under scudding clouds.

Maggie waits her turn on the deck. Soon steward John Nicol knocks the rivets from her irons on his anvil, releasing her from their death weight and earning himself another half-crown from gaolers. She is free to walk around the deck, with as much liberty as a canary in a coal mine.

She floats confined, river-bound, for another five months, watching a ragtag of prisoners rowed week by week to the ship's ladder as gaols in south-east England are steadily emptied of women. Each new group, whether brawlers, quiet in defeat, cunning manipulators or steady in character, upsets the shifting balance of relations between the convicts, who instinctively seek to find or force their place in a semblance of social order.

46

Maggie walks the deck each day as tensions rise, trying to avoid the bickering, the hair pulling and fist fights that break out, steering clear of the scar-faced brothel madam, said to be quick with a knife blade she keeps hidden in the armpit of her sleeve.

Unexpectedly, Nicol's measured, sober manner shifts the mood for the better by causing a near riot. Early one evening, after the latest mob of women has been unshackled, he falls into a contemplative mood, telling those nearest that the barque has been named for Juliana of Norwich, a mystic who survived the black plague centuries earlier.

Perhaps he aims to impress young Sarah Whitlam, for it's clear to everyone that the Lincolnshire lass has caught his eye.

'All shall be well, all manner of things shall be well.'

The Scotsman recites the nun's words in what seems like a tone of reverence, but with a thick burr that maybe conceals his pleasure at making a cruel joke at the expense of the convicts.

The women within his hearing decide it is the latter and word spreads like wildfire. It is some time before the steward and officers can quieten the uproar of outrage and threats of a fist to shut Nicol's gob, made more powerful by the fact that the women are now finally united against the common foe of male authority.

As peace is restored Maggie notices a pale Scottish girl, recently boarded, sitting against the fife rail, arms folded across her chest, ignoring thick strands of red hair blowing back and forth across her face. In the evening, the girl is still in the same spot, though now holds a Bible.

Maggie sits beside her. The girl's eyes are swollen from weeping. Nicol steps over, lowering his voice.

'It pains me to see a countrywoman in such a bad way. I lent her my holy book for comfort, but she reads it not.'

Maggie waits, asks gentle questions, offers sympathy. Tears and sighing are the only responses. At length she stands, leaves the girl sitting alone, and retires below.

The grey light of dawn picks its way across the river as Maggie returns to find the deck around the fife rail empty. A splashing sound approaches and she leans over the side to see four men stow longboat oars and wrestle with a load to be carried aboard.

The first man grunts as he reaches the top of the ladder, a bulky wet rug folded in half across his shoulder. He slings it, with relief, onto the deck. It lands with a thump and a spray of water. Only then does Maggie see red hair, stiff eyes, mottled purple lips, and the Scottish girl's skirts heavy with river muck.

It is the end of July in 1789 when the barque heads south into the Atlantic Ocean, where the trade winds will lift her sails. Maggie turns her back to Plymouth, away from her first and last view of the Devon Coast. She closes her eyes and summons her heart to tug on invisible threads of love connected through blood and marrow to her daughter, releasing a promise on the wind.

I will find you.

Every woman is on the main deck. Most have long been emptied of tears, yet their cheeks are wet as they are cast out for all time from their kin and homeland. Not all in sorrow, no, for they are tears of joy for some. Despised in their own country, as they sail away from disgrace, from their pauper past, they hope they may yet be blessed with the luck to make good on the underside of the world.

Maggie lifts her head and watches the sky open up, soaring wider overhead than she has ever seen it, swallowing their puny ship and taking with it any emotion she might chance.

She was bereft back then, as the ship's bow faced into the unknown south.

In the months at sea, though, she learned to swallow down the grief in a way she hadn't in gaol. Leaving England's shores did it, made her chew over the sorrow till what remained was an undigested lump pressing against her ribs. If she doesn't poke at it, leaves it be, she can live alongside it, which is why she resolves anew that the story starting when her feet hit the *Lady Juliana's* deck is the only one she will share with Sarah or another.

Her friend sleeps peacefully at last and Maggie goes to her own pallet. The memories have piled up too heavily, pressing down so the hard timber digs into her hips more than usual.

She drifts half-awake through the night, rising at daylight to return to the hospital. Considen arrives soon after, pausing on his rounds through the convict ward to stand beside Maggie.

'Good to see such a diligent worker, a rarity in this place.'

Maggie dips her head briefly, remaining silent.

'And an upstanding woman, too, I'm told.' He smirks and walks away.

Maggie bristles. What a two-faced scoundrel, Assistant Surgeon or not, with a family in England, by all accounts, not stopping him from seeding the babe of married convict Ann Green. And Surgeon-General John White, he makes no secret of taking liberties with his servant girl. The line once drawn between right and wrong is no more use than sand at holding back the tide. How dare men with rank lord it over others when they're no better than a ponce in a whorehouse.

She is still annoyed at midday when she is sent off for a short break. Outside, shouts can be heard above rain and wind.

'The flag's up, the flag's up.'

She rushes down the rough path as people stream from huts, vegetable gardens, sawmills and the stone quarry. No one knows what ship has been spotted by the flagstaff crew at South Head, one of two capes marking the entrance to the harbour, but each person fills with irrational elation. Women hug, ignoring wet hair, men slap each other's backs, children run and dance in the excitement, kicking up sprays of black sand with bare feet.

Within the hour the *Justinian* hoves into view. The Governor proceeds down his lawn, past the Union Jack flying from its pole at the edge of the earthen redoubt, and into his boat. The crew pushes off from the wharf immediately, the men rowing hard as the Governor is keen to reach the ship quickly. On his return, word goes around like wildfire that the vessel carries all manner of goods, the overflow that did not fit when the supply ship lying scuttled at the Cape was originally loaded.

The *Justinian* carries no convicts so has made remarkably good time. Casks of flour, barrels of pork, supplies of oatmeal, pease meal, vinegar, oil, spirits, sugar—the list passes in whispers and shouts across The Camp, right down to bales of cloth, unmade slops for convict men, blankets, and six hundred pieces of a portable military hospital.

Every woman is soon put to the task of making up the slops, whether seamstress or not, given material for two coarse convict shirts. She must work at her needle, when not at Government labour, until the work is finished, before getting the doings to sew a pair of trousers. Maggie is not exempt from her duties, either, but must sew in what little free time is spared.

Each day on her way to work she glimpses a little more of the portable hospital emerge piece by piece from the ground. First the wooden framing panels are hastily erected, then next morning the cross bearers go on, followed later that week by plates, a roof frame and finally, a copper sheath to cover it all. Praise God it keeps out more rain than the curling shingles in the old building.

The new structure is more than eighty feet long and twenty feet wide, doubling available ward space.

'A heartening touch of progress,' Considen declares. 'At least we will have space to move easily between patients.'

Less than a week later the flag goes up again, causing more excitement.

A crowd quickly gathers near the natural rock formation from which the main wharf has been built, watching as the Governor's six oarsmen pit themselves against the current, the tillerman forcing the boat's bow into the teeth of a westerly.

The longboat makes slow progress down the harbour, and it is some time before it becomes a dark dot in the grey then fades to nothing. Most of the crowd stays clustered around the foreshore despite the cold, others in small groups up the hill, scanning the water for a first glimpse of the new arrivals.

When the ship parts the gloom, English colours flying, those at the cooking fires beat their pots and the shovels used as frying pans. A great cheer resounds around the cove. Maggie sees it is a barque, smaller than the ship that bore her to the cove.

The Governor is rowed ashore, face grim. Word goes around from his boat crew that it is the *Surprize,* a convict transport. Soon after, the oarsmen take the settlement's only chaplain, Rev Richard Johnson, out to the vessel.

All around, men, women and children in high spirits celebrate with singing and raucous laughter, while Maggie is frozen to the spot.

Something dark, terrible, is coming from this ship, she's certain. Hidden in its timbers are cunning folk intent on bad deeds, commanding the restless dead, bringing terror to the living. She senses them streaming forth, riding each wave and ripple, coming closer, withered fingers reaching out to clutch at whoever they can. Though she stands three or four chains up the hill, she takes a sudden step back. She must stop such thoughts, not let demons into her head.

Below her the marine corps commander barks out orders, but she's too far away to hear what he shouts. His officers and subordinates begin marshalling convict men into small groups. The purpose is not evident to Maggie, until the swell of activity surges up to where she stands.

'You lot.' An approaching officer points to Maggie and the women nearby.

'Any that know how to help the sick, get to the hospital wharf.' He pauses to direct his group of convict men towards one of the main store huts.

'The rest of you, come with me. We need all the hands we can get to set up sick tents.'

Maggie steps towards him. 'I'm a nurse. How many need help?'

'A hundred or more. Stop yapping and get moving.'

At the narrow hospital wharf a longboat returns with Rev Johnson. Maggie edges in close to Considen and the three other surgeons, in urgent discussions with the chaplain.

'Many lie there half naked, unable to stand. The smell is so offensive I could hardly bear it. A large number are near death.' Rev Johnson presses a soiled kerchief to his forehead.

'You'll need a grave digging detail to get started now.'

Chief Surgeon White, former naval man, son of an Irish farmer, knows the ravages of disease and malnutrition. He reassures the chaplain.

'Medical supplies have run low, true, but we'll manage.' Within hours he will regret his show of confidence.

Maggie stands quietly to the side watching the *Surprize,* now anchored in the cove, as its boats are lowered. Considen signals that she is to approach him.

'Work with Mrs Hoile, quick as you can.'

They are still organising the last of the ointments, as well as bandages, lint, and the sticks they use for splints when the first longboat is rowed in.

'These three croaked it when we hauled 'em down from the deck.' The panting oarsman points at a trio of bodies slumped in the stern, then helps his crew hoist six skeletal figures and the corpses onto the wharf, before they row off.

The living are desperate creatures, barely recognisable as men. Ribs protrude, skin stretches thin over skulls topped by occasional tufts of hair, trousers are crusted with foul matter. Ankles are raw to the bone from months in slave irons, the legs unable to move more than an inch or two.

Two of the six can walk, though are bent over with painful cramps. One of the four lying on the wharf manages to roll over and attempts to crawl towards the grass before slumping face down. Maggie goes to him but it's clear his heart has given out.

Another longboat approaches, then another, waves of broken convicts offloaded with less ceremony than if they were sacks of flour. The numbers flow down the column of the ledger in the clerk's hand, but to Maggie each is a poor wretch she must comfort however she can, with soft words, water, clean dressings on wounds. The most urgent are carted on makeshift stretchers to the hospital compound, where sick tents sprout like mushrooms around the buildings.

She overhears snatches of angry talk between surgeons and officers. The ship leaked in any gale, chained convicts were often in water up to their waists. Unlike Maggie's ship, where rations were issued as intended, these contractors are slave traders who have withheld convict food to sell for profit on arrival. The Guv has called it murder, says it is barbarous, will insist the slave traders be called to account. It is doubtful convicts on two vessels still at sea have fared any better.

Maggie is chilled by what she hears, hands shaking as she forces herself to keep fear and dread at bay. The men need care, not her distress.

Twilight thickens by the time the wharf is cleared of the living and the last of the dead are lined up head to toe on one side. She can only afford them a single glance. On the other side of the globe, in London streets, English counties, Scottish crofts, Welsh mining towns, and on Irish farms, the blood of mothers, fathers, wives and children will be running cold and they will not know why. She mustn't think about the kin who will mourn these men. The torment would tear her apart.

She chews a chunk of bread handed to her, gulps down a pannikin of water from a barrel at the top of the wharf, and heads to the hospital, where chaos has overtaken the buildings as well as emergency tent shelters. It will be a long night.

CHAPTER FOUR

SYDNEY COVE, 1790

TWO DAYS LATER THE FLAG goes up again. Maggie has snatched a mere hour or two of rest each night since the *Surprize* arrived, spending a precious part of it combing her hair to deter nits from lice-covered patients.

Soon two more transports anchor off nearby Garden Island and the process of warping them into the cove begins. Maggie watches from in front of the hospital as a longboat is lowered from the East Indiaman *Neptune*, then the barque *Scarborough*. Each bobbing boat is rowed ahead and a kedge anchor dropped, then the crews haul one ship then another to its anchor.

Through a haze of exhaustion Maggie watches the ships come closer. She turns her back and walks into the hospital before she can give in to the urge to sink to the ground and rub her face in dirt, the stuff of weathered rock, abiding, elemental, unlike the horror made by men.

By noon the next day more than two hundred sick men, women too, have been landed, so many that the thirty tents pitched in front of the hospital overflow and nearby huts are full. One blanket must do for four to share, despite nights turning bitterly cold. Scurvy, the bloody flux or fever have taken hold of most carried up from the hospital wharf. Maggie stops seeing individual faces, only a blur of splitting skin and weeping sores.

One of the cleaning women wringing out bloodied rags nearby is temporarily overcome.

'God help the poor wretches. A death's head on a mopstick, every one of 'em.'

Maggie calls to her. 'Fetch more water. They need help, not yer pity.'

Worst of all are the sick raging with delusions and terrors, ulcers spreading in the final stages of the pox. The Chief Surgeon insists they be tied down to protect themselves and those who care for them.

When Maggie falls onto her pallet, well after dark, a distorted face floats in the space behind her closed eyelids, blocking the path to sleep. The woman, among the first six free wives allowed passage with their convict husbands, pleaded for her weakened man to get treatment, begging shamelessly to any surgeon or nurse who came near.

Melva Ranse's twelve-year-old son sat impassively on a rock near the hospital tent. Maggie caught a glimpse of him through the open flap. He remained motionless in a heavy downpour, as though beyond feeling or sensation. His mother, bordering on hysterical, begged for oats to make a poultice for pus-filled ulcers on her husband's black and blue ankles.

'I've come all this way, Cuddy Ranse. Don't you dare bloody die on me now.'

She plucked at Maggie's sleeve. 'I beg you, have mercy. The voyage, it did in my two youngest. My boy and me, we're goners too if we lose this man.'

The woman and her children sailed on the *Neptune,* her husband on the *Scarborough.* She told Maggie things she'd rather not know, how the Captain on her ship was a sadistic monster and the one on her husband's no better. Her husband lay chained with a dead man for days, pretending the fellow was alive to get his meagre rations, eating poultices from wounds and rats that strayed close enough to catch.

The story grieved Maggie, but like so many monstrosities in the parade of horrors passing before her she had to set it down, dared not let it slow her work.

Now, lying wakeful, the memory of the woman has her in its grip as she tosses one way, turns another on the straw until even its rustling hurts her ears.

After an hour or so the exhaustion breaks down her walls and a flood of sorrow and fear runs through her at Mrs Ranse's plight. She grasps immediately why it's unhinged her. The woman's iron will and desperation to keep the scraps of her family together are a suffering Maggie knows only too well.

She will give what aid she can.

Next morning Melva Ranse is still at her husband's side. Twice the surgeons have manhandled her from the tent, threatening to call the guards, but each time she has returned. Maggie takes her aside.

'Have you any goods to trade?'

The woman looks this way and that to see who might hear.

'A few items of his clothing is all.'

Maggie keeps her voice low.

'Take one of your man's garments to the stone quarry. Ask for Rocky Bitterman, tell him he can have it for a pot o' sugarbag honey.'

She steers the woman out the tent door as though ushering her out of the way.

'Rocky sneaks off, got a secret place in the woods where he's found a nest of native bees. The pot might not have much, take care to smear every drop on the wounds. Cover the honey with lint, Mrs Ranse, so the surgeons don't see.'

'Thank you, bless you. Melva, call me Melva.'

'I'm Maggie. Not a word to a soul. I get caught meddling there be hell to pay.'

With the human cargo unloaded from transport ships, more than four hundred convicts are on the sick list. Ten or more die each day from disease, bad humours in the blood, amputations gone wrong, organs giving out, or wasting away. From over the hill above the stream wild dogs, bigger than a fox, can be heard howling and fighting over bodies piled one on the other in the sandy burial pit.

Within five days, though, Cuddy Ranse stands tall and walks unsteadily out of the sick tent to be with his family.

Maggie is leaving the hospital around midnight a month later, walking into the gloom of night well after the evening drum has warned everyone to their quarters. Her belly grumbles with hunger, distracting her from seeing the night watchman until he accosts her.

The grubby fellow holds up a lantern, so close she can see his yellow teeth. She detests these men, convicts who've agreed to act as police, many drunk with power, worse than the London traps.

'Wotcha doin' out so late? Off to the men's camp, I bet.'

She takes a step back.

'No. I were workin' at the hospital, not that you've any call to know.'

He grabs her by the left arm, his grip hurting.

'Think yer better 'n me, do you?'

The bakehouse is nearby but no one will be firing ovens at this hour. The women in her hut will be asleep. She is alone.

Instinct drives her to shove the man in the chest. 'Let go.'

He braces and turns her own force against her, pushing her off-balance. She falls to the path, landing heavily on her right arm. The shock cuts off her breath as the fellow drops his lantern and flips her flat on her back, kneeling over her, pinning each arm by the wrist. She wants to scream yet can't get out a sound, starts to struggle, but before she can free her arms the man shudders backwards and releases his hold, knocking over the lamp.

'You hurt?'

The mouth that speaks is floating in darkness. Only when she is helped to her feet can she see the fellow's hair is the colour of night and he wears a redcoat jacket. The convict has run off.

'No, it were just a fall.'

'It was more than that. I saw him attack you.'

'He mistook my business is all, got too wound up sendin' me to my hut.'

The marine studies her face. Maggie holds to her story. She doesn't need to make enemies, especially with convict men intent on gaining favours with the military or the Guv.

He dips his head a little. 'Private Charles Ferrion. Everyone calls me Charlie.'

'Margaret Bloodworth, known as Maggie.'

'I'll walk you to your hut.'

Perhaps he doesn't believe she has proper cause to be out at night. 'No need. I often walk back at night from work over at the hospital.'

'Still, as it happens I'm going in your direction.'

The insistence irritates Maggie. Many of her peers have jumped into hasty marriages or couplings that might provide advancement or protection. Some regretted it almost instantly when they found the extra comforts they expected did not materialise. She, however, has diligently kept herself apart from the men.

Her work keeps her anchored, out of the way for much of the day. At other times she's with one woman or another, helping a birthing mother or looking in on her afterwards. What little free time she has is spent alone or with friends, foraging for native greens on the shoreline, berries in the nearby woods, or searching the bay to the west for cockles.

She is already a thief who's orphaned a child. Hard enough fighting for her soul, for what might yet be good in her, no need to add adultery to her list of sins.

The marine walks beside her and she suffers his company for a few minutes, not bothering to ask why he is out at night, glad to bid him farewell at her hut. As she enters, the rancid stink of unwashed bodies and stale rum bedevils her, along with the snoring of two women sprawled on their backs near the doorway. Despite the Guv's rules the pair are among many willing to trade favours with marines or convicts for grog. It suits the officers to turn a blind eye to the bartering of a warm body when it keeps the men happier.

Stealing food is the unforgiveable offence and several men, including marines, have been hanged for it. The knobs never miss the chance to remind convicts that the hanging tree, where backs are also flayed with the lash, sits between the men's and women's camps.

Maggie steps over one of the spread-eagled bodies towards her bed. Morals are slippery in this place, and scarce as soap.

Sarah is awake, whispering low. 'The Whitlam girl were lookin' for you. Something wrong with the boy, wants you to look in.'

Maggie waits next morning till fires have burned low at the cooking places, before going up the hill to the hut John Nicol has hastily built for Sarah Whitlam and the son born on the voyage.

'My babe, he worries me.'

Maggie holds out her arms and takes the child, carefully unwrapping the shawl that is snug around him. He squirms, bright eyes holding hers, his face and wriggling limbs a healthy pink.

'I see no sickness, only a fine, healthy boy.'

Sarah Whitlam takes her son and presses him to her chest.

'His ways be unnatural, he cries only when hungry or wet. I fear I've blighted him.'

Maggie has been with many first-time mothers fretting from ignorance, but she senses this distress is deeper.

'How so?'

'On the ship, when I were heavy with him, I took to the deck one night when sleep wouldn't come. The moon were bright. I looked up at it, should not have done so. I've made him a lunatic.

'Have you herbs, or a magic charm? Something to make him well?'

Maggie places a hand on the girl's arm.

'Old women tell such tales to amuse themselves. Ain't nobody been at more births than me, and God's truth, I tell you that seein' nature, even the moon, causes no harm.'

The girl seems relieved.

'You've the good fortune to have an easy-going baby. Enjoy it while you can. I promise it don't last.' She laughs loudly and Sarah joins in at first, before her face crumples.

'The steward, he wants to leave the Navy and be here with us.'

Maggie nods at the swift turn of conversation. Men are already deserting mothers and children so this is welcome to hear, though the girl's face doesn't reflect good news.

'The Captain refuses to let him go, says with four hands short John must leave next week on the *Lady Juliana* for China, then England.'

Nicol has promised to return for her and the boy when her time expires.

'We exchanged faith. He pledged himself to me, said I were kind and true.' Her face hardens as she speaks, making her look much older than twenty-two years.

'I am to wait, a woman on her own who bides her time for years till his return.'

Maggie barely knows the girl. What she has fessed up is discomforting, made more so because there's no reason for her to share it, least of all with her.

'What am I to do? I have the boy to care for.'

Maggie holds back the desire to scream in the girl's face, to denounce the wickedness crawling under her own skin. She's not fit to be giving advice when she's given her own daughter over to Satan's cold hands.

The pain on the young mother's face says an answer is needed.

'Strength will come when needed, I seen it often.' She hopes there's more persuasion in her voice than she feels.

They stand together in a silence beyond words.

The girl lays the baby in a crib that still has the marks of an axe, and goes to the rough sawn table pushed against a wall.

'Here, for your trouble.' She holds out a half loaf.

Maggie hesitates, she has done naught useful here. Then temptation rises and she accepts the bread, hopeful she can trade it for thread to mend holes in her stockings.

A day or two after the ship sails away late July, word goes round there will be a wedding at noon, cause for most of the women to don their best dresses and throw off shawls despite the hoar frost not long melted in the shade. They hurry, chattering and cackling louder than Brown Kings Fishers at dawn, down to the one soaring gum tree on the foreshore, where Rev Johnson waits. Body being more important than spirit in this place, there are no funds to build a church.

An icy gust rattles the leaves of the eucalypt as Maggie arrives.

The chaplain strides up to convict John Welch, waiting for his bride-to-be, seeming not to have bothered combing his hair or beard for the occasion. A group of off-duty marines stand off to the side in a long row, laughing and joking. Among them she spots the loose frame of Private Ferrion as he looks her way. In daylight it's clear he is a similar age to her, with what she grudgingly admits is a pleasing oval face and a voice less coarse than the men around him.

As a murmur goes through the crowd she turns to see Sarah Whitlam step forward, her babe in the arms of a nearby friend.

The girl calls to Maggie, waving her forward.

'Be my witness, if you will.'

Maggie wants no part in the spectacle, but too late, the chaplain gestures for her to stand to his right, at his left a friend of Welch's who will be the other witness.

John Nicol's ship has barely cleared the Heads when the woman he longs for is wed to another man.

While others cheer and hope for a tasty morsel or two to celebrate the union, Maggie slips away from the crowd, from Ferrion's glances, to work out of sight in the vegetable garden behind her hut, digging vigorously to stay warm.

She has no judgment of the young mother, only sadness. What chance for tenderness or loyalty in this savage new world.

CHAPTER FIVE

DECEMBER ROLLS IN, A STEAM bath of humidity with brief relief from an occasional southerly buster. Sweaty palms slip on axes and shovels, clammy fingers slide on sewing needles, armpits weep in widening circles at the slightest movement.

Two more days and it will be Hannah's seventh birthday. The weight of three years since Maggie mothered the child is bearing down, a crushing force that will reduce her to dust if she lets it.

She flees the shade of the hut and the cloying company of grumbling women to follow a line of sandstone ledges, working her way up the harbour's edge, hoping to find spinach growing where water runs off the cliff.

Heat beats across her shoulders, coursing down her trunk, turning her legs into logs that are hard to lift. As she slows, a shadow catches her eye in the darkness below an overhang forming a shallow cave. When she gets closer it takes the familiar form of a child, a native girl, knees bent to her chest. The girl's dark skin is dull, she does not stir. A bull ant scurries across one open eye. The child, a similar age to the daughter she once hugged for the last time, is at least a day gone, already stiff.

Hot tears course down Maggie's face as she runs up the edge of the harbour, frantic, looking left and right for any sign of the girl's people, someone to claim her, make sure she gets a proper burial. She knows the search is in vain, has heard about the smallpox spreading before her ship arrived, the way dark bodies piled up on the beaches, in hollows, and the shelter of rocks. Still she runs, faster and faster, ignoring the sun's reflection blasting off the water, oblivious to all but the need to stay in motion.

The Guv has promised those convicts who work hard a new life, opportunities to advance themselves, yet the creation of this shining future requires destruction. With every beat of her arms and legs it becomes clearer she's surrounded by what has been rent asunder for the sake of a tin-pot colony. Families split apart. Belonging breaking down. Base desires unleashed by grog.

Her legs run faster as the thoughts rush on. Death coming, not from a hangman's noose in England, but after the torture of a long sea voyage in chains. Natives disturbed from their way of life, no shield strong enough to hold back the foul wind of new diseases.

Exhausted, she slows to a walk, looking behind her in the distance towards the rocks where the group cooked fish on her first day. The area is deserted. Perhaps those natives are gone, too. Parties of soldiers or convicts who travel inland to hunt or cut timber have often had encounters, yet only the occasional dark man or woman enters the settlement, mostly wanting bread.

She will find no one here to take the girl home.

Scrambling into the next bay she is fit to collapse, in need of shade. Finding it under the twisted branches of a red gum, she braces her back against its smooth bark, where she is possessed by grief, shaken such that she has no will. Howling and sobbing, she gives in to what it demands, which is all of her.

No consolation comes, no bird, no creature, not even a breeze finding the lone figure.

The sun is slipping to the west, the air cooling a little as it weakens its hold on the day, when Maggie begins her return. Her path is deliberate, staying above the rocks and the resting place of the child, not wishing to disturb her again, not even with a glance.

At the promontory before the settlement she skirts a timber building with an odd conical tower, an observatory where Lieutenant William Dawes, an astronomer, disappears for hours on end to record the weather, the movement of the stars, matters for navigation, though there are whispers about what else he does here. Folks say a young native woman has visited in the past, teaching him the language of her people and maybe more.

She shakes her head to remove the thought. Rumours are a potent currency in the settlement, sought out like rum and tobacco, and she chooses to resist all three.

Head down, heart heavy, she doesn't see the man strolling the other way until it is too late.

'I see you're not working today.' Private Ferrion is smiling, perhaps being friendly in his reserved fashion, but all Maggie hears is the idiocy of his attempt at conversation. She nods and steps forward to go around him.

'I'm sorry if I have offended you.'

His tone rubs against the sore place the tears have opened in her chest. Best to ignore him and walk on.

'You're not like the others, are you?'

Like a fish she is hooked, and pauses.

'They take every opportunity to laze about or drink, putting more effort into shirking work than doing it. Whereas you seem steady in playing your part to help this godforsaken place.'

This man, she thinks, has tongue enough for two sets of teeth, always something to say. His remark may be praise or a slap-down, she can't tell. Perhaps he has the view of some that the whole settlement is a grand folly, and he mocks her efforts as trifling.

'I do my part, no more.' That ought to be the end of it, or at least that's her intent, but before she continues on her way a memory strikes her.

'The family name, did you say it were Ferrion?'

'Indeed it is.'

'You have kin in the weaving trade over Spitalfields way?'

He cocks his head, unsure about the way the authority guiding the conversation has swung from him to this woman.

'Yes, my father had a business there.'

Maggie can scarcely believe it. She wants to speak but a rising fury has strangled her tongue.

'Why do you ask?'

'Seems my little brother George were 'prenticed to your father. He were made to work long hours for a pittance, oftentimes in poor light. His eyes failed, so they got rid of him, shook him off like an old shoe. What would you know of honest toil?'

She doesn't need enemies, but her loathing dislodges any attempt at niceties. She walks off at a clip.

Private Ferrion catches up, touching her lightly on the arm.

'Wait, please. My father may not have been fair in his dealings with his workers, but I am not my father any more than you are your mother.'

Maggie wheels around, incensed further by the invoking of her ma.

'Take yer hand off me.'

The marine jumps back as though his fingers are aflame, his mouth falling open.

Yet it's she who feels the heat. She is a powder keg and he has lit the fuse. Her ma, Dan, Hannah, the pain has piled up over the years, deadness buried deep but now alive and rushing in her veins. She shakes with the power of it, the sense that all the hurt is a force gathering and this stupid man is where it will cut loose.

Her hands form fists, her knees brace, arms fill with the desire to pummel his face, his belly, to lash out, bruise him, split him open, to thrash free of her own torment. He may be a tall man, but has a light frame she'll pound with no thought of what cost to herself.

As she struggles to regain control in the tempest of fire and flesh she understands it's not his fault, none of it, and wants to say so but can't. Her body has become its own beast.

He steps back.

'I've no desire to upset you, I swear, only to make my case.'

It's plain to Maggie that he is sincere. She must rein in her anger, for harming this man or any other will only bring greater affliction, not peace.

She forces herself to speak, voice wooden. 'My temper runs at sixes and sevens today. Forgive me.'

His face softens and what he does next shocks the anger from her, faster than a punch might knock the breath from her chest.

He offers his arm. 'Let me walk with you.'

Still shaking, she curls the tips of a few fingers around his bent elbow, taking care not to lean in too close.

As he strolls he is at great pains to defend his character, surprising himself with the urgency of his need to have her understand what kind of man he is.

'I knew before I turned sixteen that I was different to my father. I wasn't cut from the right cloth for the weaving business.' He laughs readily at his own joke, proof he's told it many times before.

Maggie is hardly listening. She is drained by the heat, the day's strong emotions, gives him no invitation to speak further. Yet he presses on, wanting to assert that Charlie Ferrion is his own person.

'I was the eldest child and only son, destined for father to train me up as a silk trader. By then, though, the business was waning.'

The sharp edge in his voice gets her attention. 'Any man or woman in the street could have told you the new cotton fabrics and linens had overtaken silk.'

He had heard loud conversations in his father's office, seen the thunderous face of the supervisor after being given orders to reduce the wages bill for those toiling upstairs before the big windows.

Maggie glances at him, sees he is lost to his story, imagines the boy smoothing the lapels of his coat, running a hand over hair darker than the ink of night. She only sees his confidence, doesn't know the mention of her brother has thrown Charlie, sent him back through the years to Fournier Street, to the moment when he finally plucked up the courage to confront his father.

Charles senior was finishing the midday meal in their brick terrace house, workers thumping on the weaving floor above. He pushed away his plate to glance up as his son entered the dining room. Then a knock came at the door, Charlie remembers it distinctly, before the workroom supervisor appeared.

'Sir, the Bloodworth lad's arrived. You wanted to see if he might be nimble in threadin' the looms?'

Was it really the name given, did the very name of this woman's brother come from the supervisor's mouth? Could it be that Charlie's path collided with Maggie's at such a turning point in his history, or is his memory playing tricks? He shakes his head, uncertain, though his father's words that day can never be forgotten.

The supervisor was dismissed by the senior Ferrion with the mere lifting of one hand, before he turned to address his son.

'Be quick if you wish to speak. I've much work to get through this afternoon.'

Charlie remembers the way he planted his feet, felt the weight of his body, braced against the urge to get it over with, to blurt out his position. To do so would have been a sure path to failure. His father, as he often reminded him, was descended from the exiled French Huguenots, a proud and considered man, his own pater once a master silk weaver in Lyon.

Though his parents exalted the grandness of St Clement Danes, where they married, Charlie was keenly aware the church was outside the walls of the City of London, confirming that the family would always be foreigners, always excluded. His father had formed a different view, over the years shaping his Protestant heritage into an anthem he proclaimed as a blessing. And yet it yoked him to a millstone. Always striving, never arriving.

Charlie glances down at the woman walking beside him, decides to take a chance on telling Maggie how he did his best to stand up to his father.

'I told him about my longing for the sea, not just for adventure, for that would be a poor choice on its own, but for finding new chances, perhaps in trade, maybe commerce, or on the land in the New World.'

But then the boy's sentences had started hurrying as though they had a life of their own. He could not hope to slow them, worse, his tone was far too spirited, hooking out strong words instead of ones likely to flatter or appease.

He had laid out his case far too hastily, brazen about it when he should have shown restraint, telling his father that he sought work that employed his natural instincts, would fulfil his potential.

'I told him I had little interest in being bound as a glazier and painter. I begged him, do not insist.'

It had been as if he had not spoken. The gilt mantel clock ticked in its case, taunting him with the minutes and hours that would no longer be his if his father did not concede to his sense of purpose.

I do insist. I have only your interests at heart. Unlike him, his father's words had been measured, as though a metronome marked each interval.

His father, such a commanding figure in his day, had then taken the fact of the education his son had been given and thrown it in his face, as though he owed his papa a debt in return.

Charlie realises he has fallen silent. He stops strolling, and faces Maggie so that her hand drops from his arm.

'The indenture had been signed, you see, the fee paid to the Master already, and a premium at that, for I was nearly two years beyond the usual age he'd take a boy.

'I was meant to be grateful, Maggie, not vexed. How my poor father misjudged me.'

He had no choice but to do the five years of apprenticeship, for which the Master deigned to pay him a few coins here and there in the last year or two.

'I held on tight to the idea that one day I'd be twenty-one and free of my father's dictates, then I'd be bumping and swaying in the coach on the way to Portsmouth in Hampshire, to join the marines at last.'

He pauses, suddenly aware he has said too much. The woman beside him has nodded a couple of times as he's spoken, but is largely quiet. He will not tell her how he came upon his mother waiting quietly in the reception hall at the bottom of the stairs. She was younger than his father, had given him two daughters as well as Charlie, and the benefit of an even temperament that pervaded the house, soothing hot tempers and agitated minds. Charlie saw the true, kind person she was, understood her worth in a way he doubted his father could.

Her voice was full of concern. 'Have you spoken your piece?'

The grim set of his mouth was the only answer he needed to give.

'At least it may give you solace that you tried, dear boy.'

She patted his arm before walking towards the kitchen door to discuss the week's meals with cook. Charlie knew that, despite having servants, she worked harder than most people in the house, except for the weavers above. She had a knack for drawing out the best in others, listening to troubles to lighten their load, giving a gentle word when it was needed most.

He watched her disappear through the doorway, full of admiration. Louisa Ferrion had an accent that betrayed her origins as a working woman, the assistant to a cartographer, but her heart was refined, pure as gold.

He sees something of his mother in the woman walking beside him, and smiles at Maggie Bloodworth.

Probably best not to say how the gloom of the entrance hall choked him, such that he took his hat from the coat rack and hurried out into drizzle, not bothering to take an umbrella. His father had insisted he take on adult responsibilities, so he behaved like any man sorely disappointed and headed for the closest inn.

He shouted for ale like a ruffian. 'And be quick about it.' When the coins in his pocket were gone, the landlord kicked him out and he staggered home in the rain. Not something likely to impress the woman in his company on this sunny day, a woman he wants to know better.

'Tell me about yourself, Maggie. Where do you hail from?'

'Not much to tell, grew up a lumper's daughter, on the Middlesex side of St Botolph's parish.'

It is all she is willing to offer, enough for him to see she's come from the bottom of the pile, while his family has prospered. Both of them were birthed to the east of the City of London, but there's a rift between them that can't be bridged.

Maybe he's a bit daft, she wonders. Despite her saying not a thing more, he continues to chat amiably, not seeming to grasp she's spurned him.

When he asks how she came to be a nurse and midwife they are nearing her hut, and she instinctively pulls back her hand from his arm before the gossipmongers can notice. She is too tired, too defeated right now to bother answering questions.

'Another day, maybe. For now I'm in need of water and a rest in the shade.' She dips her head briefly by way of thanks, though for what she isn't sure, and steps away before he can protest.

In the days that follow, the marine tries to seek her out. The first few times she sees him coming and slips away to one of the huts under the guise of assisting with twins she recently delivered, a boy crippled by a twisted foot and a girl with staring eyes and flattened face shaped like a moon.

Maggie has seen little ones like the girl before. She'll be happy enough as she grows, though her mind will be weak. Thankfully, with no asylum at the settlement the mother is set on caring for the girl, while Chief Surgeon White will treat the boy's foot with manipulation and strong bandages to straighten it. Much harder to cure is the inclination for some to snigger behind their hands and call the babies a curse of God.

When at last Maggie gives in, agreeing to spend time with the Private, the New Year is a week under way, and she has determined to tell him why she doesn't welcome his interest.

Sarah Newcombe tries to talk her out of it.

'Maggie, for the love of God, as hard as it is to suffer, gettin' a passage back home is no more likely than dining with the Guv. You gotta settle for the better bargain, for a new life. What do you gain by declaring you are wed?'

'My dignity, Sarah. About all I have left.' She storms off.

CHAPTER SIX

SYDNEY COVE, 1791

E VERY SUNDAY ALL PARTIES, WHETHER Governor or the lowliest rock breaker, must attend morning divine service or risk reduced rations. The congregation mills about, waiting to see where Rev Johnson will deliver this week's sermon. A collective groan issues when he calls from further up the hill and leads the crowd, flies buzzing around eyes and mouths, to the tile shed in no-man's land at the Brickfields.

The chaplain stands at the edge of what little remains civil in the hearts of those milling in front of him. Maggie can't help thinking that there is no more fitting location than today's, for the reverend preaches at the place where outcasts and rebels are as far from the town camp as can be, where one step further is wild country.

Feet scuffle in the dirt, the mob wilting in heat so extreme that only days earlier flying foxes, robins and parrots dropped dead from trees. The long shed is only a timber roof and four posts, throwing just a strip of shade over the group. Impatience builds as Rev Johnson labours far too long in speaking to the twelfth verse of Psalm 116.

'What shall I render unto the Lord for all his benefits towards me?' he intones.

A loud voice answers. 'My arse. It be burnin' off.'

A burst of raucous laughter is quelled almost immediately by one of the sergeants. 'Enough, or you'll feel the heat of the lash.'

The chaplain mops his brow and continues his worn-out sermon. Maggie makes her eyes stop wandering, especially in the direction of Private Ferrion, instead pretending interest in tables to one side where tiles are moulded, running her gaze over racks where they are stacked ready for firing. The minute the Reverend's weary voice has come to a halt she hurries back to her hut.

When Maggie reappears she is still wearing her best dress, in coarse cotton once green, now sweat stained and sun-bleached, the hem so badly frayed it is past any attempt to mend it. The dress is not even hers, a payment in exchange for helping the twin's mother. A hat with wide brim, woven herself from dried fronds of cabbage palms, contains the unruly wisps of hair around her face, and shades her eyes.

She passes the Marine Barracks, expecting to see Ferrion appear, but he waits at the nearby bridge across the stream. He leans against a tree stump, wearing a goatskin haversack on his back and a smile on his face.

'Thought you might not come.'

He leads the way into cooler air, up the ferny gully fringing the stream, where occasional taller shrubs and trees throw shadows. Unlike the rest of the cove, the gully has been spared the axe thanks to the Governor's decree that land on either side of the stream be left untouched.

They emerge from the gully and continue a mile up the slope, heat beating off the hard ground. Maggie is about to object, wants to turn back, but near the Brickfields Ferrion takes a path that skirts the clay pits and leads into the treeline. In the shade of a thick-trunked eucalypt, bark cracked as though the tree is outgrowing its skin, he takes a piece of canvas from the haversack and spreads it on the ground.

As they settle, the harbour glints like a mirror through the leafy cover. Almost a hundred brickmakers, tile makers and labourers usually bang and shout at work below, but this is the one day of the week the kilns and pits fall silent. The men will be in their huts, arguing at cards, already half-way to drunk thanks to the hundred-proof grog from an illegal still.

Maggie is nervous. She tells herself it's because the woods give ideal cover if natives from the interior are lurking, then swiftly reminds herself she's never been under threat from any of them.

Ferrion disrupts her thoughts.

'Do you like picnics?'

She glances at him, his eyes looking straight into hers, and immediately turns her head away.

'Never been to one.'

He chuckles, seemingly pleased with himself.

'Well this might not be up to standard, but it still passes muster as a picnic.'

He pulls out a flask from his sack, followed by a pannikin, which he half fills and hands to her.

'You first.'

She takes a sip, expecting rum, but the liquid has a queer taste and fine bubbles like ale. She peers into the

80

mug, at liquid a brownish-green colour. Perhaps it is spruce beer, the drink of sailors.

'Not to my liking, more's the pity.' She hands it back to him.

He waves it away. 'Try another mouthful. It grows on you, I promise.'

As she takes another sip he reveals that it is horehound beer, made from native bee honey and the bitter herb, by him and a corporal mate Jim Cartwright.

'You shouldn't say such things to me or any other'. Severe penalties apply for those caught brewing or distilling.

'I trust you.' He throws back his head and laughs. 'Though I'm a better glazier than brewer.'

She takes the cue as an excuse to get him talking, and keep the attention away from her.

'So how did you find the trade you were made to take on?'

He reaches into the pack and begins pulling out bread, roasted kangaroo meat and a twist of salt made from local sea water, thinking it best not to share what the conversation has reminded him, that the coming together of his work and the grog nearly cost him his livelihood.

'I was lucky. My employer at the Westminster glass-house was a Jew, a good man. Samuel Newhouse, master craftsman, was his name.'

He saw in the first few weeks that the new lad burned with desire for his own path, knew a young fellow captured by ambition should be taught how to handle it.

'Did me a lot of good, Maggie, he did.'

She takes the piece of bread he offers, starts chewing on it to make it clear she's not ready to do any talking.

'He set me to work in the cement shop, a terrible, dim room at the back of the factory. I had to seal each new painted glass window with a mix of linseed oil, whiting, lamp black and white spirit, then pick it clean of any lead spills, before polishing it.'

She is relaxing a little as he talks, eggs him on to tell her more, finding the deep tone of his voice oddly soothing.

'My fingers were stained a filthy grey that no amount of scrubbing with the pumice could budge. From eight o'clock in the morning till six at night I pushed the gluey stuff under the flange of the lead cames. You had force it in tight, lest the panes leak, but not use enough force, mind, to crack them.'

Charlie stops himself before he bores her witless. It was the time when he first came to understand the depth of his own pride, not wanting to fail even at menial tasks, let alone break a coloured window that a team of four men had designed, cut, assembled and soldered.

'You was reliable, sounds like.' A bit of flattery won't do any harm, Maggie thinks.

'Expect I was.' He shifts uncomfortably at what she has said.

In truth, he arrived home late every night, having downed a bellyful of spirits. His mother tried talking to him, but he pacified her. His father was next.

That booming voice. 'You will do me the courtesy of entering my house in a civil and orderly state. Or you will live elsewhere.' Charlie ignored him. His father had already thwarted the direction of his life, could not expect him to live in a cage without flapping his wings.

He justified his bad behaviour back then. These days he likes to think he's capable of looking into his own character with greater honesty.

A pleasant breeze has sprung up. Maggie leans back on one hand, seems to enjoy his company, doesn't seem bothered that he is distracted.

He was a quick learner, progressing to fitting windows in buildings, starting with cheap broad glass for a new factory in Middlesex. They all knew to wash their hands after handling lead for no one wanted the palsy, though knowing and practice were two different things when they were too busy or there was no water pump nearby. Now and then he got a strange tingling in his hands, though he followed the example of the older fellows and paid little attention to it.

He moved on to his first greenhouse, then learned to fit glass to sash windows. The following year his master promised to place him on the team making a pair of Venetian windows in a pavilion at the stately home of the Earl of Grandblane.

'We'll be using crown glass, and as you know it's exceedingly costly.' Mr Newhouse had pulled him aside as the others left for the day.

'Yes sir, I understand I need to listen to my orders and take great care.'

Mr Newhouse looked at his shoes for a moment then lifted his head to lock eyes with Charlie.

'Then you will need a steady hand and a clear head in the morning.'

'Of course, sir. Thank you.' In his mind he was already out the door and half-way down the street to The Green Man, and the fug of smoke, sweat and grog.

'I don't think you do understand, not at all.'

Charlie was puzzled.

'How so, sir?'

'You can't be coming to work with a scattered mind and a tremor in your hands from the drink. I know what a temptation it can be. I've been temperate for years now because I've seen how it blights a promising future.

'You're a young man with a vision. I see that. If you want to succeed on a path you forge from your own talents, then you can't be blunting your potential.'

Charlie remembers how he wanted to run, escape the gaze of his employer. It was as if he stood naked before him, the man's directness stripping him of any pretence.

'I will not be touching on this subject again, but upon my word I won't keep on a drunkard.'

He wants Maggie to trust him, considers it only right to own up about the Master's warning and the way it cut unexpectedly deep, shame festering for days. But he holds back, given Maggie has not opened up to him so far. At least that's what he tells himself.

It ended well enough, he supposes. Though he wanted to deny it at the time he knew Master Newhouse was right and determined to shape his own life, resolving never again to let rum, or any liquor for that matter, be in charge.

Charlie stirs, addresses Maggie.

'When my time was up, the Master tried to talk me into applying to the Guild to be a master craftsman, but I still had my cap set on what I'd always wanted. A marine tricorne, as it happens.' He guffaws, pleased that Maggie laughs with him.

'Tried to talk me around, said I was turning my back on a profession based on co-operation and order, instead choosing a life of brutality and chaos.'

All so long ago. What the Master said has come true, of course. Charlie has seen plenty of violence and disorder, but there's never been a dull moment, for which he is mightily glad.

And now he has found a woman to share his eventful life. He turns to her. 'I'm still waiting to hear how you came upon midwifing and nursing as a calling.'

Maggie has been gearing up to take a turn at talking, but her work is definitely not the matter she wants to raise.

She has been enjoying the escape from the noise and nosiness of the women's camp and the woes of hospital work, stealing glances at the marine. Up close she sees how different he is to Dan. His eyes are dark, his pale skin almost white despite the strong sun, stark against the hair. Night and day, like piano keys. The corners of his eyes crinkle with fine lines, but he has none of the weather-beaten ruddiness of her man's face or the openness she loved so dearly.

Dan. It's time to make her position known.

'If I were rude to you, there's reasonin' behind it, Private Ferrion,' she begins carefully.

'Call me Charlie, I beg you.'

Maggie hesitates. They are working against each other, she pushing away while he tries to get closer. She ignores what he said and presses on. It won't do to give him cause for hope.

'I can't be courtin', you see. I wed a long while back, and was made to leave our wee girl behind. The only thing

I can give myself over to is work, that and questing for the means to go back to England and find my Hannah.'

He is silent. She brushes crumbs off her lap and sits upright, ready to leave, relieved the deed is done.

'Do you see beauty in our new world?' He waves a hand expansively, as though capturing the hill, the harbour, the entire coastline.

Maggie feels alarm. Perhaps this man is touched in the head after all.

'On occasion. Why?'

'I've seen wondrous things, terrible things. Life is short, Maggie—may I call you Maggie?' He doesn't wait for an answer.

'... The good, the worthwhile can be fleeting, and in my humble view is to be embraced to the full, even if it arrives at a time that doesn't prove convenient.'

'Are you wed, Charlie?' Her tone and the use of his given name is intended to draw him in.

'No, I've not been in a position to take a wife.'

'Then you don't know about a bond far stronger than happenstance.' She stands, angry yet again with this fellow.

He leaps to his feet, facing her squarely.

'That's unfair. I merely make the point that any good fortune in finding a kindred spirit shouldn't be readily dismissed, especially when we're so far from our old lives. I make no secret of the fact that I've much admiration for you.'

The declaration hangs in the air. Maggie is quite still, and Charlie can't discern if his words have had a positive effect or she is gathering herself to rebuff him again.

As it transpires, it is neither.

When he begins to speak, she holds a finger to her lips. 'Shhhh, do you hear that?'

He listens intently, hearing only one tree limb rubbing against another as the hot afternoon air stirs, perhaps distant voices, or the faint screeching of crimson parrots sheltering from the sun in a nearby canopy.

Maggie is already scrambling to her feet, heading through a grove of drooping firs into a darker area of the woods. Charlie follows.

'What do you hear?'

'This way.' She runs off, ducking under low branches as she goes, Charlie loping behind, then just as suddenly stops. When he catches up she is pulling leaves from a low mound to reveal a small brown parcel. Only then does he hear the baby's weak cries.

Maggie pulls away the dirty burlap from the head, exposing the newborn's red wrinkled face, then takes the baby in her arms, where its cries cease.

'Dear God.' Despite the pain and violence the marine has seen, he is shocked that such a defenceless creature has been discarded so callously.

'We got to get back, Charlie. The babe needs to suckle, its ma likely needs help.'

She hurries to the path while he collects his knapsack then catches up, full of outrage.

'The mother must have slipped away to do this while we were all at divine service. Whoever it is should be punished.'

'They already have been, on my oath. Do you think any ma could do such a thing without painful cause?' Her resentment boils over. 'Doubtless another bastard child the da's turned his back on.'

As Maggie hurries she unwraps the rest of the burlap to cool the baby. There is no sign of deformity, only a section of cord cut clumsily. It's a boy.

'Will he live?' The marine's genuine concern moves Maggie.

'Maybe, the poor mite seems like a fighter.'

The twins' ma agrees to feed the newborn, but only for the day. He is too weak to suck so she spoons drops of breast milk into his mouth while Maggie goes in search of the mother.

She suspects it is one of the youngest convict girls, only thirteen or so when transported. They're of tender years, though this is no hindrance to the knobs they work for, treating them no different to beasts in the field, then having their way with them whenever they like.

Charlie wants to help, but she sends him away with the promise she'll give him any news the next day when he finishes guard duty.

Maggie goes in search of her friend Sarah Newcombe, then remembers she's taken her chances with a sergeant and now lives in the officer's hut some distance from the convict camps, so hears less gossip.

Instead, Maggie goes to Sarah Welch.

''Tis a sad business. I've no idea who the ma were.'

Maggie can tell she knows something, but despite her urging the woman reveals nothing.

'Surely you would've taken note of a girl with a full belly one day and not the next, yet no child?'

'No more so than you, Maggie. Nothing surprises me, with so much grog and venery in this place.'

'The ma may need help. It might not have all come away clean. Maybe she still bleeds, or has weakness from the labour.'

No amount of persuasion wins her over, a similar situation when Maggie knocks at other convict huts.

She returns to the twins' mother, despairing. 'Seems it were a miracle birth.'

The woman is feeding her babies, one on each breast. The newborn lies still on a folded shawl in the corner.

'He took little more than a thimbleful of milk.'

Maggie takes him in her arms and sees his life is ebbing away. Just on dusk, in the rattle of pots and chatter at the cooking fires, she strokes his face and knows he has gone.

After a restless night she is up well before the drum beats to send everyone to work. Without tarrying to make pease porridge, she chews on a stale piece of bread on her way to the hospital. It's late afternoon when she seeks out Charlie to tell him what befell the boy.

Her eyes fill with tears as she speaks about the baby's last minutes. She doesn't object when the marine puts an arm across her shoulders and holds it there.

A week later, a sixteen-year-old girl is carried into the hospital on a stretcher, groaning with belly pain, shivering despite the heat. By nightfall the fever has overcome her. Maggie insists she be buried in the same part of the burial ground as the boy.

At the next divine service, January heat is ferocious. An aging convict man standing behind Maggie is moved to tell the throng that whatever the chaplain threatens about the hell to come, they're already there.

After the final prayer the group disperses quickly, many to find a place away from the eyes of guards to gamble, drink or both. By mid-afternoon they will have passed out in the shade, though the occasional foolhardy fellow will plunge into the harbour to cool himself before remembering he cannot swim. The spectacle of his rescue will pass for entertainment.

Maggie and Charlie fall in together from that day, with no obvious agreement to do so, except they carry the memory of the baby boy more lightly with two of them to share it.

They find themselves strolling the path past the Observatory, following the shoreline towards Cockle Bay. First one then the other takes the lead to navigate pockets of dense, low shrubs.

At the bay all is still around the lime burners. Maggie had expected to see at least a few people foraging for shellfish, but the crushing temperature has deterred them from the tidal mudflats and rocky shore.

A storm has been building all morning, and with the warning of a single thunderclap heavy-bellied clouds dump their load of rain, sending the couple scurrying for shelter. Charlie takes Maggie's hand as they run, giggling like children, into a stand of tea-tree. After the sun breaks through a short time later, they are still laughing and chatting under the trees.

What unfolds in the weeks that follow is not something Maggie invites. Despite herself she begins to bloom in the warmth of his attention, a circle of sunshine lighting up the grey of her days.

When she excites at his touch, the pores of her skin opening to drink him in, her thoughts round on her with a mean tone. *Think yer high and mighty but yer no different to a strumpet. Just as fickle, turning away from Dan and yer little girl.* Yet as the weeks pass, she finds herself fighting the nagging voice until it fades.

His touch. Despite the guilt she longs for it while she wipes a damp cloth over the lips of a man who is fevered, when she checks bandages holding a splint on a broken leg. It has been so long since she's had someone to hold her, she has forgotten how good it feels to have a firm arm around her waist, a hand entwined in hers, a man who makes her body sing when they sneak away to the woods. The hunger for it catches her by surprise, the animal of her body wanting what it wants.

Their coupling has an urgency, not like with Dan, his flaxen hair falling over his eyes as he rolled onto her as easily as pouring cool water from a pitcher. Then afterwards, the curve of his belly fitting so easily against the curl of her spine. They were two pieces of the one thing, drawn together by a natural flow. With Charlie it is like he's a magnet, and she but a pile of iron filings that must go to him.

The situation is clear, she tells herself. It calls for greater willpower on her part. The arrangement with the Private is merely a stopgap, helps bear the time till she gets back to London.

She has not come upon a plan yet. She can't work her passage back as crew, like some men hope to do at the end of their sentence. It's true she spends much of her free time helping as midwife or healer to the women, but they have little to give as payment. In any case, no one seems to agree about what the few English shillings, Dutch guilders, Indian rupees or Spanish reales are worth when traded.

Still, no matter the difficulty she must not give up. Hannah could be wasting away, starved of food, definitely hungry for love. She yearns every day to hold her close, comfort her, soothe away her hurt. Sometimes late at night, in a stupor for lack of sleep, she longs so hard to see her girl it seems the act of wishing it with every breath might just be enough to draw Hannah to her side.

Her mind remains troubled until after the Easter Sunday service when, exhausted, slumping against the hut wall under a sullen sky, she suddenly stiffens. She has not bled the past month. Dear God, no.

CHAPTER SEVEN

C HARLIE IS FULL OF NEWS when he meets Maggie late one afternoon at the end of May. He has arranged to build them a house.

'It will not be much, Maggie, but will be a home for us.'

In his excitement he fails to notice she has not responded.

'I've got permission to use some of the cabbage palm trunks from the next load harvested up the harbour. Once the frame's up, you can help me weave the wattle branches and coat them with clay.'

He throws his arms around her, pulling her in close, and is surprised when she struggles free.

'Together in a hut, Charlie? Surely we'd best be waitin' a while longer?'

What she means to say is that it's a step too far. She has been beguiled by companionship, by his touch. It has been a force that's captured her, and now he breaks the spell with a bucket of words showering her with the cold truth of her actions, of her betrayal. She's been woken from a dream.

'It's the perfect time. Do we not enjoy each other's company? I see no reason to delay.'

His good humour does not help. Such foolishness on her part, for she's already an adulterer, carrying an illegitimate child. In the world of sense and reason she has crossed a line already and can't go back, so what matter she lives with this man?

In recent days she has tossed up the idea of boiling kangaroo apple, being done with the baby, then afterwards getting shot of the man. She hasn't yet told him what grows in her belly. It may not come to that.

She tries a different approach.

'If we live as man and wife, unable to wed, it will cause harm to your good name and prospects, Charlie.'

His eyebrows shoot up. 'There's a new order rising here, can't you see it? It will be our labours, and the fruits of them, that decide our standing. Peaceful folk like us, who are moderate in drink, work hard, we can create a better place here than ever we could back home.'

This man, he knows she wasn't born on the steps of Newgate Gaol, that her crime came from need, but that's all he seems to grasp of what drives her away from his plan.

'It's too hard, Charlie.' The old pain is rising and she wants to push him away, shock some sense into him.

'What is it, Maggie? What upsets you so?'

His concerns are different to hers, perhaps as distant as the stars at night, equally out of reach. Does she really need to remind him?.

'You know I'm wed. I may never see Dan again, but I made him a pledge, it binds me. Then my daughter, the one who kept me going in the filth of the gaol, on the high seas. I must return to her, not put my efforts into makin' a life she has no part in. When you birth a child, the care don't weaken in time but grows ever stronger.'

She is fire and ice, the heat of her body as it nourishes a child is failing to thaw the bone-chilling absence of the one left behind. A wolf howl grows in her bowels, the cry of a creature calling for its pack. She covers her mouth to choke it back, shaking with the effort.

Charlie folds her into an embrace. She presses her face against his coat to smother the sound she can no longer contain.

'Come, let's walk.' He leads her away from prying eyes, up the side of the stream, to a clearing where they sit until she is calmer.

'I'm not asking you to give up your daughter. I've not experienced devotion to a child, you're right. But your situation has changed, as have you. Life brings new demands, surely we must not shy away from them.'

Maggie, who once knew the shape of her own character, feels hollow. A flood has run through and nothing remains.

Charlies wants to find a way to make it right for the woman he loves.

'Perhaps I could write to England, to a friend who has connections, see if news of your daughter can be gleaned?'

He holds out his hand and Maggie's fingers curl around his.

'If you do that, I will be forever in your debt.' Her chest softens.

Near their feet, the stream trickles half-heartedly through moss and ferns, holding on for autumn rains that have not yet come.

'Another child needs considering, Charlie.' She doesn't like the pinched lines that appear beside his eyes and mouth after she says it.

'How so?'

'Our child, Charlie. I be two months gone.'

She has not meant to tell him, undecided as she is about keeping the baby. Her gratitude has weakened her guard, opened a door. Mother Nature, on the side of life itself, has swooped in, more powerful than the weak mortal mother she is.

'What wonderful news.'

He holds her tight, squeezing the breath from her. His excitement is genuine, that much is evident, while all she feels is strange relief. Though for which child?

By early July the sky remains clear, a harsh foe for the thousand or so souls stranded at Sydney Cove. Winter has begun with only the occasional shower and the settlement's water supplies, including the stream and wells near the hospital, are almost dry.

Convicts know how difficult it is to coax vegetable crops from the sandy soil, and without water they will have little chance to supplement their rations.

'Hope lies elsewhere.' Charlie is upbeat, has been sixteen miles inland, travelling upriver on the flat-bottomed barge, The Lump, to Rose Hill, escorting officials to inspect progress on a courthouse under construction where the harbour's saltwater meets freshwater.

'Such good growing land, Maggie, a fine sight.'

The public garden and seed bank Governor Phillip established upriver in the early days is thriving. Extra work teams have been sent, clearing more land, hoeing soil by hand for wheat, corn, barley, maize. Some convicts are now free, their sentences expired, and with proof of hard work are getting land.

'The Guv this week proclaimed it a town, Paramatta. Sixteen hundred souls live in those parts now, can you believe? They've had terrible trouble with the natives, though. At least Norfolk Island is spared that, with fertile land that may be even better than upriver.'

Maggie stops herself from rolling her eyes, as Charlie flings one hand out to emphasise dry dirt stretching from their hut in all directions. 'It has a milder climate than here, which has appeal.'

What future is he choosing? She can't tell; he seems to spin worse than a wooden top. First the talk of Paramatta. Now Norfolk Island, way out in the Pacific Ocean, its shipping treacherous for men and women sent there to farm. Or has he settled on returning to England and the talk of farming's only a cover?

He kisses her on the cheek and leaves to attend his duties, not noticing his good cheer has grated on Maggie, belly three months' swollen, her faithlessness soon to be brazenly public.

'None judge you as harsh as yerself.' Sarah Newcombe, baby daughter asleep against her shoulder, chastises Maggie as they inspect the two-room dwelling Charlie has finished, with its oven built from local stones.

'Even the Guv smiles on those who settle down, wed, produce more brats to keep this place going. I'd be happy if my sergeant talked of marriage.'

She gives a full-throated laugh, the sound causing the baby to stir briefly.

'He dreams of opportunities to get land upriver, make wealth, while I've been busy makin' him a family. I hope he sees that me and his babe are just as worthy as what he seeks to gain.'

Sarah's fears have touched Maggie's restless thoughts.

'Perhaps they bark at the moon. Charlie also says he yearns for prospects, but knows nothin' of farming, has but a pittance of savings. You know how poorly they pay the redcoats.'

The precarious nature of their situation, dependent on what their men decide, or even if they will stay, is too hard to bear thinking about. The friends need a little merriment, and are soon laughing about their pathetic attempts to grow food, hooting about who grows the shortest carrots, the most blighted potatoes.

It's far easier than looking each other in the eye, asking for an honest answer to the forbidden question. Will our men stand by us or leave for England when their contracts are up next year?

Two days later the sky answers everyone's prayers for rain. A deluge falls at dawn, continuing all day and into the next afternoon, rushing down, deepening grooves in tracks and paths where shortcuts continue to be worn despite the Guv's insistence that everyone use formed streets.

Maggie is pleased that Charlie's attention to the quality of work on their cottage has paid off. Not a single drop of rain leaks onto the packed earth floor.

Despite his protests she is still working at the hospital, though for fewer hours, when the first of the next fleet of transports arrives in early July, bearing one hundred and forty one convict women and six children.

Surgeons and nurses brace themselves after the horrors of the *Scarborough* and *Surprize*, then are gladdened by early reports indicating most are in good health and the vessel has nine months' worth of rations on board for the new arrivals.

Captain Lieutenant Watkin Tench is among the first to reach the *Mary Ann*, in a party that rows six miles out beyond the harbour mouth, such is the desperation for news from home.

A crowd has assembled at the Governor's wharf for his return, each one longing for a letter, a newspaper, perhaps a parcel. Maggie and Charlie are among them.

In the jostling when Tench lands, Maggie is shoved to the back of the pack while Charlie manages to push through. He is by her side within minutes.

'Not a single letter for anyone.' It's the first time she has seen his anger flare.

'No newspapers, not a single magazine. They could easily have procured a bundle at any coffee house. It seems they can't conceive we wish to remain anything but ignorant.'

Other marines join him, grumbling together before heading towards the Barracks, doubtless to a supply of Bengal rum.

Maggie is at the hospital when the convicts are landed, a handful of sick women transferred immediately to the convict ward. The surgeons examine them and conclude that three show signs of fever. Only when Mrs Hoile directs Maggie to help care for others at the far end of the room does she realise the supervisor has guessed her condition and doesn't want to place her in harm's way.

As gratitude battles with shame, Maggie introduces herself to a pale patient in the row of beds.

'Mary Talbot. Can't say there's any pleasure in bein' here or making yer acquaintance.' Maggie grins in reply, for the woman has the attitude of a survivor.

Mary is a good five years younger than Maggie, though has also been forced to leave behind a child.

'Three, all told.'

Maggie has heard the name before, on the *Lady Juliana*.

'Good grief, you were with the ones who went over the side before we even left the Thames.'

Maggie notices Mrs Hoile has observed her lingering with the young Irishwoman. She drops her head, lowering her voice.

'I must get on. I'll sneak back later.'

After cooking and eating the evening meal with Charlie, she assures him she will be back before the nine o'clock drum beats out the curfew. In the ward, Mrs Hoile is off duty. Mary is wide awake, which encourages Maggie to ask about the river escape.

'What use do you have for my story?' The woman shifts under her blanket, wincing with abdominal pain the surgeons are treating with buckthorn syrup in the hope that purging will result.

'It be a private matter, Mary.'

Other than Charlie and Sarah, no one at Sydney Town knows Maggie has left behind a child, and she prefers to keep it that way. Yet she feels an unexpected kinship with Mary and decides, after all, it warrants an honest explanation.

'I know the same distress. I've also been made to give up a child.'

Mary nods. 'Ah, I see.' Her eyes close, as though she's too tired to say any more. Maggie squeezes her wrist gently, before withdrawing her hand, ready to leave.

'Funny thing, we got away so easily in the end.' Her voice falters, then she goes on.

'My man made contact with two of the other husbands and some of the other kin, though it took longer than he'd hoped to set things up. We'd no choice but to chance it the night afore the ship set sail.

'One of the wives sweet talked the watch after dark, loaded him with gin, while the men rowed downriver before the tide turned. After the liquor knocked out the guard, four of us and me wee one, William, went over the stern into the waiting boat. I had him at the breast so he'd not give us away going upriver.'

She manages a wan smile.

'Oh how we laughed when we got to shore, didn't matter how many potholes the cartwheels hit as we journeyed home.'

The woman is sinking further into her story. Maggie senses she tells it to hold fast to the shape of who she is—much more than a woman who met hardship, who had no choice but to take its hand and let it lead her down the road to Newgate and a convict bonnet.

'My husband were a London stonemason, a strappin' fellow. Not tough enough to take a twelve feet fall from a scaffold. Busted up, he were, for weeks and weeks. Maybe you know what it's like when your family's hungry and the rent's long due.'

Maggie nodded. 'A terrible thing when you can't provide for a child.'

'Yair, and I had two by then. William had an older sister.'

'So you stole?' Maggie feels a bit foolish asking the question.

'Seven yards of printed cotton. Hardly seems worth the trouble now.'

A year later she had been on the same ship as Maggie.

'Sad to say, only one of the four of us who got away stayed free.'

Mary gained six months with her family before she was arrested in Bloomsbury for being at large without lawful cause. This time she was convicted for escaping transportation. A death sentence.

'The jury of matrons examined me, found I was quick with child. I got a stay of hanging till the birth, a bit later a conditional pardon, then sent here for life. The baby saved me, or condemned me, dependin' on how you look at it.'

Maggie can see the woman is weary, close to tears.

'I should go now, let you rest.'

'No, I beg you, stay.' Her face contorts in pain as she grips Maggie's hand.

'The life sentence were tight round me throat, but when the beak said I were to leave without my little 'uns, not even the babe, it were a fate worse than a noose. I'd have torn out his very eyes if I coulda reached the bastard.

'I was screamin' kill me now, I'd rather die than leave my little 'uns behind.'

Though many months have passed, Mary's distress still curdles. Could it be what causes the pain gnawing like a rat at her innards?

'They bundled me onto the ship with nary a chance to take proper leave from my husband, or even get a keepsake from the young 'uns.'

It's improper, Maggie will be reprimanded if one of the surgeons sees, but she leans over regardless and kisses the young mother on the cheek.

'You're the bravest woman I know, Mary Talbot.'

She smooths a blanket across her chest, whispers goodnight.

A fading voice replies. 'The friendship of women is all the comfort given me now, other mothers like you Maggie, who know what it does to you when they take a cutlass to your soul.'

Later, curled up in bed with Charlie, Maggie tries to explain.

'A remarkable woman, risked everything for her family.'

What she doesn't say is that Mary has held up a mirror showing how little she, on the other hand, has risked for her own child.

Charlie has come to understand Maggie, senses the weight of her thoughts.

'News of Hannah will likely come soon, my dear. We're told eight more ships will arrive in coming weeks, most will return quickly to England. Captain Shea's assured our company there'll be more regular shipping carrying mail, from now on.'

As he holds her she melts into the embrace, knowing full well that when morning comes she will once again berate herself for the pleasure.

When Mary is discharged three days later, Maggie relishes the opportunity to meet her on occasion and share tea as a friend.

She is at work early the next month when Mary is brought back to the ward.

'What ails you?' Maggie now works on the ward for soldiers and officials, but has caught sight of her new friend half-carried in, a man on either side supporting her.

'Maggie Bloodworth, I will thank you to return to your duties.' Mrs Hoile appears, pointing back to the soldiers' beds in the next room.

It has been a big week for injuries in the hunting parties. Wounds need cleaning and dressings replaced, a fractured arm must be rebandaged. Wheezing lungs must be given a steam treatment. The restless and agitated are given draughts of laudanum by the surgeons, but it is Maggie who must encourage them back to bed.

When she finishes her duties hours later, she returns to the convict ward, where there is no sign of Mary.

'It was quick, Maggie.' Maeve Bilson, one of the laundrywomen, shakes her head.

'You'll find her out back.'

In the windowless room where corpses are left for the grave-diggers, Maggie lifts the bloodied tarpaulin from the body, its flesh already dull grey.

She hopes to see a face at rest, instead presented with taut muscles and lips set grim, perhaps in regret that no one dear was there to witness the end, or to speak of the bravery in one woman's heart.

The record books will say Mary Talbot died from a stoppage in the stomach, maybe a rupture. Yet grief can kill, sure as an arrow, deadly as a well-aimed blow from a fist.

'You said you'd rather die than be torn from your young 'uns. You've kept the pact, Mary.'

It's a woman's way, Maggie thinks. No fighting back with muskets or daggers, all swagger and sweat. You got to look harder than that, to everyday acts of defiance unseen by men. A fire in a hut when a man's been cruel. A touch of a special herb in a stew to loosen bowels or bring on sleep when unwanted attentions become too much. The blindness to skin colour if one of the big Jamaican convicts makes a woman's breath go faster. There's no storming the barricades. Just every morning, the simple, daring act of rising from bed and doing what must be done in the name of kinship.

'Those pages men write, it's as if we're not here, as if we amount to naught. Yet why do they leave spaces between the lines, if not to hold up the words? We're the indigo sky at night, Mary, makin' the stars shine bright. They forget we're the ground they stand on for all their damn glory, so it's up to you and me, all of us, to remember for each other.'

Maggie's tears are all the anointing her friend will get. She takes her time gently smoothing back Mary's copper hair, drawing the canvas back over her face.

'I have no flowery words, Lord, only plain speakin'. I humbly ask you to know from me, this here's a good woman. I beseech you to shelter her soul, give her the kiss of eternal peace.'

She will ask Charlie to write another letter on her behalf, this one for Mary's husband and children, to be sure they know how loved they were till the end.

The work at the hospital has taken its toll, though it's not the physical toil that taxes Maggie. Strong emotions bear down on her, as if the load of Mary's wretchedness has tipped the scales.

When Mrs Hoile suggests that at five months' gone Maggie should focus on caring for her home, the baby's father, and making preparations for the birth, she doesn't object.

Charlie has for months suffered the frequent ribbing of his peers, none of whom have convict wives or paramours doing Government work. He has been reluctant to force the choice upon her, so cannot contain his glee that she is finishing up.

The months pass for Maggie in a blur of cooking, cleaning, fetching water, washing, and mending, repeated one day after the next.

Charlie has hewn a cradle from a piece of hardwood he hauled home from over the hill, cutting and smoothing the timber with all the skill he gained as a glazier, working beeswax into the grain so that in the light from the smoking wick it glows.

He tans two possum skin pelts and Maggie stitches them together for a lining. Charlie gives her a few coins to buy scraps of fabric and old clothes to cut up and stitch into swaddling squares, bonnets and gowns for the baby.

Maggie continues to check regularly on Sergeant Clayfield's wife, an older woman due to give birth to her third child. She has attended her previously, when the second daughter was born. 'Another pot with no handle.' The husband walked off in disgust when presented with his baby. Now they desperately hope for a son.

The eldest daughter comes for Maggie at dawn. Occasionally convict women go to the hospital to give birth, though Mrs Clayfield is like most and prefers to keep the pains a secret from the surgeons, remaining in her hut. She has been labouring for a few hours and when Maggie examines her, all is well. The contractions continue all day and into the night.

As the time nears, Maggie lights two candles and sends the husband away. The baby's head begins to emerge, though far too slowly, and she knows something is wrong. Too late, she sees the arms are entwined about the neck, and slides a finger around to loosen them. The boy arrives stillborn, and no amount of rubbing or slapping him can bring him back.

Mrs Grimes once said, *whatever comes never be frightened.* She still hears the husky growl in the old woman's voice when she said it. Yet every deformity, every baby's death disturbs Maggie.

This one is worse, is cause for inexplicable terror. Her own baby seems to agitate in her belly. Charlie forbids her from attending any more women, urging a calm state for the sake of their child.

Christmas arrives and stores are running low yet again. Each woman gets only a pound of flour, regardless of status. Charlie is too low in rank to receive an invitation to the Governor's dinner, where there will be plenty of exceptions to rations.

On the holyday, despite the temperature threatening to break the thermometer at more than a hundred degrees, Rev Johnson conducts a christening and two weddings in an empty granary. Maggie, her baby now pushing against her ribcage, is too listless to attend any of the ceremonies.

That night a cunning trio break into the marine store and relieve it of twenty-two gallons of spirits, cause for Charlie's ire.

'Good luck to 'em, I say.' Maggie's flash of irritation takes him by surprise.

'Any theft robs us all, surely.'

'Yair, but we all do what we can to get by.'

The year is lurching to its end when the familiar squeezing of her belly begins. As the waves of pain build, Maggie experiences them much lower in her back than she did with Hannah, but can't decide if it is a good sign or not.

At dusk Charlie fetches her friend Sarah. He stands in the two-room hut he chooses to call a cottage, restless as a caged bear and no more useful. The two women shoo him off, Sarah promising to come for him the minute there is news.

It is a long night. Maggie's body steers by familiar stars, navigating the vast ocean of birth, troughs that threaten to drown her, peaks tossing her almost senseless into oblivion, then landing her hard into undulations pushing the baby relentlessly down its narrow tunnel.

'Lord, it don't seem like it were this hard before. Must be 'cos there's more years on me this time,' she pants in the brief respite between contractions.

Sarah has snuffed out the wick, saving the candle for the final stage. The waxing gibbous moon, no match for its solar cousin when it rose in the east mid-afternoon, now rides high, bright in the sky. Silver light steals through the open doorway, touching Maggie's sweat slick hair. She turns her head to let the light bathe her face, lets it claim her, one who belongs more to the moon than the sun.

The women set an easy rhythm together, Sarah accepting direction on how to check progress, where to place her hands to find the baby's position, learning how, when the time comes, to ease the head out with one hand while using the other to hold stretched tissue at the opening so it does not tear. Maggie accepts water from a cup, an arm from her friend while pacing, a damp cloth to cool her skin.

After long hours, her son arrives quite suddenly without fanfare, not even a single cry, arms flailing, flush with life. Maggie weeps. She prays the boy will only ever be given as much suffering as he can handle, and more love than he will ever need.

Charlie is a man grown a foot taller by fatherhood. He beams, kisses the boy's head then bends to kiss his woman. 'I have never loved you more.'

Through the doorway Maggie sees the first sunlight of December twenty-nine stream molten gold across the huts below, sweeping across rotting cabbage tree frames and patched walls, as though it comes from the divine source itself.

They discuss a name. Charlie doesn't want to follow his family's naming convention for firstborn sons, a sign of his stubbornness, signalling that time has not worn down the grudge against his father.

'My great uncle José, by all accounts, was a remarkable businessman and community leader. It's a good name, carries the promise of success.'

Maggie's not convinced. The name has not the strength to carry a lad in this hard land.

'It should be Joseph.' They agree and the matter is settled.

The one blight on fatherhood for Charlie is that he has been unable to persuade Maggie to marry. He tries to convince her again, to no avail.

'Others may be willing to lie, pretend other than bigamy, but I can't.'

The baby must be registered as Joseph Bloodworth. The boy has her stamp on him now, Maggie consoles herself. Surely he cannot be taken from her, even if Charlie decides to abandon them and return to England.

CHAPTER EIGHT

SYDNEY COVE, 1792

FOR MORE THAN A YEAR men recruited to the New South Wales Corp, not long established, have been arriving at Port Jackson, detachments sailing with convicts on transport ships. The process of relieving the original Royal Navy marines has begun.

Rumours ripple for months along the rocky streets. Whispers pass from hut to hut about who will leave, who will stay. Which women and bastard children will be abandoned by soldiers, seamen, officials. Which older children conceived on the voyage or during the first days of the settlement, especially sons, will be shipped off to England and the mothers shaken off like worn-out shoes.

Marines have been offered return to England when their time is up or the reward of a land grant if they stay. Already twenty-nine have been discharged to be settlers on Norfolk Island, among them Sarah's marine. Maggie is pleased he'll take mother and child with him in the New Year.

The most recent detachment left for England on the *Gorgon* in the weeks before Joe's birth. Since then Maggie has been consumed by adjusting to broken sleep and the baby's rhythm. It is a blessing to have not a whit of energy for fretting about history repeating itself, the prospect of fending for a child for on her own.

Early in January her composure snaps like a broken spring, leaving her spirits low. Her dark mood is not helped by the fact that new supplies of window glass mean Charlie is in demand as a glazier, working long days doing private jobs after finishing guard duty, marching at the parade ground, cleaning equipment, whatever his Captain requires to maintain discipline.

He has stopped talking about plans to have his own farm, to succeed on his own terms. A silence grows instead, lying in wait, ready to trip Maggie when she least expects it. He wouldn't be the first to feel the pull of his old life in England, to change his mind. Besides, the life he yearns for on the land has all the substance of a dream.

Her unease is not helped when a letter arrives with news that his mother, Louisa, is ailing.

'It grieves me to know I can't be there for her. She will want her firstborn at her bedside.'

Charlie opens a second letter, reads briefly, pauses with it still in his hand. Maggie wants to give him privacy, but despite Joe beginning to squall can wait no longer.

'From your friend? Has he word of Hannah?'

His eyes are dull as he turns to her. She knows the answer before he gives it.

'I'm sorry, my love. His efforts to locate her have come to naught, though he's promised to keep trying, and is a man of his word.'

Maggie lifts her blouse and puts Joe to the breast. There are those who would say this boy should make up for the one who came before, but any mother who's lost a child would willingly knock that thought from their misguided head. Each baby comes with its own signature, a particular flourish from God that never fades, even in death.

The cloudless days run one into the other without end, and their cottage is stifling day and night. She takes to carrying the cradle outside late morning so Joe can sleep in a patch of shade, catching any sluggish breeze coming off the water. Sometimes she sits alongside him, gives in to heavy eyelids and dozes a little.

She has napped too long one day when she should be hauling out the bedding, spreading it in the sun to kill off fleas. Joe is a little flushed from the heat but sleeping peacefully, arms and legs sprawled, as she goes back inside. Slow and steady does it, the only way to cope with the oppressive heat.

Mrs Clayfield walks by and stops for a chat. The sergeant's wife has harboured no ill will because of the stillborn, though Maggie wishes she had. It would be easier if the woman blamed her, better than the way she blames herself.

She goes to check on Joe, thinking there may be time before he wakes to black her boots, maybe even do a little mending. As she approaches the cradle, still five feet away, it appears he's grown an extra limb, bluish grey beside her son's arm. One step more and she sees the darker grey bands along its entire length, stretched from the baby's cheek to the bottom of the crib.

Instinct drives her forward before her mind names what it is. One hand reaches in, grips the snake behind its head, flicks it out of the cradle. The snake lands in the dirt, part-twisted so that its creamy underbelly is exposed in places, then rights itself in a flash and is gone. It was cool when she touched it, as though it was not of this world with its hot sun.

Joe is stirring. Maggie, legs so weak she can barely lift the babe, carries him inside and lays him on the table. Though he bawls loudly at being pushed and prodded, she checks every inch of skin for puncture marks. When she finds none, she weeps. Had she a birch she'd have beaten herself instead. She must be more vigilant.

Summer comes to an end, chased down in its final weeks by the cooler days of autumn. Charlie brims with excitement as he returns home late one afternoon.

'I've procured bricks to build a proper house for winter, one that will better withstand the weather.' He takes her hands and swings her around in a joyful dance.

The work of replacing rough storehouses, the Barracks, and dwellings of commissioned officers and officials with brick structures is done. What the pits produce is now up for grabs by soldier and convict alike.

'The Guv would rather convicts were properly housed than spare a thought for a dedicated place of worship.' He throws his hands in the air. It's a sore point that the chaplain still has not been given labour or materials to build a church.

'Makes sense though, Charlie. The body calls for shelter and food before it can tend the spirit.'

'Such a wise woman you are, my Maggie.'

He is humouring her, the final straw.

'You're doin' my head in. Why build a house to last when there's no land left round here for farming, and none any use for growin' grain anyway?'

He runs the answer through his mind, testing its weight. He has not wished to burden her with his change of heart, made doubly difficulty by having a woman and child to support.

'It will stand us in good stead for winter, be much warmer for our son.'

Her lips form a thin line as they do when she refuses to budge on a subject. He ignores it.

'In truth, I don't think the time is right for us to move onto land of our own. The work will be arduous, with no guarantee of success.'

Now her mouth parts a little, into a round circle of surprise, as she understands the moment has come. He is making a case to return to England after winter, when the next marine detachment goes back to England. Even if he wanted to take her too, her sentence has not yet expired, she'd be forbidden from leaving.

She will not cry or plead. She has, against her better judgment, obliged him in every way and he will repay her with a brick cottage and a cold fireside.

'Tell me, God's truth Charlie. I need to know.' Her voice is hard as flint. 'Does this mean you'll go with the others later this year? Leave the boy and me to fend for ourselves?'

His mouth falls open, yet no sound comes from it. She wants to fill it with her fist, for her sake and Joe's. She has caught him out. He has proven fickle, despite the loving words in daytime, the sweet talk, the caresses late at night.

'Damn your blood, Maggie. Why would you think such a thing of me?'

A vein on his forehead pulses red. He shakes with fury and the effort to contain it. His lively face is gone, in its place a rigid jaw, eyes flashing.

Joe, asleep in the cradle, has sensed all is not well. He stirs in his slumber and whimpers as his mother stands mute, not knowing what she's set in motion.

Perhaps it would have been prudent to hold her tongue, but she cannot go a day longer in ignorance. Let him tell her what he intends, do his worst, then she will know where she stands.

'Do you even know me at all? Answer me.' His voice rises in volume, but she refuses to shrink away, drawing herself up taller to match his rage.

'I'm not tryin' to vex you, Charlie. The boy and me, we're not things you own, to be set aside when it suits.'

She is the one now quaking, as though a tremor passes through the earth floor and any minute it will crack open, swallow her whole. Everything can fall apart in a single heartbeat, the price of adulthood. Women like her understand, carry it close, especially in the childbearing years, while Charlie knows only the certainty of what he desires, drawing him forward as a horse pulls a carriage down a road.

She faces him square on, fear flushing red across her cheeks. He sees it and begins to calm.

'I thought I'd made it clear from the beginning, more than once. You may not have a ring on your finger, but I am no less wedded to you Maggie, no less devoted to our baby.'

Tears well up as he speaks.

'Why do you continue to doubt me, tell me why?'

Maggie has gone this far, she must not waver.

'Charlie, I beg you. What are you hiding from me? Time to tell me the truth.'

He takes her by the arm, guides her to a chair and kneels so he is looking up at her.

'I've held my tongue because I haven't wanted to disappoint you. Yes, I've spoken in honest terms about getting land, succeeding on our own terms. In recent weeks, though, it's become clear we'll be in improved circumstances if we have patience, wait perhaps five more years.'

Maggie tries to untangle the puzzle she hears, thoughts swarming worse than flies on dung.

'Oh, you'll go to England, bide your time, come back to us when I get my freedom then.' She misjudged Sarah Welch, that first year. Once he returns to his own country, of course the demands of society will purge his memory of a woman and child.

'No, Maggie. On my life, I will never be separated from you.' The tenderness has returned to his face.

'If I enlist in the new corps for five years I'll get double the size of free title. The land will set us up for life. This way I'll also have steady pay, for now, to support us.'

The relief overcomes her dismay that, by rights, he should have discussed the decision with her.

Later, as Maggie combs out his long black hair before bed, she silently chides herself for the lack of trust. Her misgivings are not personal to him but to the situation. She has made the choice to be with him, glad for his love and care, with a baby who binds them even more tightly

116

and brings her great joy. Yet the fracture within needs more for a splint.

She ties the hair back loosely to make it easier for morning, when she'll prepare it in the clubbed fashion the rules require. The marines are forbidden from cutting their hair, are expert at tying it for each other. It took weeks to master the technique. Charlie's friend, Jim Cartwright, was the one to teach her, the fellow chortling despite her man's protests as he shared shipboard tales about him.

'Not one to get in trouble, your man. Didn't get the stripes, not even once, for drunkenness or insolence. One night, though, we were in calm waters when he left John Easty's mess with quite a lean up, though the ship had no roll. Then just like that, Charlie disappeared from sight.'

Cartwright was trying hard not to double over with laughter.

'Fell down the aft hatchway. What sort of idiot sailor does that?' Still holding Charlie's hair, he nudged him playfully with a shoulder.

He showed Maggie twice before she understood the technique. Now she can do it with ease. First she gathers the hair at the back with one hand, just below the collar, to form a long tail. Then her hands work deftly to fold it in half with the ends on top, then in half again to cover the ends. She secures it in the middle with a black silk ribbon.

She has learned with much practice to coax Charlie's hair, prepare it to the standard expected. Surely then the difficulty between them is only a matter of mastering another skill, practising a belief that her past won't repeat itself?

They've much to learn from each other. He is teaching her to trust again, while she may yet persuade him that leaning too hard on a plan can lead to a fall.

In April, Charlie signs up for five years, receives his bounty of three pounds, and is promoted to corporal. Maggie stitches the braided knot to the shoulder of his jacket.

Sitting in watery autumn sun at her front door, the baby's soft breath on her neck as he sleeps with his head nestled against her, she feels her body relaxing, finally, in the firmness of Charlie's commitment. Her eyes travel beyond the edge of the shoreline, over the harbour, up to a cloudless sky. Perhaps this place will, after all, let her be at home.

The boy, too, has played a part in tempering the iron of her character. With him she is soft as wax, every pore open, though the lifting note of his cry in signalling for the breast sometimes catches at her throat. When she reaches for him, sees it's not the face of a little girl, her eyes well up.

Her mind is full of her son, of the man who holds her in the cold hours, and the rough scrabble settlement. Every day she marshals the wits to survive, the effort long since erasing the throb of St Botolph's. Her flesh, though, does not forget the one who came before. At any moment the years can slip, clock wheels juddering the wrong way with the slightest thing, the weight of the boy as she cradles him in one arm, a tiny finger that curls around her thumb, the way he gurgles in the tin basin at bath time.

The pain pierces the pleasure, though she cannot wish it gone because what would be left of the girl?

Oh that she could talk to Sarah, gone months now, leaving dead air where the warm thrum of sistership once flowed. She has other friends to visit with Joe, though it's not the same as a heart sister, one who lets you say what you think and feel in all its ugly mess, with the confidence you won't be chided. It was never like that with her blood sister, Fanny.

Maggie's own changes barely make a ripple in the tide of unease sweeping across the settlement by the middle of '92.

Governor Phillip's health has begun to flag, shaking the settlement's foundations when they need shoring up. The new soldiers lack the discipline of the original marines, let alone pride in their role, concerned more about exploiting the rum trade to line their own pockets than contributing to the colony's development. The natives, at first sporadic in their retaliation to violence from convicts and soldiers, are now more organised in fighting back against attacks on their people, and the loss of hunting grounds and fishing waters.

A lawlessness has emerged.

'I despair, Maggie. Our men were no saints. Heaven knows, those hanged for stealing from the stores when everyone starved made that clear. Our lot, though, were hand-picked because we had skills. Carpenters, sawyers, stonemasons, shinglers, most with a trade like me, and a bent for work.

'The new men are a bloody disgrace, a ragtag of misfits. Some were recruited, would you believe, from the ranks of deserters at Savoy Military Prison.'

Charlie holds his fractious son during the rant, as Maggie perspires before the heat of the oven. She is cooking a pie filled with chunks of kangaroo tail and barley, covered in pastry made from hog's lard boiled with water before adding it to flour. The pastry is a small victory for tradition, one of the few old habits carried on from her ma and granny, drawing on a time and place where life was no less hard but came with a steadiness of expectations.

'I'm in a party of ten to leave tomorrow for at least a couple of nights. We're to go to Prospect Hill, near Paramatta. Some emancipists have set up farms there, and now they've been raided, two killed.'

She finishes her task and takes the baby. After so long together she hears what his voice conveys as much as she hears the words he speaks. He is worried.

'You'd rather not go?'

Joe stops grizzling, content now he's in his mother's arms.

'We are to find the natives responsible.'

'Isn't that the way justice works, Charlie?'

He lowers his eyes so he doesn't have to hold her gaze.

'Don't you see, Maggie. The Guv wants the culprits to be made a severe example. We are to hunt them down and shoot them on the spot. There will be no court hearing.'

She shakes her head.

'But Charlie, you know there's harm done to 'em first. Remember the Guv's gamekeeper? He were a week dyin' in the hospital, chest torn open by a spear. Know'd he'd blackened his soul, wanted to come clean, told 'em he killed aboriginal men, ill-treated their women.

'Hunters, shepherds have used muskets against 'em, children harmed and killed too. You'd strike back if it was me or Joe in front of a gun.'

She wipes sweaty palms on her skirt.

'You don't get it, Maggie. What you see here in the camp isn't the way it works when you get into the interior. They'll appear with no warning behind us. They're uncanny, they know where we are, how to hide. Their warriors are fierce, none more so than their leader Pemulwuy.'

He reaches out and grips Maggie's wrist.

'It's not any kind of war I've known. The Guv is right, we must strike terror into their hearts.'

Dawn is still an hour away when she farewells him, holding on so tightly he must tug her arms from his neck. She watches him duck his head as he goes through the doorway then pause to straighten up.

'Go well, Charlie.' His boots crunch on the path, then only darkness remains, as if he was never there.

The man who returns late in the week is shrunken, exhausted. He refuses to discuss what has happened.

'Charlie, you must unburden yourself.'

'There's no useful purpose in doing so, Maggie. I fear I've made a grave mistake in choosing to stay on here.'

'Because of your men?'

'The men, the convicts with muskets they got with their land, the natives … the whole bloody lot.'

He busies himself removing his boots.

'What happened, Charlie? Tell me.'

He stands and throws up one hand in front of her face, the palm so close to her mouth she can feel its heat.

'No. I shall say no more about it.'

He rubs his temples. Another of the headaches he gets from time to time.

After a cool compress on his forehead and an early supper, he leaves for the Barracks. He is so drunk when he lurches in, to the sound of the night drum, that he collapses on the bed still wearing grimy clothes.

It's the first time she has seen him in such a state.

After breakfast next day she hoists Joe onto her hip and leaves Charlie sleeping off his excess. She hardly knows Jim Cartwright's new wife, Ann, a more recent convict arrival, but goes to their cottage anyway. She has a pretext in case Jim is still home, the offer of sewing needles she can't actually spare. Fortunately, he's on sentry duty and already gone.

If Ann is surprised to see her, she doesn't show it, stepping back to invite Maggie in. The room is well-ordered, with a table covered in a dark silk cloth decorated in Etruscan red rosettes, outlined with shiny metal thread. Maggie forces herself to stop staring at it and address the woman standing before her.

'It's such a change, getting used to being wed. If I can help in any way feel free to say, especially as our men are such good friends.'

Ann Cartwright is polite, but even before she opens her mouth the dress she wears, in one of the latest styles from England, screams she is better than Maggie.

As they make careful conversation about nothing at all, Ann is quick to let it be known she has been a governess. Maggie feels the purpose of the tone, a deliberate slap to keep her in her place, but she will not be got rid of so easily. Jim's hoity-toity woman can put on all the airs she likes, but she's still washed up at Port Jackson, likely for thieving, just like the rest of them.

With no offer of refreshment forthcoming, Maggie risks a direct approach before she can be shown the door.

'The party that went up Paramatta way found a heap o' trouble on the farms out there. S'pose we must be grateful for the protection here.'

'Yes, I hear the men returned yesterday, and your husband among them.'

Maggie shifts Joe to her other hip. *What did you hear?* She wants to shout it in the woman's face.

'Is Jim worried by the goings on up country?'

If the woman understands that Maggie is fishing for information, she remains unbending.

'He prefers not to discuss distasteful matters with me.'

'Oh yair, o' course.'

She returns none the wiser to her cottage, where Charlie sits on the side of the bed, head in hands, his hair tangled, disgusted that he has let himself be a dissolute after years of caution with the drink.

'Maggie, I'm sorry you had to see this. I won't be doing it again, you have my word.'

It is a promise he keeps, even when the Guv departs many weeks later and endless pots of ale and pannikins of spirits are raised in either jubilation or despair.

First Lieutenant John Poulden was the one to march the final detachment of original marines to the *Atlantic* in early December, amid applause and acclamation. The men have endured the most terrible privations to establish the new colony, yet when they return to England not a soul, not even the poorest or lowliest, will understand what they've been through.

Eyes water from farewells and the sting of smoke where natives have set fires a few miles beyond the hill, encouraging growth of grasses for wallabies and kangaroos, luring them into the open for ease of hunting. The fires glow at night, as though the gates of hell beckon, adding to the settlement's unease.

Six days later, on December tenth, Governor Arthur Phillip boards the ship. With him are two native men, Bennelong and Yemmerrawanne, their distressed wives wailing pitifully on the shore. No one blinks an eye at the sight of the dark-skinned men. They leave of their own free will, word has it, though what that means when you have been a captive or unduly persuaded is anybody's guess.

Next morning the ship weighs anchor, sailing out of the cove at seven o'clock in a light south-westerly, accompanied by small boats on either side carrying officers and oarsmen.

Within two hours the *Atlantic* clears the Heads. The officers give three rousing cheers, for themselves as much as the Guv, then turn back. Life at the settlement will lean further their way now the military's in charge. Major Grose, 'fat Francis', will rule the colony till Philip is well enough to return or a replacement Governor is sent.

As the oarsmen straighten their backs and brace against choppy seas that have begun kicking up, a thrill of exhilaration lifts the spirits of one officer then another, for power is now in their hands.

Back at the wharf Maggie stands with the women watching the ship grow smaller, her hope for a better world for her son diminishing with it as the vessel merges with the water and is gone.

She's thinking about earlier that morning, in the wee hours before dawn when Charlie couldn't sleep, his voice little more than a whisper to avoid waking Joe.

'The Major doesn't care for civilian courts, encourages officers to trade in spirits, has no issue with gambling. He will no doubt reward their bad behaviour with generous parcels of land.

'Mark my words, Maggie, we're about to see great unfairness and even more crime. I must keep a sharp eye out so we don't come to harm.'

CHAPTER NINE

NORFOLK ISLAND, 1794

MAGGIE MISSES HER WORK AT the hospital and with mothers in confinement. While Joe thrives and brings her great joy, she has been accustomed to standing at the border of life and death, where pretence burns away to leave only the pure flame of untainted humanity.

Every day mundane tasks stack one upon the other, a teetering mound of washing, sweeping, fetching water, cutting wood, filling and emptying cooking pots. None of it a match for the meeting of souls to be found at a birthing stool or sick bed.

She is carrying another child, though at four months gone it barely shows under her apron. She and Charlie live together with ease and he is an interested father, so it surprises her that the news of a second baby has disturbed something in him.

'I would dearly like to raise our children on a farm, not in this muddy mess, with drunks and ugly goings on all around. Oh Maggie, I fear I've done the wrong thing by staying on.'

His ambitions have not waned, evident in the grumbling about others who are busy advancing their situation. He detests the officers' blatant pursuit of wealth at any cost, controlling the sale of grain and other goods, buying up spirits from visiting ships to sell at exorbitant prices, wielding power as they might a bayonet, cutting away whatever fairness and control Governor Phillip once exercised. Yet he wants the advantages they gain.

She keeps her worries to herself about Grose, no champion of those who do the work to keep the settlement functioning. For all his affable demeanour he has turned over the courts to the military, making damn sure no convict will ever get a proper hearing.

The Major favours officers with unfair land grants, and stalls public works by drawing convicts away to be free labour on the knobs' new farms. He has put an end to the equal regime of weekly rations for everyone, and now convict men do the hardest work with the least food. Worst of all, he detests the chaplain's preaching on personal salvation and has begun urging soldiers and convicts alike to treat the poor man with contempt. Some hurl insults and even stones at him as he walks the streets.

Charlie has a less irritated view than Maggie of some of the changes, so his despondency catches her unawares. Doubt has not been a state he's embraced, and it rattles her.

'With your jobs on the side, we've done better than many. The boy wants for naught and neither will the baby. Three or more years is all we must wait, the children will yet be thankful to know life away from town.'

She ignores the fact that some discharged marines have struggled as farmers, regretting their choice to go on the land, quickly abandoning it.

Her efforts do little to bolster his spirits. Gradually, as the days pass, his black disposition stirs her own dissatisfaction like a contagion and they begin to lose patience with each other, squabbling over trivial slights.

On the morning of his free day, she resolves to stop her bickering for fear it will disturb the baby that stretches her belly, and succeeds for a time. Unhappiness seeks expression, though, and that evening as they eat together it boils up like an unwatched pot, spilling over as he complains, yet again, about his circumstances.

'Dear God, Charlie. We must look to what hope we have, not descend into helpless creatures, no different to sheep in the fields or wild animals in the woods.' Her hand slaps the table hard, startling him and shocking her.

He jumps up, knocking the chair over.

'Enough, Maggie. I will not be silenced in my own home.' In the rush out the door he takes with him all warmth from the room.

It grates on her that with her son sleeping nearby she doesn't have the indulgence of storming out. She is still annoyed when he returns an hour or so later.

'You're right, Maggie. I thought about it as I walked, we must stay kind with each other and be grateful for what we have.'

The tension drains from her.

'I never meant to hurt you, Charlie. We must be friends, above all, when so much about this place is harsh and cruel.'

Later, the pair are on the precipice of sleep, arms entwined, when he frees a hand and places it on her belly. She feels its pressure on her, firm, unequivocal, holding her world in place.

The following week he is summoned to the parade ground, where a relief detachment is announced for Norfolk Island—a captain, two lieutenants, three sergeants, three corporals, two drummers and forty privates. Charlie is one of the corporals.

The news hits Maggie hard as a sucker punch. She'll be another thousand miles and eight days' sailing from Hannah. It seems the only place further from her daughter will be death. Or perhaps it already separates them, and the girl who loved all creatures, even the rats, is no longer alive. Maggie chooses to believe otherwise, wills it with all her being. Hannah would be seven now, hair grown down to her waist, her ready smile turning up at the corners the same as Dan's, the way it did from the very first time she laughed.

She pictures the face of the four year old, tries hard to imagine her taller, a face with cheekbones now hinting at the woman she'll grow into. Her mind, though, won't budge from its memory of the girl she last saw, grips with all its might on what it can recall, though with each passing year it has diminished. She is left, these days, with a strand of hair curling near one ear, a pair of skinny arms, flecks of gold in blue eyes, grubby bare feet. Soon there'll be no memory left.

It's a fool's game, this wondering, she tells herself. Does me no good. Best look to what I might gain, like the comfort of seeing Sarah again.

For his part, the impending move has set Charlie's heart racing with a glimpse of possibilities.

'In May alone the Government bought thirty-four thousand bushels of Norfolk's maize and wheat. Imagine, Maggie, I can learn so much there about growing grain.'

Spring has announced its arrival by the time she and Joe board the storeship *Daedalus*. Acacias on the shoreline opposite bloom with hundreds of small exploding suns, bursts of yellow reflecting on gunmetal water. Their belongings are already stowed, so Maggie has the pleasure of lingering on the deck while Charlie and the troops haul heavy goods below and tie others on the deck, shoulders bent as though they are coalheavers.

Maggie runs her eye up the street, across the stream, and up the hill to the front door of their cottage, already passed on to another family.

With a pang she realises it had come to feel like a refuge. Perhaps it's her fate, she muses, to only know home when she's leaving it behind, like holding up a looking glass to watch over your shoulder as the sun rises at your back.

She is overcome for a moment, remembering the many women who threaded down to the wharf a few hours earlier to farewell her before they were rowed out. Ones she shepherded through birth, eased through pain at the hospital, foraged with, shared times of tea and laughter. Even Ann Cartwright came to wish her well.

The Cartwrights will stay in Sydney. Jim has given up plans to farm, instead procuring goods from occasional trading vessels and whaling ships that now come to port, using his old carpentry skills to do ship repairs in exchange for Chinese ceramics, footwear, clothing, sugar, tobacco, tea, whatever can be sold for high prices. He's told Charlie that Ann will open a shop in the main room of their cottage.

Maggie smiles to herself. The snob will be a common pedlar turning a profit however she can, though doubtless will package herself as a respectable grocer or draper. Good luck to her, snooty schemer that she is.

Norfolk Island has no harbour and the landing is risky year-round, over a coral reef with heavy surf. As they approach the coast, Maggie, clutching Joe, prays they won't meet the same fate as the *Sirius* four years earlier. Terrible thoughts have wormed their way into her thoughts on the journey, consuming her waking moments. If it could happen to the flagship of the fleet that once carried Charlie to Port Jackson, then why not the ship they're on?

Charlie has sought to reassure her it was freak wind that doomed the earlier ship as its crew tried to land cargo and passengers, rogue gusts that blew it backwards onto the reef, where in an instant it bilged.

She has heard accounts of the daring rescue operation that saw crew, marines and convicts saved, the scene looming large. In her mind's eye she searches under the sea, where personal belongings now lie. Have barnacles already grown on coats and boots, petticoats and stockings, the ship's sextant? Does seaweed cover bottles, stone crocks, decorations from the officers' cabins?

She shudders. *Damn your foolish thoughts.*

The wind blows hard, a swell riding in wave after wave from the south-west. Charlie is at her elbow. 'Come, Maggie. Time for the longboat. We've just been told the men must stay to unload the cargo when the weather's calmer, but the women are to go now.'

He lifts up his three-year-old son under the arms and holds his face in front of his own.

'Do as mamma says, it's really important. You understand, Joe?' The boy nods solemnly before Charlie stands him back on the deck.

He kisses Maggie. 'See you soon, my dear.' Then he is gone to follow orders.

Maggie watches as the first of the women and children climb down the rope ladder, mothers going first, coaxing children one rung at a time. The jollies lower babes in arms one at a time in a basket, while mothers go down the ladder. A seamen stands at the ready in the longboat to receive the basket and reunite each baby with its ma.

The boat bounces, a hapless cork against the side of the ship despite the oarsmen's attempts to steady it. Maggie freezes when it's her turn.

'Over you go. Keep movin' missus.' The bearded fellow looks set to push her. Clinging to the handrail, she turns to face the side of the ship and swings one leg over the side. The foot floats in air, nothing comes to meet it. In the panic it lands on a narrow timber rung, enough encouragement to swing the next leg down to meet it. She takes three slow steps down, her fat belly pressed close to the timbers as the ladder sways. Joe screams as he is handed down backwards and told to place his feet on a rung.

'I'm here Joe, come with me. Good boy, I have you.' She slides her upstretched arms along the rope siderail so her hands press against his sides and he can feel her with him, but he grips the ladder and refuses to budge.

A sailor in the boat below shouts, annoyed. 'Come down, missus. I be fetching 'im.'

Maggie can't move. She will not leave Joe alone, swinging from the ship.

The vessel lurches then returns to its rise and fall with each passing wave of water. Joe begins wailing in distress.

'Mamma, mammaaa.'

Instinctively she takes a step up closer to him, but as she does the face of the bearded fellow comes into view above.

'Leave it. Go down, I got 'im.' With one smooth movement, he comes over the rail, scoops Joe under his arm and follows Maggie's slow descent.

In the boat, the boy falls into her lap and sobs.

The men bend their muscle to the oars in crossing the reef, the bow shuddering across each roll of the sea and into frothing foam. Several times the seat tosses Maggie up, only for her to land hard on the timber. She grips Joe so tightly that when they get to calmer water in a narrow opening in the reef, he squirms to get free.

Near the landing place a rope is thrown out from the shore then fastened to a ring in the stern of the boat. Each time the surf draws back the men shout to those at the front. 'Now, go, go.' One by one passengers jump into knee-deep water, clinging to the rope as they wade to shore. The woman ahead of Maggie hesitates too long, leaping into water that rushes up to her armpits. Waterlogged skirts drag her down, fit to go under, but by some miracle she keeps her grip on the rope and her feet touch sand as the water recedes.

When it's her turn Maggie slips quickly over the stern, drawing herself along with hands till only her boots are in water, then waits as a sailor carries Joe along the rope.

On the beach, her back to the surging swell and spreading white-water, she plants her feet apart, enjoying the sense of solid ground beneath them. The boy clings to her leg, needing to feel his head pressed against her, the palm of the familiar hand holding him close.

Unearthly pink sunlight bleeds through streaks of cloud, casting strange colours over the scene before them. A long, narrow strip of coastal plain is hemmed in ahead by a line of hills covered in straight pines, some two hundred feet high, green arrowheads dark against the skyline. To the right and left, past the small strip of beach and a smaller, shallow bay, are sheer cliffs.

Though they are safe she feels no relief. Here is another new place to test her.

Norfolk Island, five miles long and three miles wide. A teardrop of land spilled in the vast, mysterious waters of the Pacific Ocean. At the northern end, two mountain peaks drop away to spreading hills, valleys, basalt soils, and the final run of land to the south that exhausts itself in the cliffs and bays that greet Maggie.

From the beach at the far southern end she follows the Sergeant leading women to families where they will be billeted for the night.

For reasons best known to him, the island's Commandant, Philip Gidley King, has chosen to call the scrappy outpost Sydney Town. Like the other place, the name is too puffed up for what is little more than a camp. Maggie looks on agape at makeshift buildings, barely able to withstand the next strong wind.

Dragging Joe by the hand, she passes tired cottages facing each other on either side of the muddy street, each step absurdly transporting her back to her arrival in the other place called Sydney. Her heart drags, heavy as the soaked hem of her skirts. Any bloom of youth that arrived with her in New Holland is long gone.

A thousand souls on this speck of land, and where are they? At Sydney Cove, though some may have been mere ghosts drifting around the settlement in search of grog, a game of dice, any respite from the burden of work, everyone moved about in plain sight. Here, despite the small welcoming crowd, most are not to be seen.

At the fireside that evening, Joe wriggling on one knee, her boots drying before the flames, the host couple are lively, looking forward to returning to Port Jackson now Charlie will replace Corporal Mortimer Winstead.

Mrs Winstead's voice, shooing her ten-year-old daughter Maudie away from the grown-ups' conversation, sounds a little too bright, a tad forced, though perhaps it's because she has a guest.

Maggie has been studying the strange material used for the walls of the cottage, coral stone, she is told, though it looks less like stone and more like rubble set to wash away in the first downpour.

She realises her mistake in finding out so little about the island. It was enough effort to get her head around one new place, let alone two.

Explorer Captain James Cook is the reason she's here, damn his hide. She knows that much, is aware Norfolk would have remained undisturbed, a distant haven for petrels, had it not been for him chancing upon it two decades earlier. She could be living upriver at Paramatta or maybe Green Hills if he hadn't commended the island to his superiors as a source of tree trunks for naval masts and flax for sailcloth, keen to ensure the French didn't get their hands on any of it.

Little did he know the trunks were useless. Too dry and brittle to take the pounding of heavy weather. She senses something of their substance in herself at present, a crack at her centre that might not withstand an unexpected gale.

Mrs Winstead stacks away dishes while the Corporal pulls out a pipe, taking his time filling it generously with tobacco, a careful ritual that is a show of his means. Clearly he has benefitted from the rogue military trade, even worse here by all accounts.

As night settles on the rough cottage he puffs on the pipe, speaking to her as though she is the audience, he at the lectern.

The first wave of settlers, discharged soldiers and emancipated convicts are scattered across pockets of the island. They have pushed back some of the thickly forested areas to cultivate fertile red soils, some successfully and many not.

'We need all the grain, all the meat we can get. King has even reduced work hours for convicts so they can till the garden plots he's allocated them, take some of the load off the stores.'

He omits to say their rations have been reduced, and if they fail to produce their own food they go hungry.

'It's a mild climate, pleasantly cool nights and warm days, the soil's rich and easy to work. It beggars belief that some can't seem to grow anything. The Commandant, he reckons Polynesians lived here once, found old plantains in the interior and a few rotting canoes at Emily Bay and over at Ball Bay. Us British folk, we got the grit to persist, we'll show 'em how to make a go of it.'

Maggie wants badly to laugh, and loudly. Winstead is blowing up like a pufferfish, full of bluster, and no less spiky.

He ignores the pointed silence of his wife, the folds of her face gathered up neatly lest they betray what weighs on her mind. The state of the marriage is plain to see in the woman's careful pose.

'Mrs Winstead will take you over to Arthurs Vale in the morning. The first gardens have been created in a small ravine there, quite picturesque.'

Later, slowly drifting towards sleep with the toddler hot against Maggie's arm, a restless wind stirs the island and its creatures. Eerie moaning comes from the cliffs, low hooting nearby. The wind squeals against the walls, high pitched around the chimney, groaning through pines on the hill. The air smells of smoke and through it, the tang of sea spray. She dozes with the image of white-water creeping up the beach, the street, searching for her door.

A fitful night does nothing to lift her spirits and she is glad of the scalding tea and breakfast of oatcake next day. Mrs Winstead waits till the seven o'clock drum has summoned convicts to work and the grumbling of passing men has quietened before they head out. Maggie is glad to be free of the poky cottage, stepping out into a brisk sea breeze.

The parting from Joe is difficult, peeling his soft hands from her arm to leave him in Maudie's care, at Mrs Winstead's insistence. At this early hour scores of skinny, barefoot children run hither and thither through the huts, mostly timber like the Winsteads' but a few that are brick noggin.

'Keep him inside if you will,' she calls over her shoulder to Maudie.

The road, packed firm by plodding convict feet, winds gradually uphill for fifteen minutes or so till they pause at a break in the trees. Maggie looks on in amazement. What sorcery is this?

In the place where a wide, lazy river should flow along the valley floor, wave after wave of crops in fields glow bright green, young shoots of maize, wheat, and barley tender and fresh in the sunshine. Overshadowing the fields are steep valley walls, shadowy with Norfolk pines and tough supplejack bound together as surely as bricks in a wall.

Mrs Winstead follows the direction of Maggie's eyes.

'That woody vine they call Samson's sinew, strong as hangman's rope. Not as bad as the other hated by all men, settler or convict. Devils guts 'tis, thorns that tear the flesh as good as the lash.'

Maggie shivers. The idea of magic went into the grave with her mother, but the dark arts, she knows when they're at work. The small paradise trapped before her is intended to mock, a spell cast down by island spirits to show every mortal being their efforts are out of place, unwelcome by forces larger than their own.

The sides of the valley seem pitch black in places, impassable. Her mother's words ring in her ears. *I see it now. God has marked you, Maggie.* The darkness follows at her heels, the alleyway, Newgate, the ship's filthy bowels, Sydney Cove's desolation, now this forbidding land. God has marked her for his whip, the punishment of being born in the wrong place, at the wrong time. Born a woman, and weak at that. She was not deserving of Hannah or her bright light.

With a start, she realises Mrs Winstead is speaking, her tone scornful.

'Fool's gold, all of it.' A sweep of her arm encompasses the valley.

'My husband reckons it be easy to make a livin' on this island, easy when you'll find no dirt under his fingernails. No battle for him with winds full of salt making crops black, with caterpillar plagues, greedy parrots.

'And the rats, oh my. Thousands killed by oatmeal we laced with crushed glass, and still they come.'

Maggie can only nod, caught in awful thoughts like a fly in a web, thrashing uselessly as the spider comes ever closer.

'When we got here, women and wee ones slept on bare earth in the forest, comin' out at daybreak like wild animals. I'll be glad to get shot o' the place when the *Daedalus* is ready to sail.'

She turns to Maggie as an afterthought.

'Lucky you have our place.'

The need to hold Joe has become urgent. Maggie doesn't dare respond to the woman, who has only served to raise her level of unease. She turns on her heels, back onto the path, barely listening as Mrs Winstead follows, years of pent-up woes bursting from her faster than steam from a boiling kettle. The woman has no need of anything but Maggie's ears, emptying her bag of troubles all the way to the doorstep.

In the street it's a blessed relief when Maggie hears her name, spins around to see a familiar woman waving one hand, grateful to peel away from Mrs Winstead and greet one who was such a calming force on the *Lady Juliana*.

'Saw you come out of the surf the other day, from up at the Orphan School. How are you?'

'Susannah Hunt. What a sight.' Maggie takes a deep breath, steadies herself.

The woman stands tall. 'Mitchell now. Bill has land over at Phillipsburgh, though he's just been made head of the school here. I teach, help the children with their letters, give Bible lessons. Gospel Society folk in the old country pay me these days, fancy that.'

She touches Maggie on the arm as though the job, the allowance, the step up from the stink on the orlop deck might not be real, and the flesh and blood of her convict companion confirms that it is.

Maggie smiles, genuine warmth in her greeting. Susannah, too, has a husband erased years earlier by circumstance and a cold court room. Maggie lowers her voice as she speaks.

'Long way from eight yards of muslin hidden in your skirts.'

The pair laugh and embrace, taking a few minutes to share what has become of their lives. Susannah was among the first women sent to the island, tells how her new husband came as a seaman, a boatswain stranded on the island when the *Sirius* sank.

'The stone schoolhouse has only been built a few months. Funny how things work out. Look for your chances here, Maggie, a sharp woman like yourself can make good. You with a Corporal, mind, is in your favour.'

Maggie opens her mouth to protest, to confess she doesn't feel assured of anything, least of all having the talent to better her situation, but then remembers Mrs Winstead unburdening herself only moments earlier and keeps her thoughts in check.

Susannah is already saying her farewells, must get to her duties at the school.

When Charlie appears almost a week later, Maggie rushes into his arms, the one certainty that remains.

Within days, loading of the ship begins for its departure, all marines and seamen on hand to man the longboats, get cargo and passengers safely aboard. Mrs Winstead and her daughter are in the final group to leave, with Maggie and Joe walking them to the landing place.

As they arrive a slim figure floats nearby in a cloud of white muslin, one hand holding a small parasol. It's the first glimpse of the Big Man's wife, her young son Phillip Parker in short britches at her side, though his eyes watch with longing as the other boys brandish sticks, run through the groups of adults, throw stones into the water. Maggie edges closer, captivated by the dress, keen to see the silver plate embroidery on the bodice and skirt, to marvel at a garment that's neither grubby nor frayed.

She glances around for the Commandant's other two sons, but they are nowhere to be seen, no doubt kept hidden from official moments behind the walls of Government House up high on the rise, its windows allowing for the easy use of a spyglass over the smattering of buildings and the road leading up country.

She wants to feel sorry for the wife with the soft face and round, brown eyes. Everyone knows the upright King went to England to marry her, his cousin Anna Josepha, then returning with his prize, his seed sown in her before leaving England's shores, stopped at Sydney to fetch the eldest of his young bastard sons. Bare-faced about it, taking the boy with him as he would a spare pair of britches. No doubt in time he'll retrieve the younger one, said to be delicate, or send him to England for schooling.

Mrs King had motherhood foisted on her before she even gave birth. It would be kind to feel sorry for her, but it's not in Maggie's heart. The boys' convict mother was taken off the island, made to hand over her firstborn and doubtless will, whenever the Big Man decides, be separated from the second. A high price for keeping her master's house clean and his bed warm. That's the ma worth her pity.

The Commandant calls the group to attention. A long nose, clear cheeks and chiselled chin are growing bloated and ruddy from too much wine and food, belly straining against buttons on the blue dress coat. Some say he has the gout and bad lungs, though any illness has not dulled his sharp eyes. Maggie looks away quickly before he catches her staring and can read the loathing on her face for men such as him, who take whatever they need and damn the consequences.

The speech is brief. The drummer's beat fades. Maggie holds no fondness for Mrs Winstead, but at the last minute reaches over to give her a hug. Only then does she realise the woman shakes with fear, for what is to come may well be worse than what she's known on Norfolk Island.

CHAPTER TEN
NORFOLK ISLAND, 1794

In mid-December, Maggie's seven-year sentence expires and she is no longer under King George's thumb. She had expected to feel lighter, at least a bit happier, but is no different. She chokes back the absurd desire to laugh as Charlie congratulates her, one arm thrown around her waist, squeezing affectionately in his gladness.

'Finally free, my girl. It's all behind you now.'

He speaks as though she's had a fresh coat of whitewash that makes her look new, as if they are equals. Oh yes, she's his wife in every way, yet let him hazard taking her into a respectable parlour in England. She'd be hounded out, a worthless peculiar, barely a rung up from the harlots.

He wants her to let go of the past, has said it a few times. Never thinks, not even for a second, that the past will not let go of her. Still, not the time to argue with him. She indulges his good cheer with a smile.

They raise a glass of porter with Sarah and her former sergeant, while Joe darts around chasing his new friend Ann. Will Young is a farmer above the cliffs at

Phillipsburgh, the north-eastern settlement at Cascade Bay, the island's only other safe landing place for vessels when weather makes Sydney Bay too dangerous. He has managed to clear the better part of an acre for wheat and maize.

They've arrived bearing the gift of six fat oranges, a neighbour's part-payment for Will's efforts with a pick-axe, helping grub out a stand of coastal white oaks. Maggie peels two of the fruit, tearing apart the segments, arranging them on a plate. She fears she may faint from the pleasure of the citrusy smell.

'Good country, lots of potential.' Will's island is so different to Mrs Winstead's that they may well be entirely different places. 'Folks grow cabbages, potatoes, grapes, figs, bananas, lemons. Sugar cane along Cascade stream.'

As he speaks, Maggie studies his thin boot leather and sees it belies his talk of riches. One toe is worse for wear, a hole clean through it, a show of hard times. Perhaps it points to what may come for men like him, relying on the Government's stranglehold on the market. She and Charlie arrived soon after it declared there's too much grain and refused to buy much of it. Many are already walking away from farms, though this is not a suitable subject for today's celebration.

The men are animated as they debate Will's new plan. 'Hogs, that's the answer. Port Jackson will always want cured pork, and we've a salt-boiling house here now, though in truth it's a bit of a rough show, makes the meat a little bitter.'

Charlie peppers him with questions until Maggie lumbers over, belly now huge. 'Come now, my dear. 'Tis happier matters we be marking.'

During a visit earlier in the year Rev Johnson has married Sarah and Will, along with several other couples.

'Poor fella managed a hundred in three days back in '91. Must have been like a cattle yard on market day. Least we got spared that.' Will beams at his wife, winks.

It is Maggie's turn to propose a toast, wishing the bride and groom prosperity and a joyful life together. 'Lord knows,' she whispers in Sarah's ear a few minutes' later, 'we've little enough cause to make merry'.

The men use the excuse of lighting their pipes to step outside the door. Maggie hears a snatch of conversation about the selling price for meat before their voices drop to a whisper. It occurs to her that Will Young is a freemason like Charlie, one of the band of brothers who ignore the Government ban on secret society meetings, keeping their business even from bedmates because they are bound over, so Charlie says.

The women pay no mind to their menfolk leaning against the outside of the wall. They have more immediate matters to discuss on raising children and getting their hands on essentials—'my God what I'd give for a proper bar o' soap, Sarah'— sprinkled with a dash of island gossip.

Sarah reels off the names.

'Fanny Potts a flash piece o' mutton, got fancy clothes that come with her in a trunk. Minnie Abbott, best to have in your corner if things go wrong 'cos she makes a bad enemy. The one who works as a maid for the Kings, her lips be always flappin' so make sure to tell her naught. Grace over at the bakehouse, most ill-named woman I know, full o' gammon to yer face but just as soon run a knife in yer back. Not forgettin' the sow wife.'

'The what?'

'Sow wife. Early days, not enough swine to go round. The Big Fella ordered one sow be shared between three convicts. She an' two of the men got a pig. It birthed a litter of eight, the sow-keeper birthed one. No one knows, maybe even herself, who's the da of her boy.'

Maggie lets herself be entertained by the stories, though below the laughter worry is setting up shop. When the visitors depart, Maggie holds back till she and Charlie have supped and Joe is asleep.

'You and Will had a lot of chat outside. You'll not do anything to bring us trouble with the Guv? Tell me true.'

He pushes his plate away slowly, taking his time sizing up what to say.

'No need to fear, Maggie. The Guv knows some settlers meet to improve their circumstances. Keeps an eye on them, sees they give no threat, and neither do us in the brotherhood.

'It'd be foolishness to do anything that gives us grief. This island is our future, Maggie, the place where we'll put down roots, make a fair life for us and the boys.'

She is hearing things, what he said can't be right. Surely he's teasing. She studies his face, waiting for him to crack into a big grin any minute. This prison upon prison, after everything, can't be how she ends her days.

'What are you sayin', this place is our future?' The mellow effect of the porter is long gone.

'This is where they'll discharge me, so this will be where I get land, of course.'

146

The air rushes out of her body, she slumps against the back of the chair. In her mind, they were always returning to Port Jackson, maybe to a prime piece of land the Guv's started handing out up north on the Hawkesbury River. Not once has she thought Norfolk Island, marooned in endless ocean, will be her final home.

'No, it can't be.' The words fly out, beat against the cottage walls like moths against a lamp, then are gone, leaving a void in which both of them are rendered motionless, mute.

Charlie stirs, reaches over to take her hand, matter of fact.

'Maggie, this is where we'll be farmers in a few years. So we need friends, need to cooperate with settlers, make sure things go our way. We need to know who we can trust. The masons have always done right by me and me them.'

Who is this man eating at her table, sharing her bed? Every contour of his cheeks, nose, lips is familiar, but he seems a stranger. This man who plans, schemes, fails to make plain the path for her very life, what is he to the one with the tender caresses in the dark, who seeks her opinion on all manner of things except the ones that matter most?

The night drum will beat soon and the traps will be out to catch anyone on the loose. She no longer cares, pushes forward on the table to raise her heavy-bellied self, drags limbs that are dead weight out into the street, ignoring a couple of redcoats staggering by, their drunken voices loud, and the saucy shouts and singing coming from so many huts.

Maggie remains numb for days, sullen with Charlie until the child growing inside her makes its own needs known with pains that begin at first light. Despite Charlie's objections, she insists a neighbour will not do, Sarah must be the one to help. Charlie begins to argue but sees in her steadfast face that she will not budge. She is a woman with years of choices forced upon her and this is one small insistence she will have for herself.

He hurries inland four miles, skirting deep holes in Middlegate Road before reaching the Youngs' farm. On edge, he must muzzle his impatience while Sarah arranges for a nearby settler's wife to take Ann. He wants to run on ahead, get back swiftly, but falls in step with Sarah's pace. It is early afternoon when they reach town, finding Maggie bent over at the table, groaning, cutting a slab of bread to spread with lard for the boy.

The baby arrives, protesting, as the sun departs on December twentieth. Maggie chooses the name this time, Knox, after the grandfather she never met, a northern England miller. By her mother's account he was a kind, calm fellow, though the fractious baby shows no sign of his namesake's nature.

The New Year rolls in, though it carries no promise for Maggie of anything more than what she must deal with every day. Word has gotten around that windows fitted by Charlie have no leaks, hold steady in high winds, and his timber work is particular. He is in demand at the main settlement, on outlying farms, on the western side of the island at Queenborough, and over at Phillipsburgh, where twenty or so workers dress flax and weave coarse canvas.

With no sign of the French, or any other vessel for that matter, the marines at Sydney Town and garrisoned at Phillipsburgh are largely free to do as they please. Their uniforms have fallen apart, they look no different to convicts these days. Maggie supposes she should be grateful that Charlie chooses to work rather than spend his time drinking or gambling.

He returns home, his shirt black as the back of the chimney, carrying promissory notes or coins, the occasional bag of wheat or bananas, maybe a cut of meat or piece of clothing. On one occasion he brings an aggie for Joe, the milky marble marked by a bright band of red. It immediately becomes the boy's favourite toy.

On another, he produces from his pack a Chinese vase decorated with a singing bird, perched on a branch laden with pink blossom.

'Useless, but I thought it might give you pleasure.' He hands it to her with his boyish smile and for a moment she can see how he might have been at five or six years old, excited by a bird's nest, scrap of yarn, some small found treasure.

She would have preferred new stockings, but remembers to occasionally remark on the beauty of the decoration to please him. It is the first vase she's owned, and next morning she gathers kurrajong branches for their starry yellow flowers on nearby Mount George, its name amusing her for it's little more than a hill.

Prices have been set for trading produce and labour. When Charlie brings home a fowl worth sixpence for his day's efforts she can hardly contain her joy at the prospect of fresh eggs, while Joe delights in scattering grain for the bird. After Charlie builds a pen behind their cottage, he returns with a second white Dorking, a chunk out of its blood red comb from a contest with a rat.

Maggie insists the chickens be caged inside after dark so they are not thieved.

Soon after, on a walk to the beach along the settlement's winding lanes, baby in one arm, Joe trailing a little behind, her mind is up to its old tricks, trying to imagine how Hannah would look these days. She fancies her girl's tall at nearly eleven, ignores the likelihood she will be stunted for want of food. She has schooled herself to keep Dan in the attic of her heart, but Hannah is at her shoulder every day.

They pass the flogging triangle, then the gallows at the crossroads. As they near the Guard House the boy stops.

'Mamma, I hear sumfing.'

She has been trying desperately to recall the way Hannah tipped her head to one side when she laughed, and her son's voice pulls her back to the present. Oh dear God, the animal sound of a man buried alive, stuck in the dark hole, an isolation punishment dug into the corner of the Barracks yard.

She takes Joe's hand, drags him away quickly from what a boy does not need to know, and away from the urge to moan and shriek along with the madman. The island is its own isolation cell, goes nine, ten months, sometimes more, cut off from the outside world. Within the fortress cliffs of the coastline, the town is its own gaol. Within the town, her cottage and two sons confine her. She is truly stranded.

CHAPTER NINE

NORFOLK ISLAND, 1795-1796

AN EXTRA RATION OF SPIRITS was issued for Christmas, and although the ash of the holyday bonfires is long cold, grog-ridden mayhem has barely ceased in the weeks since. It seems to Maggie that New England rum is stronger than the Bengal spirits usually supplied by the store.

As a howling gale comes in with twilight she is expecting Charlie home, not the loud rat-a-tat at the door. She opens it to a red-faced woman and a toddler close to Joe's age, his face troubled.

'Let me in, I beg of you,' she hisses, as though unable to stretch her mouth properly. 'You be a good woman, I know'd you from old hospital days. You'll not want me to come to harm.'

It is one of the cleaners from the convict ward, yet that's not what spurs Maggie to let them pass, but the fear in the boy's eyes.

Once they are inside, she steps out, checks both directions in case an angry husband is about to swoop, then shuts the door. Despite the dim room, she doesn't light a candle or lamp.

'Mrs Webb,' the woman says, a bruise already spreading across the side of her face.

'Married to a lag these days, steady enough fella. They have no care, though, do they? Do whatever they want, take whatever they like.' She looks fit to fall down so Maggie steers her to a chair.

'He were playin' the dice, see, they were drinkin'.'

The story is in pieces, scattered about. Maggie waits till the woman can gather them up, give her some sense of what has passed.

One of the redcoats gambling with her husband decided he needed a woman, and she would do. Tried to drag her from the hut, beat up her husband when he tried to stop him.

'Gave me a thumpin' too, the bastard. Thought any minute he'd take out his knife and rip me up. He'll be making sure my fella's the one to face the justice, though. There's no winnin' with them.' Her tears turn to noisy sobbing.

'No matter a woman's married, if we been convicts they treat us worse than vermin.'

The woman's plight has torn open a scar, a raw place Maggie thought long ago sealed off, brought her back to her senses after weeks of not wanting to see or hear what goes on around her.

Just then, Charlie comes home. He is busy disentangling himself from Joe while struggling to kick off his boots when he looks up and sees the woman and child.

'This be Mrs Webb and Solly.' Maggie keeps her voice light, breezy. 'She stopped by for a little company.'

Charlie takes in the cowering child, the bruise on the mother's face.

'Getting a bit late for visiting, perhaps.' He wants her gone, knows whatever this is it will not end well.

'They can share supper with us, first.' Maggie busies herself momentarily with the stew, before fixing Charlie with a pointed stare. He is ready to send the woman home, but hesitates when he sees Maggie's flinty stance, knows the kind of fire that can happen when he rubs against it.

He stiffens. 'She is most welcome.' Spoken without a skerrick of warmth.

Reaching for his clay pipe he sits heavily on the one empty chair and begins fussing with tobacco, taking his time gathering a pinch from the pouch, tamping it down with both thumbs.

Maggie leans down to Joe, now on her lap. 'Where's your little bear, the one dadda carved from his broken pipe? Solly be glad to see it.' Joe and the boy sit in the corner and start a game with the toy.

Soon the food is ready and they eat, the strained conversation broken by the giggles of the toddlers using sticks from spare kindling as swords.

Mrs Webb excuses herself immediately supper is done, holds back the embrace she wants to give Maggie by way of thanks, to nod warily as Charlie opens the door.

'Her husband?' asks Charlie. The woman's footfalls are still fading down the street.

'One of yours. Though her man got roughed up tryin' to save her.'

'Geezus Maggie, we can't be getting tangled up in other folks' messes. This lot are not the same as the ones I signed up with, you know that. They make bad enemies, for me but especially for you.'

Another way for him to remind her that her past is still a burden. She will always be part of the sweepings of the old land, knows it only too well, and doesn't thank him for showing he hasn't forgotten either.

'I am not standin' by to let a woman, through no fault of her own, one who's properly wed, take a beating from any man, soldier or no.'

Charlie shakes his head. 'Do you not see? They've no respect for the Commandant. A Navy man, started out as a captain's servant, he's not one of them. Governor Grose, he lets them have their head at Port Jackson, and there's even less control here. Some of them are making their own rag-water, sends them half mad. It's far worse than you think, Maggie. I have to watch my step every day.'

She pauses, feels the woman of thirty or more years slide away until she's left standing in the bones of the fifteen-year-old, feet planted at the battered door of the back alley in St Botolph's, eyes meeting Mrs Grimes, refusing to back down.

'Must we always suffer it, though?'

It has been a long day. Charlie is too weary to argue, especially about the marine force he was once proud to serve. He consoles himself that Maggie is not herself tonight, so best keep his opinions for another time.

Maggie cleans the supper dishes, rubbing harder than she needs, and wonders where that young girl has gone, the one who refused to accept what morsels others thought her due. She's still thinking of her in bed and slips into sleep, smiling.

The wind whines all night, slapping sheets of rain against the walls, then dies down as the sun comes up. Maggie waits till Charlie has gone, watching from outside the cottage door till she sees Susannah on her way to the school, then waves her over.

'You took a risk. Best not stir the hornets' nest.' Susannah knows all too well the redcoats are scrapping with convicts, snatching wives, tricking the men out of what little they own by cheating at cards.

She looks at Maggie in dismay. 'You know some of 'em are gunning to kill coxswain Dring for daring to beat up a soldier who kept interfering with his wife?'

Maggie knows only too well what went down. 'Who says anything about takin' them on?'

Susannah cocks her head to one side, listening now.

'All we do is keep our women a bit safer, and their young 'uns.' Maggie tugs at her friend's sleeve, pulls her inside. 'We've no chaplain, the constables have no care. There's no protection. We looked after each other on the ship, can't we chance the same now?'

'As much chance, Maggie, as milking a pigeon. We all have to look out for ourselves, and that's hard enough.' Susannah steps towards the door.

'Wait, hear me out. What if we talk to the women we know, get 'em to agree. The ones expecting trouble could do something, maybe leave a broom against the outside wall as a sign. Any one of us who sees it could go there, plead for the woman to come look at their sick child, some reason to get 'em away from the men.'

'I dunno. Reckon the redcoats would see through it. We can't be saving them all.' Susannah stands stiffly, more brittle woman than the woman Maggie knew on the ship, yet her voice cracks a little as she speaks. It's an opening of sorts to her friend's heart, and Maggie dives in.

'No, we can't. If we help just one, though, surely that's something? Better than turning our backs. They may as well poke sticks in our eyes for all the blindness we're made to carry.'

The two women face each other, nothing more to be said. Each knows what it takes to survive on your wits and little else, to see brutality and be made to bear it, worse, required to pretend respect for those who mete it out.

Susannah breaks the silence. 'We're among the fortunates these days, you and me.'

She draws in a big breath and sighs it out. 'Let's see what the others think.'

Maggie has been in the habit of walking Joe to the beach each day, Knox wrapped in a shawl, resting in the crook of her arm. It's easy, over the following week or two, to stop occasionally to knock at a cottage door, being careful to speak only to those she knows. Or have a quiet word in the queue at the storehouse on rations day.

Unrest is part of the air everyone breathes at Sydney Town and the outlying settlements, so when Susannah seems to carry on as though the conversation never happened, it's no surprise. She gives orderly lessons at the school, stays in the Commandant's good books, protects herself by giving Maggie no indication that she has aided or hindered spreading the message from woman to woman.

It may be that a broom saved the occasional woman from a bloodied nose, a two-day headache after being slapped around the head, or being forced onto her back with a man she did not want.

Or it may be that nothing much comes from Maggie's scheming, she has no way to tell in the coming days, though she hopes a small spark has been lit in at least one convict woman, a tiny flicker throwing a light on what's been shut away far too long—the strength to see how she might gain power, however little.

Any focus on the ruse is pushed aside when Will Young, red-eyed, babbling, arrives at her door in a pitiful state. He falls onto a chair, head in hands, sobbing, now unable to speak.

'Is it Sarah? You must say what's gone down, Will.' She pats his arm when she really wants to shake him, get him to explain.

Through messy, hiccupping gulps he manages to speak.

'I bloody told her. I told her, Maggie, I said it needs cutting down, but she didn't want it, said it threw good shade.' He sobs again as the blood in Maggie's veins begins to run cold.

'Dear God, it's Ann, isn't it? Oh Will, we've got to go.' She's in motion already, taking her shawl from the peg, fetching her bag of herbs, snatching the basket she takes to the storehouse and throwing in bread, salt pork, two near rotten bananas.

'Watch Knox for me, Will.' This time she does strike his shoulder to get his attention, a little too hard, but it has the desired effect. She hauls a protesting Joe next door then returns, bundling Knox into a clean linen clout, tossing the soiled one into the washing pail. Charlie can deal with that, and Joe, when he returns.

Only then does she register that Will has run the four miles from the farm. 'Here, drink this.' She scoops a pannikin of water from the bucket. His hands shake so badly much of the water slops out.

While he drinks she banks up the fire, moving large stones in front of the fireplace and spreading ashes over either side of the coals to slow their burn. Charlie won't want to wait too long to boil water for his tea.

'Let's get to Sarah.' At the sound of his wife's name Will is on his feet, dazed. 'Come on, tell me all that happened on the way.'

Will carries the basket, letting Maggie and the baby take the lead. The dreadful report he gives drains the strength from her limbs, but the thought of Sarah's anguish keeps her upright, drives her on.

CHAPTER ELEVEN

NORFOLK ISLAND, 1795

I T WAS AN ISLAND PINE, growing tall near the house. A favourite cool spot where Ann liked to play with her two dolls and the wooden toy furniture Will had made. Unbeknown to anyone the wind had loosened the tree, its roots no longer holding tight in the soil so it leaned just a little in the stillness of days following a storm. The tree could have fallen to the south, the west or east, anywhere in between, and the girl would have been spared.

For the entire walk Maggie fights the imagining of Ann's sweet face, bloodied and broken. She is not prepared to find her seemingly untouched, stretched out on the kitchen table, no sign of the crushed lungs where a thick limb struck her. One shoe is missing, the only clue the tree has left in its wake.

They heard the wailing well before reaching the farm fence. Now they are in the room Sarah pauses keening only briefly to throw herself into Maggie's arms, almost crushing Knox. One of the friends and neighbours gathered nearby takes the baby, as Will shepherds them from the room.

Sarah is a heavy bundle of sorrow and rage, a weight Maggie cannot hold. They sink to the floor, Maggie kneeling, arms outstretched to encircle her friend. Sarah's head jerks back, she starts shouting.

'It wanted her, waited for her. Growing there, biding its time to take her.'

'It be a mishap, Sarah, nothin' but terrible misfortune.'

Sarah leaps to her feet, arms flailing. 'No, that damn tree were a dark spirit, always out to get her, others too, growing on our land, comin' for us. I told Will, I told 'im today, they have to go, every single one.' Her voice rises to an unearthly pitch, chilling Maggie.

'The wind got the better of the tree, weakened it, Sarah. The way of nature. A dreadful thing no one could tell, not you, not Will, not a soul.'

At the sound of the word soul, Sarah throws herself onto her daughter's body and screams, a long, curdling sound fit for the crackbrained in Bedlam asylum.

All afternoon she rages, out of her senses at times, a madwoman spewing words that make no sense, then collapsing in fits of weeping and keening. She refuses to let others touch Ann or prepare her for burial. Maggie stays by her side, leaving only to suckle Knox and take a little food and water herself.

Late afternoon, Will draws her aside. 'She's lost her mind. Help her, Maggie, you got to help her.'

'She needs sleep. The hospital at Sydney Town don't have laudanum to spare. I've a couple of useful herbs, though no setwall. Ask around, see if the womenfolk have anything.' They keep it to themselves, but Maggie knows some have come by medicinals from the Old Country.

Hopefully not all have been used or traded for food and clothing.

The blacksmith's woman brings in dried bark from the trunk of a Port Jackson wattle. 'Had it a long time, praise be it can still soothe addled nerves. I'm told the natives did swear by it.'

Sarah refuses to leave the child's body. Maggie boils the bark with the last of the dried flowers from chamomile she grew at the cottage Charlie built, then cools the draught and adds it to a little rum to disguise the bitterness. She goes slowly, handing the cup to her friend when she is distracted, taking it back for a time, encouraging her to sip often. It takes more than half the hour before the cup is emptied.

Eventually the concoction and exhaustion knock Sarah out. Together, Maggie and Will wrangle the limp frame onto the bed upstairs. Visitors are sent home, leaving behind a pie, cooked leg of mutton and roasted potatoes. Will eats little, says less. Maggie sups for the sake of Knox, but is so drained she would willingly let someone else do the chewing.

'Get me her best dress, Will, time to look after the poor lamb at last. Then put yer head down while you can.'

The two-storey timber house is suddenly quiet, not a joist squeaking or mouse scuttering. Knox sleeps soundly near the fire, curled in a dresser drawer padded with Will's old marine dress coat, tuckered out by an afternoon of being handed from one woman to another.

Maggie carries a basin of soapy water and a towel over to Ann, hands shaking. The girl's skin, greyish blue in the light of day, seems to glow as Maggie gently unbuttons the dress, then the shift underneath, and draws off the single shoe, the stockings.

Rigor mortis has set in but she does her best to tie a wide bandage under the chin and around the girl's head to pull the jaw into place. The eyes are fixed open, so coins will be needed to cover them. A little more than three years she's been on this Earth, all the living God has granted the wee thing, deserving every care she can muster.

She sings a little to the child, at last able to let her own heart break for this daughter, for Sarah and Will, for her own loss of a girl, old sorrow always lying in wait to enter wherever there's a rupture.

The air feels thick in the room, and she senses the girl's spirit holding on.

'Be at peace, little one. Your ma, she be looked after by your da, by everyone. Go to the Heavenly Father now, he needs you more than us.'

The fire has died down to orange embers and perhaps a flame has flared without Maggie noticing, for the room fills with white light, and she looks around for the lamp that's burning but there is none. It fades as quickly as it came, and she must light a candle to finish laying out the child.

Slowly, gently, she washes the girl's face, her hands, crooning soft words of comfort as she reaches her legs and feet. After drying the body she dresses her in the yellow cotton frock Will has found, the hem trimmed with lace daisies sewn by her mother's hand. It pains Maggie to cut the dress but it's the only way she can smooth it on, being careful to tuck the joins underneath so they won't be visible in the raw coffin Will and his neighbours have fashioned that day.

It's well past midnight when her work is done. She wakes Will and together they line the coffin with the quilt from Ann's cot, lifting her into her final home. The body is too stiff now to fold the hands across the chest. They must content themselves with nestling a ragdoll near one arm, and in the other hand placing a blue ribbon Sarah has saved in a keepsakes box. Maggie lightly crushes sprigs of pungent rosemary, tucking the herb around the girl.

Will sits vigil while Maggie gets some sleep, for Knox will wake early.

Sarah is back to screaming and wailing when Charlie arrives mid-morning with Joe to join the procession to the burial ground, on a hill overlooking the endlessness of sea. In this wretched place the old funeral rules no longer apply, and every able-bodied man, woman and child gathers under warm sun to follow the small wooden box.

Will longs to bear the weight of his darling daughter, to stumble uphill pressing her to his chest. Maggie sees in the grim set of his mouth that he's torn at letting a neighbour carry his little girl. Sarah has insisted she come, so Will and Charlie must half-lift and drag her each step of the way.

At the grave there is no passing bell to steadily toll, see Ann on her way. Instead she is lowered to the roar of ocean smashing against the cliffs, drowning out dull words recited half-heartedly from a prayer book by local garrison chief, Lieutenant Dankworth.

Afterwards the Ferrions stay for an hour or so, then must leave while there is daylight to get home. Sarah is making less sense in her grief than the day before, fixated on the sinister intentions of the tree, quite far gone from mourners milling around in the house.

'Get her in the vegetable garden if you can, Will. She needs to touch something that grows, it might help set her mind right. I'll come back in a week.'

Will wipes red eyes with fingers still sap-stained from the struggle, barely two rounds of the sun gone, to drag the limb from his daughter's warm body.

'She's with child, not yet four months gone.'

Maggie wants to cry with him, tells herself not to add to the poor man's suffering. What good will a mad woman be for a babe?

'Time will heal her. I ain't seen a woman yet who didn't come to her senses for the sake of new flesh 'n blood.' She hopes her voice doesn't betray her concern.

They say their goodbyes and set out on the dusty road, Charlie carrying Joe, Maggie the baby, lost in their private thoughts. Grief is a boat that takes you a long way from land, and Maggie fears her friend has no stars to find her way back.

'It's a bad business, dear girl. Sorry times for them.' Charlie's words are all that break the silence as they trudge home, the road winding up steep hills and down.

Near the town Maggie fancies she hears a voice on the breeze, maybe with a touch of wheeze like old Mrs Grimes. *Once a handywoman always one, and nuffink you can do 'bout it.*

Herbs, potions, easing babies into the world, the dying on their way out. It's part of her, and she can't expect Charlie to understand. The soul of her is made to be in the world this way, unlike what he does fixing frames, fitting glass, painting walls, labouring for money with those gone settler, enjoying the satisfaction of a task well done. It's

164

burrowed deeper in her than that, she knew it at fifteen years.

It's not something she will be persuaded from again. Her weary legs no longer drag around the final bend towards home. Only when Charlie calls to her, 'steady Maggie, no need to run,' does she realise she is striding out towards home, well ahead of him.

The island has no secrets, other than those buried in a garden behind a cottage here and there, a small bag with a few coins, maybe a pilfered pouch of tobacco kept in the earth till the heat of thieving has gone from it. Or the secrets buried deep in the hearts of those who did harm before leaving England's shores.

It doesn't take long for word to spread that Maggie Bloodworth, skilled handywoman, midwife, will attend birthing or nurse the sick. Like Charlie she is paid with coin and in kind, some of which she shares with the young mother who cares for Joe and Knox when she is called out. It's a relief to be doing work beyond looking after home and family. She might not know her letters but she knows her sums well, embracing the pleasure of counting the pence and shillings.

The reasoning she gives Charlie for taking up her old role is simple enough, appealing to his sense of duty.

'This speck o' dust in the ocean needs every upstanding woman to do what she can.'

He goes quiet for a bit, stands from his chair, the legs dragging on the packed earth floor. She has fired a shot and waits for the kickback, but it does not come. 'Alright,' is all he says.

She is sensible about it, being careful to stay well clear of the surgeon and the hospital on the edge of the settlement. Thomas Jamieson has been elevated from Surgeon's First Mate on the *Sirius*, made into a far more important man, and has made no bones of the fact that he hasn't an ounce of patience for any woman who, as he would have it, tinkers with herbs.

Maggie's resolve has spurred Charlie to remember the woman she was before the babies came, the way she bit into the sour apple when others looked for the pleasure of the sweet, the times she willingly did work that needed to be done. He hatches a plan.

A month or so later he returns as dusk settles, excited as he enters their cottage.

'Thought an outing on Saturday would be a good thing for you 'n the boys.' He has been working at a farm at Charlotte's Field, officially called Queenborough, though the old name holds sway with the settlers. He has arranged for them all to visit.

'The farm is a good un', one of the early ones, best part of three acres cleared and sown, plenty of hogs, fowls, geese, a few goats. The settler's bound to be off the stores soon.'

Maggie is struggling with a fretful baby and a grizzling toddler, only half listening. Might just slap her man if he stands there a minute longer without helping.

'It'll be a long walk, Charlie. Maybe another time? Here, take the boy while I get supper ready.'

'Think you'd like her, Maggie. The farmer, she's but a year or two out of her sentence.'

He has her attention with his cunning slip of the tongue. A woman tending her own land, so rare she could be Mab, queen of the fairies. Of course they'll visit.

'Oh, I dare say she'll be glad of a woman's company, then.'

They leave early morning, the day unusually windless, its calm carrying expectation Maggie can't name except for the small joy of a day that is free of the ceaseless demands inside the cottage.

The road up country, little more than a wide track, is quiet with convicts on their day off, and soon they have passed Arthur's Vale, beyond the furthest point north she has gone.

They stop often, when Joe has tired of running ahead and waits for Charlie to scoop him up in his arms and onto his shoulders or when Maggie needs help adjusting the shawl acting as a sling for Knox.

Eventually they come over a rise, the land opening like the gap between plump, smooth breasts. Nestled in the centre are cottages strung in a line, a gaol, and a few modest homes for officials. The land is bare save for what's been grown through clearing, tilling and sowing. Sheaves of wheat stand drying on three or four plots, not a pine or creeping vine till the furthest hills.

After the mud and dust of Sydney Town, the towering cliffs and ceaseless battering of the ocean at Phillipsburgh, the softness of this patch of country seems to sing, the air caressing instead of stinging with salt. It works its way into Maggie's shoulders. She feels them drop, the sublime ease of tension draining away after more months than she cares to remember.

The farm is another mile on towards the foothills of Mount Pitt, and soon they spot a row of banana plants providing a windbreak for a field of tall corn. A worn path runs alongside it, leading to a small timber house with a brick chimney stack. As they get closer, Maggie sees dark dots of tree stumps scattered about, in places thick as raindrops at the start of a storm.

A slightly built figure emerges from the shady side of the house, hoe in hand, silhouetted against the white wall. The small woman is dwarfed by the monumental work it has taken to clear the land, make a farm. Only when Maggie gets closer does she see the tough streak running through Ellen Dorset, leathery skin dried by sun, wind and ceaseless motion, dark as the hides that came out of stinking tanneries near the Thames at Bermondsey.

'Good day to you.' Charlie is jolly, full of good humour at giving his family an outing.

Ellen ushers them inside, where Joe is handed cool water and the adults take a tot of rum to slake their thirst, clear dust from their throats. Maggie and Charlie have brought onions and turnips as a gift, though Ellen already has carrots, pumpkin and potatoes roasting in a deep pot over the fire, and sizzling in the centre of the vegetables a fowl, doomed, they are told, because it no longer laid eggs. The smell is heavenly, though they are glad to leave the heat in the cottage and follow their host out to a rough table in the shade, where five or six sections of sliced tree trunk provide makeshift stools.

Behind the cottage a large vegetable patch flourishes, with peas and beans climbing stakes. Nearby, a pear and apple tree are each about ten feet high, small fruit evident on both.

'How'd you come by the fruit trees?' Maggie doesn't mean to be direct but curiosity has overcome her usual care with a stranger.

Ellen laughs, full-throated, unexpectedly loud for a woman with such a light frame. 'Begged, borrowed, but not stolen.'

Maggie instantly warms to her host. She admires the industriousness, of course, and the tenacity to dare such an enterprise as an independent woman, though what strikes her most is the way she sits so comfortably in her uncommon life.

Ellen is canny, too, employing convicts in their free hours in return for a share of her crops, giving them a stake in their work to help protect what grows. Despite the threat of the iron collar and a hundred lashes, plenty are still willing to steal corn or an occasional sheep.

The progress made on her land in two years is testament to her foresight.

'It's all about growin' what I need to get by, o' course, but soon I'll have the means to profit from it.'

Maggie is busting to ask how she got her land, though it would be rude to ask her outright. The woman's an unmarried convict, would have scarcely owned the clothes on her back when she went before the beak. Chances are she's been mistress to an officer or an administrator, the usual way a woman gains advantage.

Later though, after they have eaten and Ellen is showing them around some of the twenty acres she has been granted to carve out her homestead farm, the answer slips from her with nary a question needed. She has made herself a land-owner through her own merit and the strength of her nature.

Charlie has by now taken Knox and Joe back to the shady side of the house. Maggie knows he is scheming to get her leaning towards farm life, but is happy to play along in such good company.

'My sentence was nearly done, there was no one to take my part, so I put it to the Big Man himself, got it written out that my hard work and good behaviour showed I was worth getting land. Lord knows, others less deserving had been given it.'

She bends to pull out a few weeds pushing up through a row of potatoes.

'Didn't get it, o' course. Not that I expected it.'

'What did you do?' A woman with no work, no man, it would be easy to give up. Maggie wonders what her own circumstances might be if she hadn't met Charlie.

'You got to remember, like many I had a plot of land behind the hut at Sydney Town, and a lot of time to myself. I worked it hard, growing vegetables mainly, nearly came off the stores, would have done so if not for thieves takin' about half of what I growed. Give me enough, though, to get a couple of fowls and a goat.'

A clever woman, she proved her capacity to succeed, then petitioned again on the grounds she was an honourable woman and land would give her a home for the rest of her life, make her less of a burden to the administration. The second time she succeeded.

'What a stroke of luck.' The words are dirtied by envy. Straight away Maggie wants to bite them back.

'No luck in it, me dear. Knew from the get-go I could stand on me own two feet.'

Clearly the woman has farming in her blood, walking the fields talking to the corn stalks, calling to the sheep, naming the goats, a small flock of fowls following at her heels as they stroll the fence-line.

'Not a skerrick. Da was a clerk, toiled in an office for a merchant. I've come by all I learned from trying new things, watching to see what happens, or by asking those with more knowing than me.'

They turn and work their way back to Charlie and the children. For the first time Maggie, born and bred Londoner, lungs once clogged by soot, glimpses herself beyond the force of circumstances that struck her with the bang of the judge's gavel so long ago.

Her man's caresses, the baby curling pink fingers around her thumb, Joe throwing himself into her arms if she's been out, all of it has smoothed her hard edges till she is the river stone you hold in your hand, marvelling at the way it's been worn by water yet not diminished in strength.

She will need it, a ferocity she is creating as she goes, the kind that can bend a little when harsh winds blow, yet hold its ground.

CHAPTER TWELVE

NORFOLK ISLAND, 1797

RAIN HAS THUNDERED DOWN IN torrents all night, in such constancy that channels dug to drain the lowland cannot contain the water. Despite the string of swamps and fens across the commons, as soon as it eases Maggie lets Joe and Knox out the door to play. At almost five years old, Joe can watch out for the brother two years younger. She would rather not let them hear their parents butt heads, turning into a pair of old billy goats when they get riled.

She turns back to Charlie, seated at the table she scrubbed clean only minutes earlier, and hefts her large belly and the rest of herself onto a chair. This baby is pushing up under her ribs already, though it is just after Easter and by her reckoning she still has the better part of two months to go.

'Thought you would get it by now, Charlie. Naught to be gained in treating me like a fool. I been hearing the whispers good as you. The new Guv at Port Jackson wants the island shut down, force all of us off.'

Charlie shifts in his seat, stretches out the leg he strained Monday last while helping fell a tree.

'Now Maggie, nothing will come of it. Too many settled on the land here these days, they wouldn't risk an uprising.'

He's pacifying her like a she's a troubled child. Nothing makes the blood rush faster to her vocal chords, twice as swift this time because she's already warned him off trying it.

'Geezus Charlie, any day now your discharge comes through, the papers for the land soon enough after. Why in the name of God would we break our backs for a farm we have to leave, only for the vines to take over again?'

A woman shouts in the distance like she is chasing off brats. Maggie wonders if it's Joe and Knox up to no good in the water, yet doesn't have the strength to get up and look out the door.

'There's no threat, Maggie, just idle rumours. At the brothers' meetings we talk about this sort of thing. Letters have been coming, we share them with each other. No one at Port Jackson thinks it likely the island will be abandoned. Besides, everyone would stick together and they'd be needing a hell of a big army to shift folks off their land.'

She thinks of Will, expanding his farm over at Phillipsburgh, the stock including nine hogs Charlie's come by in the past couple of years. Despite all that Will and Maggie have tried, Sarah is lost to her world of demons and mean sprites, unable to sleep for days at time then fit for little other than sleep for a good many more. At least baby Mercy has thrived, thanks to the girl she helped Will find to care for her. Then up at Charlotte's Field there's

Ellen, rooted in her soil as deeply as pines on the nearest hill. Not a woman likely to walk away from what she's made, not without an almighty fight.

Maggie leans across the table as far as her belly will allow and takes Charlie's hand, callused from the years of fitting glass and labouring.

'Give me your word, Charlie, that the blood, sweat and tears we're ready to pour into a farm will make good for the boys.'

He smiles, his face seven years more creased and weather-worn than when they first met, though the strapping marine still dances in his eyes.

'Hand on heart, my girl. We'll do them proud.'

The tenderness in his voice is always there when he speaks of his sons. It loosens a closed-off place in her chest, words bubbling up, leaving her mouth of their own accord.

'Charlie, your last pay, it'll be nearly three pounds when the money comes. With what's been earned by both of us, it be enough for my passage to England. I could settle once and for all what's become of Hannah. You sent letters I know, but maybe if I turn up myself, talk to familiar folk, I can find out what's become of her.'

He's a father now, knows how the love for a child has no bounds, surely understands the way her heart still beats, still breaks, for her firstborn. How such feelings, incandescent, never dimming, can't be parcelled up, tied with string and put away.

He stiffens. She sees he is trying to stop himself from dropping her hand.

'Oh Maggie, how can that be? The baby, it will need you. And the boys. We all need you, especially when we have so much work ahead to clear our land and get things growing. We need the funds too, how else are we to buy seed, timber, nails?'

There it is, that posh voice he used with his da, not the marine who roomed at the Barracks, learned a rougher way to speak.

He releases his hand and lifts it to pat the back of hers. She wants to hit it away, not least because she knows what he says is true.

She rises slowly from the chair and without a word goes to find the boys, tells herself it's the moist air outside that makes her sight momentarily blur.

As she walks along the street towards the sound of children's voices, she looks over at Government House, distracts herself by wondering if new Commandant, Captain John Townson, will be a better or worse fellow than King, forced back to England by ill health. Though he has no interest in trafficking rum himself, Townson turns a blind eye to the grog shops, and uses convicts in Government employ to farm his own land, feather his nest. She tells herself to take comfort, that it's good he's on the settlers' side in frequent disputes with Port Jackson merchants, and has sympathies about lengthy disruptions to shipping.

Her mind turns away from the new Guv, begins running along a well-worn rut of late, the wondering about Mrs King's maid, Mary Tippett. What might have become her fate? The young woman, it's well known, turned her back on Private Mackler's proposal of marriage for a berth with her mistress on the ship back to the Old Country. A fortunate woman, unencumbered by children or the need for a fare. It's a bitter pill that Maggie, on the other hand, must stay.

She thinks of her ma, not one for sentimental thoughts. Knows exactly what she would say if she stood in front of her now. *You made yer bed, best lie in it. A waste of yer breath to be moanin'.*

Oh ma, it's not the slightest bit fair. You, your sisters, friends, neighbours, your whole generation of womenfolk, what could you possibly have known about a world upended? A place where choice is only glimpsed through the thin cracks of rules made one day then just as quickly changed the next, and chancing your own path leads more often to a bog than a cobbled road.

If it's not the marines arguing with each other, stirring up fights with convicts, vexing settlers by boasting about their advantages in using free convict labour, getting drunk and abusive, then it's convicts rumbling with each other. And always the thieving and the battle to keep belongings safe.

Townson's administration has proven more lax than his predecessor's. He neglects the school, has none of King's vigour for standards of behaviour. Soldiers rough up convicts, take what they want from them, deny them any rights.

Joe and Knox are growing up within sight of men flayed till chunks of flesh fly off, backs dowsed afterwards with buckets of sea water to the sound of screams that cannot be stifled. Women stagger in the street, skirts askew, sometimes falling on their faces or sitting in the dirt, cackling, making lewd offers. Older boys scrap for a few coins, while men who should know better egg them on, placing bets on the winner.

Maggie has grown weary of the effort to give Joe and Knox a better start in life than she got, so when Charlie says he's bought a tent and why don't they move onto their land at Charlotte's Field, she stuns him by immediately agreeing.

The sixty vine-ridden acres won't be official for a few months, till the Guv at Port Jackson signs it off.

'Townson says it's ours for the taking, though. The district has the best farming land on the island, think of it Maggie.'

Charlie leaves a few days later with a couple of hooks freshly made by the smithy. He will spend a week clearing a patch big enough for them to live on, with space for a vegetable garden and a pen for the fowls.

He has worked hard to persuade the powers that be to grant him land at Charlotte's Field, near fifty acres Townson has claimed for himself and a further fifty held in the name of King's seven-year-old son Norfolk, proof of the district's worth.

In his absence Maggie packs their few pots and pans, the worn clothes, gardening tools and provisions, cleans the cottage and whitewashes the filthy fireplace. Once the land is official they will be given an allocation of grain, farming tools, poultry and swine, hopefully convict labour, but for now they'll have to make do.

When Charlie returns the fowls are loaded into their cage and the handcart packed high, chairs lashed to the top of the load. Maggie has already made her farewells to Susannah, Mrs Webb, the women she's befriended, and walks off from the cottage without a backward glance.

It is a slow trip, with Charlie pushing the cart, stopping occasionally to balance a weary Knox on his shoulders. He has another one of his heads, and though he says nothing the tightness around his eyes, the furrow of his brow give it away.

'Let's rest, Charlie. Don't make your headache worse.' When they get to their camp she will boil some of the blue gum leaves collected at Port Jackson, get him inhaling the sharp vapour.

'No need. Let's press on.' He forces a smile.

Maggie carries Knox a while to give him comfort, but her legs can't hold out for long with the weight of him and the unborn child. She must jolly the boy along, get him to walk as much as he can up Country Road, through the pleasantly moist air of a long stretch of tall tree ferns.

Joe darts about finding a fascinating rock here, a bird feather there, excited by the adventure and the promise of all the new things his father says he will teach him.

Despite a cool breeze Maggie sweats as she tramps up the final hill, numb to anything but the need to place one foot in front of the other. They pause at the top, catching their breath, Charlie gushing about the beauty of the protected valley with its scattered cottages, the sweep of cleared fields stretching towards Mount Pitt, where a ridge of volcanic soils connects it to Mount Bates.

'We're going to have a grand, two-storey house as good as Will and Sarah's, upon my word. It'll be a proper home for you and the boys, built with my own two hands.' He beams at her, pleased with his vision.

Maggie is not imagining a ghostly house or looking at the view, nor even the farms laid out in neat blocks before her. She's never felt more care-worn, bones already aching at the prospect of all the toil ahead, the weeks, months, years of hacking, burning, digging; of animals with hungry mouths, children dragging on her skirts, fires to keep alight, food to be got on the table.

Thirty-six years old and as much to show for all her industry as one of the shiftless ones lost to the siren call of grog, or the nether world of forgetting that comes with the pox.

The dark thoughts are thick today. She raises her eyes to escape them, up to clouds scudding long and grey across the pale autumn sky. It's then she sees the shape gliding overhead, a silver bosun, white against blue, its long wings stretched wide, soaring closer, floating on the currents till its bright red beak is visible, along with thin red streamers trailing from tail feathers.

With the dip of one wing, a salute seen only by her, the seabird turns, flies west towards Anson's Bay, leaves her churning and certain it's a sign, but of what?

The thought strikes her then, knocks the breath from her so she has no choice but to sit heavily on a rock. She is the same age as her ma when she went to meet the worms in the pit for the dead.

Maggie is overcome with a rushing wave of responsibility, not the one she already carries for the loss of her ma, but a new one, so big she fears she may not have the strength to bear it. For it occurs to her that it's not just the rest of her own life she must live out, but the part of her dear ma's she didn't get to inhabit. She must make what remains of her time on this Earth count enough for the two of them.

Charlie is at her elbow, helping her to her feet. 'Almost there, see?' He waves an arm cheerily. The boys, sensing his excitement, their energy renewed, run ahead. She stands on the track while he points into the distance to a place she cannot see.

The sun is riding high when their ragged cavalcade skirts the lease settled by Noah and Mary Cottle, some of the first convicts to arrive on Norfolk. Maggie remembers Mary, a Middlesex lass barely eighteen when she was loaded onto the same ship as her, then at Port Jackson hastily married before sailing to the island. It's hard not to stare as they pass by neat fields, maybe two acres or more cleared, a two-storey house, thatched barn, log outbuildings. Oh that it was theirs, the work already bearing fruit.

Charlie is gesturing towards the house. 'Noah Cottle was on my ship. Skipped the hangman's noose, highway robbery. Upstanding man now.' He brings his announcement to an abrupt halt, flicking his eyes onto Maggie's face. With so many emancipated convicts, talk of convictions that brought them here is less than wise.

'Oh, a fine citizen like me.'

Her fractious retort has irked him.

'Not what I meant. You know it.'

They remain silent after that. Best not to risk any grumbling, the snapping that might get a mood started that will ruin their first day together on their own patch of ground.

Soon after, she spies a large tent in a clearing at the northern end of their long, narrow block. With the cart unloaded, the boys exploring, Charlie leaves her to make their canvas shelter into a home, while he treks over to Will's to collect a promised goat for milk.

The canvas rustles, flaps a little in the breeze, but at least it will keep out the rain. She must try to be grateful. Charlie has gathered rocks and made a firepit near the entrance, with a supply of kindling and small logs stacked neatly nearby. A tripod over the firepit has a long hook to hang a pan. She finds the tinderbox, is relieved when the iron hits the flint and sets it alight on the third attempt. Soon a fire burns hot and she can boil up pease for their meal.

Mercifully, as the days unfold the weather remains mild, a smattering of occasional rain not enough to keep her and the boys confined to the tent. At twelve feet wide, high enough only in the middle for the two adults to stand upright, there's barely room for their table and chairs on the swept dirt, or the five boxes of provisions, utensils and clothes stacked to one side.

Charlie has promised to dig a well, but for now water must be carried from a stream half a mile away, along a track hacked from vines and around stands of bloodwood and the good-for-nothing bastard ironwoods, the small trees a deceit, looking for all the world like they make good fence posts only to rot away in no time.

He brings two full pails each morning, and if she runs short she sends Joe with one of them to fill. Once a week she carries their washing to the stream, wrists aching from wringing the wet clothes and linen hard as she can, squeezing out water to lighten the load for the walk back home.

Nights are spent tossing uncomfortably on the sheet-covered straw on the floor, the hot bodies of Joe and Knox on the bed with them, the baby just as restless, kicking her ribs all hours. It seems to punish her for the lack of rest in the day, though what opportunity passes to pause for more than a mug of tea?

At least Charlie is content, working hard, snoring into the night, waking eager to gobble down bread then go back to sawing, slashing and burning. He is teaching the boys how it's done, a pair of toy soldiers dragging lighter tree limbs and scrags over to the fire, basking in the approval of their da.

'Don't be workin' them so hard.' She chides him while he shovels the leftover stew into his gob, keen to start the afternoon chores.

'They love it, Maggie. They only do as much as they want. If you see fit, though, I'll get 'em to take a rest this afternoon.'

She nods, taking the dishes outside to scrape them off, glancing up at the thickening clouds of a mackerel sky. Rain is a coming. The first pain grips her as she bends down to the basin. Mid-June, she thought maybe she had two more weeks, plenty of time to go over to Mary Cottle, see how she went birthing her own three young 'uns, whether she'd be up to being her helper.

Tears are stinging, she wants the old Sarah here, the one who knows her rhythm, reads her ways in the good times and the bad. Ellen is closer to what she holds comfortable, but she has no birthing experience.

'Ma, what's wrong?' Joe is at her side, his face troubled.

'Just bent a bit fast, dear boy. Run and get da for me, would you?

By the time Charlie has knocked on Mary's door, persuaded her of the urgency and got her to come with him, the afternoon is running low and the beginning of a gale is kicking up loose leaves and twigs.

Mary wants to send Charlie off to her house with the boys, but he is reluctant to leave Maggie, nervous like she hasn't seen him with the other two births.

'Best not to have yer boys here. The girl who keeps an eye on my little 'uns when I'm helping Noah in the fields, she can watch 'em if you must come back.' Mary fixes him with a firm expression, lips pursed. It's no time for interfering with what a woman must do.

Once he has gone with his sons, she sets to work helping Maggie lay old cloths on the floor, gather a clean basin and rags, boil water, count the length of time between the pains. Maggie has misjudged the girl, no longer the soft piece of clay she was in the days of sailing together, but a strong vessel hardened in the heat of change.

'Your three babies, it all went well?' Her voice betrays her concern.

'Yair, fit and well, no harm to me. The first, the one before them, were born lifeless but t'were not my doin'. Cord around the neck, and the useless woman with me didn't get it loose in time.'

The wind has picked up, shoving the tent walls one way then the other. Charlie returns as rain hammers down.

'No place for a man,' Mary shouts as he lifts the flap and steps in. He lights a lamp for the tent and gets a second one, kissing Maggie on the cheek before taking it with him out to the shed with the goat.

'Shout if you need me.'

The tempest outside fast becomes a frenzy, rocking the tent, straining its ropes. They hear Charlie hammering the pegs further in, then the thump as he drops logs to pin the skirt of the canvas walls to the ground.

After that he is lost to Maggie in the roar outside the tent, the grind inside, its own maelstrom as her belly squeezes seven pounds or more of flesh and bone, arms, legs and skull down the birth canal.

She cannot let anything else matter but this passage, losing herself in each agonising constriction of muscles, breathing back to her centre, then gone again.

Mary covers her with a blanket when she shivers, is gentle when she examines Maggie and reports progress, stays near, waiting for the final birthing stage when her help will be needed most.

In Mary's touch Maggie knows the young woman is nervous, worried she may fail the baby as her own was once failed. 'No need to fear, Mary. This babe be doin' what it needs to.' She hasn't the energy to supply any more comfort.

The lamp dances in the raw gusts despite the glass surround. It gives the only glow in the black of the tent, a small comfort in a world gone mad. Mary has re-lit it twice already, sitting it close by on a low box where it shines on both their faces. Suddenly, a fist of wind hits the tent flap hard as a cannon ball and tears it open along a rope seam. A blast of air knocks the lamp to the floor. In a flash the flame sets fire to the straw below Maggie.

For a brief moment it is merely a flicker, but as Mary reaches for water it bursts into a high flame, driven by the rush of oxygen from outside. Frozen to the spot, she swears. Maggie is at the height of a contraction, struggling to breathe.

'Throw the water Mary, damn you, throw it.'

Maggie hears a scream, can't tell if it's hers or her companion's. She rolls to one side, away from the fire,

184

pulling her shift in tight to keep it from the flames, covering her hair with her hands and closing her eyes.

When she opens them Charlie's beside her, an empty pail in one hand while the other steadies Mary with a firm grip on her shoulder. The sheet and straw are scorched and stinking.

'You hurt?' He kneels beside her, touching her face. She manages a shake of the head before grimacing as the urge to push comes on.

Mary has recovered herself and helps Maggie onto her knees.

'I'm staying here now. I'll sit over there, out of your way, but I'm not leaving.'

Every convict woman will say that if there's one thing they have learned it's that being amenable to what a situation demands is how you survive. Mary studies Charlie, makes a reckoning.

'Well, if you must stay, make yerself useful.'

The wind is at a pitch, still flinging debris at the tent, when Maggie gives birth to her third son on her knees, arms wrapped around Charlie's neck, leaning on his sunburnt chest while Mary guides the boy's head out.

In the moment after the baby's hot body slides free and he gives his first surprised cry, the torrent outside ceases to exist, the tent fills with the timeless wonder every newborn brings, a fleeting brush with eternity. Maggie holds him, feels his fragile lungs rise and fall, knows that whatever happens she will be okay, they will be okay.

They wait till daylight to name him, after the wind calms and Mary has gone home. They try several names but none seem right, eventually settling on Wesley. Despite its Methodist touch they agree it's a sound name, suitable for one who, like the preacher John Wesley and Charlie's own forebears, must blaze his own trail.

Charlie gives Maggie and babe an hour or two to sleep then goes to fetch the boys. Knox studies the baby's little face, still creased, eyes closed as though not yet ready to take on the world outside the womb. He promptly calls him weasel.

'Wes, we're calling him Wes.' Charlie tries several times to dissuade Knox from the nickname, but not having a brother himself fails to understand that the more attention he gives it the more it will be used, for the lad has discovered he can get a reaction.

If Maggie was once dispirited by the limits of domestic affairs, she is far too busy for that now. Once the land was officially signed over they secured the use of two convict labourers, and in the blink of an eye she has gone from servant of sorts to mistress, slowly getting used to the men calling her Mrs Ferrion, though she is not.

She has more mouths to feed, more mothering to do, but also does her share of watering and feeding the fowls, swine and goats, as well as digging and sowing.

Charlie has kept his promise and water can be drawn whenever she needs it by winding the crank on the windlass at the well dug nearby. The island's master carpenter has turned up with a convict team to help build their house. The skeleton rises up from the ground, frames for two wooden floors and beams for a snug shingled roof. Oh the joy of dropping something and not picking it up covered in dirt. She can hardly wait. The stone chimney is already done, such a sight, so tall it clears the roof.

Charlie will leave at first light tomorrow to help the men haul timber boards from the sawpit at Sydney Town. Once the walls are clad and the shingles on she will have her first real home. She is overcome by the pent-up wanting for a place that's her own, something permanent. A woman needs to rest deeply in the home she creates, she senses it as a powerful desire moving in her veins, handed down in blood or learning from one generation to another.

The island is good for two crops of Indian corn a year. Despite Charlie only managing to clear enough land for a small planting in late June, it flourishes, producing twenty bushels to the half-acre. The centres of the eaten cobs are dried and dipped in tallow, good for fuelling a hot fire in minutes, while the husks are mixed with feathers from plucked fowls and stuffed in their mattresses.

Maggie has planted potatoes, onions, lettuces and cabbages in a small vegetable plot and is trying a new plant from Ellen, a red berry called a tomato. She has also planted seeds for medicinal herbs, the packets obtained from the ship that took Governor King away.

The sow thrives on scraps from the garden and fern tree fronds gathered by Joe. It produced a litter of seven, though one of the piglets poisoned itself by eating a local plant of some kind, and now Charlie has fenced them in. The goats disappear for days at a time, grazing happily on leaves in the underwood, wandering back when Maggie calls them to the vegetable scraps she throws down.

They plan to celebrate their first Christmas on their land with a harvest, maybe a little income from the Commissariat. Charlie has whittled toy wooden horses trimmed with rope to surprise Joe and Knox on the holyday, working on them late at night, but Maggie insists on buying a special treat for them after so much work they've done with their da.

In truth, the walk with baby Wes to the town's few ragged shops will be a blessed relief from days surrounded by men, sour with sweat and smoke, endlessly shovelling down the food she cooks with only a grunt for thanks, sprawling in the shade on Sundays with bare chests while she does their washing. One of the fellows, lugs either side of his head that are big as open barn doors, squealed like a stuck pig when she yanked a rotten tooth from his jaw. Something about the sight of the pulpy root seemed to get to him.

She will relish a quiet hour or so on the road and the same on the way back. She goes on a Saturday in the hope of seeing Susannah or one of the women who might offer her tea and regale her with gossip.

Shopkeepers, a grand word for the women who sell motley goods from a room in their cottages. They have little to offer, given the last ship came in a good six months ago and toys are well down the list of what folks seek. Maggie, though, has the haggling power of a roasting fowl, head severed on the chopping block that morning. It is enough to get a jumping Jack for Knox, a trio of tin soldiers for Joe, and a length of linen to make a new shirt for Charlie.

The woman who sells the toys disappears out back when she sees the fowl. Maggie suspects the toys have been taken from her own little 'uns, but puts them in her basket anyway. She had stopped to feed Wes before reaching Sydney Town and he now sleeps wrapped against her chest, giving her time to seek out a friend or two to be sociable.

At the doorway, farewelling the woman, Maggie registers the town is particularly quiet, few people moving about.

'Something go down today?'

'Lizzie Blackhall, got forty-eight stripes for bein' drunk and noisy. After all the bloody knobs get away with every day.' The contempt in her tone is undisguised. Maggie may be a settler, but the woman knows she is safe to complain, can recognise a fellow convict a mile away.

'Nearly caused a riot. Constables had to call in help from the Barracks. Go carefully, now.'

Disappointed, Maggie decides it's not a good day after all to go calling on folks. She retraces her steps along Country Road, fixing on a visit to Ellen instead.

At the homestead there is no answer. Instead, a lone figure toils along a row of wheat sheaves, a sagging straw hat pulled low over her face.

'Where are the men?' She is close to Ellen now, sees how thin she has become.

'Give 'em time off to thank 'em for all their work in getting the wheat cut. Once it dries they'll be needing plenty o' muscle to do the flailin' and winnowing.'

Not like Ellen to send the men packing, Maggie thinks, but she doesn't dwell on it. She is keen to show she's a farmer now, that she is learning the language of the land that farmers share, couched in weather patterns, hogs fattened, portents for harvests.

'It'll be good when we have land cleared for wheat. Must be a relief getting a better price than us for corn.'

Ellen shakes her head. 'Best you can feed yerselves, get off to a good start.'

It feels good to bond with another woman over more than babies, though why it should be the case is a mystery to Maggie, when it all comes down to hard work in the end.

Ellen has grown a strangler fig from a cutting procured soon after arriving on the island. They pick the fruit, shaped like stunted purple pears, and she sends Maggie home with all of it despite her protests that the gift is too generous.

'You got a family. I won't be needing it.'

CHAPTER THIRTEEN

NORFOLK ISLAND, 1798-1799

T HE YEAR IS GOOD TO the family, better even than they had hoped. As winter of '98 turns to spring, they have more than an acre of fertile soil cleared, much of it planted in corn, barley and wheat.

The swine and goats are breeding well and they have sold their first consignment of pork to the Government Store, though Charlie had to go against his better judgement and do the deal through an officer, paying him a fee for the privilege. He and fellow masonic brothers have been recruiting other settlers for a fraternal society, hoping to pressure the authorities into breaking the monopoly the knobs have on the swine meat trade.

She knows he doesn't want to worry her with the prospect of trouble, so she skirts the subject, for now anyway. Nothing good will come of it. Townson may tolerate the men banding together, but once word gets to the current Governor at Port Jackson, John Hunter, he'll be afeared of an uprising and heads will roll.

The fowls have multiplied and proven good layers, as well as the occasional tasty addition to the cooking pot. Will has sold them two Bengal ewes and offered the services of his ram, promising the sheep are good breeders and will triple their numbers in two years.

They have a cow, a red Afrikaner from the Cape with long curling horns, shared at first with a nearby settler then the share bought out when he left to live at Paramatta. The beast is docile enough, pulls the plough and gives milk, the latter sufficient to warrant the tender care Maggie gives it. Though what she would give to smell a slice of that meat in the cooking pot.

Daily she ignores the aches in her back, her limbs. They are the price for bending to sow seed, taking her turn to follow Charlie's home-made plough, shaped from timber he cut and pieces of iron from the blacksmith at Pittsburgh. The men allocated to them aren't shirkers like so many, they do a fair day's work, for which they are well fed and given stout clothing. If they return to the farm stinking of rum after their Saturdays off, it's a small thing to be forgiven.

The shingled house is a miracle of space, convenience and light, with a kitchen and separate living quarters downstairs and two bedrooms upstairs, glass in all windows fitted with great care by Charlie. Wes is recently weaned and now sleeps in the room with his brothers. Finally, Maggie can count on a quiet space each day where she is not bound to one child or another and their ceaseless need of her.

If Charlie grows stooped from long hours bent over spade, sickle or axe, well it's to be expected, with always more land to be cleared and cropped. In truth, he has surprised her with his farming skills and knowledge. Whatever they discuss at the masonic meetings has sharpened his ability to read the weather, know what to expect of the soil, when best to plant and when to reap, how to fatten pigs with a little corn but not too much.

She supposes there is cause for gratitude, too, that the London lodge Charlie's old employer got him into was a temperance one. While her man no longer practices abstinence from liquor, he is inclined to moderation, unlike settlers who've lost their land, sometimes their lives, to the ravages of grog.

They have taken to remarking on their good fortune in bed at night, in the brief space before exhaustion snatches them away to sleep.

'Things going the way they are, some of our family will be off rations next season.'

Her face is on his chest, one of his arms beneath her head, though his pride warms her more than the embrace. He has travelled such a long way to find success.

'Your da, he'd be mighty proud of you if he'd lived to see it.'

Charlie laughs. 'Papa, I promise you, would never have dared express such a feeling regarding his son.'

'It just may be, Charlie, he's up there on high, looking down on you, smiling with regard in a way he'd never be doing in earthly form.'

The sentiment pleases him. 'Every day, Maggie dearest, you remind me with your ways about what a wise choice I made in pursuing you.'

She gives him a playful slap. Within minutes they are fast asleep.

Soon Christmas approaches and their harvest is done, though it takes more than one wash to get the chaff from their hair and dirt from fingernails.

The climate is bountiful, for which they give thanks, but is also a merciless master. Two seasons mean that no sooner is one harvest done than they start planting the next crops, with no rest in between.

They take a break on the holyday, walking to Sydney Town for public worship, though it's the company they seek and not the preaching. A convict beats the head of an empty cask in the absence of a church bell to ring, or for that matter a church or parson, calling them to attention. Townson does a reading, takes the opportunity to deliver a lecture on proper behaviour, they sing a hymn or two, recite the Lord's Prayer, and the service is done.

The crowd quickly gathers on the commons to share the extra ration of spirits that's been issued, celebrating in rousing fashion in the heat while officers dine on four courses at Government House.

Maggie peels off to the women in the shade, Wes holding her hand while Joe and Knox scoot hither and thither with other children running and tumbling through the crowd.

Mid-afternoon, as the family makes its way home, Charlie is unusually quiet, brow creased.

'You feeling off? Maybe the heat got to you. Or is it a headache?'

He shakes his head. 'I'm alright. Maybe something's not right with the weather pattern, though.'

Concerned, she turns her face towards his, but he is determined not to ruin their day and laughs loudly, perhaps a little too harshly.

'T'were Henry Hussey raised it, mind, and what little he might know would fit in a thimble.'

The small crop of wheat sown back in August is ready for the reaping hook in late January. By then the rains are brief, sporadic, not the subtropical downpours they have come to expect. Come the end of February Maggie is drawing water from the well to keep her vegetable and herb garden alive.

Soon the corn stalks, tall and full of promise, droop and turn brown. The main stream on their land reduces to a trickle, while the smaller one stops altogether.

Day after day they scan the sky towards Mount Pitt and its sister peak, Mount Bates, hoping to see clouds gathering. When the sky darkens they wait for the expected six inches or more of rain, but instead what falls is barely enough to settle the dust.

Will leaves Sarah and their daughter with the house servant and comes over to see how they are faring, though truth be told he seeks a friendly face.

'Lost two ewes the other day. Must have been hungry beggars 'cos they went over a cliff trying to reach a stand of green plants. And here's me worried about foot rot.'

Gallows humour, Maggie thinks, but what else is a man in his position to rely on.

By April they must face the fact that their crops have failed, all except the potatoes, a situation repeated across the island. Soon after Easter they begin the thankless task of pulling out or digging in the remnants of what they had planted. Work piled on wasted work, and still no sign of the drought breaking.

Maggie's not one for praying, but is moved to speak silently to the Heavenly Father as she goes about her chores, begging for an end to the drought on account of her family, all the others on the island, and not least the baby that has taken hold in her womb at the end of summer.

Neighbours help each other clear the fields, wordless as they go about destroying what remains of hope for the season. Charlie's small plots are soon cleared, and he and the men go over to help Ellen with her much bigger holding. Within the hour Maggie sees smoke rising, the sign that they are burning rows of half-grown sugar cane, Ellen's latest experiment now a folly.

Charlie returns late afternoon, face streaked with dirt and sweat.

'Bad enough we lost what we planted, Lord knows how hard it is when you got so much more at stake.'

Maggie sees he is feeling it, perhaps thinking it could be them in a couple of years' time, with more cleared fields and the burden of extra years on their weary bodies.

'How's she taking it, then?'

Knox is leaning against Charlie's knee and he rubs the boy's hair absent-mindedly. 'As you'd expect. Sold most of her stock to get by, she says, which is a shame. Though she was cheered by us showing up to help.'

'I might go over next Saturday, say hello.'

At least she and Charlie can share their woes, take turns leaning on each other, though maybe this wasn't a time to do too much leaning. They might knock one another over without intending to. She saw it with her ma and da, how they got wound tight in the times when his work was scarce, her sewing dried up. Never thought she would grow up and be like her folks.

Wes, nearly two, is grizzly with a sore ear when Saturday morning comes. Charlie is unlikely to tolerate keeping an eye on him so Maggie will take him with her to Ellen's, leaving the two older ones behind.

With the labourers on their day off, the midday stew is served and the washing up done in record time. As she sets out she's not more than ten steps from their fence when a great weight lifts from her shoulders. The day is mild, as winter days generally are on the island, and the taste of freedom gives zest to her step. Wes has also brightened with a new adventure, giggling when his mother joins him for a short burst of skipping along the path.

As they approach Ellen's farm Maggie marvels yet again at the order her friend has created in neat fenced plots, the house and outbuildings, everywhere the rewards of the woman's efficiency and the long hours devoted to work.

The soil in most fields is bare, bereft of what should be growing, sad as the disturbed dirt of their own farm. Perhaps the lack of green is what gives the land an eerie quality as she gets closer, the fields undisturbed by footfalls of a single person, neither Ellen nor her workmen. No sound of industry can be heard, only Maggie's own boots echoed by Wes' lighter ones.

At the house no one answers to the knock. She opens the door a little and thrusts in her head. 'You there, Ellen?'

Grey ashes lay unswept in the fireplace, the tabletop is tidy, an old jacket hangs on a hook at the ready for Ellen's next stint in the fields. The room is stale, air thick like it hasn't been stirred for a time.

Maggie goes behind the house, Wes trailing behind, and checks the coop where the fowls are kept. Nothing, not even a chicken. The silence begins to raise more questions than answers. Charlie said she was selling stock, but now it dawns on Maggie that she saw neither hog nor sheep on the approach to the farm. It's a jigsaw puzzle, and she has dropped some of the pieces, so that the picture makes no sense.

At the barn where Ellen pens ewes during lambing the door is heavy, and she must press her shoulder against it to shove it open. The rough hinges scrape and creak as she does. Perhaps Wes has remembered his sore ear, for he suddenly wraps an arm around one of her legs and begins to cry, distressed. Maggie is looking down, shushing him as she takes a small step inside, does not want to raise her eyes but must. Then she is carrying him, hurrying back to the kitchen, fumbling in the bread box to pull out a short loaf, tough and dry. She tears a fistful from it, sits Wes at the table and gives him the bread.

'Stay there, Wes. Eat this.'

She shuts him in the kitchen and runs back to the barn, her friend's sharpest knife in her hand, Wes' screams following. 'Mamma, mammaaa, come back.'

She stands the stool upright and climbs on, bumps the stiff body as she does, causing it to swing a little. When she reaches for the rope she turns her face away, doesn't want to see the final minutes laid out so plain. The twisted, distorted face, the fingers tight against the rope. Dear God, she didn't get the drop right and must have hung there writhing for a time.

The rope is rigid, resists the knife, so she must keep sawing at it for five, ten minutes, maybe more, swearing and cussing at the lifeless woman, angry she did it this way when other ways would have been easier if she'd made up her mind.

Maggie shouts in the echoing barn, giving in to the only chance for screaming out her fury. She saws back and forth with one hand, swearing, can find no word foul enough to get out the anger.

'Sod you, yer a dried out doxy, stupid bitch.' She is still trying to cut through the rope when her hands start shaking as the tears come. 'Oh God, Ellen, you should've come to me, I could've helped you.'

The rope frays, lets go. The body drops with a dull thud, scattering hay and sheep shit.

The bundle of rags is barely recognisable. Maggie looks on, aghast at where the wiry, strong woman went, so thin at the end, turned to a beanpole by death. Illness has shrunk her, that much is clear, but whether it's been of body or mind can never be known.

It can't be the drought. Surely her friend was made of sterner stuff than that? Yet the clues were there in the December visit when she'd sent the men away despite the wheat harvest, given away all the figs she had grown. And what had Maggie done? Been too damn busy showing off, blind to her friend's struggles.

'Why, Ellen? Why?' Dust shifts and settles around her. No answer comes.

She can't hide what has happened, give her the chance of a decent burial with the proper rituals. Even if she cuts the noose away, gets rid of it, the surgeon will see the purple bruise across her neck, the bulging eyes.

Her friend has hung there maybe a day. This will be the only chance to help her cross over. Maggie senses a spirit in turmoil, the need to ease her friend over the river to the other side. She falls to her knees, makes the sign of the cross over the body.

'Dear Lord, forgive this woman for what she's done, though it be a sin. She were a kind hearted one, worked harder than many a man. Don't judge her life by how it ended, I beg you. Whatever drove her to this must've been a terrible millstone. Have mercy on her soul.'

She remembers Wes then, and rises to her feet with great effort, stumbling back to the house.

The boy is hysterical, banging on the door, sobbing, she must push him aside to open it. Inside, she falls to her knees, pulling him into an embrace, drawing in his softness and heat, the life flowing through him. Once he has calmed, she fetches a blanket and returns to the barn, warning Wes to wait outside.

He ignores her words, wants to get into the barn. His instincts, even at two, tell him it will be better to face what disturbs his mother so greatly than deal with the brooding monster his mind has conjured up.

Later, after Charlie has sent one of the men to fetch the surgeon and the fellow has examined the corpse, Maggie insists on preparing the body, despite his protests that it's not necessary, she will go into unconsecrated ground.

Next day she still picks at the scab of what caused her friend to do it.

'It were not in her character, least not what I saw of it.'

Charlie can't see anything to gain by dwelling on it.

'We can't ever truly know what goes on in the heart of another, Maggie. Best to let it go.' He smiles, though it has no warmth to it.

'That may be so. She were my friend, though. If I failed her I want to know how.'

By August the drought has broken, in time to water grain they have risked planting. Joe, Knox and Wes gambol like lambs in the rain, splashing in puddles and slinging handfuls of mud at each other till Knox cops Wes in the eye and Joe gives him a belting for it.

Maggie has come round to the good sense of Charlie and most of the settlers banding together. The numbers of former seamen, marines and convicts on the land are now greater than those of the garrison and administration combined. If any order and discipline remains on the island, it is down to what committed settlers achieve on their land.

If pressed, Maggie would admit it is because of Ellen that she has overcome her unease about agitating for a better deal, looking out for their boy's future. If they stick together to improve their lot, share their worries, it will get them through the hard times. Maybe it could have saved Ellen.

Charlie is careful with how much news he shares at home, but Maggie talks to the women queued at the Government store, waiting for victuals on ration day. The menfolk forget how much they hear and understand.

She knows the settlers' society has rogues in the mix, some Irish, and a handful of marines gone settler, all troublesome, querulous men with a bent for brute force, keen to change things their way.

Yet the benefits of standing together outweigh the dangers, and it's good that level heads like Charlie's will keep them straight. The pair of them are in agreement on this score, for they won't give in to pressures from those in power who seek to hold their family back.

Maggie has taken to walking out her front door with a mug of fresh tea in the mornings, waiting for the sun to greet her as it pulls its golden orb away from the horizon. The rest of the day will see her with eyes cast down to her feet, her hands, as she deals with one chore then another till the light fades. Now, though, she is alive to the see-saw calls of the black noddies clustered in groups in the pines, the kek-kek of green parrots in palms near the stream, can lift her eyes up to the hills and let them dance across the spreading farm.

In these moments she feels what has taken root in the land, their land. She belongs to it in a way she has never belonged anywhere, not even in the narrow streets below Tower Hill, has found herself giving her soul to what they are creating. It has sunk deep in her, is a prize worth fighting for. She pats her fat belly, pleased for the baby that will be born into far better circumstances than her.

She is a thief. An adulterer. Mother of illegitimate sons. A displaced person. Every word of it true. Has wondered so often if she can still call herself a good woman, if she can still be worthy if she's done bad things. Is there a ledger kept in each heart, for surely any reckoning must start there and not with God?

Much of it has been cause for great suffering, and still is. Yet in the moments when morning gifts her its peace, she feels healed. Charlie has long since mended the loss of Dan, but it is this patch of earth that's soothed the hurt left after Hannah.

In mid-October Charlie fetches Mary, who arrives as the gap between the birthing pains narrows. The two women are now firm friends, Maggie attending her the past year when her previous baby was born.

'Lap of luxury for this one.' Mary laughs as they recall the tent flapping in the wind, the fire that marked Wes' arrival.

Spring has brought calmer weather, and the bedroom is awash with light flooding through the window's glass panes. Charlie has taken the boys to the bottom paddock to help drag dead vines, lopped weeks earlier, into a pile ready for a bonfire. He is bound to turn a blind eye when they sneak away to splash in the stream.

The room is quiet, save for an occasional gasp from Maggie or an encouraging word from Mary, though within the hour the labouring has slowed. Mary presses her hands on her friend's belly, checks for the head and the bottom of the baby.

'Maybe this one's a big 'un, Maggie?'

'Seems to me the same size as Wes, but you never can tell.'

Maggie stays on her feet, pacing to keep the pains going. She hears Charlie and the boys return, eating their supper downstairs. More hours pass, and still it's not time to start bearing down. She has carried this baby low, had hoped it would be an easy birth.

It is after midnight before she has the urge to push. Mary gets her on her side, confident the time is close. Each push brings little progress.

When Charlie knocks at the door to see how things are going, Maggie shouts at him to go away, says she's too knackered to answer any bloody questions.

'God Almighty, Mary.' She sucks in breath after straining yet again. 'This one might be the death o' me.'

Mary massages the belly, hoping to prod the baby to work harder. Maggie drifts a little in the pain, then startles with a memory, one of the last births she attended before Newgate.

The baby was unusually big, the labour so prolonged she had no choice but to get the da to fetch the surgeon. He examined the mother, then gave the father a most terrible choice. 'I can save your wife or save the infant. Which do you want?' The fellow, trembling with misery, came down on the side of his baby, seeming to hope for a son. The mother wasn't yet thirty years when the doctor cut her open, let her bleed out, and lifted out a wee girl.

'Push, Maggie, push.' Mary calls her back to the room, urges her on.

She takes a big breath, locks it deep in her chest, and pushes down, keeps pushing even when the spasm is gone and Mary tells her to take a spell while she can, desperate to get her and the baby safely to the end.

She concentrates, bears down with each contraction till she is spent, convinced she has no more to give. Then goes again, and again, until nearly an hour later her fourth son slides free.

When Mary calls Charlie in to meet the newborn, as it turns out no bigger than the others at birth, there is no energy to talk of a name.

'No more, Charlie, no more. I'm gettin' too old.' It's all she has the will to say. Anything more will have to wait.

Her forty-year-old body is never the same again, the dropped womb often painful by the end of the day, chafing where it bulges when she walks. She loves the baby dearly but late at night, everyone else asleep, she picks up bawling Gilbert to feed him and wonders if it was worth it.

CHAPTER FOURTEEN

NORFOLK ISLAND, 1800-1804

P HILIP GIDLEY KING HAS RECOVERED from what ailed him and has been promoted, returning to Port Jackson as the colony's Lieutenant Governor. He has commissioned ambitious Major Joseph Foveaux as Norfolk's Acting Commandant.

Charlie has grudging respect for the island's new Guv, remembers him when he arrived at the mainland colony on the *Pitt* in '92.

'Landed as Captain, now look at him. Mind you, he's earned a reputation for getting things done, is a man of morals, too.'

Charlie has just walked home from his monthly masonic meeting, full of news to share with Maggie for a change. The Major is committed to the island, has been Port Jackson's largest landholder and stock owner, with more than a thousand sheep and not much fewer in acres. Yet word has it he sold the sheep, gave it all up to make a name for himself on the island.

'Could be he comes here to make a difference. We can only hope so.'

Maggie agrees wholeheartedly. It's daunting to see how rundown the settlements have become, especially Sydney Town, while military men pursue self-interest and damn the rest.

The hope is dented three days later when she goes to collect supplies from town, for it seems the Major may not be the upstanding fellow Charlie knew.

The ropemaker's wife, Jane Good, has invited her in for tea, keen to show off her latest baby given Maggie delivered the first years earlier.

'Took a Sergeant's wife on the ship coming out, they say. Promised to do the Sherwin fellow an injury such that he'd never work again if he didn't let her go to him. She's coming here as the Major's wife, we hear.'

Truth or lies, impossible to separate the two in this place, rumours growing fatter than a turkey fed for the pot. Maggie once met Ann Sherwin at Port Jackson, a practical, forthright woman with her own mind. She'd have her own reasons for deserting her husband, might have followed her heart, or caught sight of a better prospect and jumped at the chance.

She says none of it to Jane, simply shakes her head as though sharing the woman's disgust. Later, back home, she deliberately mentions none of it to Charlie. They will keep a clear head and see for themselves what mettle the new Guv might have.

The Major wastes no time when he arrives, pulling back ill-used convict labour from officers' farms, putting the men to work repairing neglected buildings, starting a new construction program.

At the end of leading his first divine service he speaks to the crowd, swollen to a decent size with so many settlers trailing in to Sydney Town for the chance to size up the new man.

'Let me be clear in my intentions, which are to make progress in the service of King George, as much as it is in my power to do so. I promise to give every encouragement to the honest, the industrious, to those observing propriety. Woe betide those who are idle or dishonest, for they will not avoid the punishment due to those who are undeserving or destructive members of society.'

Honesty, propriety. Maggie stifles a bellowing laugh, makes a choking sound instead, wonders if she let it go would the laughter start up the whole crowd, spread like a bad case of the pox.

The Big Fella has no doubt been told about the island, but his fine words show he knows little of its undercurrents, the treacherous shoals lying in wait for anyone who gets in the way when one of the knobs sees something as his right, to be taken as he pleases. As for punishment, likely things will stay as the same as they always have, applying only to those tarred with the convict brush.

To her surprise the new man keeps his word on one score at least. Plans drawn up to develop Sydney Town, the drawings languishing for years on a dusty shelf at Government House, are put into action.

Soon officers get their own stone cottages, a house is readied for a chaplain, public buildings are mended, rotten shingles replaced, walls lime-washed or painted. The mill's worn grindstones are dumped for new ones, rusted saws and tools brought back to life. Moves are even afoot to school nearly two hundred ragamuffins who run loose at Sydney Town with no supervision from their parents.

On the Ferrion farm the new appointment makes little difference, though the convict labourers report that the Major is fond of ordering the lash for the slightest misdemeanour, and puts women prisoners to good use, providing entertainment for soldiers at the Barracks. Maggie needs no imagination to know what that would be.

She and Charlie still work hard, sell as much of their grain to the stores as they can spare, and a little swine meat. At least the Guv has given settlers the chance to sell it direct to the Commissariat.

Charlie is one of the first to try a new crop the Major encourages, coffee plants to start a new industry. A couple of them grow like weeds on the farm, promising a decent harvest that will fetch a good price thanks to senior officials at Port Jackson, who have a taste for the bitter drink.

Four years at Charlotte's Field and Maggie finally can relish what it is to have freedom. She and Charlie make their own choices, cope with their own mistakes, and continue to steadily build up the property. The boys flourish on the good food, have become true colonial cornstalks, taller than if they'd been born London-side, and apart from a few bruises and scratches have been mercifully free from illness or injury.

Maggie doesn't agree with every opinion of Charlie's, yet they argue less these days, and she has come to understand that his predictability gives her steady ground, even if there is little to surprise her as time passes. So she doesn't expect the turn of conversation that evening.

'I've been thinking. You're a clever woman, Maggie dear, maybe the time is right for you to learn your letters, help with the farm papers and accounts.'

She turns the idea over in her mind.

'Best for the boys to learn, I reckon. They stand to gain the most.'

He is undeterred, has given the matter a great deal of attention, evident in the way he lays out the case.

'Anything happen to me, I've no doubt you could take over, run the place. You know your numbers, that's a fact. But if you learn to read and write there'd be nothing to hold you back from keeping the farm.'

For weeks afterwards, in the hour between the boys going to bed and the pair of them getting dopey for want of sleep, they work together at the table, Charlie writing the letters in flour scattered across the table and Maggie copying them.

'You're a natural, my girl.'

Soon she has progressed to quill and paper and there is no longer a need for his tutoring.

One morning Maggie is emptying a pail of hot water into the wash tub in the lean-to behind the house when she hears a voice calling her name. Circling to the front door, she is surprised to see a stranger standing there, a slip of a girl, sixteen or seventeen years.

''Scuse me ma'am, would you be Mrs Ferrion?'

Maggie grins and holds out a hand. 'Maggie will do. What's your business, if I may be so bold?'

The girl announces she is May Batten, second kitchen maid at Government House, and has come on a confidential matter. Maggie's eyebrows shoot up, but she manages to keep her face composed, inviting the girl in for tea and an oat cake.

May is doing her best to sound like the proper servant she is supposed to be, unaware that the way she stuffs the oat cake into her mouth gives her away.

After she has finished chewing and the tea is made, she is ready to talk.

'No one is to know. Not a word, by Jesus.'

Maggie wants to stop her, this can only be a bad business.

'The Major has the wheezing disease. They keep it quiet 'cos he's not wanting to be seen as havin' a weakness. Had it real bad since Monday, when he went over to Cascade Bay in the wind.'

Maggie's stomach sinks.

'Guv's wife knows you work with herbs, wants you to give him something to help.'

The stakes are high. Maggie reckons it up, her mind whirring. Life is good on their farm, they are bothered little by the politics of the place, the big and petty power plays that hobble real progress. Even the small ones can have the same effect as a stone in a horse's shoe. She wants no part of it, has no desire for Ann Sherwin to set her up for blame, even if she is the Guv's supposed wife.

'The surgeon should see him, May. He won't want the Major being subjected to ministering from someone like me.'

Ann has evidently predicted what Maggie will say, has prepared May well. 'The mustard plaster hasn't worked, nor the bloodletting. Doc Redfern's an old Navy man, using old ideas. She has faith in you.'

Maggie decides to appeal to the girl's own vulnerability, pointing out that they're in the same boat, both needing to take care, not get important folks offside or worse, promise something they can't live up to.

'You wouldn't want to take that chance, May, and neither would I.'

'I'm not here to argue. Mrs Foveaux says no matter what you say you're to come. I'll be seein' a clean plate instead 'o dinner, and maybe a wooden spoon around me ears if I turn up without you.'

She'll be insisting on some things herself, Maggie mutters, as she gathers what she needs, fetching a small a piece of inner bark from the whispering pines on the harbour's edge at Port Jackson, brought with her in case of consumption. She hopes it will ease a different kind of illness in the lungs.

May refuses to go on ahead, hopping from one foot to another while Maggie informs Charlie so he can watch the older boys. She takes Gil with her as he is not yet weaned.

The kitchen at Government House is not as grand as she'd expected, the floor on a bit of a lean, though Maggie admires the large oven where the cook and her helper are flapping about preparing a massive pie to be served at the noon bell.

Ann Sherwin appears quietly, is at Maggie's side before she realises it.

'I'm grateful you came.' She is well-spoken, gracious. Not what Maggie remembers, which throws her off guard and she almost forgets to address her as Mrs Foveaux.

At first Maggie tries to dissuade the Guv's wife from any involvement in his health.

'I'm a settler's wife these days, not a handywoman, as you'll have known me. And not the right thing for me to attend the Major when the surgeon's just up the road.'

Ann Sherwin is unmoved.

'I have faith in you, Mrs Ferrion. Besides, you'll not attend him. Any treatment will be given by me, and no one, least of all the surgeon, needs to know you've been here.'

Maggie wants Ann to understand the wheezing disease is a tricky malady with no known cure, only the chance to damp down the ways it can blight a person. She explains the situation, finishing up in a firm voice.

'I make no promises, you see.'

She has spoken in a fashion far too blunt for Ann's new standing, and waits to be put in her place. But the mistress of the house shows no sign of offence, instead busying herself with questions about what is to be done and how she should do it.

By the time Maggie has given instructions for the steam bath, how long to boil up the bark decoction and the dose to be administered, Gil is unsettled and she wants to get away to feed him, put some distance between her and the Guv's kitchen.

'I will remember your kindness.' Ann farewells her and the baby at the servant's door, insisting that May accompany them part of the way back.

'Nothin' to eat either way,' the girl grumbles as they climb the hill.

Maggie hears nothing in the days that follow, cause for anxiety. Charlie is the one, returning from market day, who gives her the low-down. 'The Major seemed in fine form. Let's hope he remembers us when we need his favour.'

The settlers group continues to meet, despite the authorities' earlier efforts to ban it, and when that failed, to blunt its role. It has fashioned itself as a benefit and burial society, paying part-passage to England should a new widow wish to sell up and leave.

'Down in town they get fearful because we're oath-bound, as though we're plotting against them instead of looking out for ourselves. They can call us a secret society or whatever name makes us sound bad, but we'll keep meeting. We don't need a name at all.'

Charlie beams. After years of taking orders as a marine, he's come to enjoy finding his own authority.

'Good to keep 'em on their toes.'

In December the smile is wiped off his face. He returns from taking a load of grain to the stores, breathless with what's gone down.

More than fifty Irish convicts were landed on the island back in June. Then in November another thirty were sent packing to the island after their role in an uprising at Paramatta, aimed at doing away with Governor King.

'They've been really careful. None of us had a clue that some of the Irish were hatching a revolt. They'd even won over five soldiers to their cause, can you believe?'

Maggie shakes her head as a no, while her heart says she does believe it. Hold people down for long enough and of course they fight back.

'Maybe a hundred wooden pikes sharpened. Could have turned nasty. A thirst for blood, no doubt about it.'

As fate would have it, a convicted rapist in the group saw the chance to give himself a leg up, going to the Guv to empty the bag.

'Lord knows what would've happened if he hadn't turned. The Major wasted no time, two ringleaders hanged already, no trial. Floggings of some of the others going on today and all through tomorrow.'

Maggie counsels caution with settler meetings or any other. 'No sense in diggin' a hole for ourselves on this, then having all the work we done here fall in.'

For once Charlie's in wholehearted agreement, committing to keeping to himself until the situation dies down. Neither of them says what they are thinking, that they doubt they've the will or their strained bodies the strength to do years of toil all over again if their good fortune at Charlotte's Field is snatched away.

In the coming days many settlers are taken to Sydney Town to be shaken down so the Major can hand out punishments for those even remotely thought to have offered the rebels encouragement. A few get away with harsh warnings about untoward activity, but some are threatened with the lash, have convict labour removed, and promises of further land quashed.

Charlie works each day with an eye towards the road, waiting for redcoats to come for him. It's known he speaks his mind at the meetings, has the power to sway others. Day after day he waits, yet is spared their attention. Maggie can't help but wonder if Ann Sherwin has had a hand in it.

The brig *Norfolk* arrives before Easter to collect salt pork for Port Jackson. It causes a stir on two counts, the first being it gives hope of a regular shipping service because Governor King has actually bought the ship, originally named the *Harbinger*. The second is that it brings the island's first resident parson. Word spreads like wildfire that he's an Irish hellraiser with a reputation as a do-gooder, a convict given a conditional pardon at Port Jackson days before they packed him off to save the island's lost souls.

The novelty of a chaplain, let alone a convict one and an Irishman to boot after the attempted coup, means many heads are craning at Rev Henry Fulton during his first service, where he is accompanied by wife, Ann, and four-year-old daughter, Jane. From the middle of the crowd Maggie casts her eye over the wife and sees a woman who's had to swallow what is disagreeable.

'She's no different to the rest of us,' she whispers to Martha Edward, hushing Gil in the next breath before his fidgeting causes him to break away from her hand.

Martha lowers her head, busting to share what she knows. 'The manservant has put it out they hope to be gone when the year's out.'

Charlie has heard the same rumour. As the family makes its way home through the hills, the boys darting about, he tells her what he heard from the men.

Fulton studied at Trinity College in Dublin before turning cleric, was a political prisoner who supported the '98 rebellion against British rule in Ireland,.

'Clever fellow, good at mathematics, the law, literary matters, they reckon.'

Maggie interrupts, snorting. 'Fat lot o' good it be doin' him round here.'

'Doubt the books are where his interest lies these days. By all accounts he's keen to buy up folk's goats. Going in with one of the sergeants and the Harbour Master. Might be a man of the cloth but looking to be a man o' commerce now.'

Charlie's not one for gossip, has been known to chide her for it, so she receives the news with delight. She nudges him, teasing. 'You like a good yarn 'bout folk as much as I.'

He enjoys the joke and taps her playfully on the back. Knox distracts them, calling their attention to a dead morepork owl chick, its white down flattened by rain that has left the tiny skeleton exposed.

The walk is a rare, restful family break in the relentless routine of the week. Maggie drops behind, happy to straggle along at the rear, delay even for a few minutes the return to the farm and the chores lined up.

Charlie slows till he is beside her.

'We must take our chance, Maggie, while we have a parson. Time for us to wed.'

Her mind turns in, ready to gather the old arguments used long ago to prevent such a thing, though none come. She will never lose her love for Dan, but the man has become a thin puff of smoke blown away by the wind. She's a long way from the days of being tied to him, a woman who can wed if she's willing to look the chaplain in the eye and lie that she's single.

Most of all, she's the mother of boys who need the protection of their ma and da being properly churched. They might even have a chance to get their surnames changed to Charlie's in the register.

On the seventeenth day of August 1801, Maggie officially becomes Mrs Ferrion and likely a bigamist, a new sin for her list. The four boys are looked after at home, it not seeming right to parade them in front of the parson.

Standing beside Charlie in the yard of Fulton's house, she shivers a little in a sharp sea breeze as they make their vows. She has worn her best dress, wants the moment to feel special, to have meaning, yet there is none of the joy she had when she wed Dan, a young woman full of excitement about the life they would build together.

She has done it backwards with Charlie, building a life first, though is happy to have contentment and the love of a reliable man, which these days is more than enough. The pair of them have rubbed along with each other for ten years or more, long enough to wear away any rough edges between them. It helps that she still enjoys reaching for him when they turn in at night.

He flashes her a pleased grin as the simple ceremony ends. It is over quickly, one of twenty or so Rev Fulton performs that year, along with thirty baptisms, part of his conviction that he can stem the tide of the island's vice and moral corruption, an idea that leaves the locals laughing behind their hands.

Maggie has a girl to help around the home now and has left her tending to a large piece of beef roasting in a pot over the coals. The delicious smell greets them before they reach the front door.

Will has come over for the celebration meal with Mercy, nearly six years now, having long given up on trying to persuade Sarah away from their home. Mary and Noah Cottle arrive with their three bairns, while witnesses to the marriage, John Barnes and Martha Edward, bring their two year old, James, and baby Elizabeth.

John and Martha grew up in the chaotic back lanes of Middlesex, over Smithfield way. Their sentences now expired, they have earned Charlie's approval for their willingness to work, having cleared and begun cropping three acres of land allocated to them on the other side of the hill.

On a day such as this, Maggie is mighty glad to hear folk speaking the same as those she grew up with.

Her ma had a vision she was marked. It seemed meant as a curse, a blight on her soul like the purple birthmark she once saw covering half the cheek and forehead of a newborn. As everyone sits on benches in the shade of the house she watches the children run about, relaxes in the ease of friends laughing, chatting, and decides that maybe her ma saw something else. That the young Margaret Bloodworth would eventually prosper and be blessed, would do better than all her family put together.

The peace of mind stays with her when the family trails south to Sydney Town the following Sunday for divine service.

As the congregation gathers in the empty granary, Major Foveaux is the one to step up with the prayer book to lead the service.

A whisper spreads through the crowd, turning to a murmur. By the time the Major apologises for Rev Fulton's absence, the reason is known to all. His wife will not let him leave her side, their daughter having succumbed to peritonitis the day before, the onrush of grief made worse by the fact that their boy lies a thousand miles away, left in the burial ground before they departed the other town called Sydney.

Despite Maggie having heart for the stricken woman, she can't help but feel grateful she has been spared such a thing. She doesn't have a family that is whole, of course. It will never feel complete till Hannah's story somehow weaves itself into the boys'. Yet she's not had to watch a child waste away from dysentery or brain fever, slowly choke with croup or diphtheria, or die convulsing.

The Major finishes reading the psalm and calls for everyone to bow their heads as he prays for the parson and his wife in their hour of need.

Maggie lowers her head, not listening to the Major, busy with a silent prayer of her own.

Lord, thank you for all you've seen fit to grant our family, for our health, for the gift of shelter, for all that satisfies our wants. We thank you.

What she really wants to say remains unvoiced, even to herself. For it is the devil's work to be saying *thank God it's not my turn.*

CHAPTER FIFTEEN

NORFOLK ISLAND, 1804-1807

THE WHISPERS DIED A LONG while back, but now are fanned like a northerly behind wildfire. Soon the whole island is alight with unrest and fear about what is to become of the place.

When a pair of redcoats turn up at Charlotte's Field, Maggie has no hesitation in stepping up with Charlie to find out what they've got to say. They are working their way through all the settled areas with the news that Foveaux, now a Colonel, has called a meeting for early winter.

'It's compulsory for every adult to attend. Mind you're there on time, no stragglers will be tolerated,' the taller one says. The tone is far too pompous, and were it not for the news Maggie would be of a mind to take him down a peg or two.

'High-handed buggers,' she mutters, as the two men disappear down the track.

Charlie is also unimpressed. 'We're not some lowly outpost of Port Jackson any more, to be treated like children. We're our own community, they should show us a bit of bloody respect.'

On the day of the meeting Maggie and Charlie have been waiting in the crowd for some time when Foveaux steps up onto the speaker's box.

The Commandant knows he is in for a fight, has worn his ceremonial uniform to emphasise his authority, especially as he is unhappy the matter is not as black and white as he would prefer. The British Secretary of State, Lord Hobart no less, has decided the island is nothing but a drain on the Government purse, has ordered it be cut loose immediately. However, Governor King at Port Jackson still has a soft spot for the island, and his instructions are to start a more gradual wind-down of services and support.

Wes, nearly seven years old, studies the Commandant and decides that whatever the man is about to say won't meet with his parents' approval.

'Lording it over us,' he says, far too loudly for Charlie's liking. He clips the boy on the back of the head to shut him up.

Foveaux has heard the boy's remark, knows immediately he made a mistake with his garb. It smacks of officiousness, of unpalatable news. He takes a square of linen from his pocket, wipes away sweat beading on his shiny forehead, and speaks at a booming volume.

'The time has come for new opportunities.'

He pauses, unable to be heard over the outburst of shouting and jeering that ensues, signalling to the Captain at his side. The officer bellows to the constables and officers to step up, before hollering at the throng. 'Quiet down, or you'll be thrown in gaol.'

Foveaux wrests back control. 'Hear me out, for what I have to convey is in your interests.'

'Let 'im speak.' Jacky Black, one of the settlers' group leaders, roars out his command from behind Maggie.

As the Colonel delivers the news, describing what is on offer to seduce settlers from their farms, she wonders if others feel a weight pressing down on them as she does, the hand of God finding her, ready to pluck her away, yet again prove her will is but a trifling thing.

The Commandant has learned much in the way of oration during years of swaying troops to action for the greater good, particularly when it might get him a promotion. He appeals first to reason, sly as an old fox, for King doesn't want the useless and idle as volunteers, only those willing to give their work to the cause. England has a new colony to establish, more territory to make its own.

Those willing to be transferred to newly-claimed Van Diemen's Land, an island off the furthest south-east tip of New Holland, will be generously compensated on the basis of what they have achieved here. It is not the time to tell the crowd the southern island is more isolated than Norfolk, more than one and a half thousand miles away as the crow flies, or that only heaving ocean separates it from the South Pole, which burdens it with a harsher climate.

The Commandant lowers his voice, pivots to a softer approach.

'Understandably, those of you who have laboured long and hard, who have carved valuable farms out of forest and vines, have no wish to be ruined by giving up your land.'

A cheer goes up.

He is on safer ground now, speaking directly to those who've succeeded, the ones who have the greatest attachment to their land, the ones who will give all they have to the new southern colony.

'Four acres will be granted for every acre cultivated on Norfolk and two for every acre of wasteland you have.'

A hush falls over the crowd as the full terms are given. Settlers and as much of their stock as possible will be removed at public expense, surplus stock bought by the Government at valuation. Rations will be given to each household for twelve months after arrival, and the use of two convicts for the same period.

By the time his speech is done, the assembled throng is strangely quiet. Maggie looks over to Charlie, now standing with Will, sees him give his head the barest shake of disapproval.

Foveaux has done his duty. 'Those interested are asked to come to Government House and the clerk will take down your names and details.' He gestures over to the verandah, where the fellow is already stationed at a table, then steps down and swiftly walks away.

Maggie turns to Martha. 'The Guv reckons we're done for, don't he? He don't know us at all.'

Martha purses her lips, points to a gap in the crowd. 'Let's go over there. His fancy words have quite cut the air from me.'

They stand away from the others, watching settlers mill around as though they've lost their bearings, either unwilling to be the first to sign up or unable to begin the trek home. The air buzzes as though a lightning bolt has struck the earth and everything near it shakes with the force of its energy.

By the end of the hour forty men have climbed the stairs to the clerk and their names have gone in the ledger, declaring they are willing to leave holdings from thirty acres up to one hundred and twenty. They have laid down one condition, that they stay till their crops are ripe so they can take corn and maize with them.

Maggie is still with Martha when Charlie appears, somewhat harried. 'Come now, let's find the boys and get away home.'

As they set off he is worked up, unmoved by the fine speech.

'Let George Guest give up his six hundred sheep, foolish man, the others give up their holdings. They will regret it.'

He turns to her, tall and steady. 'You and me, we've been through our share of privations. We won't budge.'

She hugs him, right there on the road, grateful they are of the same mind, though it doesn't stop the fear about what may come in the years ahead.

By the time the cutter *Integrity* arrives the following month, carrying further dispatches from Governor King, heads have cooled. All but ten on the list have withdrawn their names.

With so few settlers leaving voluntarily, and no instructions from Governor King for forced transfers, Foveaux concludes there is no choice but to start withdrawing services. The settlers are fools if they can't see the Government is serious about forcing them off the island, maybe not this month or the next, but it will happen. He will make a show, flex his muscle.

At Charlotte's Field, Maggie puts the day behind her. The bigwigs are always threatening something to make a person worry, keeping lesser folks on their toes so they know who's in charge. Those on farms have been tested, have proven they can't be tempted away from what is rightfully theirs, homes built with bare hands and empty bellies, a living wrested from naught but hope and determination. Perhaps the way everyone stands together is the hard-won reward for all the time Charlie and the others have given to endless meetings.

The sense of being weighed down returns in February, but this time Maggie feels it more as a thumb screw tightening than the hand of God, for this threat of island closure is the work of men.

They are mucking out the pig pen after one of the sows has given birth when she stops and leans on the shovel.

'I could do with cheerin' up, Charlie, I need to get away for a bit, get my head straight.'

It's not like her to be so down in the dumps. They all need her strong, he knows that much. 'Go to Sydney Town tomorrow, then. I'll keep an eye on the boys.'

She returns from town early afternoon, cheered by some chat with Susannah, and with the news that some of the civil officers have been discharged, others transferred to Port Dalrymple on the northern coast of Van Diemen's Land.

'There's talk the southern island's a wet and woebegone place.'

Charlie nods. He's already heard the talk at meetings and said nothing to her.

Her news is just the start. Soon the military guard is almost down to half what it was, the number of officers hardly sufficient to form a court.

A month or so later, Maggie is hanging wet washing when their convict labourers return from a day off. She sees Charlie speaking with them, can tell from the way he's waving his hands that he's angry at what they have to say.

After setting them to work he comes over. 'They're taking our men away at the end of the week. A big group of convicts are being taken to Port Dalrymple. They're making sure none of us have help on our farms.'

Maggie resists the urge to cry. 'What are we to do, Charlie? They be puttin' the squeeze on.'

'We hang in there, Maggie, that's what we do. They can't force us to go.'

She wants to argue the point with him, though holds her tongue because he hides worry behind his big words.

'What a mess, Charlie.' She stops herself from moaning. He needs her at his back.

They've starved here, buried loved ones, sweated away to nothing in making their farm, endured famine, the distress of failed harvests, near destitution. She knows why he clings on, why others do too. They've spent so many years adjusting to the rhythm of the island that now the red of their blood runs with a streak of green from its fields.

When Foveaux is instructed to resign his charge, leaving the island immediately, Maggie and Charlie are relieved to see the back of him.

By now they have thirty-one acres cultivated, twenty-six sheep and thirty-one swine. Along with Charlie being a discharged marine, they are officially classified as first class settlers.

'They may let us be now, leave us to get on with earnin' our living.' Maggie wants to sound certain but the sentence comes out with the unexpected lilt of a question on the end.

Charlie has just finished his midday meal, He works harder than ever with their men gone and Joe and Knox not yet up to a grown man's labour.

'I reckon, or they'll have an uprising on their hands. We've been through enough. Everyone here is the same, just wanting to get on with raising our own, handing down our farm in good time.'

They are circling around the truth that has become evident to all the settlers now. Van Diemen's Land, a frequent stopover for ships sailing to Port Jackson, has resources the Government wants to stop the French from claiming, which means a forced population must occupy the place.

Charlie sees the strange joke in it, that Norfolk's been a dismal failure for masts or a decent supply of canvas, while scuttlebutt has it the French found the island after Cook but sailed off, declaring it fit only for angels and eagles.

He must stay calm, Maggie likewise. Nothing good comes from expecting catastrophe, and the terror of ruination stops a man from keeping a clear head.

He has helped write a letter to make the settlers' case to the new Guv, hoping to flush him out on where he stands, see if they can secure extra years on the island or advantages. Lieutenant John Piper, thirty-one years old and soon to be made a Captain, is now the island's most senior military man.

'He was an Ensign here, remember, that first year on the island, before he went back to Port Jackson? Bit of a charmer, though he understands us folk more than Foveaux ever did.' He skirts around the fellow's willingness to accept half pay without the full commission, no doubt keen to impress those senior to him and pave the way for future promotion.

Charlie is wasting his breath trying to put things in a good light. Maggie knows him only too well, and when he seeks to comfort her it only makes her more anxious.

As the days roll on they begin to live two lives, or rather, their one life splits in two as though the surface of it has separated from what is underground. They rise each morning to work the soil, plant seeds, fatten pigs, flog at more vines to increase cultivated land, go to the occasional wedding, funeral, Sunday service. They trade at market days, still occasionally go to a dance or sing-along at one of the settlements for a few hours of forgetting, as former sailors, soldiers or convicts pull out a fiddle, fife or drum and beat out a tune.

Below it all another reality makes itself known. Maggie feels it as she might a leech sucking on her blood. It weakens her spirit, dims any vision of a future, leaves her full of unease.

She and Charlie take turns bolstering each other when their disposition gets low, one reminding the other that every bit of striving is for their boys.

Charlie takes a cheerful tone as they undress for bed. 'Piper's acting as though he favours us. Besides, he's taken a sixteen-year-old girl into Government House, is fixing to marry her when he can, they say. That'd be the mark of a man who looks to stay.'

Maggie is the one struggling today. 'He'll have his orders, mark my words.' She doesn't bother to say what they both know, that it's impossible for a man with a commission to marry the daughter of convicts.

Charlie is bone tired, does not bother lowering himself gently onto the bed, instead flopping down with a thump.

'Be that as it may, what are they going to do? March us off our farms when there's not enough troops to shine the brass doorknobs at the Barracks?'

Any confidence Charlie might have in the solidarity of settlers soon wears thin, with about a quarter weighing up the risks of staying, only to take a chance by late 1805 on the promised recompense for a fresh start.

Two hundred and fifty men, women and children, many of their worldly possessions, and enough livestock for breeding, have departed on small vessels, one or two of them hardly seaworthy, which puts Charlie in a black mood.

'Can't even see fit to send decent ships.'

Many of the Government stores have been sent to Port Dalrymple or to the south of Van Diemen's Island, where a second fledgling settlement is already starving on the Derwent River.

Even Charlie can see there are only two reasons for the seven hundred souls left on Norfolk to stay. They are either stupid or opportunistic.

He has chosen to be an opportunist, telling Will on a family visit to Phillipsburgh that it would better for him to stay on as long as he can, increase his stock numbers, clear more land to benefit himself with greater compensation.

'I dunno, Charlie. It'll only be a year or so, by my reckoning, and we'll have to go anyway. It's already hard gettin' what we need, what with officials gone.'

Maggie is listening to the conversation, having spent half an hour or so in the bedroom with Sarah, leaving reluctantly when her friend became jittery and wanted her out. The sadness of a demented wife and mother fills the house, seeps into every nook and cranny so that even the furniture is dull, the windows grey. Little wonder Will has lost heart.

Charlie has already talked Will out of leaving once before, a few months back.

'It's true, Will, though the more stock we have before our time comes, the better off we'll be. It'll give us a better start when we go.'

A better start. Will rears up a little, spraying some of the rum from his mouth.

'My oath, Charlie. Ain't nothing better waitin' for me, God's truth. I got no wife, no sons to help carry the load, and a lot more years on me than when I came. I can't stay but I got no appetite for doin' it all again.' He downs the rest of the rum in one gulp.

Charlie backs down, sorry he's chosen the wrong moment and words. Meanwhile, Will's despair infects Maggie, or perhaps it is the hopelessness of Sarah's condition.

They are back home by late afternoon, talking in the swine shed out of earshot of the boys, when Maggie fires up.

'Why are we waitin'? Beggars belief. We'd best make the move now, while we've a few more years in us to get a new farm shaped up.'

'I know, I know, but we have to think of the boys. It's not just about clearing more land, buying up more stock to benefit ourselves. Every year we're here, the boys are another year older, another year more able, even Gil is growing fast. Me and the boys, that's five of us to get things off to a good start.'

The reasoning stacks up, yet still she sighs.

'The waitin' is driving me silly, flogging me bones to get through every day, all the while watching for the axe to fall. I just want it over.'

'I know, my girl, I know. The time will come soon enough.'

Will has given them a sack with a couple of eels caught in Cascade Creek, near where it spills over the green lip of the cliff and plunges down to the bay. They must be cooked that evening as the flesh breaks down quickly. She takes them outside and begins bashing them, one at a time, against a large stone to make sure they are dead, each strike a little harder until their heads are almost pulp. Still the bodies wriggle.

The task is too horrible. She drops them in the dirt at her feet as a rush of images intrudes, of her deranged friend, a dead girl in a yellow dress, of towering seas, a ship dropping down a mountainous wave and her trapped below decks on the way to the ends of the Earth, of a golden-haired child with a green ribbon in her hair.

She can't stomach it a minute longer, disgorging her guts in one violent heave.

Straightening up, her instinct is to grab the eels and pitch their dark, slithery bodies into the woods. Instead she goes to the water pail, washes out her mouth, then hangs the eels by their tails. One at a time she slits the skin in a circle, working a small piece of it down to grip with an old rag, then dragging off the skin as if rolling down a stocking. It is done.

Next to leave the island is Rev Fulton, recalled to Port Jackson. He delivers the Easter services in 1806, then departs with wife Ann and their new baby. An aging missionary, mysteriously turning up from a Polynesian island months earlier, is left to give the occasional garbled rant that substitutes for a bout of preaching.

The Irishman's departure affects Maggie in ways she doesn't expect, as if the walls of her house are no longer solid. She can't shake the feeling, pours herself into baking, cleaning, tending her garden and animals with more thoroughness than usual, thankful that sleep comes quickly to claim her when the day is done.

It's not so much that the man gave succour, ministered to his flock with compassion and care, showed qualities hard to come by in the world she inhabits. More that he was a weaver of sorts, tying threads of island life together to make a fabric that had structure and predictability. And in its absence, she is falling through a gaping hole.

Charlie returns from the August masonic meeting, the numbers much reduced these days. As Past Master and one of the most senior members he has access to Piper, so has heard from the horse's mouth that the island's ally, Governor King, has left Port Jackson for England.

'The bad blood between him and the Corps, it got him in the end.'

Maggie is dismayed. 'A new broom will stir up more dirt. Have we been wrong to delay?'

Charlie is doing his best to stay hopeful. 'It might work in our favour. The new fellow, Captain William Bligh, seems to hold settlers' welfare in high regard. He's opposing the corps and its power, despises trading sharks taking money folks don't have, is already making new deals with farmers.'

Maggie has known many officials in her time, not one of them a saint. She stifles a groan. 'Do tell, what failings do you hear?'

'Well, the man's temperament is rash. I'm told he is prone to outbursts, and speaks his mind freely.'

Maggie doesn't need her ex-marine husband to tell her what this will mean for the naval man. He is setting a collision course with the redcoats.

'Charlie, we be ruined if things go bad at Port Jackson, sent packing with naught.'

He slumps in weariness, unable to disagree with her. Although the settlers like the new man, especially those in the Paramatta and Hawkesbury districts, the knobs who've held power for so long already hate him with a passion.

'I'm sorry, Maggie. Guess it's a roll of the dice now.'

In the months to come, Piper, now officially a Captain, is under his own pressure. He becomes more strident in urging everyone to leave. He gives glowing reports of the two settlements at Van Diemen's Land, the success of those who have ventured there, the opportunities for farming and trade.

Charlie and many others stay resolute, though more than one wonders why they are obstinate in holding out. It's as though the act of refusing to leave has become its own force, a reason to get up every day, a shot of vigour that charges the spine and gives purpose.

It bothers Maggie that, unlike her, Charlie has only ever known life to work out according to his own plan. She worries that he doesn't give sufficient weight to the possibility of failure, that he delays out of puffed up pride rather than a canny nose for advantage.

It's a relief, then, on New Year's Eve, when he returns home carrying thirty-seven pounds and thirteen shillings for twenty-five sheep and one hog sold to the Commissariat. He has begun making calculations about how best to run down stock numbers.

Piper, meanwhile, knows something the settlers do not. Bligh is busy overcoming the main obstacle, the true one that prevents full evacuation of the island, which is the lack of suitable ships. The Lieutenant Governor earnestly seeks out vessels of suitable size and reliability, and he is a man made for prevailing.

On the Ferrion farm, whatever misgivings lace their way through the days, the work continues unabated.

The rains fail once more and they see drought, yet again, turn most of their crops to dust. By Easter they have cleared a further five acres and are well through banishing vines from a sixth.

Joe at fifteen and Knox, twelve, now put in a full day alongside Charlie, while Wes, nearly ten, and Gil, at seven, are expected to do what they can.

Winter is almost over when Piper puts out the word that a special meeting will be held at Sydney Town the following Saturday. He has spent weeks travelling to farms, talking one on one with settlers or in small groups, listening to their concerns, allaying fears, bringing calm with his respectful manner. He is determined to put an end to this.

The Ferrions arrive in town to busy scenes that, were it not for the lack of bunting and stalls selling food, could be mistaken for a festival.

The families jostle together on the common as they did three years earlier, though with fewer numbers and more dread. Piper steps lightly onto the box to speak, a slim, poised fellow. Maggie half expects him to break into a jig or lead a reel, for it's known he is fond of music and dance, but quickly sees that levity is the last thing on his mind.

With great care he lays out one fact after another, building a ladder they will all be climbing down soon enough. Ripples of discontent spread through the crowd.

After all his fine listening and talking, the deal is sealed. Every one of them, man, woman, child, and as many animals as can be accommodated, will be gone by the time next year is out.

'And what if we bloody refuse?'

Piper bats the question away as though it is a nuisance mosquito.

'There's no option for refusing. Once the last ship sails away there will be none seen again, no contact with the outside world, no way to get goods to market, no services in the towns, no protection from invaders.'

As he pauses, perhaps for effect, a voice comes from the front of the gathering.

'Not much different to the last eighteen years, then.'

The crowd erupts into laughter, leaving Piper stranded at the climactic part of his response. He presses on regardless.

'Not a man among you can deny that it will be a perilous situation for anyone left behind. We cannot allow it to happen, for the sake of your wellbeing and safety, and that of your families.'

Four vessels have been scheduled to begin the evacuation, starting November and continuing till winter next year, one running two trips.

'The schedule will be posted in public. You must indicate how much time you need to get families and stock ready for the journey so you can be assigned a ship. You will then be given a likely departure date.'

Piper is no coward, but he is a student of human nature. With the last sentence spoken he steps quickly from the box and marches off, flanked by officers. There is nothing to gain in staying for questions or comment. Talking is over, they need to see the matter is closed, as will be the island soon enough.

Maggie and Charlie are not in the mood for discussion as they make their way home, not for want of things to say but because they plan to say them to each other away from the boys.

They are not far up the road before Knox explodes, angry his parents seem so calm about what they've just heard.

'Bugger it, da. This is foolish. Why do you dig your heels in? You could have put our names on the list. Least we'd know what comes next.'

The boy is always in a hurry, impatient with others, though it is the first time he has dared take on his dad.

Perhaps, Maggie wonders, he's seen her anger simmering below the surface in recent months and wants to wield his own to see if it lances what ails her. She stiffens, ready to step in if Charlie chooses a backhander by way of reply. He's not one to spare the whip when the boys get out of line. He settles for shouting.

'Mind your tongue boy, or it'll be a beating for you. It's not for you to tell me or your ma what's best.' He roars it, trying to sound fearsome, but all Maggie hears is a man past his prime. She hopes Knox doesn't hear the same. The last thing they need is fighting within the family when there'll be plenty of it to come from outside.

Knox storms off ahead.

That night, Maggie and Charlie lay in bed, murmuring well after the moon has set.

She will suffer the situation no more. 'It's a wretched business. I've had a gutful, let's sign up and go now, or I'll not do another thing around here.'

Even Charlie can resist no longer. He slips out the front door soon after daylight, carrying in his pocket a list of what they own—forty-two and a quarter acres cleared, seventeen and three-quarters not, the two-storey house, the thatched and boarded barn with two floors, three thatched outhouses, and one boarded outhouse.

At Government House he hands the list to the secretary, telling him that wheat and oats are under cultivation, and there's a flock of sheep and large herd of pigs. He requests a word with Piper, and after a brief conversation with him returns to the farm.

Charlie has cashed in his good standing with the Guv.

'He'll give us time to run the stock down to the numbers he'll let us take, and a chance to get in the harvest.'

The boys have heard their da come back and crowd into the kitchen with Maggie.

'We go on the last sailing, which suits us fine because it'll be the biggest ship they've got.'

Maggie would sooner they left earlier. She'd go tomorrow if she could, but Charlie, as usual, has been keeping his ear to the ground, keeping abreast of letters and reports coming back from those departing earlier.

'We wait till then because it'll be the ship taking the most stock. I put us down for Hobart Town. The ones gone to Port Dalrymple have fared badly, were given land at a place called Norfolk Plains, along a river, and got flooded out.'

He is studying her face, watching how she receives the news, what she makes of the future he has set in motion.

She says nothing, overcome by the sense of the unknown years ahead, teasing at the edge of her vision, confounding. Far too big to grapple with for now.

Her lack of reaction has unsettled him, thrown him into an old place where he once had to work hard at winning her over, get her to see his word was something to count on.

'You trust me, dear girl, don't you? I'm truly of the opinion that this is our best course of action.'

She knows him well. As much as he's solid in his temperament, certain in his views, despite the fact that she is filled with misgiving, up to the brim after months of worry and waiting, the quaver in his voice means she must be the one in this moment to give steady counsel.

'Of course I trust you, Charlie, always have. With all my heart. You've made the right choice and we'll prosper for it, I'm sure. Won't we boys?' She looks around at every one of their faces, full of zest for adventure. Oh that it was already nightfall and she could climb the stairs, sink into the bed and sleep, maybe for a week.

'Think of it, Maggie. When we get there we start afresh, husband and wife, a respectable family of free settlers. You boys will take your proper place in the new society.'

He stops, seems to grasp that he's gone too far. She knows exactly what he infers, sees it has exercised his mind that her convict stamp, weakened by time, should now be wiped away by distance. She will be presented as Mrs Charlie Ferrion, wife to a former marine, mother of four legitimate sons. He is turning his back on the thieving adulterer with a daughter left behind, as though that part of her can be cut away like a limb.

Maggie's too weary for arguing. He is the worst kind of fool if he believes who she has been, the way she has loved Dan and especially Hannah, can be excised for good.

Charlie continues to sell stock to the Commissariat and within weeks is down to forty-four sheep and sixty hogs. Only twelve acres are in grain, the rest left to pasture, though he has two hundred bushels of maize on hand.

After three years of living in a suspended state, island folk are blasted into action by winds of change circling the southern Pacific Ocean. The *HMS Lady Nelson*, a sixty ton brig that has plied the route from Port Jackson to Norfolk Island on many an occasion, arrives to collect the first group of settlers.

A small crowd gathers at the Sydney Town pier at to wave off thirty-four men, women and children and the few animals the vessel can take. Passengers will get to know their cramped quarters well, and the women will have ample chance to master cooking on the deck before they reach the River Derwent in about twenty days.

Joe has gone with friends to see them off, not because he has any particular feelings for the families who are leaving, but out of the need to mark the moment, pointing the way to a direction he can't wait to take.

Maggie has no need of such nonsense, for there's nothing to mark except the certain slog of one day giving way to another, and the need that will be upon her soon enough to summon all the old wit and resourcefulness she once needed to survive.

The next sailing comes soon, uprooting the usual celebrations of Christmas, pushed aside in the bustle and chaos as possessions and animals are loaded onto longboats and ferried to the *Porpoise*.

More than a hundred and eighty folk, along with large numbers of cattle, pigs, sheep, goats, poultry, and some of the last grain harvest, sail off on Boxing Day into calm weather and high hopes. Seventy-five sheep have been jammed into one of the longboats on board, leaving an onlooker to remark that 'the ship best not come to grief an' prove sheep more of value than a few human lives'.

This time Maggie, Charlie and all the boys go to the foreshore. They feel their time closing in and need to stay watchful, study how well others have prepared. They wave as the final passengers are ferried out to the ship, and are none the wiser.

Charlie searches his mind for something cheery to say to Maggie.

'The minute we're on our land I'll build you a fine house, the boys and I will, won't we?'

'We will,' they chorus.

She has faith in his purpose and industry, she tells him, and means it. Out at the washing line an hour or two later she is free to be with the crippling doubts she harbours about herself. Forty-six years old with a waist that's filled out, muscles losing their power, pelvis battered by childbirth, and pains in her back from lifting and digging more than she should.

She is more a bruised old tent boxer with too many rounds under his belt than a farmer's wife flush with vigour, ready to make a new home and enterprise.

CHAPTER SIXTEEN

NORFOLK ISLAND TO
VAN DIEMEN'S LAND, 1808

T HE SHIPS KEEP COMING IN the New Year, while
the number of people left to stand on the shore
for farewells dwindles away. By the time a mid-
May departure leaves, those who have come to see the ship
off can barely raise a wave, they are so weary of goodbyes.

Early in June, Sydney Town is disturbed by a gun fired
soon after dark, announcing the arrival of the merchant
ship, *City of Edinburgh,* for the final group of settlers.
There is no white flag flying on Mount George to signal it
is safe for the vessel to approach. The winter gales have set
in with a timetable of their own and the vessel is forced to
shelter at Cascade Bay.

Maggie, Charlie and the boys herd their remaining
stock to town, finish packing, and begin ferrying their
possessions to the foreshore, by which time the ship has
returned. The winds drive it out of sight for days on
end and the vessel fares no better as the days pass, high
seas causing loss of an anchor and serious damage to the
fore-rigging.

In limbo on the farm, Maggie and Charlie become shrill as tin whistles with each other, the older boys taking their cue from the tension, harping at one another. Soon easy-going Gil can take no more. One evening, the meal finished, his parents continue low-key bickering that began late afternoon, while Knox works on riling Wes. Gil bursts into tears.

'Stop it,' he splutters, ashamed that at eight years he's crying like a girl. 'We can't be acting like the fowls, fighting over scraps.'

Every person turns to the boy, shocked into silence about their behaviour, called out by the youngest, of all people.

'You're right, Gil. We ain't doin' ourselves proud.' Maggie resists the urge to draw him into a hug, knows it would give him more cause to feel weak. Instead, she touches him lightly on the shoulder.

'Too true, Gil,' Charlie chimes in. 'We must stay on good terms, get through all this waiting as best we can.'

By now they have finished preparations. Charlie's decision to stay on till the last ship has paid off, given them time to benefit from advice that has finally come, in a letter from Irishman William Maum, one of the earliest settlers taken to Van Diemen's Land.

Writing to his friend, storekeeper and miller Robert Nash, he has let it be known that it's every man for himself in the new place, that there's things needed to shore up a family. To Nash's credit he has been quick to share the contents of the letter with many folks, including Charlie.

As a result he has followed the recommendations, storing wheat and flour in sealed casks to prevent others overstating what bushels they've taken and short-changing him. He is taking more tools than originally planned, given the report that they are in grievously short supply, and plenty of corn for livestock to avoid the exorbitant prices Maum has warned against.

Many animals have died from thirst on the ships so Charlie will carry plenty of coin to bribe one of the crew, if need be, to make sure his stock do not suffer from want of water. He is also taking twelve good ewes, made sure a few of his sows are in pig, and sent three cages of fowls for loading. It will be a hungry town and the fowls could have greater value than money.

There will be shortages of all kinds, he tells the boys. 'Life will be tough, at least for a time, but we're a strong family and will soon be back on our feet.'

It has only dawned on Charlie in recent days that as a youth he failed to understand the power of forces that shaped his father, forces that he must now face. He has not escaped the Huguenot legacy after all, it is upon him.

He discerns at last that it runs in his veins, is inescapable. A story of alienation, of starting from nothing in a land that holds no welcome. As a lad, he'd imagined he would break loose from the family heritage that so clearly weighed on his father. Yet here he is, Charlie Ferrion, facing dislocation and the need to begin again with little but the poor bargain of resolve.

On the final morning at Charlotte's Field, Charlie is using an old broom to clean urine-soaked hay from the swine shed, listless at the task because it serves no purpose other than filling in time. Maggie stands by idly for the same reason. The ship is finally loaded, waiting for passengers, and anything left on the farm will be abandoned.

They will walk away mid-afternoon, go to Sydney Town and wait for their turn in the longboats, however many days it takes.

'Promise me, Maggie, you won't look back when we set foot on the path.' Charlie's question is uncommonly urgent.

It's a promise she finds easy to give. She has no desire to needle the misery of their leaving.

In the stillness surrounding them in recent days they hear Will calling, a high, fractured sound that ricochets ahead of him as he runs up the track to their door.

Even at a distance they see his face is red, his arms in a fierce rhythm as they pump his chest and legs towards them. Maggie takes one look and begins striding in his direction, then running, Charlie close behind. As they reach him he stops suddenly, teeters to the left, needing Charlie to steady him with a firm hand on his shoulder.

Will gasps, struggles to suck in air so he can speak.

'She's gone, she's gone. It were terrible, oh Lord, such a terrible sight.'

Maggie's panic makes her blunt. 'Who Will? Mercy? Sarah?' Why, oh why does she ask. Either way it means pain upon pain, loss piling up in the cesspit of sorrow with all the other losses. Deadness rises to save her from what he will say, rolling over her like thick London fog.

Will bends over, hands on knees, unable to straighten up, forces out broken bits of sentences.

'I hated it. Hated every bit. Knew the only way to get her out o' the house, make her safe on the ship, would be to tie her like a trussed fowl. Oh God … .'

Charlie has gotten him upright, tries to lead him to a log to sit, but Will can't move. His eyes bore into Maggie's.

'She asked me to go with her to Ann's grave, make her goodbyes. A load shifted from me, 'cos I thought if she were agreeable to leaving the house maybe, just maybe, she'd walk on her own two legs to the ship.'

He pauses to cover his face for a moment with his big workman's hands.

'Can't get any bit of it from me mind.' He sobs again, agony stretching his face so he's barely recognisable.

'Will, I beg you, tell us what went down.' Maggie's sharp tone is met with a glare from Charlie.

'The wind got up while we were on the hill, the sea pounding against the rocks, gulls squealing. Mercy was chasing a swallowtail butterfly, close enough for me to see the red spots on its tail.'

His face is suddenly blank.

'Then I looked over at Sarah. She weren't there.'

Maggie feels sick, the image forming in her head has cut through the fog. She wants to turn and retch, rid herself of the awfulness, strike Will so he won't say what she already knows.

'She were running towards the cliffs, me takin' after her.'

Maggie wants to plead with him to stop, to leave her dear friend right there, feet dancing, skirts flying, the bright, laughing girl who twirled in the muddy street at Sydney Cove and laughed in the faces of those who would keep her meek and small. But Will must finish, must say the unspeakable or it will never be real.

'She got a head start on me, kept running full pelt, right to the edge. Threw herself off.' He begins to shake.

'By all that's mighty, I swear she were cackling as she went down.'

The boys have heard the ruckus and come to see the cause. Maggie insists they go with her back to the house, leaving Charlie to help Will round up some men. They'll need to move quickly if they're to get the body before the tide rises.

Back near the house, Maggie's knees start to buckle. Joe, a handspan taller than her these days, grips her across the shoulders, pulls her against him, leads her inside. Rough sawn slabs of logs function as seats with their chairs gone. He guides her to one of them while the other three stand there, not knowing what to do as the woman who is their reliable centre crumbles before their eyes.

Joe pretends anger, a way to keep himself together when he, too, would sooner fall apart at the sight of his mother weak and hurting.

'Whatcha big lumps of nothin' doing. Get the fire built up and make your ma some tea.'

The departure of the *City of Edinburgh* is delayed by yet another day, not to allow Will to bury his wife next to their firstborn, but to give the ship's captain a chance to sign off on the passenger manifest, the crew needing to track down two men who ran into the woods to avoid evacuation.

Charlie wanders off to do a few last minute things, despite Maggie shaking her head. 'Why bother? It don't matter any more.'

Finally they leave, without ceremony, making the final trek across to Phillipsburgh, and up the hill to the burial ground. Sarah's body was retrieved late the previous afternoon, and there has been no time to make a coffin, no loving preparation of the broken woman's remains.

Maggie wants to see her face but Will says no, she's already bundled in an old sheet, though in truth he wants to spare her from the sight of what the rocks did.

The body is lowered into a grave beside Ann, while Charlie mumbles a few words remembered from the prayer book.

Only a handful of those who knew her are there to witness the end. Plenty more already down at Sydney Town could have made the effort, Maggie thinks, but it's as though they hold back now, saving their feelings and efforts for the next place. Only a neighbour family of Will's, and the girl who's worked as housekeeper and carer since Mercy was born, watch the earth swallow so much promise.

She understands why Will would want her buried with their daughter, though it's hard to think of her dear friend being left behind, far from those who love her.

Lost in memories, Maggie lets her eyes drift over to the girl, now grown into a woman, a frightened Mercy clutching her leg. The old midwife expertise stirs and, with no effort whatsoever, recognises the slight bump under the hands the young woman has deliberately clasped in front of her. Suddenly it makes more sense that Sarah will be left behind.

She wants to rage at Will, to judge him harshly, find every mean word she knows and hurl them at him, stone him till he bleeds. But she walks off with the others, says nothing, will never speak of it to him. Who is she to say a man should not find comfort in a world where there's so little of it?

Maggie, Charlie and the boys leave Will to a private moment at the grave, and the others to their final chores. The family sets out on Middlegate Road for the last time, even the boys subdued. At a familiar rise on the road that gives a wide view over the island, Maggie looks across to Charlotte's Field from habit. On the spot where she figures their house stands, smoke pours into a clear sky, forming a large, black plume.

'Charlie, look.' She shakes his arm. 'Our place, goin' up in flames.'

He ignores where she's pointing, looks straight ahead.

'I know. Set fire to it myself just before we left.'

She understands now why he lingered at the last minute.

'Geezus Charlie, why? Why ruin what we made?'

He faces her, arms locked by his side, fists clenched.

'They will burn the lot, Maggie, mark my words, every house and outbuilding on this island once we're gone. They'll make sure the French or any other country gets nothing if they come.

'I couldn't let a stranger be the one to set a torch to every piece o' timber we nailed, every floorboard we laid, every log laid down for a shed.'

She wants to cry, her chest so tight it might burst, but her throat closes, will not allow a single sob or word to escape. What paltry thing might come from her mouth, anyway, to carry the weight of all that's been destroyed.

They are among the last to be loaded late that afternoon. The ship, with its new spar deck, takes two hundred and fifty people, nearly a hundred of them children. They set sail at ten o'clock next morning, watching behind them as gathering storm clouds wipe the cliffs away until there is only ocean, and it is as if the island never existed.

Later, much later, when enough time has passed that they can tell the story without wincing, they will call their month tossed on some of the world's biggest seas the great journey of suffering.

They have barely faced into open ocean when waves fifteen feet high, sometimes more, kick up and send the ship bucking and lurching, flooding the deck. Winds thirty knots and rising lash timbers and sails, a sickening omen that doom awaits down south, if they make it.

One thousand and four hundred miles to go, and every one of them clawed from the teeth of a gale. They stay in wet clothes until some can stand them no more and go naked. Animal shit mixes with sea water, washing back and forth. Children scream for days and go quiet, animals die.

Maggie is called urgently to a bunk where a girl barely fifteen, rigid with terror, is fighting against the birth of her babe. Her mother stands by helplessly, a queer frozen look on her face as though trapped by an old panic of her own.

She shakes the girl's mother, sends her in search of hot water though there is none, to be rid of her so she can calm the girl. The son that's born a few hours later is small but squalling, his cries drowned out by the whine of the wind. There is no joy to mark his arrival, no way to keep him warm and dry. Maggie doubts he'll see Hobart Town.

Back in the family's quarters, eleven-year-old Wes is complaining about Mary Cottle's baby, Salome, the ten month old's screams at such a pitch they penetrate the thin partition separating the families. Little does he know the day will come when she will be his bride.

Water and food are strictly rationed, adding thirst and hunger to the discomfort of damp and overcrowding. By the time the ship nears the shelter of Hobart Town's harbour, those on board are in such a wretched state they've forgotten their shrunken bellies, thinking of nothing else but the craving for hard ground under their feet.

Maggie, Charles and the boys are taken off thinner and quieter. They stand together on the landing, having waded across a sandbar from the rocky island where the ship has moored, and watch as the dark flanks of Mount Wellington and its soaring summit suck the light from the sky.

A crowd mills around and Maggie recognises the set of so many faces, wearing the same disgust encountered at Sydney Cove fifteen years earlier, folks grim that they will have to share what little they have with newcomers.

It is early October and spring has failed to dislodge winter's grip on the southern island, a flurry of sleet leaving white specks on jackets and shawls. Maggie forces herself to look away from the strangers' faces, towards a town that's little more than five years old. Rows of rudimentary huts and cabins splay out from the waterfront like spreading claws, rough accommodation Maggie thought she'd long left behind, some wattle and clay daub, others made from turf and split logs fit only for fence rails.

Many men wear kangaroo skin jackets and opossum skin caps, some have kangaroo skin shoes covered in mud. She can't tell who is convict or soldier, finds herself ill-prepared for the primitive, noisy chaos of the town after the quiet of the farm.

Port Jackson, Norfolk Island, now Hobart Town. Three times she's been forced along the narrow ledge of survival, made to give every breath, every beat of her heart to the

British Government's hunger for a bigger empire. She fears this time the precipice is too great, one slip is all it will take and she'll be falling, falling, her loss rating no mention in a single despatch sent to London.

'This is no town, Charlie. We been sent back to hell.'

Gil has fared worst on the journey. He turns nine in a couple of weeks, has always been on the thin side, though Norfolk's mild climate protected him from illness. Maggie fears he has dysentery and not much ability to fight it.

She sends Charlie to agitate with the authorities, try to get him quickly to warmth and a place where she can prepare tea of garlic and honey. Regardless, it's hours before they are taken in a cart along Sullivan's Cove to the edge of what looks like a slum. They are dropped at the crooked door of a cottage where they will be billeted, sharing three rooms with a family of seven. The father opens the door under sufferance, ignores introductions and shows them directly to the room they will use, no bigger than the confined space on the ship.

'Don't be whining to us about your lot. The salt meat ration's been cut by half, the stores got next to nothin' left. Those up in Sydney give no help either, what with floods on the Hawkesbury washing away crops.'

The sullen fellow shuts the door behind him, leaving a stunned silence that Charlie feels he must break.

'They care nothing for a single one of us, damn it. Then they wonder why a place like this is full of thieves, liars and law-breakers.'

He feigns anger when he hasn't the strength for it, Maggie knows. She hushes him anyway, the boys don't need to hear their father overcome.

Two days pass before they are victualled from the stores, and the better part of the next day before Maggie can obtain dried garlic and a little honey to treat Gil, who barely keeps down water, becoming steadily weaker. Their hosts have insisted he be quarantined, kept in the one room the Ferrions share, where they are all forced to endure the stink and the boy's frequent groans.

Late in the afternoon Maggie hears the wife speaking to her husband in a stage whisper.

'Get 'em to dump him at the hospital. We're not wantin' his disease here.

She jumps to her feet, and despite Charlie's attempt to hold her back by the sleeve, is out the door to confront their hosts.

'You think we want this any more than you?' Spittle flies from her mouth.

'He will not be left in a place for the hopeless, hurried to an early grave. You dare try it and I be puttin' you in a hole with me own bare hands.' She draws breath to say more, but Charlie drags her back to the bedroom.

'Come now, stop upsetting yourself, dear girl. The town's crowded, us islanders are all in cramped quarters. Tomorrow I'll go in search of better accommodation, surely there'll be something.'

Water seems to run through Gil, but overnight he manages to hold onto some of the garlic tea, and in the morning a little more. By lunchtime he has eaten a few spoonfuls of porridge to no ill effect. At last he is on the mend.

They are all cheered when Charlie returns to say that he has found them two small rooms at the back of a blacksmith's shop in return for his help making charcoal for the forge by burning timber at the edge of town.

Soon the repetitive clank of hammer striking iron and anvil beats out the length of their days. Spring has finally settled in, though the family still enjoys the heat from the smithy, warming the thin wall between them and the shop. Summer will be another matter. For now Maggie must ignore imaginings about a random spark rising high from hot coals next door, coming to rest on timber boards already crisped by heat.

Their perilous state seems to grow ever worse. Rations get shorter, some of the Cape beef is thin with rot. Extra food for purchase is scarce and expensive. Maum's warnings, written a year earlier, were no exaggeration. Maggie can scarcely believe soap sells for four shillings, potatoes threepence a pound, flour a shilling a pound, prices for provisions nearly a third more than what they'd been paying.

The Commissariat has no clothing or shoes for the arrivals, no bedding. Word has it the Guv has few convicts to spare for settlers when they get land, and even fewer who know a jot about building or farming.

Charlie is no fan of the island's Lieutenant Governor David Collins, remembers all too well that as Judge Advocate he was one of the Port Jackson men who pushed for Norfolk to close. Yet even he can see the dilemma the Guv is in.

'Turns out he's been told to expect a hundred of us in the past year, not the better part of six hundred. What's a fellow supposed to do?' Hobart Town's population has exploded by nearly a quarter.

'Feed and clothe us is what I reckon,' Maggie snaps, the memory of Collins coming to her, thick eyebrows creeping across his face like caterpillars, that tight little smile. How many more men will be in charge of starving and degrading those she loves, while expecting them to slave away for bloody King and country.

Charlie insists Joe must help with wood burning, though the lad takes every opportunity to head to the cove where he is fascinated by the merchants, and seeks out hardened whalers for their boasting tales of battling southern right whales in the river or out from the bays facing the Southern Ocean.

Knox and Wes wander the streets, drawn to new sights and sounds, thankful there is no Government school for them to attend and no money to pay fees to the elderly schoolmistress teaching in a hut at the bottom of Collins Street. They would rather make slingshots or enjoy drunken commotions spilling from slapdash inns. Sometimes they make themselves useful fishing for native trout at Wellington Rivulet, on the town's southern edge, using sticks from a stringybark tree tied with old twine.

Domestic animals are needed for breeding stock, so the boys' occasional catch is eaten with gratitude, a change from the kangaroo meat the stores are rationing in the absence of beef. Maggie has learned how to cook a local dish, the kangaroo steamer, stewing chunks of the tail meat in its own gravy with a few rashers of salt pork and handfuls of cut potatoes.

When the blacksmith gives them a bag of mutton fish he has come by, he shows her how to slide a knife along the gap in the shells and prise out the flesh. She roasts the morsels as she would beef, rendering them so tough even their teeth are fit to ask for salt pork that's been laid down too long.

Maggie keeps Gil close by under the pretence of needing his help, keeping an eye on him while he rebuilds his strength. Her mind is blessedly occupied with the immediate needs of her family, a fortunate convenience holding back the tide of worries about the future, preventing a sudden flood.

CHAPTER SEVENTEEN

VAN DIEMEN'S LAND, 1809

HOT NORTH-EASTERLIES BRING IN THE New Year, along with confirmation of the land grant Charlie will be given as a first class settler and discharged marine.

Under General Orders issued before the Ferrions arrived, Norfolk settlers have had to apply to the Deputy Surveyor for their preferred location. Charlie, after careful inquiry, has opted to go down the Derwent, near the mouth of a tributary they call Brown's River.

Their home will be past the southern edge of existing habitation, well beyond the site where Mary and Noah Cottle will farm, with not even a rough bridle track past that point, the only access by boat.

'Why, Charlie, when most of the others have taken holdings upriver?' Maggie is perplexed, wanting to go close to friends, the women she's familiar with, at least have the comfort of knowing others are nearby.

'We'll be getting a lot more acres than them, for starters, and there's plenty more land around us to take on in time. We need sufficiency so the boys can have their own places when they come of age.'

There he goes, she thinks, making sense again, though it rankles. *Gawd, will there ever be a time when a choice might be what suits me, not him or the boys? Selfish on my part, shouldn't bother me, yet it do, gnawing at me just enough to keep me out o' sorts without needin' a dose o' herbs.*

She remembers then that Will, after marrying his housekeeper in Hobart—thankfully not asking Maggie or Charlie to be witnesses—has taken his family to land north of the town. Perhaps it's better not to live up that way after all.

Charlie interrupts her thoughts.

'Those in the know say land along the river flats is prime growing soil, and the river winds so slowly there's no risk it will burst its banks.'

He has been short-changed with the land, however, not given his due. He sets to work immediately, protesting that one hundred and eighty acres is not a fair allocation, petitioning in his best handwriting for the rest. Before leaving Norfolk he was promised a further one hundred and fourteen acres as a non-commissioned officer of the marines, and has not received the full indulgences pledged to him for services to the King.

His plea succeeds and his grant is enlarged.

In no time they are provided with a boat for the first trip, nearly ten miles south from town. Charlie and the three older boys go ahead with a tent, tools, and what building supplies they've been able to buy, desperate to clear land to graze what few of the family's hogs and sheep have survived the sea voyage or not been sold since.

Charlie has relieved the Governor of his obligation to provide them with a house, knowing it may never come, in return for three sheep and two Bengal cows.

Walking to the wharf with Gil three days later, Maggie is a bear emerging from the long slumber of hibernation, ears twitching at shouts, clatter, and clangs so loud they land as blows to the head.

It's good to be moving again.

Their pots, pans, what little clothing they have, their rations for the next month, some bedding, four chairs, all of it has been loaded on the ketch earlier that morning. Any other furniture will be whatever Charlie and their sons can make.

When they pull away from the shore, out into the hush of the broad harbour, Maggie turns to see behind her. The town is melting away, yet the mountain towers over it, stronger, bolder than ever.

No sense looking back, she chides herself. *Best look to where you be goin'.*

Gil is excitable, can hardly keep on his seat with the thrill of the adventure. She laughs at his joy, grateful he's with her, showing in his youthful way that whatever awaits them will be good, will give them more than what they've left behind in town.

The river spreads wider as they go, languid, the boat sending ripples into long sandy bays, where they disappear into half-hidden coves, the scrub growing down to touch the water. The sun has not yet had time to gather heat and she turns her face up to it, eyes closed, enjoying the rocking of the boat. When she opens them, a sea eagle glides above, white wings outstretched as though leading her home. She smiles, finds she cannot stop smiling, the pleasure of the moment running unexpectedly deep in her.

An hour or so later the skipper interrupts the spell, brings her back to the mass of her body pressing down on the seat beneath her.

'Go out that river mouth …'

He waves one hand wildly, pointing a finger to where freshwater, ocean and sky turn pale grey and become a vast nothingness.

' … and keep goin' in a straight line and you hit icebergs at the South Pole.'

He manages to say it with a pipe clenched between his teeth. If he was trying to impress her he fails, though Gil's enthusiastic response is enough for both of them.

'Icebergs, ma, do you think we'll see icebergs?'

A little before ten o'clock they pass cliffs on their right, light striking the tall folds of rock, looking all the world like the craggy edge of Norfolk Island the first time she saw it. The boat rounds a final headland, blowing its horn. It noses towards the middle of a curving beach, past a small river spilling its guts across a swale of sand pushed up by wind and tides. Marshes spread wide either side of the dirty river, she sees the rushes growing there. Surely that wasteland can't be theirs.

'Brown's River, by name and by nature.' The skipper likes his joke.

'Named after a Scotsman, a surgeon fella. Stumbled on it a while back, looking for plants he were gatherin'.'

Maggie ignores him, a history lesson is the last thing she needs. He guides the boat into shallow water with a sandy bottom. She and Gil take off their boots and wade to shore.

Charlie and the older boys call out as they thread towards them through a thick stand of tea-trees, emerging wearing shirts with armpits stained to their waists, filthy hands, faces streaked with black. Knox reaches her first.

'We got the tent up, ma. Let's get you home.'

Wes is next, not too old to give her a hug, tell her he's glad to see her. Charlie smiles, letting the two brothers have their moment, before calling them to help Joe and the skipper unload.

A path the width of two feet has been beaten through loose grey soil from the landing place, the forest and scrub hacked back so they can pass. She and Gil follow the others, ducking their heads occasionally to miss an overhanging branch. The boys have insisted she carry nothing, they will do as many trips as needed. She hears the pride in their voices, knows that wherever the path leads they want her approval at what she finds.

Their land is upstream half a mile, straddling the river, with the flats either side rising up to tightly wooded hills. She spies the mould-spotted tent in a circle of packed earth, a grey tongue of dirt marking the entrance, and nearby, six log seats neatly surrounding a firepit. She summons all the energy she can muster, giving a performance worthy of a few pounds in London's finest theatre.

'Well done, me lovely boys, well done.'

Charlie is keen to show off, too.

'Make your ma some tea, she'll be parched from the journey. Then we'll show her the house site.' A fire is burning low, held in by stacked stones. Wes busies himself building up the coals and filling a pot with water from an oilskin bag hanging in a tree.

The beauty and peace of the Derwent River has worn off. Maggie is wide-eyed, as incoherent as a person whose dose of laudanum fades. She sits on a log clutching her mug of tea, a life buoy in the whirling thoughts of a house to be built with no convict help, few building supplies, and little furniture to make it habitable. She sits on the bare bones of her arse yet again.

She must make the best of it. They have most of autumn before the frosts nip at their heels and chill winds find them. She trusts in their ability to work hard, it will carry them through. She says it to herself a few times, as though chanting a magic spell.

The tea finished, Charlie leads her to the level place they have begun clearing for the house, then takes her across the river flats, pointing out the place where the water curls lazily back on itself before heading to the marshes at its mouth. Later, they eat flour cake Maggie cooks on the coals.

When they have finished, only then, does Charlie speak of the natives.

He directs what he has to say to Maggie and Gil. The older boys already know the score.

'Don't go off on your own, whatever you do. We've been told the blacks might stray down to the marshes and the beach certain times of year, maybe winter when they're on the move from colder parts. Only seem to pass through, not hang about too long.'

He says nothing of the report that came his way, made by Hobart's chaplain, Rev Bobby Knopwood. Happened a while back when he and his servant were returning to town from a fishing trip. From their boat they saw maybe two hundred and fifty, up to three hundred natives camped on the flats around the mouth of Brown's River. Mainly women and children, looked like the men were out hunting. Long time ago, no reports since.

Charlie also fails to mention those seen paddling bark canoes from their camp near the head of North West Bay, only a few miles south as the crow flies, the group heading over to the long island of Bruni, its northern tip lying just beyond where the Derwent empties into ocean. Or the three hunters some time back, picked up by a schooner further down at Oyster Bay, all their provisions burnt by the blacks, two thousand kangaroo skins lost.

'The darkies won't be any trouble to us. Soon see it's our land now.' Least said the better, besides he has his gun and isn't afraid to use it.

'They won't wanna, or we be giving 'em grief.' Knox is too young for such swagger. If it weren't for the disturbing news Charlie's delivered, Maggie would be having a quiet word with him about knocking a bit of it out of the fourteen-year-old.

Come April, Charlie is obliged to travel to the market square in town for the annual muster, counted with other men in Hobart and outlying areas, declaring his circumstances so they can be recorded. He returns with three ewes, a cow, and great delight in the conversation he had with Deputy Commissary Len Fosbrook.

'Five hundred and thirty acres we got here along the river, I told him. You know what he said?'

Everyone sits around the firepit, scraping spoons across the bottom of tin dishes as they eat stew.

'You, Charlie Ferrion, have secured for yourself the largest landholding in Van Diemen's Land at this time.'

Maggie laughs along with him. 'Land enough to make the gentry back in the Old Country go green-eyed.'

A few weeks later she is bent over the washboard, stiff fingers scrubbing clothes, when she suddenly throws down the soap cake and straightens up. She can't stand it a moment longer. The sound of men's voices, not a single woman to be heard. The strange mist the sun refuses to chase off. The smoke from fires lit to burn what's been felled. The bush on nearby hills bearing down in ever darkening green.

Winter already shakes its cold fist at her. She fears her mind will turn like Sarah's if she doesn't do something. She is in need of sharp, salty air to clear her head, and begins scrambling through scrub in the direction of the beach, looking for the sandy path. In a clearing, Charlie and the boys have left two fires burning fiercely in tall piles of branches and twisted trunks, too useless even for fence posts.

Smoke stings her eyes as she rounds the furthest fire, so she doesn't see the figure standing there until the last minute.

It's a young woman, hair close cropped, a baby tied to her back with a short cloak made of kangaroo fur, in one hand a pendulous woven basket that carries something, Maggie sees it has heft. The woman's breasts, belly, all her dark, gleaming skin is uncovered. She doesn't move, watching flames devour the pyre of what has been an old eucalypt.

Maggie is close enough to see raised scars on her forehead, eyes dark as the bottom of a well, and the tears that fall from them, knows immediately that the woman cries in sorrow at what is broken and burning. The figure startles as she hears the older woman, then is gone, slipping away on silent feet to merge with tussocks of tall rushes and sedges thick in the marshes.

The encounter is over in an instant, leaving Maggie rooted to the spot, unsure if she's sad or glad the young mother has gone.

As the months pass, Maggie comes to understand that on this wild island the word convict rarely passes anyone's lips. It's a nasty word to be avoided, even among the lowest orders. Some prefer to be called servants of the Crown.

She finds it strange at first, but gradually understands that every soul in this new colony, whether damned to the island by a beak or come of their own free will, is busy stitching a new self, a better one.

Even the hard core shysters and crooks, of which there are many at Sullivan's Cove and creeping between rough timber buildings that stand for Hobart's small commerce district, have a hankering to be seen anew.

It is to be a society of free persons, not ex-convicts, a confection that consigns the truth to a secret cave in history, where descendants may one day stumble upon it and wonder, maybe even tremble, at what runs in their veins.

Out in the harbour the *Porpoise* tugs at anchor with Bligh aboard. He has been ousted in a military coup at Port

Jackson, turning up when he is supposed to be en route to England, hoping for support from Collins.

The banished Governor hovers in the Derwent, an angry, demonic God who has failed to smite his New South Wales Corp enemies and wrest back control of the economy and justice system. Collins has declined to give assistance for his cause, focusing energy on requisitioning stores from passing ships to keep the population alive, no doubt furious that the man who once criticised him for wanton administration of the island's food supply now wants his help.

Charlie is agog at the news passed on by old marine pals, full of events that saw Bligh placed under arrest. Maggie, for her part, can only see the coup as another reason to believe that wherever they build their lives it's on shifting sand. Even their land, like everyone else's, is subject to temporary location orders, with the authority to issue formal grants withheld from Collins.

Meanwhile, at Brown's River progress has taken up its axe and in the course of a year has felled what stands in the way of a new farm for the Ferrions.

Using timber cut from their land and materials bought or scrounged they have finished a three-room house, moving in as winter descends. It is little more than a large hut. They stand by its fireplace the first night, taking turns extolling the dwelling's virtues, each one, even Gil, ignoring sawcuts on corner posts, the dirt floor, shingles that had no time to season properly and will curl to let in rain, bedsteads slapped together from wattles. Every one of them secretly thinks of the glorious two-storey house at Charlotte's Field, the way it wrapped around them with space and comfort.

They have two fenced-in paddocks on the river plains for the sheep and cattle, who grow fat on native grass growing there and the corn they brought with them from the old farm. The Teeswater sheep, with a bit of Leicester bred into them, seem to be thriving despite the unforgiving climate. Charlie is keen to get them lambing, sell meat to the Commissariat Store in the next year or two.

Three acres of forested land are cleared. One field, its rich soil hoed by hand in the absence of a plough or a horse, has seen a crop of potatoes planted, for surely the last frost is over. Another field is being prepared for the first appearance of spring's warm fingers, ready to chip in wheat, maybe barley. Maggie has beans growing in her vegetable patch and peas ready to be sown.

Victualled and clothed for two years, given the use of four convicts for nine months and two for a further fifteen months longer. What a hollow deal, none of it available, everything they need other than stale, weevil-ridden rations must be conjured up by their own sweat.

At least the boys are proving solid workers alongside their da. Joe does more than his share, but while he's keen to own land, Maggie sees his heart doesn't quicken at the work of farming. Knox and Wes, Gil too, they are different, their strong bodies bending easily to flow with the elements, the alchemy of soil, weather, water. Somewhere in England, on green fields long ago, perhaps she had forefathers who took their bond with the land so profoundly into muscle and bone that it's travelled down the generations, a mysterious spark igniting a natural bent for farming in the three lads.

Maggie sees the black woman again, this time at a distance in a group passing along the shoreline. Knox spied some of them earlier that morning, women and children looking in the rushes for swan's eggs he supposed, while others dived off the rocks near the cliffs in search of molluscs.

She doesn't know what idea or force has impelled her to the beach when she ought to stay away, be scared as Charlie says. She watches from the cover of tea-trees as they bend heads to the children, the women talking excitedly to each other in a language Maggie can't fathom. What she does understand, from her hiding place, is that they enjoy each other's company, sharing their work and the raising of children, like women the world over.

It strikes a hard note of loneliness in her, the longing for female companionship, the way it gives succour through talk, a knowing look here and there, and laughter, especially the kind that shakes the belly and loosens troubles.

She turns her gaze away, it's an intrusion that brings a hot flush of shame. Hurrying back to the house before her husband or one of her sons see she is missing, she gives herself a talking to about the dangers. If native men had been marching up the beach with their clubs or spears she could have been in peril, everyone says so.

Her family is no longer alone in this far-flung place, others no doubt willing to help if the blacks become a threat. Sawyers and shingle splitters, lured by good timber, have set up camps further up Brown's River, rough fellows, not the kind she wants to invite to their fire. They have no right to be in the district, but the dire need for timber in the town means officials turn a blind eye.

Soon another family moves onto neighbouring land. Charlie and Maggie go over to greet them, taking peas from their garden. The couple are familiar faces, the husband a marine who came out in the same fleet as Charlie, working on Norfolk Island as a master mason. The wife was on the next ship after Maggie. A counterfeiter, she escaped the hellish sentence of death by burning, given instead the slower death of exile, and what Maggie sees is the wasting disease, in the bluish colour of her skin and the way it hangs from her bones.

Maggie mentions none of it. Privacy is the only gold folks own.

Another year passes, more land is cleared, and a proper house is built, clad in timber palings with a roof of serviceable shingles, a wide verandah along the northern side to catch the sun all day, and a spacious kitchen. They have no master carpenter or convict labour for the work so they settle for a single storey farmhouse, using oak-like timber from their own land, cut by the local sawyers and left to season for the past twelve months. The new home is sealed well against the south-westerlies that hound them with no regard for the hill on their southern border.

Funds have run low, but Charlie has managed to build up the flock of sheep to twenty, four of them ewes in lamb, with Gil given the job of keeping them herded together. With a bit of luck they will start selling some mutton in a year or two.

At the end of winter the natives return near the river mouth, more than a hundred of them gathering, fires burning to cook wallaby or kangaroo caught by the men and shellfish gathered by the women, many voices rising and falling late into the night like it is a celebration. Charlie and the boys see the men occasionally, moving in a line through the bush on the other side of the river, skirting the farm fences, the day's catch slung over a shoulder. When the wind blows their way in the evenings they can smell roasting meat.

On an unusually warm morning Gil leaves to carry water to the wooden sheep trough in the log stockyard, where the flock are penned. Charlie and the others are on their way out the gate when Gil comes running towards them at a clip, shouting.

'Nineteen, only counted nineteen, da. One of 'em has gone.'

Charlie goes with him to check. The fence has no obvious gap.

'Probably strayed, go down to the river and look for it boy.'

Maggie has heard the ruckus and caught up with Charlie. She waits till Gil has gone and the older boys have been sent packing to help.

'What if that meat roasting down at the blacks' camp last night was our mutton?' She is immediately sorry she put the idea in his head.

'They'd be fools if that's the case.'

The missing sheep cannot be found and Gil is given a stern talking to about keeping a closer eye on them, bringing them nearer the house at night from now on.

Charlie is bone-tired, bowed by work and responsibility, now lamenting the loss of a valuable ewe. What he has to say is for his wife's ears only.

'No point stirring the natives up when we didn't see anything to prove it was them. By God, though, if they try it again there'll be hell to pay.'

He stops, holds his tongue, no need to press the point that upriver near the town of New Norfolk, and inland too, there've been attacks on 'roo shooters pushing onto hunting grounds used by the blacks, and once on an overseer on the Government farm, who fended off Aboriginal men after he tried to take one of their women. There's more, too, bloody encounters that seem to get worse on both sides. Stockkeepers speared through the chest after chasing native women up trees, shooting them like it was sport. Or the man at a whaling station, recently cornered then stoned to a pulp for kidnapping a dark-skinned girl.

'Leave it, Charlie. Seems they lookin' after their kin, no different to us. They stick to the marshes and beach. We let 'em be and they leave us alone.'

'Let them be? Not if they come back for more sheep.'

She hears his outrage, senses it comes from his own fears about whether one aging man can protect her and the boys from a mob.

'Better a sheep or a bag o' flour than one of us.'

'They're not the same as us settlers.' He is near shouting. 'What would you know, Maggie, what would you know about the terrible things they do?'

He thrusts his way past her, picks up a hoe, and heads in the direction of his sons.

The natives are gone within the week, of their own accord, leaving the ground clean except for the remains of their fires, a mound of empty shells, and the tide taking away their footprints.

Charlie knows his family is more fortunate than others, what with the natives coming and going up and down the coastline and never staying nearby for long, but he keeps the gun handy just the same. Hobart has a newssheet now, the *Van Diemen's Land Gazette and General Advertiser*, and he's read about the hundred natives surrounding the farm across the river at South Arm. It may have ended peaceably when the elderly farmer gave them food and clothing, but he won't be parting with what belongs to him.

Some of the black men have been coaxed into town. The Guv is a fool, wanting to save them from uncivilised ways, as if the ribaldry, drunkenness and unruly goings on in that town could rescue a single soul.

CHAPTER EIGHTEEN

BROWN'S RIVER, 1814

THE FERRIONS ARE ONE FAMILY of many dealing with hostile weather that taunts them, any knowledge brought with them from the old island about growing grain, with its two harvests a year, has been nigh on useless. Only one main harvest now, and much riding on it as each year passes.

Maggie is glad about the lack of a decent mirror, only a small one in their possession, barely big enough for her husband and sons when they occasionally shave. Her waist is gone, brown hair mostly grey, while the years weigh heavily on her face, lines cracking across the skin as they do on the glaze of the vase Charlie gave her so long ago.

Each week she peels a small potato, dips it in vinegar and presses it between her thighs to push up the bulge of the dropped womb, securing the arrangement in place with a strip of cloth hooked up to a belt she's sewn. The discomfort is often aggravating, but at least she can walk and work without causing an abscess. Besides, Gil has proven he's worth it, has cleaved to her while the older three are their da's sons.

Challenges never end. The Commissariat prefers to buy from merchant farmers keeping grain in warehouses near the store, with outlying farms left to a cheaper rate. Then there's the boat costs for sending grain up the river and bringing goods down, the isolation, uncertainties. The work is wearing out Charlie, his body more gristle than fat.

They will go mad if they look too hard at what is stacked up against them, so they set their gaze always on the future. At night, in the quiet minutes before sleep lifts their load, Maggie and Charlie remind each other that they're up to managing the challenges, but each goes to sleep with a head full of worries.

The first wheat crop of the season grew well then a week before harvest, on the heels of a wet spring, Charlie found smut balls in the heads, dashing his chances of selling it at a premium. It had to be screened and sold for milling. The paddock should have been left fallow, but they couldn't afford to leave it empty and have planted barley.

The potato crop fared better, giving them their first small income and a little encouragement that their efforts would yield results.

Slowly the land is teaching them new ways, when to chip in seed, how long to wait when the frosts are upon them, when the rains will come. Their lives are shaped by what the land gives and what it takes away, and though they may feel they have control with their slashing of scrub, burning of trees, with their hoes and spades and sickles, it is always the dance of soil and weather that decides when the balance will tip in their favour.

Maggie grasps that what they could achieve through force on the old island, with its temperate nature, does not apply here. This is an island that resists.

A rough ten mile bridle path now extends from Hobart over the Mount Nelson ridgeline to Brown's River, the final section having made its way from the edge of the Cottle's farm at last. Knox walks it once a month for their stores, Wes sometimes going with him.

Maggie wants to keep her sons from the town, its drunkenness and violence. It's a terrible place, flipped on its back, the pulsing underbelly exposed, ready to be slit open at any time. Hobart is a town that bleeds, and often.

The boys are good lads compared to some, but she fears for their safety around staggering whalers needing no excuse to throw fists, pickpockets on every corner, sailors carrying knives, unafraid to use them for any slight. The men with strange faces and even stranger ways, jews from London's East End, Poles, Germans, Dutchmen, hulking men from Africa, Indian lascars.

Her sons share none of her concerns. They are fast becoming men, desperate for fun to make the ceaseless work more bearable. They go to the occasional cricket match, watch crews from merchant ships and whalers battle it out on the river for a purse, or sometimes show up for a dance, sleeping on the floor of a barn or shed, limping home worse for wear next morning.

Perhaps it's not a bad thing they're around others their age. The shortage of women means they'll be in competition for a wife when they are ready.

They share a ram with the neighbours and Charlie has gone to retrieve it. He returns along the track, his gait stiff. Time passes so quickly that Maggie hasn't noticed before how his joints have seized, so that he rocks from side to side as though the bones in his knees and hips have rusted together. Her love for the man needs no words, it shows in what she does, every small thing that eases his life a little. It rises now in a rush of care, causing her to lean her spade on the garden fence and go to meet him.

'I take no pleasure in it, but I was right. Word has come from Norfolk. The handful of men left behind on the island were given orders to burn every timber building, smash the ones made of stone. A fine job.' He takes a scathing turn, but she knows it's only to cover his hurt.

'A ship has picked them up, so they say. Not a soul left there now.'

Maggie should feel sadness or at least a little surprise that the death blow has fallen, even if it has taken till 1814. Instead, she feels nothing. Charlie may just as well be telling her a folk tale, it's so distant.

The watermills will lie smashed, the dam on Watermill Creek breached. Abandoned pigs and goats will feast on wheat, barley or oats springing up from seed left behind, no human ear to mark grunts and bleats as they nose through the streets of Sydney Town, gobbling redcurrants in the Guv's garden, avoiding the pack of dogs left to kill them. Doubtless the vines have already worked their way into soft ploughed soils, reclaiming what they never truly gave up.

Sarah's body lies decaying on an island now an entire graveyard, hopes and dreams smouldering in one wasted pile after another.

'Say no more, Charlie.'

She walks across the flats to the shallow place on the river where they've made a ford. It rained heavily overnight and she stands at the edge of grey silt, watching the dusky surface of the swollen river, water stained by tannins leached from peat. She ignores black cockatoos screeching overhead, doesn't budge, watching the moving water always coming, always going, while the river itself remains. She waits for it to call forth what abides in her despite endless change, but emptiness is all she feels.

The years roll by, there's no point trying to stop them. The seed in the girl has sprouted into the grown woman, come into a fertile self that now fades fast. A cycle ancient as human memory, and she but a flea on its skin.

Joe, now twenty-four, has left to make his own way, leaving the farm nearly two years earlier after getting location orders for his own land. He is busy building up business interests, proving canny at finding ways to spin money. Charlie resisted him leaving, bickered with the son now a man until Maggie stopped him with the reminder of harsh words spoken decades earlier in a house at Spitalfields, where another father fought the natural urges of his son.

To her husband's credit he relented, saw the wisdom in backing Joe's obvious head for business, selling an uncleared block of land on their upper boundary to fund Joe's bay whaling activities, going in with him and a boat builder to make a schooner for sealing and whaling. All of it on condition his three younger brothers will be the only ones to inherit the farm.

Maggie shakes her head, looks up the river and down. The advance of change never ends. Better to make peace with it than let it knock you to your knees.

The bread waits to be baked. She marches off across the paddock, not breaking her stride till she reaches the house.

In late October Maggie is making starch from potato scraps, to spruce up Charlie's good linen shirt, when she hears a commotion outside. Two rough-looking men are in loud conversation with Charlie, one of them punching his fist in the air. She starts walking towards them, but Charlie sees her and waves her away.

When she looks out the door a while later the men have gone, and Charlie and Knox are hurrying towards the house.

'We're needed down at North West Bay.' Charlie reaches for his old musket, checking the powder in the pouch is dry. Knox fetches the second gun the boys sometimes use for hunting.

'For what purpose?' Charlie's haste is making her fearful.

'Timber cutters had a disturbance with fifteen or so blackskins living down there. They've asked some of us to give them a hand, scare them off.'

'Bloody hell, why do their bidding? They're ugly brutes, you know it, likely takin' the women, making the men riled. It's been peaceable here, no trouble. Leave it alone, Charlie.'

He ignores her, busying himself filling a knapsack, telling Knox to get food, blankets.

'We'll be out till early morning.'

In her mind's eye she sees the young native woman and baby in front of the burning eucalypt pile that first year on the property. She stands in the doorway, hands on her hips, and shouts.

'Stop, I beg you, stop this foolhardy business.'

Charlie comes up to her. 'They're more daring in recent times, Maggie. You don't know the half of it. Could be us next, so we got to stick together, protect what's ours.'

She hates being treated like a fool. She knows plenty, knows that this was never the Government's land to give away, that others were here first. She can add a new sin to her list, it's plain as the nose on her face. She may be a woman banished from her own country but now she and her family, with their fences, their fields, ready to use threats or force to push the natives back, she's a party to driving out others.

She gets scared sometimes, most settlers do whatever their district. Even here, when the natives have their big seasonal gathering down at the river mouth, she's on edge, mindful the mob has the numbers to easily overwhelm the few of them on farms nearby. Yet the natives soon move on, have given little grief.

'Makes no sense, Charlie, not our fight down at the Bay.' She opens her mouth to remind him that only the previous month the Guv was thundering in the newspaper about stockkeepers and settlers being cruel to natives, *repugnant to humanity and disgraceful to the British character.*

He refuses to brook an argument with her, instead acting the bully.

'I gave my word we'd go, and that's that.'

They leave in time to meet up with two other settlers and reach the timber cutters before nightfall, planning to use the cover of darkness for their foray.

Maggie goes to bed with images of campfires glowing, men, women and children sharing food in the firelight, bark shelters behind them, families safe together. Her thoughts disturb her bowels and she must get up and go out in the dark to the pit toilet. On the way back to the house shadows rear up around the lamp, and the terror of what lies out of sight leaps up to her throat so it's hard to breathe.

Back in bed she falls asleep twice, each time waking for hours on end. She rises, groggy, sick at heart, before the sun appears.

Charlie and Knox return a couple of hours later, tired, saying little. Wes attempts to question them, but Charlie shuts down the conversation. Maggie's not having it.

'What did you get up to? Tell me.'

Knox is not one for silence. 'Gave 'em a helluva fright, that's what.'

'Enough, Knox.' His father is fierce, face flaming. He turns to Maggie with a quieter tone.

'Won't be any more bother. They started clearing out this morning, heading over to Bruni in their canoes.'

She wants to say it, *the ones that weren't hurt, you mean*, but stops herself. Her husband, her son, were among those to pull the trigger. Like it or not, she's already chosen a side.

The guilt is slick on her skin, slimy as the eels she once killed at Charlotte's Field.

Maggie is the first one up a couple of weeks' later, when the mild spring has begun giving way to summer's heat. Her weak bladder often wakes her before the others, though she has come to relish the quiet walk across damp grass between the outhouse and back door. On the way back she leans as usual on the fence, casting her eyes over the fields where crops grow and animals graze, enjoying the small, satisfying space in the day.

The sun starts to break through tall peppermints growing on top of the hill, picking out shapeless dots in the paddock on the other side of the river, slowly showing the outline of their cattle, heads lowered as they feed. She smiles to herself, ready to go inside, before her attention is caught by something out of place. Two of the beasts are on the ground. They must be sick.

She walks down to the edge of the water for a clearer view, all the better to report back to Charlie. As she approaches the river the sun bursts clear from the hill, shining bright on the scene. Dark blood stains the cattle's flanks around blacker gashes.

In no time, word goes around the district. Two cattle speared at their farm, one at the far neighbour's, and another in the small cove between Brown's River and the Bay. One for each man who took part in the raid.

'They'll bloody keep,' Charlie growls, as he and Gil sharpen knives ready to cross the river and cut up the carcasses. She hears a slight quaver in his voice.

'You gonna let 'em get away with it, da?' Knox looks at his father in disbelief, but before he can answer Wes chimes in.

'We got to do something, don't we?'

Maggie feels their fear, is scared herself, but damned if she'll let it beget more violence. 'No, we don't. They were settling the score, we leave 'em be.'

She ignores the raised eyebrows of Knox and Wes as they stare at each other across the table.

'Don't you be doin' anything stupid, boys.'

Less than a day passes when they smell smoke. Maggie's first thought is that the natives have come back, set fire to the wheat. She joins the others in walking half-way up the hill, where they see a haze of grey blocking the outline of Mount Wellington, its foothills and the country between them and town. They've seen it before, the natives setting fire to hunting grounds, making way for new grasses to attract their prey, making them easily caught.

It happens most years, though Maggie never finds it an easy sight. Where she grew up, a blaze meant someone had a grudge or people had a beef with the authorities. Either way fire got out of control, caused harm. It was terrifying.

'Probably worse in Hobart Town.' She says it to remind herself they're a long way from there, where folks will be going about their business while keeping an eye on nearby hills.

A north westerly picks up early afternoon, quickly turning to powerful gusts that swing to the north east and back again, over and over. By evening the glow of fire from the foothills has spread closer than it's ever been, sweeping around them towards North West Bay, where the sky burns in reds and oranges. Any thought of two dead cattle is gone.

She serves up corned beef and cabbage as the men discuss the danger. Her stomach must be playing up again, she is queasy.

'We'll be alright, unless there's a wind change. We'll take turns overnight, keep an eye out just in case.' Charlie and the boys stack old potato sacks near the back door, within easy reach if they need to hurry to the river to soak them. He appoints himself to the first watch.

Later, as Maggie is about to leave him brooding on the verandah, a question occurs to her. 'What chance the fire will get to the timber cutters down at the Bay?'

'Every chance, but they've got a dory if they need to get away.'

She washes her face and hands, thinking it's a shame they have the boat. Maybe they should be getting what they deserve.

The wind has died down by first light next morning. The smoke clears by late afternoon, and it is as if nothing has happened.

CHAPTER NINETEEN

BROWN'S RIVER, 1815

HOBART HAS DEVELOPED LITTLE, STILL clings in a square mile to its cove, backed by the mountain's low-lying foothills. The new Guv has decreed that the name no longer needs 'town' after it, as though convincing himself it is past needing that kind of shoring up.

The wharf is more frenzied than usual when Maggie arrives late winter for a rare trip to get supplies. Charlie and the others couldn't be spared, needing to get the redskin crop in the ground before the next heavy rains.

Soldiers are searching vessels, while more mill about on shore, stiff and scowling. Curious, she stops beside a labourer leaning on a crate, smoking. 'Smugglers, was it?'

'Gang of armed lags, seized a schooner night before last. Got away even though there were a guard and constable on board.' He takes the pipe from his mouth and laughs. No need to guess he was once a lag.

'They reckon the captain was in cahoots with 'em, so yeah, smugglin' it were. Offloaded the two soldiers and constable into a leaky boat in the dark, left 'em a long way downriver.'

No longer interested in his own story, he taps the pipe against the crate to empty it and shuffles off.

Maggie shakes her head, walks away. Nothing surprises her any more.

She is on the hunt in the town's few shops for nails, calico shirts, lamp oil, and castile soap. Wes needs boots, the hand-me-downs from Knox have worn out. A few hours later, having arranged for the heavier items to be carted to the wharf, she has an impulse. Six harvests gone and money from their grain has been used to build up stock numbers, which now include the herd of cattle. She can afford to throw coin away, for once, on a few fripperies. She ignores the handsome black silk cloak inside the door of a Liverpool Street shop. A few silk flowers to freshen up her best hat will do.

Back in the street, noise and activity all around, she yearns for the hush of Brown's River. Streets are full of hustle, shouting and coarse language spills out of frequent inns, drivers call to horses dragging carts through mud, what excitement it once might have been, but now all of it too much. It's a relief to head towards the harbour for the ketch home.

The whaling industry is taking off, ships, longboats and dinghies jostling for space at the wharf. When Maggie turns a corner expecting to see the ketch, it's not there. She must be mistaken about where it's moored, and hurries to the next street leading to the docks.

Intent on looking towards the water, she doesn't see the rotting corpse till its stench causes an unwitting shudder.

This is where they hung him. The town was full of talk about it.

Van Diemen's Land, nearly two thousand times the size of Norfolk Island, has vast tracts of wet forest, dense undergrowth, gullies and caves offering hiding places galore for bushrangers. In a land where felons outnumber settlers and colonial administrators, where law and order is no more substantial than a piece of gauze, some armed convicts sent out to catch game have gone rogue, a few military deserters joining them.

The leader of the worst gang has boasted he will set the colony on fire end to end. Collins is long gone, having succumbed to stress and a stoppage of the heart while sitting at his desk. The new Guv, Thomas Davey, in between frequent bouts of heavy drinking, is spooked about a convict uprising and has proclaimed martial law.

Maggie instantly sees the corpse is his public statement on the murderous gang who terrorised the New Norfolk district. The mess liquifying, putrefying under a gunmetal sky, was the twenty-six-year-old fellow who aided and abetted them, his body bound in chains after hanging and left to slowly rot as a warning.

After years as a nurse she should be used to the horrors of fetid flesh, but the wretched stink and the awful public display of what was once a human being stirs the contents of her stomach. She manages to keep it in check by letting out a long groan.

She finds the small ketch, stout as a Thames barge, though crafted from the island's own celery top pine. It seemed so big when she boarded it from Brown's River beach, yet now it's a flimsy bobbing thing dwarfed by the other vessels, the water around it clogged with garbage from the town's rivulet. At three o'clock the skipper pushes off into the river, where she turns her face into the cool southerly, gulping in lungfuls of river air to force out the foulness of the corpse.

She is going home.

The river breathes beneath the wide beam of the boat, its rhythm a slow up and down, rocking her as if she were a baby. She sits away from the other two passengers, inhaling with each lift of the vessel, slowing the exhale to match each dip down. She has seen the Derwent and its shores many times, yet this afternoon it's a new river, winter colours shimmering and dancing, the water widening in its welcome as they sail south.

This way, this way. You belong.

She leans back, surprised to find contentment stealing upon her for the first time in years. Her family thrives, unlike so many. Destitution is behind them now they've rebuilt their lives. They've been spared attack by bushrangers and natives. Her sons will stand on solid ground, will progress beyond what she and Charlie have created, the kind of success that's the wish of every parent.

It has been months since she attended divine service, the last time being when Rev Knopwood took time from his duties as Magistrate to go south, offering the sacrament to ensure heathens were reclaimed by the Lord. He was genial enough, though failed to spark inspiration with his sermon, urging the need to support the man and maintain the Christian, whatever that meant.

Now, sailing towards home, it is the spreading river that unexpectedly touches her spirit, lifts her up as Norfolk's vast sky and hills once did when she stood at the door of their house in the moist air of early morning. As it was then, she can accept this small gift of time that is hers alone.

Rounding the final headland, it pleases her to see Gil waving enthusiastically from the beach. Her own boy, fancy that, extending the welcome given by the big river. Her goods and shopping basket are loaded into the dinghy and she climbs down into it, rowed to where the boat bottoms softly on the sand. As she scrambles out into the shallows, Gil runs to her. Only then does she see his gestures are frantic.

'Come quick, come quick. It's da.' Gil's face is white. She drops her basket on the sand and starts running towards the house.

'He was dragging the harrow, me and Wes following with the seed potatoes … .' Gil is gasping, running ahead, turning his head back to spit out each sentence over his shoulder.

'He fell down, sudden like, were a strange colour, said he were dizzy, overcome.'

He spins forward to see where he is going, then shouts again towards her.

'Knox took off for the surgeon, should be back soon.'

Charlie, oh Charlie. She was travelling down the river full of peace while her husband was in agony, her son running eight miles the other way to get help.

They are nearing the house. 'We got him inside ma, been keepin' him warm.' Gil throws open the door. She needs to get to her husband, but her feet want to stay on the step where she won't have to face what awaits. Once she steps inside, nothing will be the same.

Maggie brushes past Gil, into the bedroom. Charlie is ashen, lying still, the blanket barely rising and falling over his chest. His eyes stare up at the ceiling, not moving when she says his name, though his lips twitch in silence. Wes sits helplessly by, jumping to his feet to give her the chair, pleased at last to have something he can do.

She squeezes Charlie's hand, brushes away grey soil smudged on his temple. No hospital experience is necessary to judge what his body reveals. He is done for.

She must be crying, for Gil is squeezing her arm.

'It'll be alright ma, he'll come good.'

She lays her palm against her husband's cheek. 'Charlie, it be me, your dear wife.'

In his crumpled state, undefended by constant motion, she sees how the heavy load of regret has weakened him, that he had to turn his back on all he'd made on Norfolk. It has eaten away at him like borers hollowing out solid wood.

By the time Knox returns with the surgeon the fellow doesn't even need to open his bag. His only task is to declare Charles Ferrion officially dead and to record the date, the twenty-ninth of August, eighteen hundred and fifteen.

It doesn't seem right. Maggie struggles to grasp this is how it ends with Charlie. Her mind is all awhirl.

'He were a glazier for years, back in London, out here in the colonies. Suffered bad sometimes with head pains. Was it the lead got him?' Maggie doesn't know why she wastes her breath asking. What does it matter now?

'Could be. His feet and legs are swollen. If it's the lead palsy sometimes the kidneys give out. I'll know more if I do an autopsy.'

Charlie sliced up, his innards exposed, weighed, tested. Not a private piece of him left. Oh God, this is happening, he is gone from her.

'No, I'll not be havin' him cut up. Leave him be, let him rest.'

Two days later they take him upriver, a sombre journey made in silence, not even the skipper daring his usual chat. The body is loaded onto a cart at the wharf and taken to the undertakers, where it is lifted into a coffin of golden pine from the island's wet west coast forests. Maggie takes some comfort from knowing it's a special timber, doesn't seem to decay, keeping her husband safe in his grave for a long time to come.

Shortly before three o'clock she walks behind the funeral bier, her sons pulling it, two on either side, down Harrington Street towards the burial ground at the edge of town. She ignores onlookers. No doubt they tut-tut that a respectable woman goes to the graveside. She has no care for the airs and graces they pretend worse than Old England. Let them talk behind their hands.

A hundred mourners or so gather in the walled park of St David's cemetery, many Norfolk Islanders. No church affords shelter since the timber building blew down in a storm four years earlier. Proof, Maggie thinks, that good Christian ways have no chance of taking root in this town.

Members of the Lodge of Freemasons wait with the Worshipful Master, standing near Rev Knopwood. The Master will follow the cleric's prayers with a brotherly oration, then place Charlie's masonic apron on his grave, though who made the arrangements is a mystery to Maggie.

Mount Wellington mourns along with former marines and settlers, a shroud of snow on its summit. Maggie ignores the faces in the crowd, lifts her wet eyes up to the peak soaring high above her, unfettered by such a trifling thing as one human life. She has the absurd urge to scream up at it. *He mattered, he matters still.*

She is flanked by her three younger sons—Knox, wearing twenty-one years' worth of muscle, Wes, grown into his da's lanky form at eighteen, and Gil, his face more careworn than it should be at sixteen. Joe has taken over as head of the family, greeting the chaplain on behalf of his ma.

Fifty-six years was the toll Charlie carried, nearly thirty of them spent at her side. Stupidly she'd bargained on maybe thirty more. Maggie hears few of Knopwood's words, even fewer spoken by the Master. She is straining instead to hear the familiar voice, recall its comforting tone, the wholehearted laugh, the way he soothed her when she worried. There's only silence in her head. She stifles sobs behind her hand, crying because she longs to be back on their farm, where his presence lives in each field, in every room of their house.

Charlie has named Maggie an executor of his will, along with two men he greatly admired, both of whom arrived with Collins as voluntary settlers. She is but a lowly church mouse alongside them. Richard Pitt is one of the island's wealthiest men, renowned for his grand Georgian house at Pitt Farm, while Scotsman Robert Littlejohn, watercolour artist and botanist, has developed Montrose Estate into a fine property.

She finds her copy of the will in the lean-to at the back of the house, where their first rough table now functions as a desk for farm accounts and correspondence. She has sat here many times to fill out the ledgers, file receipts, fill out official forms, though it was Charlie who took care of the letter-writing.

It's unsettling to see her name appear alongside Pitt and Littlejohn's. Charlie has had his way, made sure she has good standing. She should be glad, for the sake of her sons. The unease makes no sense, she tells herself to stop being so foolish.

I give and bequeath with love and affection to my beloved wife Maggie … He wants the world to know theirs was a love match, not a union of convenience, the letters on the page her assurance should there ever have been any doubt. A flood of affection rushes through her, emerging in messy bawling. *I never doubted it, Charlie, not by the time we were wed.*

He has left her the one hundred and eighty-two acres of land and house they call Ferrion's Farm, to go to Wes and Gil when she is gone, along with stock and household goods to be shared between all four sons at that time.

Knox gets the nearby one hundred acres they call Nash's Farm, while Joe has already been advantaged.

Hobart has no solicitors, so she and her co-executors must apply to the Supreme Court in Sydney for Letters of Administration of the estate and effects. The process will take months and includes calling in any debts. Richard has asked her to check for records of such.

The boys have fences to mend, fields to till, hogs, sheep and fowls to fatten. Maggie barely gets beyond the kitchen, so many visitors coming by in the following days. Her husband was a good man, they want her to know, a loyal marine, a friend to settlers, an esteemed masonic brother. It seems he's becoming a saint.

She wants to hold onto the man, not the folk tale, wants to set them straight. Though he aimed to do good he had his own frailties, could be bloody-minded, strong-willed, the Charlie who would get his own way, curry favour with the right folk to help his cause, the man who set his mind to something and saw it through no matter what she might say.

She's glad when they stop calling, leaving her to search out the memories so she can grieve the truth of him, choose what she will hold close, what moments or feelings can be carried forward and which ones let go.

CHAPTER TWENTY

AS THE DAYS UNFOLD AN aimlessness sets in.
Maggie decides to be practical, give herself over
to the sorrow in the hope it will lead swiftly to
healing her heart. She finds herself wandering the river
flats for hours, other days drifting through the house like
a ghost or following the path to the beach, drawn to the
gentle lull of waves kissing sand.

When the pain doesn't lessen she changes tack, must
throw herself into what needs to be done. She takes herself
to the desk and starts sorting the farm's papers, making
a pile for slips relating to farm debts, then bringing the
accounts up to date.

An afternoon passes quickly and she is sorry to step
back from the work, to find the grief still waiting, still
raw. She must go to the kitchen, cook their evening meal,
but first she looks for brown paper and string to bundle
papers for sending to Richard. She pushes back the chair,
overcome with exhaustion.

The string and scissors are in a wooden storage box on
the desk, made from four small drawers salvaged from an

old apothecary cabinet, secured in a frame Charlie made years earlier. She pulls out one of the drawers, forgetting that none of them run straight. It jams and, impatient to be gone from the room, she tugs it hard, yanking the box so fast it drops from her hand and spills its contents onto the floor. Her knees hurt as she lowers herself to the string, crawling under the table for the scissors and a couple of half-used sticks of sealing wax. As she backs out, she spies a piece of paper caught between the table and the wall, reaches to tug it out.

It is getting late. She straightens up, glances at the paper ready to toss it on the desk, but sees it is a letter written on thick, creamy paper, more fancy than anything she or Charlie used. The seal is already broken, and curious, she opens it. The first page is headed by the grand mark of a Sydney merchant company, in fulsome, swirling print with the flourish of a crest above it. She flips to the second page, recognises the name below the signature, Charlie's old friend Jim Cartwright.

The first paragraph has the usual pleasantries to be found between friends. She lowers the letter, ready to set it aside, for even death shouldn't mean meddling in business that's not hers. Besides, she must hasten to fetch turnips from the larder. Distracted, she wonders if her eyesight is going when some letters dance forward from the second paragraph, a name forming itself, alive with meaning. The emotions register first, a torrent of feelings that crash through what the years have walled up.

Hannah. It is her darling girl's name, in iron gall ink already eating away at the paper.

The letter is dated seven September, eighteen hundred and six. Two whole years before they left Norfolk.

Your ward, Hannah Jarman, is to marry a most suitable man, therefore your patronage will no longer be necessary. At twenty-one, she has grown into an amiable, accomplished young woman. In previous correspondence I have assured you of the admirable service she has provided as an assistant in my shop since you sponsored her passage to Sydney six years ago, but in the circumstances it seems fitting to remind you of her steadfastness.

My wife, as you may rely upon, has assisted your ward to ensure funds you provided are allocated most judiciously. In this instance, she has helped your ward select a modest though comprehensive trousseau, as well as a wedding dress and bonnet that befits her status. The wedding will be held at ten o'clock in St Phillips Church on the first Wednesday of November. My wife will loan her a family heirloom to wear on the day, a fine brooch set with pearls.

Hannah's intended is a respected shipbuilder with sound connections, his business flourishing in one of the colony's fastest growing industries. In terms of temperament, they are well suited to each other. I have no doubt she will be a fine wife and mother, an asset in supporting his business prospects, and will advantage him in society.

As per your standing instructions, I will continue to ensure our arrangement remains confidential.

The turnips are forgotten. Hannah is alive, married, has a home in the same country as Maggie.

And Charlie? Right now Charlie is a stranger, and maybe deserves to be dead.

Maggie folds the letter carefully, places it in her pocket. It burns against her hip and she pulls it out, opens it again to check the writing hasn't disappeared, that Hannah lives on the page. Puts it away to read and reread until Jim Cartwright's message becomes real.

Friends and neighbours who have acted as though Charlie's a saint, they would strike off his halo if they knew the truth, but not if she got her hands on him first. His deceit is a cuckoo in their nest, crowding out every good thing they once shared, every good deed he did in her name. So much has been turned upside down that she can barely remember how to move her own limbs.

She says nothing to her sons as she stumbles through the days, the secret bending her into a bitter old woman, warping memories of Charlie more than acid on skin. The boys rarely speak of their father, but he is with them every day in the way they mound potatoes, treat sheep with tobacco water against scab, wield the hay knife to cut sections from a stack to feed sheep.

Waves of despair catch her unawares. It's as though she walks in a dream, fighting to wake up and set her life back to rights. So many letters must have passed between him and his friend in England as he sought out Hannah's whereabouts, then a string of letters with Jim. The knowledge mocks all she held dear, the times he sat with her at the table or pulled her in close at night, all the while denying what would heal her sorrow; the way he adored his boys, learned from them about the bottomless well of love for a child, yet kept her from her own.

Dan had no guile, wore his character lightly. But this husband, it seems he has hidden a black heart, made worse by the way she didn't see it. Oh that she could talk to him, shout in his face. *Why? Why pain me like this, Charlie? Why lie to me? Have I not done right by you?*

The only answer she can find is in the pleasure she saw on his face that first year on Norfolk, when she was freed from her sentence. It was there in his smile, the shine of his eyes. He was already fixed on wiping out her past, and any arrangements he made for Hannah were nothing more than a salve to his conscience.

He said not a word to her, and there's no forgiving such treachery.

A week goes by, then another. Household chores still get done, though she has grown ever quieter, speaking little to the boys, filled with the idea of Hannah, the imaginings of who she is, her circumstances, swelling so there is space for nothing else in her waking moments.

'Ma, you don't seem well.' Gil is studying her, the other two still clattering knives and forks on their plates, discussing plans for the next day with mouths full of pork and potato.

'I be fine, Gil. Just a touch tired, is all.'

He looks away, loads his fork.

'You don't look it, ma. I know it's been hard without da, harder for you in some ways 'cos of the way you cared for each other.'

Her beautiful boy, still innocent about the ways of men, seeking to reach her with understanding, ease her load. She tries to focus on her son's gentleness, but too late, a reaction explodes through the numbness at the mention of Charlie's care.

She slams down her knife, harder than intended. Knox and Wes stop their chat in mid-sentence, stunned by her fury.

'I have news. I be goin' to Sydney the first passage I get.'

Within the month she is ready to board Her Majesty's brig, *Kangaroo*, in a new sapphire blue dress purchased that morning in Hobart. It's a scandalous choice for a new widow, who by rights should still be wearing black in public.

Joe's in town selling meat to the Commissariat, so she takes the chance to see him for the first time since the funeral, though can't bring herself to explain the true nature of her trip. She has given all her sons the same explanation, that she needs to get away and recover, one thing she will do for herself.

She is anxious about telling Joe, the one most likely to see through her ruse, to insist on the real reason for leaving. Fortunately, he is full of news of his own. He will marry before the year is out, Constance Ealey, a farmer's daughter with a steady personality like his. Maggie knows the young woman, like Joe, has convict blood, though what good would there be in telling her son? Constance would hardly want to let on her da was once a London nightman, the son of a despised sewer scavenger, a fact he was known to brag about in his cups at the grog shanties back at Sydney Cove.

Joe walks her to the edge of the shallow channel separating the shore from the wharf on Hunter Island, hugging her before two able seamen carry her across in a sedan chair. He is gone before her feet touch the deck.

She leans on the rail for as long as her aching legs allow, while twenty or more of the crew check sails and clear the last few barrels of grain off the deck. The main mast soars eighty feet above, a perilous climb in darkness when any delay in shortening the sail could spell doom. Not a concern for her, though. She plans to be asleep in her bunk well before then.

On the stern, the boom points out into the river, eager to leave just like her.

Before the hour passes the helmsman is at the wheel, barking out orders as the crew sets enough sail to catch the north-westerly and drift out into the harbour, saving the effort of kedging.

The brig picks up speed in full sail and soon the beach at Brown's River hoves into view. She strains to see if Wes stands there, maybe even Gil waving her off, but of course they're busy on the farm. Only when the vessel clears the river mouth does she let herself feel the deep ache of loneliness, an unwanted lodger that's taken up a room in her marrow.

The moment she read the letter Charlie's presence was gone. Not fading slowly, but cleaved by the axe of betrayal. It cut the cord that bound her to him and she can no longer decide what to mourn—the years of believing her husband was a man she could count on, or the missed opportunities with a forbidden daughter.

If there's a place between the otherworld and the crust of the Earth she is journeying in its thin air, suspended where time and the pull of the tides can't reach her. The only touchstones are ocean touching sky and the purple edge of coastline the brig clings to as it makes its way north to Port Dalrymple.

From there, with final cargo and passengers loaded, the vessel crosses Bass Strait, making good time up the east coast of New Holland in favourable conditions. Maggie takes to her bunk, gathering the store of energy she will need when they land. At least that's what she tells herself in the hours and days lying still, blanketed by permanent twilight below decks.

They arrive in Sydney on the half hour of nine, far too early to find accommodation. She leaves her bag in storage and sets off on foot into a town no longer recognisable, except for the uphill road where she once took her first steps. Now called George Street, it has a fancy stone wall running up the eastern side.

Under the latest Guv, Colonel Lachlan Macquarie, new public buildings have sprung up. The place finally has a church, St Phillips, a squat stone building out of keeping with its tall castle-like tower on one end, flaunting a large clock. Maggie doubts Rev Johnson, if he's still alive, would approve of such an ugly beast, not worthy of the Lord.

Maggie is agog at how commerce now flourishes, with Macquarie breaking the military stranglehold on trade by importing Spanish dollars. The new mint punches the centre from the coins and New Holland has its first currency, the holey dollar and the dump.

Services and goods are on offer everywhere she looks, shoemakers, barbers, watchmakers, toolmakers, carpenters, more trades than she can count. Shops no longer operate out of the front rooms of houses but have their own buildings with large signs proclaiming what they sell, with discounts for those who pay in gold, silver or Government bills.

She wanders aimlessly, an explorer in new territory.

The Governor has flexed his authority, determined the colony will at last bend to the law and the rules. Bare-knuckle fighting and gambling have been banned, cricket and athletic pursuits encouraged. Good luck to him, Maggie thinks, for he surely needs it.

The town buzzes with possibility, an excitement that only serves to remind Maggie she's a weary old woman. She loses her bearings until she finds the crossing over the stream towards The Rocks, heading towards the site of the old hut shared with Sarah. As she strolls in her new blue dress a constable approaches, dipping his hat.

'I wouldn't be goin' down there, ma'am. It ain't a place for a good woman such as yerself, all pickpockets and crooks down there.'

His responsibility discharged, he walks away, saving her the awkwardness of explaining just how much she has in common with those who thieve.

Further on, she barely recognises her surroundings. The convict huts are gone, though the hospital is still there, a string of sandstone buildings replacing the leaking wards where she worked. Stretching out of sight towards Cockle Bay are rows of hovels, cheek by jowl.

New streets have been forged in a grid across the town, narrow lanes she once knew blocked or built over. She is weary by the time she works her way uphill in search of the brick cottage Charlie built for them. Three times she walks this way and that, checking the outlook, trying to figure out where it is in relation to the harbour in front and the windmills behind.

At last she accepts that the cottage has been knocked down, replaced by a row of officers' quarters. The destruction bewilders her, perhaps because she wished for the cottage to anchor her to a time when Charlie was her whole world, when Joe was just an idea forming in her belly. Its disappearance leaves her more groundless than ever, sending her nerves skittering.

She must find lodgings, rest up. Tomorrow, with renewed vigour, she will go to the address carried in her coat pocket.

The morning is humid, an invisible fog of moisture penetrating hair and clothes. Maggie sweats as she makes her way to the end of York Street, where successful businessmen have their offices, some with brass plates shouting their good fortune.

At one of the more modest doors she enters from bright sun into dull light struggling through two small windows. A clerk sits at a desk. She summons the confidence to address him, annoyed the words sound halting.

'I am here to see Mr Cartwright.'

The clerk, half her age, stands and squints. 'He is not in, I'm afraid. Is he expecting you?'

It's not how she had seen it. Jim would be there, surprised. She'd have the upper hand, throw him off balance.

'No, but I come on a matter of great importance. He be wantin' to see me, of that you can be sure.'

The clerk studies her straw bonnet, the travel-worn dress and the matron wearing it, weighing up whether the visit warrants sending a boy to fetch his employer.

'May I inquire about the nature of your business with Mr Cartwright?'

'No, you may not.' She has travelled the better part of a lifetime to this dingy office, and bristles at the indignity of a hand-wringing accounts-keeper blocking her way.

The sharp edge of her retort has unnerved the clerk, not one for a scene.

'Very well. Please return on the hour, I will endeavour to ensure he is here.'

She leaves her name reluctantly, before departing for her inn near the military precinct and the hope of a settling cup of tea.

When she returns, steadying her hands by gripping her black embroidered purse, the clerk ushers her into a large rear office.

The man Maggie once knew is shorter, more stout. As Jim Cartwright stands, she considers the perspiring purple face and sees nothing of the energetic, laughing marine. The strain of building his wealth has drained what was good and likeable, leaving a sour, miserable man.

So taken aback is she by his degradation that she almost misses the edge of the chair when he gestures for her to sit.

'My sincere condolences, Maggie. I have heard the sad news about Charlie. I trust he didn't suffer.'

She hastens to reassure him, desperate to get through the pleasantries and explain her purpose. He also seems keen on the need for haste.

'I gather you're not here to inquire about my family, Maggie. Perhaps you would care to enlighten me about the purpose of your visit.'

He knows, of course he knows why she's here. Why must they play this game? Better to be blunt and have it over with.

'In sorting through Charlie's papers I came upon a letter by your hand from some time ago, about his ward, Hannah.'

Jim stiffens, as a boxer might brace for an expected blow. 'I see.'

Maggie presses on. Three decades a victim is enough. 'Did he tell you why he felt a duty to the girl?'

'It was not my business to ask. I'm sure you would appreciate that even between friends some confidences must be kept.'

She wants to throw her hands up in his face, put a stop to this idle patter. Before she has the chance to do it, a thought jumps into her head, fresh, startling. He believes the girl was fathered by Charlie.

'She were no child of his.'

Jim exhales, nodding, ready to hear she was a niece, perhaps an orphaned child of a late marine colleague.

'She were mine, Jim.'

He rears back a little, floored by the disclosure, then recovers quickly and composes his face.

'It's James now, if you don't mind.'

Maggie's hand starts to rise. She wants to whack the pompousness from him, wrestle him to the ground for insolence when she'd hoped for understanding, or even a little compassion.

305

The merchant in him, made rich by exploiting the vulnerabilities of others, knows instantly he has taken a misstep.

'Then you must have been delighted by news I sent, back then, of the good match she made in her marriage.'

She rolls her eyes, makes no attempt to hide her disdain.

'I had no word of her after leaving England. For decades I thought her likely dead. Charlie hid her from me, along with his part in bringing her to Sydney Town.'

James stands, taking control. 'I shall call for some tea, perhaps something a little stronger if you will. We have much to discuss.'

She accepts the whiskey, sips it slowly, lets the burning in her throat stop any chance of choking sounds as James outlines the arrangement between him and Charlie, assures her that he was determined the girl would have a good start.

'I have no idea, Maggie, why he kept the information from you when she was your child. I can see, if she was his daughter, he might do so to spare you pain, but ... .'

She leaves his statement hanging in the air, has no desire to shield her husband. He fooled his friend as well as his wife.

'I want to see her. Where might she be?'

He is in a quandary, fiddles with his glass while he mulls over what might be best for his ward and especially, his wife.

'Hannah and her husband are held in high repute. They dine occasionally with officials, even once at Government House. They have some standing here, you see. Look, I don't believe I am at liberty to give you the address.'

Whatever friendship once flowed between them now runs putrid as the Tank Stream. Ann Cartwright no doubt has a hand in his reluctance, for she's the one who pretends to be better than others.

Maggie sizes up the situation. Confined by the demands of his wife, the former marine pretends power, seeks minor victories to puff himself up. *You've turned into a petty bastard, Jim.* She thinks for a moment she said it aloud, but he continues to sit, unruffled, behind his big desk.

The shame of what he implies stings, despite the mellow glow of the drink. She puts down the glass, slowly and carefully, marking out the time she needs to gather herself. She has known worse bastards than this.

'She were but four years old when I saw her last, would be twenty-eight now. I won't go to my grave not knowing the woman my girl has grown into. Sure as day you must see that, James. If you give me no help I will find her another way.'

The leather squeaks as he shifts on the seat, leaning on its wooden arm, smiling unexpectedly.

'Always a determined woman, Maggie, you were. I see nothing's changed.'

He agrees to act as a go-between, requesting permission for a visit. Maggie departs the office with two things: a promise he will send word to her inn next day, and the dread of so many yawning hours to fill until then.

She wanders to the waterfront, a little dazed, reluctant to walk too much further and aggravate the old pain from birthing days. A Jamaican fellow, getting on in years, wearing a torn military jacket from a foreign army, shouts to her and others nearby.

'Blues Point or Milson's Point, the only waterman offerin' safe passage over the harbour. Cheap rates, fast service.'

Maggie has no call to go to either location, has had enough of boats and water after her trip from Hobart, yet an impulse seizes her. She finds a coin and hands it to him.

'Billy Blue at your service, ma'am, known to all as the Commodore.'

He rows with strong strokes, telling tall tales, assuring her of the good fortune that she's got him on the oars today. 'Two other boats o' mine out there. My men may be young lads, but they ain't a patch on me.' A canny fellow, she thinks, doubtless once a lag, with the perfect set-up to smuggle in plain sight.

She returns to the Crown and Kettle hours later, sore from the hard timber seat on the boat, heart aching. The inn, unfortunately, is popular with noisy soldiers from the nearby Barracks. She takes a light meal in the dining alcove to avoid them, and falls into bed.

CHAPTER TWENTY-ONE

SYDNEY, SPRING 1815

MAGGIE HAS STAYED IN HER room, not venturing out for breakfast, straining so hard for a rap at the door that she opens it three times, certain she's heard one. While waiting she plumbs the storehouse of faded memories of young Hannah, tries the game from years ago of growing her up in her mind's eye, imagining a pleasing face, an upright form. She'll want to see her old ma, of course she will. All the years behind them will mean nothing when they meet.

When the knock comes Maggie jumps, is at the door in a flash. James has written four words on the note. *She will see you.* Below is the address and scrawled next to it the appointment time, two o'clock this day.

She needs a new bonnet, the straw one is far too shabby, yes she definitely must go out this minute to get one. The rush of nervous energy sweeps her down Pitt Street to a shop, where she stands frozen before an array of silk bonnets, looking for all the world like she's eyeballing the place for no good.

An assistant is quickly at her elbow, his voice slippery with suspicion. She asks his opinion on the latest fashion for matrons in Sydney, though what he would know as a man is questionable. He spreads flattery thicker than butter when she tries on his recommendation, in plain grey silk with a purple velvet trim. As she studies herself in the looking glass he holds up, the reflection is far from pleasing. A solid woman, face with as many wrinkles as a currant, peers back in a bonnet that shouts her advanced age.

She wants to flee from the shop there and then. Instead, she forces herself to calmly remove the hat and pay the exorbitant two shillings and sixpence, not giving the weaselling man the satisfaction of seeing her upset.

A few hours later Maggie presents herself, sick to the stomach, at the front door of a two-storey sandstone villa. As the handle turns she fears she may faint, though it is the face of a cap-wearing maid that appears. She follows her down the echoing corridor of a home that seems unnaturally quiet, into a sitting room with tall windows, curtains half-closed to block out the afternoon sun.

A figure rises at the edge of a stream of light. 'Mrs Ferrion, how do you do?'

They stand across from each other, neither moving.

'I am Mrs David Hayter. Please take a seat.'

Dumbstruck, Maggie sits as the maid brings in a tea tray, placing it quietly on a side table. She doesn't want tea, damn the tea. She's come a long way, around the globe, through years that snagged worse than thorns on a blackberry bush, has waited a lifetime in the hope of seeing Hannah. Where's the person for whom she has borne such love, walking barefoot with it across the broken glass of time? What does such a bond have to do with the cold, stiff woman sitting before her?

It's not a time for falling apart. She is in her senior years, must take the lead to spark their knowing of each other.

'My showin' up must be a shock. So many years have gone by, for you and me both, leaving us in this uncommon state of affairs.'

She wants to call her Hannah, say it softly the way she did in the quiet mornings together, see if it will warm the cool eyes raised from the teapot to meet hers.

The figure, hair flaxen like Dan's, gives nothing away, is a slow-moving statue bearing the stamp of Ann Cartwright. Doubtless that dreadful woman has moulded her in her own likeness, trained her in calculation for serving in the shop, and in the wiles needed to gain favour in society.

'You must remember, Mrs Ferrion ...'

'I don't expect you to call me ma, though I beg you, call me Maggie.' She didn't mean to plead, but the formalities do nothing to narrow the distance between them.

'Very well. You must understand that, there is no delicate way to put it, you have been deceased in my mind since I was a young girl.'

The word, so final the chill of it creeps through the room, and even the flame in the grate flickers low.

Hannah, oh Hannah. Dumped at the workhouse and told, as many a prisoner's child was, that her mother was no longer in this world. The space her mother once occupied in her heart eaten up, instead, by the need to survive.

'It seems both you and me were misled. We've much to share, dear daughter, from all the lost years. May I call you Hannah?'

A scuffling sound draws their attention to the doorway, where a golden-haired girl has been listening. She leans in as though hoping for an invitation to join the women.

'Cora, go back to practising your letters right now.' With a flash of muslin, she is gone.

'My apologies, she is a curious child.'

Maggie has a granddaughter, a new limb grown on her family tree and her ignorant of it. She attempts to paint Hannah a picture of the other branches, the half-brothers, their successes, even presenting Charlie in a good light.

It's as if she talks underwater, the words bubbling up to the surface where they break and disappear into air, with no interest from the woman seated nearby. She tries again.

'Hannah, I got no choice but to leave you, I were taken from you, much as you were taken from me. I loved you with every heartbeat, never stopped lovin' you all these years.' Maggie is close to tears, while Hannah seems unaffected.

'Your da, Dan, he were a good man. He doted on you, would swing you up high in his arms. You'd say higher, higher, and laugh so hard, all the while me fussin' and saying take care, set her down. Surely you remember?'

A flicker of a response passes Hannah's face and is gone. Maggie is pushing too hard, she senses it and pauses.

'I have no memories beyond the workhouse and coming to Sydney. Once here, Mr and Mrs Cartwright became all the family I ever had. It serves no purpose to speak of what I can't recall.'

'Don't you wish to know about your blood kin, know how you started in life? If you're afeared I seek forgiveness, Hannah, I dare not. You got a hard life back then, no two ways about it. Though would we not gain, each of us, from coming by a little kindness in hearin' each other's story?'

'I disagree, Mrs Ferrion … Maggie. There is no gain in lodging ourselves in the past. I have a good life now, I will allow nothing to interfere with it.'

Maggie looks on in shock. She is this woman's ma, not the 'nothing' she goes on about.

Soon Hannah Hayter's stiff skirts rustle as she stands to end the visit. She has spoken honestly, Maggie will give her that.

Any idea of a warm embrace, a grateful reunion, lies in pieces on the floor. Her daughter has no desire to embrace who she truly is, or bring disrepute to her husband and child by acknowledging a convict ma.

Below the coolness her daughter must feel something, even if it's spite or wretchedness. For a moment Maggie stands in her daughter's shoes, feels the charge of it, that the man who was her anonymous patron paid her off to stay out of his life and the lives of his sons. Now Hannah repays the favour by keeping her mother out of hers.

'I am not heartless, Maggie. For that reason I make my position clear, so that you do not suffer from false hope. I will seek no further contact. I entreat you to respect my wishes and not approach me again.'

Maggie's daughter, the child yearned for, grieved for, has taken up a sword and sliced the old wound deeper, cutting through to the very marrow in her bones. Maggie bleeds pain down the hallway, through the streets, all the way to her room at the inn, where she wraps herself in a blanket and sits on a chair, too stunned to crawl into bed.

She waits three days, as long as she can bear, then sends a note to the Hayter house, for surely Hannah's resolve has softened now she's had a chance to think about her ma. They can meet again, talk properly.

The note is returned with the address crossed out, replaced with the name of the inn, written in tight, curling letters.

Next morning Maggie books a passage back to Hobart. Downcast, she will return to the only moorings she now has, the wearying work on the farm. May it hasten her to Judgement Day. Then Charlie can answer for the wickedness of destroying love not once, but twice over—the love for a mother, and the love of a wife for her husband.

Back at Brown's River she says little about the Sydney trip, making light of the townsfolk, their posturing and pretensions, ignoring mention of anything but the hospital, where her sons know she once worked.

She hides the grey bonnet at the bottom of an old trunk. Its open brim, even in her hand, is a mocking thing with the power to make her cry. She has fought the urge to take to it with the scissors, her thriftiness the only reason it's been spared. Silk and velvet, ridiculous for an old workhorse, wearing the convict mark to boot.

The boys have made some changes of their own in her absence, unaware they have tossed her aside, have started making her invisible.

Knox, for his part, has gone to the farm he will inherit.

'It makes sense, ma. He can start getting it the way he wants, make his own way with it.'

Wes is not asking for her approval, there's no hint he thinks it should have been raised with her first. If she cares

314

about what they've decided or the fact that her opinions are being ignored, she's in no mood to argue about it.

She nods. 'Looks like a native cat got through the back o' the henhouse, if one of you can see to it.'

Far from daunted by their father's death, the younger brothers are full of excitement, renewing their efforts, full of their own plans. She should feel pride in their hard work, their willingness to try new ideas. It's the way of the world, that sons will stand on the shoulders of their father and see a bigger view.

In their eagerness to value their own ideas, though, they've forgotten she may have some of her own, that she's more than a mother, maid, baker, washerwoman. They unwittingly shrink what makes her human. She doesn't blame them, her sons. They're not so different, in the end, to her daughter.

The illusions that have propped up her life are in pieces, moth-eaten remnants of all she stitched together after she left the *Lady Juliana*. She can never go back and start over.

Bitterness towards Charlie, irritation with her sons, distaste for her cold daughter, these can only eat her up if she lets them, and she will not. Her soul is the fingerprint of who she is, no other like it. She tells herself that it's worthy, beyond the gaze of others, unaffected by any description left on a page. Believing it is another matter.

In the meantime, toiling for family fills up her days, bringing her one morning to the washtub. The water has boiled before she remembers the soap is all gone. She gathers ashes from the pile dumped on the edge of the garden when she last cleaned out the fireplace, mixes them with a few handfuls of lime, and boils the paste with a quart or more of water, skimming off solid matter as it rises.

She waits for the lixivium to settle so she can pour it off the dregs at the bottom, before adding lard and a dash of castor oil. As she waits, her body begins to shake and tears fall, a queer experience out of her control, as though another woman inhabits her body and weeps.

It is family that calls her upriver to Hobart a year later. Joe's wife has birthed their first child, a daughter Betsy, and she is being baptised. It was a difficult confinement for Constance, who remains sickly even though the birth was nearly two months ago. Maggie selects dried nettle and a little tansy from her herb pouch and mixes a tonic to take to her daughter-in-law.

The baby wakes during the service at the touch of Rev Knopwood's cold hands, crying forlornly in her mother's arms. Maggie offers to take the baby from a weakened Constance, pacing with the child while the parson continues to pray.

As the girl quietens she burrows into the fold of her grandma's arm, the softness of her breast and mound of hip. The baby's soft body fits easily against Maggie, awakening a forgotten sensation in her, a tidal pull of flesh and blood belonging that reaches from one generation to another as if the years are no barrier.

In the brief visit with Hannah, back in Sydney, she had seen the inquisitive girl with her own eyes, proof that she'd become a grandma. But it never landed in her being, the proper progress of kinship had been severed. Betsy, on the other hand, is free to follow her instincts, to ask with her body for the protection and care of her granny, and Maggie is free to respond with all of herself. The baby has blessed her life with new meaning.

When Constance approaches for the girl, Maggie hands her over with reluctance.

They retire to Joe's house to wet the baby's head, soon shaking off the solemnity of the baptism with raucous laughter and singing. Maggie goes to fetch fresh glasses for latecomers when she hears loud rapping at the back door.

The lad on the doorstop removes a grubby cap, informing her he has a message for Joe from the Captain of the *Rosetta,* and must get an answer before she departs for the sealing grounds.

The sound of the celebration spills out from behind Maggie. 'He has the afternoon off for his babe's christening. I doubt he'll want the bother of business affairs.'

The fellow, barely fifteen, is undeterred, his rough demeanour belied by a natural charm.

'He'll be expectin' me, missus. If you tell him George Ranse is here, he'll be pleased to hear it, I give you my word.'

He has Maggie's full attention now. Surely it can't be.

'Ranse? Any relation to Melva Ranse, of Sydney?'

His wide grin is the answer. 'You knew my ma?'

She forgets to call Joe, with so much to ask the youngest Ranse boy. He tells her he was apprenticed as a sailor when eleven, often now journeying between Port Dalrymple, Port Jackson and sealing and whaling grounds in between, occasionally washing up in Hobart.

It turns out that after Melva Ranse and her husband walked away from the hospital tent, the honey having done its work, they went on to have four more children, developing a prosperous farm up Paramatta way.

'I nursed your da, but your ma was the one to save him. What a strong woman, young George. Don't you be forgettin' it.'

She wags a finger at him, laughing loudly.

'She's gone, missus. Some years back.'

The lad makes no attempt to disguise the hurt. She admires it, the way he stands in it despite her gaze, tenderness in his eyes yet no weakness in the set of his jaw, a face that's open for a brief moment before the shutters come down.

What a curious fellow, she thinks, hardened as a boy would be when sent to sea at a young age, though clearly he's kept hold of something true that runs deeper. She catches herself staring, then goes in search of Joe and the glasses she was fetching.

The sense of fascination remains with her long after returning to the celebration. She will see that young fellow again, she is sure of it. A shiver passes over her, foreboding bearing down. Just like her mother, the future cracks open and for the briefest moment she glimpses what it holds. George Ranse is marked in some way.

For good or bad, it will change her family forever.

CHAPTER TWENTY-TWO

BROWNS RIVER, SPRING 1827

A BROKEN HEART NEVER STOPS ACHING, but like an arthritic joint it serves no purpose to let it seize up. Maggie has kept moving as one year after another rolls on, through a drought that decimated crops, pummelling rains, the hail of an unseasonal spring that flattened tender barley shoots. They have bought a plough, enjoyed bumper harvests, and finally have convict labour to extend the farm. She marvels that they've survived a cholera outbreak, two more Governors, and rising threats from bushrangers attacking farms to steal food, valuables and sheep, sometimes a whole flock.

Only the previous year Knox, a settlement constable and pound-keeper, caught three armed convicts on his land, while Wes, now a Police Magistrate, helped escort them to justice. The Hobart gallows are not empty for long; in the past month alone twelve criminals have hung there. Lawless men, now called bushrangers, are often aided by convict labourers and shepherds and are such a threat that scared settlers are fleeing their farms.

Aborigines are in much smaller numbers on the island but are more daring, too. Their people have been shot, women raped, children stolen for labour, and trade routes and hunting grounds taken over by thousands of sheep, thanks to the Government encouraging a new breed of free settlers from the Old Country.

Little wonder, Maggie marvels, that the natives fight back, newspaper reports making them into a violent race by ignoring what sets them off.

At North West Bay a convict sawing station has taken over and no natives are seen, only a handful showing up on occasion at the mouth of Brown's River or over on Bruni.

Despite the dangers, and everything that might have defeated them, her sons have thrived.

Maggie sits on the verandah in her favourite sunny spot and counts their many blessings. Joe's business interests have gone from strength to strength, with a string of bay whaling stations, farmland, a stake in boat-building, and a licence as victualler at the City of London Arms in Campbell Street, where his family lives. All of it helped by free labour from assigned convicts. He and his father-in-law have secured the right to operate a passenger boat between Hobart Town, Green Point and New Norfolk two days a week.

The other three are capable farmers, supplying seven hundred pounds of meat at a time, sometimes more, to the Government stores. They too enjoy the benefit of convict workers. Their potatoes, grown in the deep, sandy soil beside the river, are feted as some of the island's best.

She imagines their dad watching on high with a smile. The prosperity and the balm of twelve years passing have softened her feelings towards Charlie, though the old, deep love can never be again.

As for the Sydney visit, she has long stopped torturing herself, replaying the conversation with Hannah as though it could be made to turn out differently. It resides now as an occasional needle stab in her heart, instead of the sword blow it once was. She has schooled herself to let the warm glow of Hannah's first four years fight off the memory of an unyielding woman in her fancy house.

Knox married a widow not yet a year after Joe was wed, a woman already forged by the deaths of a husband and a sixteen-month-old girl. Maggie sees something of her own toughness in Martha, trapped as a girl with a father who cared only for grog that made him a guzzling, raging beast, her mother gone for years to England, claiming an inheritance. They have given Maggie six more grandchildren.

Wes married the Cottle's daughter three years earlier. Seventeen-year-old Salome gave birth to their son two weeks after the wedding, so the house is full of life. With four men to every white woman in the colony, Gil has not yet found a wife.

One time only Maggie accepted a convict servant to work in the house. The girl was fond of Salome's toddler, taking him for a daily walk. When she failed to return one afternoon they searched, panic rising. As twilight deepened, they found her in a drunken stupor by the river, the boy nowhere to be seen. Wes came across him on the edge of the marshes at the river mouth, curled up with the wolfhound they used for hunting.

Maggie refused after that to have *a drunkard or a slattern* in the house.

Almost seven score years have slowed her down. She lets Wes' wife do the heavy lifting on washing day, gets grandchildren to carry wood for the cooking fire. She still bakes the bread, tends the kitchen garden with its vegetables and fruit trees, but the bench Gil made against the fence gets regular use.

She is sitting there late one afternoon, weak winter sun on silver hair, when Gil returns from town. She follows him into the kitchen to boil water for his tea.

'For you, ma.' He is sorting the post and tosses a letter wrapped in brown paper across the table to her. She stuffs it in her pocket while she makes the tea. Rarely is any mail of interest to her these days.

In her bedroom that evening, about to turn down the lamp, she remembers the letter. Inside the cheap outer wrapping is a neatly folded sheet of thick writing paper.

As she reads, her knees give way and she sits heavily on the side of the bed. The handwriting carries a clear voice, full of quiet confidence. It's the voice of Cora Hayter.

Her granddaughter has never forgotten the brief glimpse of her grandmama all those years ago. In a few short lines, Cora explains how she eavesdropped, heard the mystery visitor refer to her mother as 'daughter'. After she was sent from the room she pestered the maid till she confessed it was Cora's grandmother, swearing the girl to secrecy.

Had Cora been in Sydney, she writes, she would have been forbidden from reaching out. As she is now eighteen and lives in Hobart, having arrived three months ago as governess to the children of banker John Jenkins, there is no barrier now. She made inquiries to James Cartwright before leaving Sydney, and has finally found the courage to pen the letter.

> *My mother has done what she believes best for our family, I do not reproach her for that. I, on the other hand, must do what is best for me. It would make me exceedingly happy should you agree for us to meet.*

Maggie can't continue reading. She fights the impulse to pass the letter over the lamp, let the flame burn it to nothing, pretend it never existed. She has come to terms with her life, has no desire to invite in disturbance, abrade the skin on old scars.

Yet the girl is of the same flesh, has the same determination. Surely that must count for something, balance out the harsh knockback from Hannah twelve years ago?

Maggie curls in bed, cold despite the opossum skin blanket, her mind in a whirl. If she chooses not to see the girl will she die sorry there wasn't a chance for a bond to grow? If she does want to know Cora the boys will have to be told, her past will be laid bare, and what will it mean for them, for their children's prospects of marriage or prosperity?

Maggie rolls over, taking the weight off her painful right hip. She will meet the girl, with interest and warmth. To turn her request down would make her as cold-hearted as Hannah. A single meeting, to nail down what Cora wants.

Ten thousand people now live in Hobart, and like a needle in a haystack one of them her estranged granddaughter.

Maggie travels to meet her full of worry, and with a sliver of hope. It may be that Cora can sway her mother, help her see that Maggie's no threat, maybe encourage a letter or two.

Cora has Sundays off and one Saturday a month. Travel is discouraged on the Lord's day so Maggie waits four weeks to sail upriver for the meeting, pretending she will visit Joe. The best course, she decides, will be to avoid any awkwardness by stretching their legs, perhaps up Barracks Hill, where a promenade leads to a small park near the military base.

A lone woman waits on the new causeway to the Hunter Island wharf, hands clasping a drawstring purse. As Maggie approaches the figure comes to meet her, the young face breaking into a smile.

'Thank you for coming. I was unsure if you would, given the manner of your departure from our house those years past.'

She is taller than Maggie, surprises her by reaching down immediately to kiss her on the cheek. If her granddaughter is nervous, she shows no sign of it. Maggie, though, needs movement to settle herself before she can speak of the past.

'Shall we stretch our legs?'

They begin slowly working their way up from the harbour, faces turned to the mountain. Some days it looms over townsfolk as a foe, hurling down daggers of ice or winds full of chill from snow. Today Maggie wants to see it as protector, as she must strive to be with Cora, respecting what they share in their bloodline.

'I hold no ill will for your ma, Cora. The visit were a painful business, yet I did come to a reckonin' on why she hadn't the desire for contact. I wish it were different, though it weren't in me to stand against her wishes when she was so terribly clear.' *Clear as cut glass and just as cold.*

The girl tucks her arm through Maggie's, the gesture of familiarity disconcerting to the older woman, intent on biting back any mean spirited remarks.

'Grandmother … may I call you that?' Maggie nods at the stranger on her arm.

'You're the only grandparent I have. Papa's parents are now gone, though I never met them because they were in the Old Country. I hope it doesn't sound selfish, for I have no wish to be, but I need to know who I am, what's shaped mother and me.'

'Ann Cartwright had quite a hand in that.' Maggie purses her lips, annoyed that the sharp rebuke has escaped, striking out at one who is blameless.

Cora gives no indication she is offended.

'It's not the same though, is it, as what we are given by our forebears in the way of eye colour, hair colour, traits, or temperament?'

'True, Cora, it ain't. Beggin' your pardon for speaking so sharp.'

In lashing out, Maggie has released anger, giving space for curiosity. The pair are soon deep in conversation, Maggie answering Cora's many questions. The sky is overcast, but it is as if the sun only shines on the two of them. They stroll until Maggie can walk no longer, then find an inn where they are served tea.

The past flows forth in Maggie, the pleasure of sharing it a relief, like lancing a boil. She's never talked so freely about Dan or young Hannah, not even with Charlie. The old feelings for her girl come back to life, flushing out years of dross, invigorating her aging body.

'Your ma, Cora, I never stopped lovin' her, and I know whatever happened to Dan it were the same for him. He did his best, but a weak moment got 'im, and in the end I'm to blame for what went down for me and her.'

Maggie glances at Cora, wants to offer a brighter note. 'Funny how things go. Without all that, you wouldn't be here, so I've cause for thanks.' They smile at each other.

When they finish, Cora walks her back to the waterfront, hugs her goodbye. The young woman's arms are strong as they wrap around Maggie. In their embrace she feels at last that they belong, that Cora is of her, as she did when she held baby Betsy.

There is no question of it, she will tell her sons the truth.

'We'll meet again, Cora, hopefully many a time. First I must tell my family. The boys know nothin' of your ma or you, Charlie made sure of that.'

Tears spring to Cora's eyes.

'I'm so grateful we've met. It saddens me to think we may have missed this chance.'

Sailing home, Maggie is light as a summer cloud, can only think of her family gathered around the big table at the farmhouse, Cora in their midst.

The news is not something to blurt out in a rush, she must take care. It may shake the foundations for her sons, who hold their beloved da dear, and rattle the way they see her. They will soon, however, come to see the rightness of Cora belonging in the family. Maggie's in no doubt of it.

Joe's the most sensible one, she will bide her time and start with him.

He and Constance now have three more daughters and a son. At the end of the month the family comes down the Derwent to Brown's River, showing off his new schooner, *Contest*, soon to be fitted out as a whaler, ready to leave on the first spring tide.

At the house, Joe is distracted, fusses over Constance. Each of her births has drained her a little more, and since the youngest arrived five years earlier she has suffered terribly from the bleeding disease and painful cramps.

Maggie wonders if she should wait for another time till her son is more settled, though it could be a long while, with Constance showing no sign of improvement.

After the midday meal, Maggie decides it's now or never. She draws Joe away from the family, pretending to need advice on some papers kept in the desk out the back. At first he is shocked at her news, as much by the secret as the realisation that, at thirty-five years old, he might not really know his mother and father.

As she talks she watches him grapple with the two people who step from the shadows of his ma and pa, claiming stories that leave him drowning in a wave of ignorance.

'I don't know what to make of it, ma. Truly, this is quite the surprise.' He shakes his head, then steps towards her, plucking at her sleeve. 'Yet I do know how I feel about my daughters, so I can see this must be dreadful for you.'

The dash of sympathy emboldens Maggie.

'Your da, he had yer best interests in mind, but now you've all found success, surely it's no skin off anyone's nose for Cora to be welcomed.'

Joe is so quiet she can hear his breathing, almost hear him assembling his thoughts in his careful way.

'Look ma, I don't think we should stand in the way of you seeing Cora, and I'm not against meeting her, but she should be introduced as our distant cousin. Then there's no need for folks to know anything more.'

A scheme, she hadn't expected that. Now she is the one surprised.

'Joe, I need her to be in her rightful place in our family. Her ma may never have anythin' to do with me, so Cora's my only hope of having family all together.'

She hadn't meant to cry, but without warning her face is wet.

'She can, ma. This way she can, without any backlash for us.'

Her own boy, refusing to let her muddy the fine reputation he's built as a businessman and victualler, the newspapers calling him a respected colonist. He doesn't need to spell it out, but he is his father's son. The way she came from England's a burden to him.

What of his sister, or his niece? Maggie expects a few questions, but he shows no interest in them.

The conversation has come to a halt. Maggie's spirit is worn down, scraped thin by the friction of so many days left behind her, the last one fast rubbing out the new one to come along.

At least it's an arrangement of sorts. She agrees to his proposal, on condition he leave it to her to tell the others.

'It ain't for you to shoulder this duty, Joe. I be the one to break it to 'em.'

Another week passes before she can speak to Knox on his own. He has dropped in on the way back from town to his farm, bringing their share of an order of seeds. He finds her in the vegetable garden at the back of the house.

She explains the situation carefully, conscious he's more prickly than Joe, less inclined to patience.

'It's not okay for her to waltz in as though she has the right. She and her ma, they done nothing to build up these farms, or the old one on Norfolk for that matter. We did the hard yards, busted our guts, every single one of us.'

'No need for worryin' about your due when I go, Cora wants naught from me. Her ma and pa have made provision for her, and she's content with that.'

He snorts, rolling his eyes.

'Yeah, that's what she says for now.'

Maggie can't persuade him otherwise. He vows he will never accept her as part of the family or have anything to do with her.

'And the others bloody well shouldn't, either.'

Her second-born son, so stubborn. Always has been. She wants to remind him of the sacrifices she's made to give him a prosperous life, but what good would that do. She thinks of her own father, broken by hard labour while she saw a better life for the taking.

'I beg you, Knox, don't be doin' the same as your da and keep her from family.'

It was a mistake summoning the memory of his father, she knows it the minute she's spoken.

'Do as you like, just don't include me.' He collects his goods and is gone.

Gil is alone with her in the kitchen next morning, mending a boot, with Wes and his wife gone to the fields, the children running amok outside.

Precious Gil, the one who looks into his mother's eyes as she speaks about the past, sees the deep well of sorrow, made worse by his father's well-intentioned deceit.

'Oh ma, what a thing to carry. I see now why you looked so heartbroken after Sydney.'

She outlines Joe's proposal carefully. She's already agreed that Cora's true place in the family will be covered up, so there's no gain in setting Gil against his older brother.

'If that's what you want, ma. Hard to see that telling the truth will cause a fuss. Scratch the surface of any colonist, and though he deny it, he'll bleed with at least some convict blood.'

Wes, when she gets him on his own, is matter of fact about the situation. Sees why his father acted the way he did, why he would hide Maggie's conviction, her husband and child. Her son's practical response is grit in her shoe, causing her to fire up.

'It were all unfair, Wes, what he did on his own account. No chance for me to choose for myself.'

'Yeah well, it changes nothing in the end, does it? You clearly plan to see Cora.'

'Changes nothing? Changes nothing, Wes? I were kept from my daughter, my only daughter, your sister, and my granddaughter. That's somethin', it's a hurt that never goes away.'

He is quick to correct her. 'My half-sister, ma.'

She needs to calm herself. Wes is not one for shouting or arguing, he will think what he thinks of his da, that's not for her to change. What matters is that he agrees to Cora being part of the family.

Wes supports Joe's plan. Best she not be the granddaughter, but a distant cousin of well-regarded settlers.

With the boys all informed, Maggie is keen for Cora to visit the farm soon. They wait till she has a Saturday free from her governess duties, both deciding that it's best for her to use the river service and not get one of the boys to fetch her. While the Ferrions now have a four-oared boat with sail for delivering meat and grain to the Commissariat and bringing back heavy supplies to the two farms, neither of the women want to invite strain into the visit.

Maggie leaves beef roasting over coals to wait on the beach. She wants to go alone, but Wes' three-year-old daughter, Lill, refuses to let granny out of her sight. The two of them walk onto wet sand near the water's edge, one leaping and spinning, the other leaving slow, deep footprints.

The surf is up so they go along to the river mouth, where a dinghy will have to be rowed in and the passenger let out in the calm place behind the curving sandbar.

As Maggie stands on the beach, stomach churning, her mind turns unexpectedly to Charlie. A sense of his disapproval sweeps through her, that she would dare bring the girl to the farm. She shakes it off as the vessel appears around the headland. Who knows after all these years what he might think? And damn his hide if he would stand in the way of a family reunion now.

Cora is nervous when she arrives. Maggie is glad Lill's there with her innocence and excitement, keen to make friends with the new arrival, who bends down to meet the girl with an easy warmth.

Cora wears a pale brown dress, not nearly as showy as the one she wore in Hobart, where she must maintain appearances as a governess. Maggie is quietly pleased she wants to show the family she's not so different to them.

Knox was invited for the midday meal, the reply a grunt before walking off. To Maggie's surprise his wife, Martha, has said she's happy to meet Cora, probably because of her own origins. Odd, Maggie thinks, that it has become a wedge between the two of them, as though history is determined to repeat itself.

Cora has already agreed to be known as a cousin. The grandchildren will not meet her as one of them.

Lill leads them home, full of chatter and the joy at having a new person to share it with. She bursts through the door to announce their arrival to her mother, Salome, who is laying out plates.

Martha is already there with her three, and the room is full of children from the toddler to six-year-old, all drawn to Cora as they might the pied piper, shouting and jostling, pulling at her hands to get her attention before Maggie can even finish introductions.

The clattering of knives and forks and the ruckus of the children covers a wariness as the meal proceeds. Maggie sees her sons avoid Cora's eyes and say little, while the wives are friendly, full of questions. She tells herself to let the visit unfold as it must, that the point of it is for everyone to get to know Cora. Yet she finds she can't bear to leave matters to themselves.

With most of the beef, potatoes, turnips and beans eaten, Maggie decides to speak up. She calls for the children to hush.

'We're so glad to have you at our table, Cora. Welcome to our home, welcome.' She pauses to blink, stop her eyes welling up.

'I long since thought this day would never come, so it be a great blessin'.'

The wives are smiling, the children scuffling but quiet. Maggie feels her heart will burst. Cora is smiling too, opens her mouth as if to speak, but before she can Wes' voice cuts in, calm and firm.

'We're pleased for you, ma. We know how important this is. Me and my brothers, though, we've no need of getting to know Miss Hayter. No offence, Cora, but this is naught to do with us.'

Not one of the adults moves, not even Maggie. Wes turns to Cora.

'Don't get me wrong. Come to the farm when you like, but let's not fool ourselves, it's for ma's sake, not ours.'

He stands, wipes his hands down his trousers as though something sticky, unpleasant needs removing. 'Now if you don't mind, I'll get back to my work.'

Gil stammers, struggling to choose which side he's on. Maggie watches him battle it out, wonders which loyalty will win.

'I'd best get back to it, too.'

Martha is the first to speak after the men have gone.

'Don't you mind them, Cora. They'll come round.'

CHAPTER TWENTY-THREE

BROWNS RIVER, 1828-1832

THE TRIP UPRIVER TO HOBART no longer agrees with Maggie's old bones, so Cora is the one who travels every month or two to visit.

Knox keeps to his own place when Cora's around, remains aloof, though Gil shows no issue with the young woman's presence now and then in their kitchen. Wes has thawed a little, not enough for Maggie to say he's on friendly terms with his niece, but at least makes attempts at polite conversation.

Cora, for her part, has remained understanding of the mixed reception, perhaps bolstered by the exuberant greetings of the children each time she visits Brown's River.

'I don't want to cause trouble, granny. It's enough for me to have time with you.'

After a few visits, Maggie must raise the subject neither of them wishes to discuss.

'Your ma, Cora. Have you sent word, told her we meet?'

Cora lowers her eyes to the tea she is sipping. 'I have, yes. I felt it only right to tell her the truth.'

Maggie waits. She wants to know the outcome, though perhaps it's better not to. If she sits here, shuts down this conversation, it may be kinder than hearing the path to Hannah is forever closed.

'I know you're hoping, granny, that mother will come round. I've truly hoped so, too.'

Here it comes. She'll wager her daughter remains unmoved, feels no quickening in her blood towards her old ma.

'She's shown some interest in your circumstances.' Cora is softening the blow, Maggie sees it, holds her nerve against what will come next.

'Unfortunately, she can't be persuaded to write to you. I'm so sorry.' She doesn't need to say that her mother disapproves of Cora's visits. It's written all over her face.

'I will keep trying, I promise.'

Maggie's flicker of a smile says she understands the situation. 'Enough talk, now.' She leads Cora to the garden where she's teaching her how to grow herbs and vegetables, a skill Cora's unlikely to need if she marries well, though one she has professed genuine interest in learning.

'It's the same as nurturing the seeds of young minds, granny, only with dirt on your hands.' She chuckles at her own joke, a young woman who laughs often and freely.

'Your pa, Cora, you rarely speak of him. He is well?'

'Very well, thank you. He works hard, I hardly saw him when I was growing up. It's why I enjoy seeing your sons working with their children nearby, the older ones helping, a more natural way to grow don't you think?'

Maggie hears the yearning in her voice, through the silence between them understands that Cora carries what her mother has denied in herself, a longing for the completion of family. It's a longing Maggie knows only too well, serving to bring her closer to her granddaughter.

Cora was raised in a household privileged by learning and money while her half-brothers had neither, yet they are the ones to have benefitted from belonging in a circle of kin.

Maggie has not the gift of clairvoyance, both a blessing and a curse. Had she second sight she would see the future of her grandchildren unwind in the years ahead. One grandson a prominent ship-builder, another a solicitor and parliamentarian. A granddaughter marrying into one of the island's wealthiest, most long-lived farming dynasties. Others with mixed destinies, like the master mariner who drowns, the abandoned mother of seven who keeps her family together by running a house of ill repute, and the grandson widowed twice by pulmonary consumption.

More than one is destined to have a child die at birth or soon after, while Joe, temperate in his ways, will live to see one of his daughters become a total toss pot.

No, the future's not a destination to which Maggie can travel, cause for her to be grateful. Best not to know when it might be coming for you. As it happens, she is hoeing weeds in her beloved garden, her back warmed by sun, when it finds her, a flock of black cockatoos screeching overhead to announce its presence.

As she glances up at the bright yellow flashes on their tails, her right arm stops dragging the handle, goes numb and drops by her side, then the right leg gives way. She falls softly onto the soil as if it's a feather mattress, sinking into the turned dirt, her mouth moving but unable to form words to call for help.

Salome finds her, light spring rain beading on her hair, face turned to the side, drool spreading from the corner of her mouth, and eyes full of terror.

'Ma, dear God, what's happened?' She lifts Maggie's cold head onto her lap and begins screaming for Wes, the farm hands, anyone who can lift her inside.

Apoplexy, the surgeon announces after the examination. 'Bed rest, lots of fluids, keep her calm. I'm not one for bloodletting in these cases, or any painful and cruel endeavours, particularly for the elderly.'

He administers a dose of belladonna immediately, then another an hour later for her difficulty in speaking, leaving a bottle of arnica, one drop to be administered daily to reduce paralysis in the right limbs and swelling in the foot.

Maggie lies on the bed, a lumpen shape, for three days. She dozes often, hears voices, sees figures come and go as in a dream. If she stops trying to force her limbs and mouth to do what they once did, a peaceful feeling comes over her, as though she no longer has a body.

On the fourth day, she manages to speak in a drawl, the words slow and thick. Knox is sitting closest, hears her first word.

'What did she say?' Martha is at the foot of the bed.

'What does it matter what she bloody said. Come on, we need to get home.'

As they leave, Martha presses him for an answer.

'Hannah, she damn well said Hannah.'

The return of Maggie's speech coincides with recovery of some sensation in her right limbs, though she cannot use them gainfully. Movement causes pain but she wills herself to keep trying. Either she stops eating and dies here in bed, or she fights to regain use of her hand and leg.

Salome has been feeding her, perhaps because she can't bear her own discomfort at seeing her mother-in-law spilling food with her left hand. Maggie insists, with grunts and a few decipherable words, that she will feed herself no matter the mess. She keeps a clean spoon on the bed, spending waking moments trying to grip it with her useless right hand.

Gradually, in the next few weeks, she recovers the use of her fingers, though she cannot raise the right arm far, and it must be tied in a loose sling above her waist. Next she moves to a chair propped against a wall so she can lean on it, building up her muscles and balance for sitting while the others pretend to look away.

After breakfast and in the evenings, the adults take turns holding her under the arms, one on either side, so she can shuffle along and strengthen her legs. A month or so later she can manage to hobble independently with a stick Gil has cut from tea-tree, though the right foot drags badly.

She is left with permanent palsy on the right side of her face, one eye staring ahead, half her mouth frozen. She carries a large piece of cloth in her pocket to wipe the spittle that leaks from the corner.

Her unsteady gait, even with the stick, confines her to the house and verandah, where Wes has set up a chair to which he has attached thick handles either side so she can't tip out. Gil has made a pretty side table from the fiddle back burl of a musk tree. It's their way of acknowledging their ma's state is permanent, that she will no longer be a reassuring backbone to their days, glimpsed over the distance from one field or another as she weeds the vegetable garden, carries water to the fowls, hangs their wet trousers and shirts on the long washing line.

She sits outside for hours, away from the busyness and noise of family life in the house, chin often on her chest. It is the crying that disturbs her family the most, tears often falling for no apparent reason. It disturbs Maggie too, as though a stranger within grieves for something, though try as she might she can't recall what it is.

Mary Cottle visits often, as do other friends. It's as if they must always make one last visit in case there can never be another. It amuses Maggie. She tells them, word by halting word, that she's had a good life but it's not done yet.

With her condition more stable a sense of relief pervades their lives. Their matriarch has survived. Maggie's one keen eye watches on, sees the love that surrounds her, pushed aside over the years by work and striving.

With nothing to do, she rests on the verandah in the still place of no expectations, nothing to force, a knowing that all is well without the need for an ounce of effort. Sometimes she wonders if she's slipped the veil and gone to the netherworld without noticing.

Wes has sent word to Cora, who comes as soon as she can, walking three hours alone on the rough, muddy track, having ignored warnings of the dangers of escaped convicts or bushrangers. She reaches the farm early, when her grandmother may have energy for a visitor. Having not seen her granny at her worst in recent weeks she only sees what Maggie has lost, not the hard-won gains.

She stands on the verandah in her filthy boots, the bottom of her dress stained grey from wading across the ford, trying not to cry, wretchedness writ large on her face.

Maggie is the one to soothe her, placing her left hand on Cora's arm when the young woman sits, setting off a flood of tears.

'I'm sorry granny, so very sorry for you.'

Maggie doesn't remember what she ate for breakfast, how she got to the verandah, the names of her two new grandchildren. What she does know is that Cora isn't talking about her granny's illness.

'No frettin', dear.'

Cora cries harder, pulling herself together only when Salome approaches with the teapot and joins them.

'She tires easily, I'm afraid.' Salome has become protective of Maggie, fussing over her as she does her children. 'Best keep your visit short, my dear.'

When Cora makes her farewells, she hugs her grandmother gently. 'I'm terribly fond of you, granny.'

Maggie wants her to know not to worry, that she's found acceptance about never seeing Hannah, for that's why the young woman is full of tears. Her tongue is too tired to shape the letters, so she remains mute as Cora departs, waving from the garden gate, carrying a small gunny sack Salome has filled with turnips, lemons, and carrots. Gil takes the sack from her and waves to his ma as well. He will accompany Cora as far as Mount Nelson, where she will be in sight of Hobart.

On the giant scales of the universe, Maggie's decline is balanced by a surge in her sons' good fortune, the men flourishing, each in their own way.

Gil has succeeded with his application to rent fifteen hundred acres, taking over Wood's farm nearby, and has stables in town the Commandant uses in return for a substantial fee. In October, Wes secures the tender to rent five hundred acres on North West Bay Rivulet. Joe's whaleboat, *Tasmanian Lad*, wins a hundred pounds in a rowing race against a British ship's crew unbeaten in Singapore and Sydney, cause for the swelling of local pride.

Win or lose, to Maggie it's now all the same. Day by day, week by week, she lives from the untouchable self, the one who never needed a title or moniker, She revels in the sound of children's voices at play, bird calls in the mornings, the howl of wind even as it jerks the heads of gum trees, causing her to tug her shawl a bit tighter.

Some days she thinks of Charlie, wonders if he'll come to meet her when she crosses over. The heat of her temper has cooled, they can be together again as friends, as the lovers they once were. And Dan? The memories have gone out, as an unsmoked pipe will die and go cold.

Cora continues to visit, has taken to bringing a book and reading aloud to her grandma in a voice as melodic as the birds. She does not mention her mother again, and Maggie is grateful the young woman has found a way to spend time by her side without anguish.

The family can never be whole, every one of her children gathered around the same table. She was a selfish woman wanting it, believing that needing it badly for herself mattered more than the wishes of others.

The day will come when she's buried beside Charlie, her tombstone saying for all time that she's mother to Joe, Knox, Wes and Gil, no mention of Hannah. But her bones, they will never lie, they carry her daughter's mark for eternity.

St David's Church, opened in all its glory seven years earlier in the centre of Hobart, well away from the burial ground, is packed for the October funeral. The death of a young person is inclined to draw a large crowd to the cedar pews, let alone the wife of a prominent publican and businessman.

Constance's coffin is carried in by Joe and his brothers, all eyes turning to watch, Gil recounts to Maggie when he returns home. She insisted on attending, despite her infirmity, but they were all against the idea, citing the effort needed to get her there, though the main concern, kept from her, was the fear she might get emotional and cause a scene. Two years since the dropsy and she still cries at the slightest thing.

Gil promised to give her a full account and now he delivers on the undertaking, starting with the slow walk behind the coffin from the City of London Arms, Joe a little portly in his hat wrapped in a black crepe band, and wearing black gloves.

Her eldest son is not a religious man, though he has paid pew rents of ten shillings a year for himself, Constance and the children, giving them the privilege of sitting among the front rows of the church, as befits the family of a successful man.

Maggie imagines the coffin near the altar, hushed folk kneeling on embroidered hassocks the colour of old blood. Dear Constance lying stiff in the finest white satin Joe could buy, no more cold baths and compression on her belly, free at last from the disease eating at her womb. Her four daughters and their only son at the inn, huddled and tearful in their quarters with the convict kitchen maid, who has been keeping an eye on the two littlest ones.

Gil has brought home a copy of *The Tasmanian* newspaper. He reads Maggie the obituary, how Joe's wife died after a long and painful illness which she bore with the greatest fortitude. Always easier, Maggie thinks, to see it as a badge of honour, the bearing of pain without complaint after the business of giving birth. Better that Constance had railed against the disease, died fighting, flailing, than quietly succumbing, letting others believe she was a weak woman, the illness a kind of failing on her part.

She has left a large family to deplore the loss of an affectionate, exemplary wife and mother. A faultless woman, oh yes, another way of saying her beloved daughter-in-law fulfilled her duty without disturbing others, making sure she'd be another woman the world soon forgets.

Gil has entreated Joe, on Maggie's behalf, to bring the young ones to the farm. They arrive ten days later, the children neatly dressed, hair combed, so the world can see her son is up to the task of caring for them on his own.

Salome is not one for idle hands, even in grief, organising Betsy, fourteen, and Violet, twelve, to help with the cooking. The younger three, Ada at nine, Joe junior, seven, and May, five years, are free to run squealing outside with their cousins.

Joe finds Maggie on the verandah despite the unseasonal spring chill, a blanket around her shoulders. She has so much she wants to say to her grieving son, but the strong feelings glue her tongue to the top of her mouth and all she makes are low growling sounds. She cries with frustration.

'Don't cry, ma. There's been enough of that. We must look to the children and the future.'

He sits so close she can feel the warmth of his shoulder, the stiffness of the effort he makes to be stoic. As her chin lowers to her chest, the children run past in a burst of laughter and shrieks, chasing chickens to the bottom of the garden. When Maggie doesn't move, Joe decides she must be asleep.

'I loved her so much, had more love for her than I ever thought possible. We were true friends, ma, not many can say so as husband and wife. I don't know how I'll do this without her.'

Maggie makes no sound or movement, lets him lean forward, head in hands to hold the unbearable heaviness, as he sobs. Her presence is shrinking these days, but she gives him all of it, fighting against sleep till the choking cries subside. He is quiet by the time Salome calls them to eat.

After the plates are cleared Betsy pulls up a chair at the end of the table to sit alongside her granny. She holds out her hand, uncurling the fingers to reveal on her palm a plain silver locket on a chain. She opens it, showing Maggie a curl of her mother's hair secured inside.

'She knew she was going, granny. She made me cut it, gave me the locket for it.' Her hand trembles a little, though she sheds no tears. Maggie sees her fifteen-year-old self in her granddaughter, who has helped care for her ma for months. She works her lips, pleased when they form the right words.

'Not yer fault, Betsy love. Only God. Could save her.' She reaches over with her good hand to hold the outstretched palm. 'Not yer fault.' Betsy has understood the clumsy speech. She leans over and hugs Maggie for a long time.

When the girl straightens up, her voice slices the air between them. 'Well, it's done now. Seems I'm to care for the others. Not like I got a choice in it.'

The girl's mix of pain and anger puts Maggie to mind of Hannah, how it was when her ma was wrenched away, with far less support than Betsy's given.

In her granddaughter's eyes she finally makes sense of Hannah's coldness. It was all she had left to shield herself, a barricade she dare not drop, even now. Hannah has made it the thread from which she's spun her character, and picking it undone would unravel her sense of who she is.

The realisation soothes her, makes Hannah's rejection less hurtful, more about an orphan's need to survive.

Knox has given up on Nash's Farm, says the soil was poorer there, not yielding to his work the way it should. He's been gone five years, left it to Wes and Gil to manage, taking his family to a farm he rents at Black Brush, on the Jordan River north east of Hobart. He is doing well, by all accounts, and Maggie is pleased to hear he has engaged a teacher for his children. London-trained, no less. An education will give them a leg up.

Gil has returned from town and is relaying the news of the tutor, along with what else he gleaned while downing a pot of beer with Joe at the Arms.

'A drunkard, I'll wager. Why else would he be stuck out at Black Brush? Joe says he's got a reputation as a good musician, plays piano. Gawdsakes, he's a drawing master. What farm kids need with drawing is beyond me.'

He's on a roll about Knox, saying nothing about Joe. Maggie wonders if there's something wrong that he doesn't want to tell her. She struggles to ask, while Gil continues.

'One of his bull's strayed, worth a fortune o' course, saw the notice in the gazette myself. You know how fast an animal like that'll be made to disappear.'

At last he notices the guttural sound she is making.

'Joe?'

'Yeah, he's good ma. Also saw Betsy, not the others, though she says they're all doing okay.'

Maggie's puzzled, convinced Gil is keeping something from her, but when she tries to figure out what question to ask, the cloud in her head is no help. She is forced to leave it be.

Gil walks off without saying what else Joe has heard on the grapevine. Knox is in trouble financially. The Sheriff's Office is set to advertise the auction of a hundred bushels of his wheat in the straw if debts cannot be met.

During the coming weeks, Maggie's aware of hushed words spoken between Wes and Gil. She may as well be an old coat hanging on a hook for all the credit they give her in having eyes and ears that still work perfectly well.

It falls to Wes one evening to explain.

'Remember how I got that tender, ma, to rent fifteen hundred acres down at the Bay, near where Gil got his five hundred?'

She nods, knows they've been given convicts to work the farms, though the boys go there often to check on progress.

'Well, Knox is coming back. I'm making him my overseer.'

She tips her head to the good side, indicating she wants to know why.

'To tell you the truth, he's gone bust. We've only just gotten to the bottom of it. He was persuaded to go guarantor for a neighbour and now the fellow's defaulted.

'He's in the Debtor's Prison, but I'm going to sort it out, I promise. No need for you to worry. There's a house on the farm at the Bay, and Martha and the kids will move there, wait for him to get out.'

Tears spill down Maggie's face.

'It's okay, ma. All of us brothers will do right by him.'

Maggie doesn't have the wherewithal to tell Wes she cries because, what with Constance dying young and now this, it's starting to feel the good life their family has wrested from the wilderness is turning bad.

The next event makes her wonder if Knox is blighted, paying for his part in what happened years ago with the natives down at the Bay.

His eldest son, apprenticed six months earlier to Hobart wheelwright Will Copperwheat, has been accused of stealing four shillings and sixpence from a basin on his employer's mantlepiece, and in the heat of the moment has fled.

The accuser, Mrs Copperwheat, immediately marched to the *Hobart Courier* office and placed a notice in her husband's name, warning the public from harbouring the thief.

The first Maggie knows of it is when the boy turns up at the house two days later.

Wes meets him at the door, refusing to let him in.

'I know what you done. Get away, we'll not be having you here. You're a disgrace to the family.'

'I didn't do it. I don't know who took the money. I tell you true, it weren't me.'

Wes continues to block the doorway.

'Turn yourself in, there's a notice gone round saying there's a warrant out for you.'

Maggie sees the lad, barely fifteen, is crying, begging for help. *Four shillings, for chrissakes,* she wants to say to Wes. *Let the boy in.*

Before she can move, he is gone. This is what it's come down to. Her son denouncing his nephew as a thief, knowing full well his own mother was one.

Fortunately for the boy, he has a stroke of luck. Martha's da happens to go into the same shop as Mrs Copperwheat, and when pressed for proof the lad was responsible has none for the grandfather. It is clear she has blamed the first person she clapped eyes on after noticing the theft.

Knox decides to sue Mr Copperwheat in a Supreme Court civil case. Wes goes to the hearing, on his return telling Maggie that the Chief Justice agreed the Ferrion reputation had been slandered. He ordered the wheelwright to pay twenty pounds in damages.

Wes, somewhat contrite after assuming the boy's guilt, praises the eloquent work of lawyer Joseph Gellibrand, and the fairness of the justice's remarks.

'Twenty pounds is a sizeable sum, ma, but you can't put a price on good standing.'

Maggie's mind goes to strange places these days, as though rehearsing for life without flesh holding it back. Some days it flies, soars so high all she sees is the river, the land, marshes and endless ocean, and her barely a speck. What it means she can't tell, though it places her as part of something greater, much bigger than the farm, the district, the island. She feels oddly at peace with her paltry part in it.

Sometimes she pictures Charlie coming to meet her, or Dan, or both. For all she knows strange things may be possible on the other side, though in the celestial ledger will she warrant a companion or a hellhound baying for her soul?

On darker days, she knows nothing beyond the failing body that traps her. She's not yet a corpse, yet is restless as one whose spirit has failed to ascend, chained to the Earth by its sins. Had she the ability she'd stand from the chair, walk away, keep walking until she had no skin on her feet, till nothing remained of her failings, the dark flaws.

Maggie wants to tell her sons to fetch a sin-eater when her time comes, someone to absolve her, though she doesn't know of a single one in Van Diemen's Land, a thought that gives her a laugh because if ever a place needed one, it's sorely this island.

With a jolt, she wonders if she got it all wrong. Maybe the weight that presses down shows she is the one who is sin-eater. She's been blind to it, her soul slowly tangled in final words spoken by loosened tongues of the dying, drawn towards the shadows while tending corpses.

Their sins have come upon her with not even a few pence of payment.

What bitter thoughts. Her soul has been tarnished by her own deeds, hard enough to carry without the sins of others sticking to it like blowflies on birch tar.

In London, once, she saw a sin-eater do his work for a couple of coins, called by the wife of an old fellow from Herefordshire when the body was still warm, Maggie waiting to lay him out. What sins the wife feared her husband had not atoned for Maggie couldn't say, but the woman begged the fellow to do his best.

The man, poverty-thin, hungry-eyed, asked the wife to mound salt on the dead fellow's chest. Then she placed a piece of bread on the salt and passed across a bowl of beer. The sin-eater ate the bread and guzzled the beer in one draught, swallowing the dead man's sins with it, at least he said so.

'I give easement and rest now to thee, dear man. Come not down the lanes or in our meadows. And for thy peace, I pawn my own soul. Amen'

After the prayer he melted into the night without giving a name, for he would face punishment if caught. Only the parsons were meant to absolve the dead, though the risk was no match for an empty belly or a craving for grog.

Did she look the sin-eater in the eye as he sat by the bed, see the evil he'd absorbed during visits to the

350

lamented? Was that the moment it started, a key turning in a lock? She searches within herself for a memory, desperate to prove she spared him no glance as he walked out the door, that he left her untouched.

The strain of looking inward exhausts her. Sin-maker, sin-eater, cursed, cursing, blessed, blessing. Tomorrow she'll wake and with luck her mind will soar again. The marrow of her life will be one, gathered into a single, singing whole, and none of the past will matter.

Destiny is not a thing granted, she understands at last. Death creeps closer, pulling back the curtain to show fate was a force she lived one step at a time, choices made or unheeded shaping the hills and the steep, dark valleys of her life.

She stretches her good leg, easing the pain in her hip. Her sins have plagued her for so long, divided her spirit. She's running out of time, wrestled them forever. Will she go at peace, knowing in her heart she's a worthy woman, or face eternity as a hungry ghost?

The question moves through the air, shifts this way and that, doubling back on itself. With a jolt, Maggie sees the verdict can only come from beyond her death, not from her, not from the Heavenly Father, but from the Earth-bound.

She looks up to the ceiling, gives thanks for the newfound freedom as all the old anguish lifts. The burden is not hers, it will fall to those who carry her fingerprint. Her children, their children, the generations to come, they'll be the ones to pass judgment on her worth. They will do so in what they carry forward in their hearts and deeds, in how they live out their own days.

Two years pass as Maggie grows weaker, though not so much that she can't recognise the guideposts leading her down the final road travelled.

In bed one night, everyone else asleep, she decides it's finally time.

She lost the ability to speak weeks earlier. It came as a relief, no more struggling to form words, to get understood. No need for any of that now. Yesterday she began refusing sips of water, no need for that either.

They can't see it, her family, but she's climbed a mountain since the fall in the vegetable garden, scaled the layers of her character, steered around failings and strengths, picked her way through patterns in her temperament, higher and higher to what remains when all the rest is gone.

She is within reach of what endures, and tonight it will release her. She will fly like the silver bosun on Norfolk, up into the wide blue sky towards the sun.

EPILOGUE
HOBART TOWN, JUNE 1832

THE PROCESSION PREPARES TO LEAVE the City of London Arms at noon under a pewter sky, blacker around the summit of the mountain.

The body was rowed upriver that morning by Maggie's four sons, the coffin lid closed, though they have seen their mother at rest.

Salome found her gone in bed the day before. She and Martha, helped by the older granddaughters, carefully bathed the face and limbs, brushed the hair, prepared Maggie with gentleness, as she once honoured the dead.

Joe arrived at the farm late in the evening, having made funeral arrangements. They ate together then took turns for the overnight vigil. Gil was first to voice what they all felt. They sorrowed at the loss of their ma, but they had no wish for the body that failed her, that leaked, could no longer hold her upright or speak her needs, they had no wish for it to go on. It was for the best.

Reverend William Bedford arrives unexpectedly at the inn before they leave, remarking that it's only right he lead the procession for such a well-known colonial family. They wait, heads politely bowed, while he delivers an extempore prayer, then the coffin is carried to the bier. Gil, standing behind Joe, squeezes his brother's shoulder briefly, letting him know he remembers the first coffin to go out the side door of the inn.

The mourners slowly file down the street, the four sons standing tall, two on either side of the bier, its wooden-rimmed wheels juddering a little as they steer it along.

There will be no service in the big church, Maggie made that clear. The parson guides the family along streets now lined with civic buildings, shops and offices in sandstone, each block of hewn rock rising up from the blood of the original people to walk on the land, from the rib bones of dead whales, the hard hooves of sheep where rare creatures once roamed.

The town's funeral bell is tolling as Cora joins the end of the procession winding through the stone gateway at St David's burial ground, coming to a halt at an open plot beside the grave of Charlie Ferrion.

Maggie didn't want anyone to fuss over her in life, so Joe and his brothers are certain she wouldn't want it in death. They have arranged for the service to be brief.

She is farewelled as a respected pioneer, devoted mother, steadfast wife, and a resolute widow. On the slate that is her life, each uttered phrase wipes away chalk marks that measure the truth of her humanity, the sacrifices made, contributions given, guilt that lingered, and the shame.

The angst-ridden girl is gone. The blood-covered hands of the midwife and nurse, her talent for healing, disappeared. The abandoned mother who stole for her child, the woman stripped of everything familiar, the spirited convict, all wiped away. Every shade of colour for the capable, culpable, complicated, courageous woman now turned to grey. The price of a clean slate.

When the others straggle away to the inn, Cora hangs back, remains standing at the graveside in light misty rain that now sweeps down the mountainside. The two gravediggers, shovels at the ready, shelter nearby, keen to start piling in soil so they can go home.

A woman in her mid-forties appears at the gateway, the wide collar on her woollen coat pulled up around her neck. She walks up to Cora, greets her. They stand side by side, umbrellas dipped a little to keep falling droplets off their faces. When the woman opens her mouth, she speaks to the grave.

'I came, mother.' She wipes her eyes.

The wind begins to shift, a southerly driving swollen clouds towards the town. As they reach the burial ground they release their load in pelting rain that turns to sleet against the backs of the two women.

The mother and daughter link arms and hurry off. They are hardly out the gate as dirt thuds onto the coffin.

AUTHOR'S NOTE

This is a work of fiction, set in the era of my five times great grandmother, Ann Howard, and based on her extraordinary life. She was an interloper in a foreign land, forced to contribute to the expansion of the British Empire through colonisation.

Ann was largely erased from history. What she gave and what she did was of little consequence to military commanders, politicians, record-keepers, or those grasping at power.

Yet, through her beliefs and actions, sacrifices and deprivations, dreams achieved and denied, the many small moments of celebration and joy, she contributed no less to the nation's character than the leaders and lawmakers.

It is a family history that weighs heavily. A second fleet convict, Ann and those sentenced to New Holland before and after her—as well as members of the military, administrators and free settlers who all came willingly— were part of an invasion that alienated and decimated Australia's First Nations people after living undisturbed for centuries in connection to country and their strong, continuous culture.

She eventually married first fleet marine Thomas Lucas, and their family now has hundreds of descendants in Australia and around the world.

While I have tried to stay true to known dates, events and historical figures, this is a work of invention. It includes the creation of a first husband and daughter for the character Maggie, derived from speculation by historians that Ann was well into child-bearing age, and the fact that the goods she stole included a child's cap.

Likewise, Charlie's early life is speculative, though there is some evidence to suggest Thomas was descended from exiled French Huguenots, came from a family in the weaving industry, and chose a life at sea after an argument with his father.

ABOUT THE AUTHOR

Anna Housego has always been
fascinated by the currents that
ebb and flow in us, and in our
lives, bringing strength or creating
havoc, depending on how we meet
them.

A former journalist, she
has worked in a range of jobs,
from roustabout at a frontier
pub to political adviser, and
for two decades was a freelance
communications consultant. The storytelling gene comes
from Irish ancestors. Growing up in a wilderness town full
of eccentric characters switched it on.

She lives a long way south on the island of lutruwita/
Tasmania, off the south-eastern corner of Australia, close
to her two adult children and their families.

This Savage World is her fourth novel.

ALSO BY ANNA HOUSEGO:

The Way to Midnight
One Small Life
Crows on the Roof

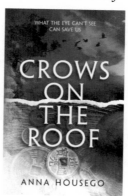

www.annahousego.com
@annahousego
@annahousegoauthor

Made in the USA
Thornton, CO
11/04/24 07:47:56

30be0b3c-8d5b-4f6d-a242-bbf67253c912R01